DESPAIR OF THE SEER

PITHOS DOMINION SERIES
– BOOK ONE –

ANTONIO GUADAGNO

DEFIANCE PRESS
& PUBLISHING

DESPAIR OF THE SEER

ISBN-13: 978-1-959677-67-3 (Paperback)
ISBN-13: 978-1-959677-66-6 (eBook)
ISBN-13: 978-1-959677-68-0 (Hardcover)

Published by Defiance Press & Publishing, LLC

Bulk orders of this book may be obtained by contacting Defiance Press & Publishing, LLC. www.defiancepress.com.

Public Relations Dept. – Defiance Press & Publishing, LLC
281-581-9300
pr@defiancepress.com

Defiance Press & Publishing, LLC
281-581-9300
info@defiancepress.com

For the woman who saved me from my own pithos dominion.
It's only been two decades; I look forward to seven more.
I love you, Bear.

Pandora's Pithos

Pithos was the Greek word for a large jar, often used to hold wine or oil. In the 16th century, Erasmus, translating Hesiod's Greek poem "Works and Days," came across this word. He mistranslated it to the Latin word, pyxis, or box. The pithos in the poem belonged to Pandora's husband, and when she opened it, she released evils upon the world.

Since Erasmus' mistake, the word box has become synonymous with the story.

Since Pandora's mistake, the world has never been the same.

Welcome to the Pithos Dominion.

Fenced In: A Short Story

A Week Ago, in the Pithos Dominion.

To tell this story, I must go back, back before its beginning. You see, this story is not like every other one. Sure, it has love and hate, friendship and betrayal, peace and war, celebration and heartache, the One True God and many false ones, a Controller and a speaker, fences and fields, mythical creatures, seers, and, of course, zombies.

Every story should have zombies of one type or another, but this story, this one here, it has two types. I'll get to them soon. The real story is about two friends, some traveling, daddy issues, and what many would call destiny. To understand that story, however, I need to tell you this short one.

You see, you need to know more about these dark lands, this dominion the old ones refer to as the Pithos Dominion. Yours they called Alpha before the Creator locked them into the Pithos Dominion for what they did. They're just a few doors down from each other, so they have a lot in common. A long time ago, they played a trick on an honorable man and his wife. They gave him a jar, and he was to keep it safe. They did this in both dominions. Ours contained evils, but in this one? In this one they put every horror, evil, and dark god they could scoop up.

But that's just an introduction.

This story, the one I'm telling you now? The one that will introduce you to the twisted lands that serve up hideous monstrosities and evils as if they were Sunday dinner? This short story? It begins with a brother and sister. They live on a spider-cattle farm in the Midwest, behind the First Fence, in the safest part of the most dangerous area of North America. But before I get ahead of myself, we should check up on Luke and his little sister, Cyndi.

They're running home.

Fast.

Luke held her hand as he ran, though he should have held his shoes. They'd been sewn back together so many times they were little more than spider cow silk all the way 'round. He kicked up dust and ran as his right shoe began to unravel.

It wouldn't rip. Spider cow silk is too strong for that, but it wasn't woven together; it was sewn. It held together what was left of the spider cow leather that originally made up the main part of the shoes. This leather was not as strong as the silk and it did rip, allowing the silk to unravel.

Luke slowed and dropped his sister's hand.

"Come on, Luke! Keep up!" she yelled back at him. "Even Snuffy's ahead of you!" She waved her teddy bear in the air as she smiled.

Without stopping he bent over to pick up his shoe and then he looked back.

The sides of the canyon rose high and steep beside them, but he wasn't looking at the sides of the canyon. He noticed the sun disappearing behind the horizon. The shadows of the canyon were growing too long, and he knew they'd never make it home in time.

Then he saw it.

A shadow of a man standing on the edge of a cliff grabbed his eye; then it was gone.

They're coming.

Cyndi looked back, but she couldn't see her brother through the dust. His yellowed clothes were held together with leather and cloth and a lot of love and hope making him nearly invisible. For that reason, she was surprised as he ran past her.

"Come on, Cyndi, keep up! You know they're due back soon." Luke looked back, but the figure was gone. "A group was seen only a few days ago near the Jade's farm."

"I'm coming; besides, we have at least an hour. They only come when it's actually dark." She lowered her voice, "if they come at all."

"I heard that! You know they come," he glanced back again, "and not just at dark. I've seen them during the day. Now hurry up!"

You'll have to forgive Luke for being so severe. Sure, he was nervous because of the shadow he saw, but that could have been anyone. What he was really upset about was the attack that caused them to have to move in with their aunt and uncle.

He still remembered the recent attack. His uncle came in at the last moment and saved the two children. He was too late for their mother and father, however. Luke was eight at the time and had covered his sister's eyes as he watched what happened to them.

As he watched what his uncle had to do to his parents.

For his parents.

Let's skip ahead a few minutes, though, shall we?

They made it to their aunt's house safely and arrived just as their uncle was coming in from the pasture. Aunt Bayna was standing at the back door, giving all three her most stern look.

"How are the calflings doing, Uncle?" Luke asked as he knocked off his shoe and started in the door.

"Don't you dare, Luke," Aunt Bayna interrupted. "You will explain to me why you're running home late and with one shoe."

"Well, we were on our way home, on time, I promise, and, well, my shoe started to come apart." He held out the mass of silk and leather. "The leather ripped again. I only slowed down for a moment to take it off, but," he looked at his sister for help, and she offered nothing, "Well, we ran home as fast as we could after that."

"Running? So that's what happened to them, huh? You'll be sewing them tonight, little sir."

Uncle Arlen waited a moment as Aunt Bayna gave him a look that he knew meant they'd discuss the rest later and that it was not going to go well for him. It was that universal look all women are granted upon adolescence. The one any man can recognize and learns to fear.

The four walked inside and began setting the table for dinner.

Drought plagued the area for weeks before the rainfall two nights ago. The spider cattle would all eat whatever they caught in their web: small animals, large insects, and if they were fortunate, they'd get to suck a zombie dry. But despite their eight, tough, leathery legs, they still had eight stomachs, and grass was a necessary part of their diet. The spider calflings had been sucking their mothers dry lately, and the family was nearly out of hay.

"Well, Luke, to answer your question, the spider calflings are doing better, for now." He turned to his wife and held his breath. The plate in his hand hung there as if the next thing he said would break it.

Aunt Bayna noticed and put her hands on her hips, looking at him expectantly.

"Well, Arlen? Out with it," she said.

"Kurt Jade stopped over. He said they're going to make for the fences tonight. Wanted to know if we'd go with 'em."

"You told them 'no,' right?" she said as she resumed laying out dinner.

His lack of a quick response made her pause with a hot dish in her hands, much like the plate that remained in his hand. She looked him in the eyes, and the children held their breath. "Arlen, what did you say?"

He sighed as if defeated and set the plate down, "I told them they could cross through the pasture. That's all. And I told them that we would not be attempting it. We all know what happened when the Lonelys tried last year and... well, not in front of Cyndi, huh?"

"You can tell me, Uncle Arlen. I'm eight now. I can handle it."

Luke started in, "Well, when they got there, the guards... "

"No! It's not something an eight-year-old should hear, Luke," Arlen said and he was right. No eight-year-old should have heard, or lived, the story Luke almost told his sister. "Anyway, this smells good, honey," Uncle Arlen sat at the table and pulled his chair close.

Aunt Bayna smiled sadly and sat down to eat her dinner.

The two had discussed the fence in great detail and always

disagreed about it. Arlen knew the danger but thought they could make it during the day. Bayna thought it was too dangerous at any time and that they wouldn't be safer outside the fence.

They argued about it so many times that each could argue the other's points perfectly. The problem was that they still couldn't agree. So, Arlen, respecting his wife, decided they would stay for now.

Secretly he hoped the Jades would make it over the fence, not only because they were friends, but because he thought Kara Jade, Bayna's best friend since Libby Lonely died, would be over the fence. And with her over the fence, he hoped his wife would want to join them.

Soon after dinner, they all went to bed, except Uncle Arlen. He had the first watch. It was uneventful and boring, so let's skip ahead to three hours later when Aunt Bayna came to take her shift watching the property. That was when they heard the spider cattle. The sound of the barn creaking beneath the weight of the one-ton, eight-legged, mammal-arachnid mutants was unmistakable.

Something had disturbed them.

"It's probably just the Jades; I'll go check it out. You stay here, Bayna." He gave her a quick kiss on the cheek and squeezed her hand.

He went outside, loaded shotgun in hand, and crept through the pasture, toward the barn. A clang rang out, and the sounds of all the cattle padding up and around the barn grew louder. He cocked his gun and rounded the corner. He saw an adult moving out of sight around the far side of the barn; then he noticed a shorter shadow creeping into the barn.

The moonlight gave him a brief but clear glimpse, and he knew immediately who it was. He lowered his shotgun and called out, "Hey, Mara! You better keep up with your family; they went around the other side!"

He pointed to the far side of the barn.

Mara was ten years old. She had on her brother's old overalls, worn and dirty, but holding together and not too loose on her.

Arlen couldn't see her freckles in the dark, but if not for them, her green eyes and her red hair, he would have thought it was Cyndi. She stopped and looked at him, then back to the other side of the barn.

She began to wave and turned to run toward the other side of the barn as she called out, "Thank you, sir!"

Then she disappeared.

Arlen heard noises and knew the Jades were heading back and looking for Mara. He couldn't see her at all.

Something pulled her into the barn. It must have. She couldn't have just disappeared.

Arlen ran up to check it out, but the barn was dark. He brought his gun up and aimed into the barn. The moon only lit a small patch of ground near the entrance.

Soon the Jades were right behind him.

"What happened? Where is Mara, Arlen?" Kara, her mother, asked.

"She just disappeared into the barn. Stay back," was Arlen's calm response.

He was slowly stepping into the barn with his shotgun raised.

"It couldn't be one of the spider cattle. Could it, Arlen?" she asked.

He stopped and turned, looking at her with irritation. *Why doesn't she let me go in there and check?* Then he realized that she was worried. He would be too if it were Cyndi. Even though he knew the cattle were safe. He sighed, releasing his frustration.

"Nah, they'd never hurt anything human, unless they went Revenant, and we'd know that long before we put them away for the night." Turning again toward the barn, Owen called for Mara. "Mara, where are you, hon?"

"She is right here," a dark voice answered.

Arlen stopped breathing for a moment.

"It's one of them!" he yelled finally. "Get to the house and get locked down, now!"

The others ran and listened to him. Arlen wasn't the only one who had seen a Revenant in person, and everyone knew that voice. He was the only one who had killed a Revenant, however.

But not in time to save Joe and Anna. What he did to them was horrible; he deserved his fate. But what I had to do to them—

He snapped out of it and focused. Walking slowly, he approached the dark voice.

"You are the murderer of Luc Bennet," the dark voice slowly annunciated from somewhere to Arlen's right. "Plead your case, human."

"He deserved that bullet and a thousand more for turning my brother and sister-in-law into filth like you."

"This filth—did it deserve what you did to it as well?"

The voice came from another corner, so he turned to face that one. Arlen knew it was playing games, and with Mara in here he couldn't fire at will.

"He killed them by turning them into flesh-eating monsters. I just put them down."

"Put them down?" he asked from behind Arlen again. "Like a lame horse?"

"No. Like I'll put you down," Arlen looked around. If only he could see the Revenant's eyes. "Now, give me back Mara, and you can walk out of here."

"You wish to have the little girl back?" he laughed lightly. "Of course."

Her body flew from a corner to his left and flopped on the ground, lifeless.

"Now that I have had a snack... I will enjoy the main course."

Now, we leave the spider cattle to witness Arlen's fate. For I have found that describing the atrocity that happened there in any detail does nothing to convey its gruesome and carnal nature. So we return to the house.

Bayna heard a gunshot as the Jades, without Mara, showed up at the back door. She rushed them in and asked what was happening. They told her what Arlen said, and she immediately ran to wake the children.

Now, for Cyndi, this was a terrible thing. She was dreaming of her parents and candy and days before there was worry of Revenant or zombies. She was shaken out of it by a fearful aunt who was telling her to get up. She could see in Bayna's eyes what was happening and reached back to grab Snuffy, her teddy bear.

For Luke, on the other hand, this was something he looked forward to. Like any twelve-year-old boy, he wanted to protect the family and had been dreaming of taking them to the fence and what he would do there.

For him this was a dream come true.

He would quickly come to regret that dream.

Bayna came back with Luke and Cyndi and heard Mara before seeing her. She looked around for Arlen, but he wasn't back yet.

"And then that thing jumped down from the spider cow web, onto him and... " Mara started crying and couldn't continue.

Then a sound came from the front door, a subtle knock.

The knock was so low that nobody heard it over her crying. Mara, however, heard the noise clearly and quickly wiped the tears away and grew calm. She briskly walked toward the door.

"I better go let my brother in," she called over her shoulder.

"Your brother is right here, Mara," said Kara, gesturing to her son.

Her father, Kurt, reached out to stop her and with no more than a slight contraction of her arm, she flung him across the room into a wooden chair. She continued, unfazed, to the door and opened it as horror, shock, and realization came to the rest of the families.

Then it hit Bayna. She realized what Mara was saying and that Arlen wasn't coming back.

Nor was he the one at the door.

"Thank you, my new sister," said a well-built Revenant soldier who bent and caressed Mara's cheek. "The Controller is happy; now go tell them why we are here."

He stood to his full height of 6'9" and folded his hands in front of him. He smiled at them like the polite dinner guest he was, then laughed to himself at the thought.

He patiently waited for Mara to tell the family that they were here not only to feed. *No*, he thought, *but for revenge. You're the ones who killed Luc Bennet, one of my First Brothers. And now, I,*

First Brother J'Nou Nguyen, and my new sister, Mara, will destroy you.

"We come to your home, not only to feed," Mara said. "The death of Luc Bennet, my First Brother's First Brother, is on the heads of all of you. There were only a few, and now there are less. For their death, y—"

Everyone's ears rang in the small room, and blood dripped down the wall near Mara. A hole went through her left cheek and out the right side of her skull. Mara fell to the ground and her mother, Kara, leapt onto Cyndi who was shaking, holding the smoking 9mm pistol she'd pulled out of Snuffy.

"You shot my daughter!" Kara, Mara's mother, screamed. Kara tackled Cyndi, crushing her, but Aunt Bayna dove on them and pulled Kara off as she grabbed the gun.

"Now for you, zombie!" Aunt Bayna exclaimed as she pulled the trigger.

A hole opened in J'Nou's chest.

"Do you not know how to shoot? Do you not know what we are? The zombies roam outside. We are Revenant." J'Nou squared his shoulders and looked down on Bayna. "Only your man was a worthy adversary."

Sneering, J'Nou walked to Mara and helped her up. She was wobbly, with her right ear missing, but she could function. "Now you will need to feed more to heal that wound, little one," he bent down and spoke in a fatherly tone.

Mara looked up at him and nodded. She looked at her brother and lunged at him. He screamed for help as she feasted. The injury made her ravenously hungry.

"Come on! We have to leave now!" shouted Bayna.

Everyone followed her except Kara who tried to wrestle Mara away.

"I won't leave my children," she said.

Bayna called for her to follow, but it was too late. J'Nou and Mara were already upon her. Kara looked up and saw her daughter chewing her flesh as the hole in her face filled with blood and then skin. Kara smiled as her last thoughts were of giving her life for her child.

Mara thought nothing as a new voice pushed its way into her mind.

Kurt raised his gun and fired at J'Nou. He missed because tears had filled his eyes. Time seemed to slow as he emptied his gun. Only two bullets hit J'Nou, and neither was a killing shot.

So he charged at the Revenant, knowing that he had no hope of overpowering either of them. J'Nou tapped Mara's shoulder and pointed. She followed his finger toward her father and stood slowly. Then she grabbed him and laid him down next to her mother.

Bayna led Luke and Cyndi through the hall toward a back room and to a shrine made for Spinner, the goddess of the spider cattle. She was worshipped to protect the herders of spider cattle.

"Aunt Bayna, why are we here? I think it's too late for Spinner to help us now. She let us down," Luke said.

Bayna swept the totems, wooden and silk figures off the shrine and pushed it aside. Now this Luke couldn't believe, and his sister got one last giggle from his mouth hanging loose. Bayna pushed aside a door built in the wall and revealed the side yard.

"We have only a short moment while they feed; hurry through," she said.

Cyndi didn't realize until much later that she'd dropped Snuffy here.

As they came into the yard, they noticed they were not alone. While the two Revenant inside were very dangerous, twenty zombies outside shambled toward them and were not a welcome sight.

Luke raised a six-shooter to fire. It had been given to him by his uncle. Bayna pushed his hand down gently.

"If you fire that, they'll come from all over." She pointed toward an area with fewer zombies and pushed her hand forward. "We need to run through them."

"Do you really think we can make it, Aunt Bayna?" Luke asked.

"Yes. The real problem is what to do at the fence."

The group was a study in how to play tag. They bobbed and weaved and darted as zombies lunged. Cyndi scooted by three of them to get around a tree while Luke slid recklessly between the legs of another.

Nobody wanted a Revenant to visit, but zombies could be handled in small groups, and were almost fun. Their slow reflexes and stupid demeanor meant that the now twenty-four zombies shambling toward the group would likely remain behind them and be no trouble anymore.

Now that they were through the zombies, the group ran toward the fence, five miles east of their farm.

Let's not forget J'Nou and his new sister, Mara, though. They surely haven't forgotten revenge. They finished eating and watched from the roof as the group slipped past the zombies.

"Dolts," J'Nou said. "Simple, mindless dolts. If we did not provide them with humans from the Farm, they would crumble into nothing."

He watched for another moment as Mara sat there quietly.

"Promise me, Mara. Promise me that you will kill me if I ever become like them."

"I promise, First Brother," she said.

Now, my dear friend, the next few miles were mostly uninteresting, so please allow me to summarize. J'Nou and Mara followed stealthily behind their prey, teasing them, calling out to them, and reminding them that they were being followed. The group grew tired many times and fell from exhaustion, but as much as their bodies cried out to slow or even stop, J'Nou reminded them what they were running from and would speak in his unearthly, dark voice, the Shadow Voice, a voice thought to be unique to Revenant.

This unending taunt inspired them to keep moving. Luke would carry Cyndi; Aunt Bayna would push Luke; and they all scrambled toward the fence. Finally, over an hour later, they arrived at the fence, bloody, dirty, sweaty, and tired.

Cyndi and Luke leaned against it to rest, while Aunt Bayna sat in the dirt.

"We are still here," J'Nou said again, just loud enough for all to stand and try to get the attention of the guards on the wall.

J'Nou and Mara crept quietly behind a large boulder to a spot where they could watch as Luke tried to climb the thirty-two foot, sheer, concrete fence. He had no luck. J'Nou was purposeful and loud with his snarl from behind the boulder. He flashed his red eyes and waited for the guard to see him.

The guard on the wall shouted to his fellow soldier, "Over there, behind that rock! It's one of those damn Revs!"

He aimed and shot. J'Nou watched as the bullet streaked at his jugular. He pulled down behind the rock as fast as he could, but not in time to keep away from the bullet. It took only a piece of skull and skin with it however, so he was relieved.

"Come my brothers and sisters; we will take them. Climb the wall and then we will take the nearest city." J'Nou spoke again in his pitch-black Shadow Voice.

You see, in these dark lands, well-trained soldiers were in short supply, and since the wall ran from the Canadian wall down to the Gulf of Mexico, the rest of it was guarded by locals who volunteered or were conscripted by city lotteries. They had no formal training, had never seen a Revenant in person, and were replaced often.

The guards could clearly hear J'Nou's threat, however, even over their radios. It scared many of them and, though a couple remembered to order more men to their point, most of them began to tremble and shake.

Then they saw the group crying for help and trying to climb the wall. These cries were not loud enough to break through the radios, however, so to the guards they were like any other zombies.

"That is it, my siblings. We will breach the wall and feast in their cities," J'Nou continued as he smiled to himself, knowing what would happen next.

As Cyndi lifted a rock to bash through the wall, a shot went cleanly through her eye and she slumped over. In the eternity before she hit the ground, her only thought was to wonder where Snuffy was.

As the guards opened fire on Bayna and Luke, J'Nou and Mara were on their way to a farm ten miles southwest of their current position. They needed to eat and gather supplies.

"We must go feast, sister; we have a long trip ahead of us. A lost key has been found."

The Controller knew all that J'Nou had seen and heard; he and the other First Brothers were happy; revenge was finally theirs.

So now you know more about these very dark lands. There is much more to learn, but the story, the one about love and hate, friendship and betrayal, myth and legend, the Speaker and the Seer, the One True God and many other gods, and so much more—that story can begin.

A dark voice invaded Mara's mind. It drowned out any guilt as she attacked her brother. She recalled her father's face, blinking back tears, but the voice grew darker, twisting his image in her head and striking her.

She ran from those thoughts.

She was on top of her mother, teeth tearing into her mother's shoulder; she savored the taste; then looked down. Her mother was calm and at peace as she croaked, "Mommy will nourish you, Mara."

Tears formed again, but the voice wouldn't allow that. It calmed her and cleared her mind. She blinked and all she could see was the desert rushing past. *Am I running?* She saw J'Nou running beside her.

They stopped.

How long had they run? She couldn't remember. Where were they exactly? She knew they were still in the fence, but then she saw a large hole in the desert. It reminded her of the holes left when her mother cut out biscuits for breakfast.

Then she recognized what it was.

This is the Farm? The voice rushed in to quiet her again.

"We keep them in a pit so the zombies cannot get to them. We must protect our food supply," J'Nou said to her. He leaned in and smiled, "They would eat all of them and have them turned. Then how would we feed ourselves? Zombies do not taste very good."

She looked back at him, but he was distant. Or was she the

one far away? She understood and took in what he said, even laughing at it, but she could not consciously consider it.

The voice grew stronger.

Three hundred feet below her was a sight that fueled the nightmares of millions of children around the world. In a pit over four kilometers in diameter, thousands of children were watched over by a handful of Revenant adults.

But the voice wouldn't let her think of the word *children*, instead replacing it with the word *cattle*.

"That's a lot of ch... *chattle*, First Brother. Why do we need so many?" she asked.

"As they ripen, they feed us and our zombie fellows. We must keep enough to satiate our hunger," he replied.

"But why are there no *ripe ones* here?" She wanted to say *adults*, but it came out *ripe ones*.

"A few are close. And we will pick two of them for our snacks; the *ripe ones*, however, are taken to more heavily patrolled farms for controlled reproduction. Then when the *calves* are weaned, we bring them back here," he sighed. "To the one Farm we tell the humans about."

"Come. We need some snacks for our long voyage," J'Nou said as he jumped from ledge to ledge down into the pit.

"Where are we going, J'Nou?"

"Over the fence."

1. Spider Beef Stew

Terrance Bonifacy wore only his shorts as he juggled a soccer ball in his bedroom. Looking at the reflection of his dark-skinned chest in the mirror, he pulled out a small box and held it close. He pried it open so only he could see what was inside.

It took months to save enough money, and several more to get the ring shipped from the United States of Africa, but tomorrow was the night. He and Sara would go to Paxton's house for dinner, and there in front of Paxton and Paxton's mother and grandmother, he would get down on one knee, show her the ring, and finally propose.

Paxton's mother, Cynthia, promised to prepare something special. They acted happy for him, but he knew what they thought of Sara.

Sara walked in the bedroom and climbed into bed, "Put the ball away, Terrance. It's time for bed."

He closed the box and hid it in his pocket.

She rolled over and put out the candle on her side of the bed. His was the only light left. He kicked the ball into the corner and climbed into bed, snuffing his candle and shoving the box under the mattress. They snuggled together and quickly fell asleep.

A wave of saltwater crashed into Terrance's face and he gasped for air. It forced him backwards and into his father's arms. His father smiled down at him, "Be careful there, son. You don't want to drown."

21

"Oh, I won't," Terrance said. "I'm gonna grow up big and strong so I can kill all the zombies, and Revenant, and everyone can come back." He was eight years old and thought he was the only child in Miami, which was very close to being true.

The waves raised him up and let him back down where his feet could touch. He watched his father walk back up the beach toward his mother. He smiled up at them, but sadness hit him as hard as the wave before.

His father sat next to his mother as Terrance dug in the sand. He never liked sandcastles, so instead he dug trenches. Watching the water flow into them, out of them, around bends and islands, and into pools—that was the best thing in the world to him.

He hadn't done this in years.

He was nineteen again, even though he was still wearing those hideous, short, green swim trunks with ducks on them. He knew where he was now. He looked up the beach and saw *them* coming before he was supposed to. This time he knew to look for them. This time he could stop them. This time he would stop them.

He ran toward the pirates; he knew they were pirates because only pirates wore sandals like that. He wasn't moving. He couldn't lift his legs and began to panic. He was stuck in one of his trenches and couldn't get to them.

That's when he felt the hand on his shoulder. It always came at the worst time.

He stopped in place and watched the pirates stalk up to his parents.

"Terrance?" his mother said.

It was Sara's voice, though. Why did he hear her voice now?

"Terrance, honey, are you alright?"

He shot up in bed.

Sand poured off of his feet, and the ocean water evaporated; then everything disappeared, and his bedroom returned. It was pitch black and he was sweating.

"Another bad dream?" Sara asked.

"Yeah." He lay back.

"Your folks?"

"Yeah."

"What was it this time?"

"The hand again. It held me in place." He still felt stuck.

"You want to talk about it?"

"What's there to talk about?" he answered.

"Ok. If you change your mind, just wake me back up."

"Yeah, good night."

"Hey, Sara, I'm going out to kick the ball around with Paxton," Terrance yelled into the bedroom the next morning.

She was getting dressed in the master bathroom.

"Of course you are. You wouldn't want to spend too much time with me, would you?" she said.

"It's not like that, baby," he called on his way out.

Sara heard the door close as Terrance left.

"Sure it isn't," she mumbled to herself. "Four years and you're still the same. I should have just left on the first pirate ship I found; instead I had to get wrapped up with you."

Four years ago, on her way to the docks, she saw him seething in a corner. He had a knife in one hand and an empty bottle of scotch in the other. He was staring down any pirate that came close to him, and she knew what that look meant.

So Sara walked up to him. "What's the knife for?"

Without taking his eyes off the pirates, he answered, "One of them."

She followed his eyes to the pirates walking by and nudged up next to him, on the empty-bottle side. She didn't want to take a chance next to the knife, "Anyone in particular? Or just whoever comes up here first?"

"All of them."

"Well, I think you may stick one or two, but you're pretty out-numbered. Why don't you let me take you home, honey?" She grabbed the bottle from him. "Where do you live?" she said and reached for the knife.

He started to pull it away, but then submitted. She knew her family would not accept a dark-skinned boy like Terrance, but as much as she missed them and loved them, her need for Terrance was too great.

He helped her forget them.

She sighed as she watched him walking down the street in his soccer uniform.

"I love you, Terr. I just wish you—" She stopped. *What am I doing talking to myself?*

Paxton Roald was a pale, dark-haired, young man who took care of his mother and granny. The three of them lived a few houses down the street from Terrance and Sara.

"Mom, what's for dinner tonight?" he called into the kitchen.

"I'm making Terrance's favorite, spider beef stew." Paxton's mother, Cynthia, leaned around the corner and whispered "Tonight's the night."

"I heard that, Cynthia, and I know already." Gail, Paxton's granny, yelled from the couch. "You don't need to whisper. That boy has no sense; he needs to get rid of her, not marry her."

"They're in love, Granny."

"Love? She just wants someone. She doesn't care if it's him or some pirate. I can tell." She pointed to her nose. "I can smell it on her. She's a hussy."

"I don't care for her either, Mom, but we have to support Terrance," Cynthia said.

"Mom's right, Granny. Will you at least not say anything in front of them?" Paxton asked.

"I'll try, but I'm getting old, Paxy," she smiled. "I can't always remember, and if her hussy stench is in my nose, I may blurt something out."

"Yeah, yeah, old woman," Cynthia smiled at her mother as she walked into the kitchen again. She turned back on Paxton and said, "The stew should be done in time for the alarm tonight. I expect you to be home by then. Tell Terrance that he and Sara can come over as soon as they're ready."

"Sure will," he said.

"Did you pray for your father, Paxy?" Gail asked.

"No. I don't pray for scum, Granny."

"That's no way to talk to your grandmother, Paxton Eugene Roald. Now go apologize to her and don't let me hear you talk about your father like that again. He did what he thought was best," Cynthia said.

"If he'd done what was best, he'd—" he stopped, noticing his mother's glare. "Yes ma'am."

Paxton walked into the living room to his granny who sat on the couch; he bent down and hugged her noticing how frail she was, and he grew sad.

"I'm sorry, Granny. I shouldn't be rude to you," he said.

"It's ok, boy. I know how hard it can be. After what he did, I—Well, let's just say, I still pray for him, and so should you. He left to protect us, and that's something to be grateful for," she said.

"I know, Granny. I just can't forgive him for Laura, or for leaving us, or for everything else he's done," he said and laid his head on her lap. "None of it." He looked up at her. "I'm sorry, Granny, but I just can't pray for him."

"Give it more time, Paxton. Give it more time."

"I love you, Granny." He stood up. "I better get going or I'll be late meeting Terrance."

Paxton left quickly and jogged up the street. He saw Terrance ahead and raced to catch up with him.

J'Nou Nguyen walked steadily down the street with a child at his side. Mara Jade stood on the other side of this child, looking almost like her twin. The two skipped, played, and laughed together while J'Nou stopped to smell the air.

He was a tall Asian man in good physical condition. His skin was turning gray and his eyes were red, but otherwise he looked like the soldier he was nearly twenty years ago. His close-cropped black hair and muscular build competed with his posture to impress power on those who saw him.

The man across the street paid attention to none of this.

"Hey, Gook, go back to your empire. We don't want your Oriental ass in our country," he yelled. "And put our kids back where you got 'em. You hear me?"

The man raised his rake and began to cross the street.

J'Nou turned sharply to meet the man in the street and then stopped short. He looked around, as did Mara. The child between them bent down and tried to catch a grasshopper.

"I do not see anyone else here, sir. You may beg for my forgiveness now, you ignorant piece of—" J'Nou said.

"Hey now, there are children around, Ninja-Boy." The man made a gesture with his hand to imitate a martial arts movement as he called J'Nou a Ninja-Boy. "And why would I apologize to you?"

"Can't we just kill him?" Mara asked.

Mara was ten years old. Her hair was a deep shade of red, and her skin was pasty and smooth. She only recently joined J'Nou as a Revenant, so her eyes were still their natural green.

J'Nou looked at Mara and smiled.

"Oh, aren't you cute, little girl. Who's gonna kill me? This robo-chink?" the belligerent man asked looking again at J'Nou and grasping the rake more tightly. "Come to think about it, aren't you ninjas supposed to be silent and unseen?" Looking back at Mara, he added, "He's just a—"

The man stopped talking and gasped for air. He looked down to see J'Nou holding his heart.

"I do not mind when people insult me, or try to kill me, but there is no need for such blatant and ignorant racism," J'Nou said. "My mother was killed by a bigot like yourself, and if you are going to hate me for any reason, it should be that I am J'Nou Nguyen, First Brother of the Revenant."

The man crumbled to the pavement, dying, and watched as J'Nou ate his heart. J'Nou and Mara turned and walked over to the nearest house. He turned on the hose and washed his hand and arm, splashing bloody water on the side of the house.

"Why are we here, J'Nou?" Mara asked.

"There is important information here. We must find the key. He is lost to us."

"So they know where he is?"

"Yes. I believe they do. We are here for that information." He smelled the air again. "I think they are having spider beef stew tonight, Mara. Does your friend want some?" J'Nou asked.

"No. I think she just wants to play; we'll go back down the street," Mara said. "I'm sure you can handle them."

J'Nou nodded and continued toward the back of the house. As he came to a window, he looked inside.

A pale, blond woman screamed when she saw J'Nou,

"Hello again, Cynthia Roald. It has been a long time."

2. Bam!

While horrors lurked near their homes, Terrance and Paxton played soccer. Terrance's dark skin was covered in sweat, but the humid air didn't slow down either guy as they laughed and played.

"Over here, Paxy," Terrance yelled, laughing.

Paxton squinted and kicked the ball as hard as he could at Terrance's face.

Oomph!

Paxton cursed. He'd only hit him in the chest.

Terrance continued laughing after he caught his breath. Then he paused, looking at the orange glow of the Miami sunset. In his mind, nothing could be more beautiful.

Paxton's pale skin took on the orange color of the sunset, but he didn't share Terrance's opinion, "Hey! Are you gonna kick it over here or just stare at the sun?"

He kicked it hard at Paxton, "Have you talked to any of those missionaries, Paxton?"

"No. Why would I listen to them? I mean, come on, one god?"

"I know, but I've been reading the book they gave me and it..." he was distracted by the sun again.

"Come on, Granny's gonna have dinner done soon, and it's gettin' dark. Are we gonna play or talk about African missionaries?" Paxton continued.

"What's wrong, Paxy? Scared the Revenant may come? They never come here; all we ever get are those drills."

Paxton's mood turned a bit sour. He knew they would be

coming soon and tried to shake it off, but Terrance noticed. "Hey, I think we should go soon."

"That's what I'm saying." Paxton tried dodging the conversation. "They made a special dinner for your special night."

"You know that's not what I mean," Terrance said and kicked the ball back to Paxton. "We should go find your dad and bring him back here."

"I'm not leaving Mom and Granny home alone." Paxton caught the ball and juggled it some. "I can't do that and they can't come with me, so I'm not going."

"Listen, after the wedding, Sara can take care of them and I can go with you. Your father should be here."

"Yeah, that'd go over great; you know how they feel about her. To be honest, Terrance, I don't want him here. I want to find him and let him know how I feel." Paxton kicked the ball as hard as he could to Terrance. "I want to beat him within an inch of his life. We shouldn't have to live this way."

"I'm sure he knows how you feel, Paxton. He lost his daughter, and now he's away from his family."

"He doesn't have to see how it affects Mom."

Terrance kicked the ball back to Paxton who barely missed it, letting it roll off into some bushes. Walking up to the bushes at the edge of Captain's Field, he felt something in the air. Just then, the siren started its whine.

Terrance looked at his watch and smiled. "Exactly 7:30 on the dot. See what I mean?"

"Those drills are done for a reason, Terrance." Paxton grabbed the ball and both of them ran home.

The sun cast long shadows in the small suburb on the north side of Miami. "We'll be over soon," Terrance said and waved to Paxton as he walked up to the small, white, modest home he shared with Sara. It was stucco, and the yard was full of crab grass. A single palm tree stood in front, and drawn shades shielded the two windows to keep out the sun.

He opened the door and heard a man curse and stumble from his bedroom. Terrance sprinted ten feet down the hall to his room.

Grabbing the doorjamb, he swung into the open doorway.

His eyes focused just enough to see a shirtless man, shorts around his knees, dive through the window. Terrance noticed the man's feet and swelled with anger.

Only pirates wore sandals like that.

Five houses down, Paxton opened his door and walked in, "Granny, the stew smells so good." When he didn't get a response, he called out, "M'ma? Granny? I'm home."

Paxton's home was just like Terrance's and every home on their street. As he walked through the front door, their small kitchen was on his right. To the left and in front of him was the living area. Past the living area was the guest bathroom on the left, and beyond that was his small bedroom. Across from there was the master bedroom. It wasn't much bigger, but it had its own bathroom.

His mother and granny should have been cooking, but nobody was in the small kitchen. They should have yelled at him for being late, but there was no sound at all. He walked a few steps forward and noticed them sitting silently, completely still, on the couch.

The man sitting between them slowly turned his head toward Paxton and said, with blank eyes, little expression, and in his unmistakable dark tone, "My name is J'Nou Nguyen, First Brother of the Revenant. We have been waiting for you."

Normally, Terrance would chase the man down, but he noticed that his sweaty half-dressed girlfriend looked frightened, but not of the pirate.

Sara was frightened of him.

This enraged him more and he said, with a dark voice he never knew existed, "Come back here." The bass of the words rattled the house. Dishes in the kitchen fell and broke, and pictures vibrated off the shelves.

The calm in his face belied the anger and power felt by Sara and the pirate who came back through the front door, blank eyed and expressionless.

Terrance stared at Sara as he asked in a disturbingly calm voice, "What the hell were you doing with him?"

Paxton watched as the only family he cared about stood and turned toward him in unison with J'Nou. He knew what J'Nou was. He remembered the Revenant attack on Los Angeles nine years ago. He was grayer, though, and his eyes were a deeper red.

He knew they'd be found eventually and that it would be bad, so he'd practiced. He thought he could handle a few Revenant attacking. He thought he would be home when it happened. He thought they had more time.

He was wrong.

The three spoke in unison, "Tell us where your father is."

"No," Sara cried as Terrance walked to the kitchen. "You can't kill him. They'll send more and kill us both.

"Jeff said he would kill you if I didn't do it, and that his buddies would come looking for him if he didn't return soon. I wish you were here; I know you would have protected me." She knew he kept his pistol under the sink. "Please, let's just take him to the docks and give him to his crew."

Jeff. So that's his name. He couldn't let someone do that to her, but he didn't entirely believe her. He knew there was something more, so he reached into the cabinet below the sink.

Letting the pirate go wasn't an option.

"No," Paxton yelled as he stretched into the kitchen and grabbed a revolver out of the bowl on top of the refrigerator.

His father taught him to shoot at a young age and he'd had plenty of practice, like most kids. With one fluid motion, he switched off the safety and shot the intruder in the neck, severing the jugular. Unlike most kids, his senses were fine-tuned.

J'Nou calmly reached his hand to his throat, and the blood congealed almost immediately. Its sick gray/pink color was odd, but Paxton didn't notice. Barely bothering to aim, Paxton fired again at J'Nou, missing the spinal cord by millimeters.

Very little blood came out, but J'Nou's head snapped back from the force of the shot.

Paxton dove out the door. He knew his mother and grandmother were lost, but he couldn't bring himself to shoot them, so he ran to Terrance's house for help.

Terrance held the muzzle to the paralyzed pirate's temple and began counting down, "You have five seconds left to live, Jeff. I hope it was worth it."

"No, Terrance, please don't," Sara said. "You don't know who he is."

"Five."

"Please. You don't understand."

"Four."

"Terrance. You can't do this."

"Three."

"Please, Terr!"

"Two."

"He's the Captain's son!"

Terrance looked up at her, "One."

The door burst open and Paxton, shocked by what he saw in front of him, could only point toward his house and say, "Revenant."

Paxton's father, Eugene Roald, watched the news as he worked on his life's work.

Hell's Kitchen, a slum of New York City, was the only place where he could afford a room large enough for his supplies. He couldn't afford a net connection and didn't condone theft, but he missed his family, and tapping into the local network was the only way to watch the Miami and National news so he could keep up with what was happening.

Only Paxton knew where he was. *If I told Cynthia, she'd come after me. It's just too dangerous.*

The blonde woman on television was talking about the Revenant, a normal topic for the local news, ". . . and in the

Everglades yesterday a Revenant alligator was captured. This is the first Revenant seen on this side of the fence in two years. We now go live to Eidan Nogmi with the officials who caught the alligator. Eidan."

Eidan, a handsome, brown-haired man, in his late twenties and wearing a red shirt, cleared his throat and spoke into the microphone, "Thank you, Emily. I'm here in the Everglades where US Army Ranger Nate Gordon has captured the Revenant alligator alive. Ranger Gordon, is it safe to keep the alligator alive?"

Ranger Gordon, dressed in camouflage and waving orders to his men, replied, "Yes, we have the means to keep him contained, even when the Revenant is at its hungriest. This alligator will provide a means to study not only the disease, but its animal variant which before was only a rumor."

"But in the past, haven't Revenant in the care of 'capable' individuals escaped, sir? Isn't that how Atlanta was nearly lost ten years ago?"

"Yes, but those were researchers who didn't know how to handle an infected individual. We have captured, contained, and hunted down several human Revenant inside the fence in the past months. We know what we're doing. Now, I have to get back to work."

"Sir, will you use Death Metal to contain the 'gator, or does that affect Revenant?"

"Yes it affects Revenant, and we will be using it in the truck. Now—"

"One more question, if I may? Do you have any idea how this alligator came to be here?"

"No. Now, if you'll excuse me," Ranger Gordon. Five men and the Ranger lifted him into the back of an army truck as the other twenty men climbed into the other two trucks, rifles in hand.

"And that's it from the Everglades," Eidan said and turned back to the camera. "It seems we may never have an answer to how this 'gator got here. I'll give it back to you in the studio. Emily?"

Emily, truly interested, asked Eidan, "Have you seen any other animals around or anything suspicious?"

"Now that you ask, it has been amazingly quiet here. Normally the 'glades are teaming with sounds, from insects to the occasional airboat, but we've heard nothing since we got here."

"Creepy. Thank you, Eidan. Be careful and make it back to the studio safe. In other news, we received a report of a group of Revenant attempting a break through at the wall near Dodge City a week ago. Fortunately, the guards at their posts along the Second Great Wall stopped them. With us now is that guard... "

"Damn it!" Eugene cursed himself as he realized that this latest batch had the same problem as the first. *I'll never get this formula right. Even then, what will I do with it? I'm in no shape to storm EA51; nor would I want to.* Eugene was more than a little stressed, but he had to continue. *No one else can do this.*

The sun finished setting in Miami, and Paxton saved Jeff's life with his intrusion.

For now.

He didn't stop Terrance from knocking Jeff out cold with the butt of his gun and leaving a deep gash.

"I have to go, Terrance," Paxton said. "If they turn me into one of them, they'll know where Dad is."

"How would they know that?" Sara wiped the blood from Jeff's head.

Terrance glared at her.

"The Controller can know anything a Revenant knows," Paxton explained. "He not only controls them, but he can also read their minds. He's the reason that the government hasn't just bombed Einstein's Area 51. He's in a bunker that would let him ride out a thousand A-bombs, and he can make more Revenant any time he wants; they already have the Farms. Anyway, they want me now and they already have—" he choked before finishing, "they have Mom and Granny."

"They've been... " Terrance couldn't finish that thought.

"Granny... " Sara mumbled. Then her head shot up, "You mean the Farms are real?"

"Yes. My father knows a lot about the Revenant."

Jeff mumbled, "Don't *they* know where your Dad is, dude?"

The pirate was slowly waking up and Terrance planned to change that.

"No, don't," Sara pleaded.

He scowled at her, "Tonight wasn't supposed to be like this," he mumbled. Then he snapped, "Keep him quiet then."

"No, they don't know where he is, *dude,* or they wouldn't need me to tell them where he is, would they?" Paxton turned to Terrance. "Anyway, I need to go before they find me."

"Too late for that, son," Paxton's mother replied from the bedroom. With a sad and desperate, yet oddly plastic look, Paxton's mother pleaded, "Paxton, J'Nou said he would heal me and let me go free if you just tell him where your father is. Don't you love me?"

"I did, Mom. I loved you very much," he replied, as he raised his gun, turned his head a little to the right, and squinted. One tear rolled down his cheek.

The front door opened; it was J'Nou. With his mother in Terrance's bedroom and this First Brother at the front door, there was nowhere for the group to go. Terrance leapt up and aimed his gun at the neck of J'Nou.

"You tell me where your father is, and we leave you all alone." J'Nou spread his arms, smiled, and looked at everyone present. "This is a good deal for you."

"Do what he says, Paxy. He only wants to help." Paxton recognized his granny's voice, but it wasn't as frail as it used to be, and it was much darker. She stepped out from behind his mother and continued: "The Controller doesn't want to hurt your father; he wants to help him."

J'Nou's evil grin was undeniably mirthful, and Paxton knew he was ready to feed. He began to lower his gun, realizing the group was outmatched.

"I will submit to you, but only after you let my friends go. They leave first."

"No, Paxton, I won't let you do this," Terrance said.

"We're not leaving you," Sara said.

"I'm out. My head is killing me," Jeff said.

Terrance elbowed Jeff back to the ground.

J'Nou took a step forward, "I will not be—"
BAM!

A hole opened in J'Nou's belly as blood splattered on Jeff, Sara, and Terrance. Seriously wounded, but still living, J'Nou bent over on all fours and ran past the group, toward Paxton's mother and grandmother, and through the window in the back of the house. The two of them helped him along and protected him.

Paxton shot at J'Nou as he watched the Revenant's spine growing back. Even without it he leapt on all fours, like a rabbit escaping with its life, out the window and away from the house.

At the door now stood a patch-eyed Captain holding a shotgun with his cutlass at his side. His clothing was the finest, though not the cleanest, and he spoke with authority and a strong accent from the sea, "Where's my man? Jeff? What happened to 'im?" As he took in the scene with a now blood-soaked Jeff, Sara, and Terrance, the Captain raised his gun again.

"He's fine, Captain. It's from that Revenant you just shot," said Sara, feeling he would likely shoot Terrance or Paxton before either of them could explain the situation. "We need to get away from here before they come back. They want Paxton, so we need to get him somewhere."

"Wench, why you be talking to me?" The Captain scowled at her. "I be taking my man back and that be that. Uelese, come. Get Jeff and bring 'im back to the ship."

Uelese ran in, threw Jeff over his shoulder, and turned to leave. The Captain was already out the door.

Paxton stepped outside and hailed the Captain, "Ahoy, where are you going? I need to get away from here."

"I don't take no passengers. We be headin' to Haiti, then N'Orleans. If you want to come, you work the trip, and it be a long one." The Captain looked Paxton up and down. "Ever been on a ship?"

"Yeah, I took one from LA a few years ago. I can help."

"Alright then, y'can come."

"I'm coming too. You're not going without me, Paxton." Terrance leaned in to Paxton's ear and whispered, "Not even on a pirate ship."

"No, you... " Paxton stopped short when he saw Terrance's face. "Ok. We'll go together."

"What are you doing? This is crazy. You can't leave me here, Terr. I'm coming too," Sara said.

"No. No wenches on me ship," the Captain said.

Sara stared at Terrance and waited for him to change his mind or stick up for her. His silence destroyed her, "Please, don't leave."

He ignored her pleas and walked out the door behind Paxton and the Captain.

"No, don't go, Terr."

As they got a little ways down the street, Terrance admitted, "I never liked it when she called me Terr, y'know?"

Paxton forced a smile.

The Captain urged his First Mate along, "To the *Falcon*, Uelese. We have some new recruits."

3. Penelope

I n New York, Eugene waited until dark. The docks were always crowded and well lit, but the shadows provided enough cover. He pulled the hood on his jacket further over his head, "Susan. Hello. Did it come in yet?"

"It's comin' from China, Eu. May still be a while. You only commissioned the expedition a month and a half ago. That's barely enough time to get there and back, let alone get a—"

"Just promise that you'll let me know when it arrives, ok?"

"I always do," Susan smiled.

"Thanks." *I need that package. If only you knew what it was for, Susan ...* He hurried away and bumped into a pirate who stumbled toward the docks from a nearby pub.

"Hey, buddy, watchwhereyou'regoin' a'ight?"

"Sorry. Here," Eugene tossed a Naught to the pirate to prevent any trouble. "Buy another one on me."

The pirate turned and walked right back into the pub he'd just left. Eugene glimpsed the Hell's Angels Director tattoo on his neck. *Dodged a bullet there.*

No he didn't.

Eugene then headed to the local netBar, the Net Cafe, a place where he could relax. *Well, at least I can try to.* He walked in and found a seat. It was near the runway-like stage and close to the TV. Soon a woman walked out and sat on a black stool with her band behind her.

The Chipmunk Cherry Velcros played swing music and relaxed the crowd, sometimes playing more up-tempo and encouraging dancing, but often it sounded like a swinging dirge about the man she lost to the Revenant or the child she couldn't feed.

The horns, bass, and drums were key to the sound as was the southern, classic voice of the lead singer. Their irreverent approach to serious subjects was also part of the reason they drew in crowds at the Net Cafe. Nobody wanted to think of the atrocities outside, and Eugene had more reason to avoid them than others.

Her voice alone is enough to sooth me, but the best thing is that it drowns out these tabloids. All they ever cover is Nazi Europe, the terror of "Zombie America," and what this or that captain is wearing, drinking, or doing. A bunch of trash and not worth my time.

Ahh, but this music...

The walk to the docks was almost ten miles and all five men were very fit, even the Captain. But with Uelese carrying Jeff, there was no way to hurry. It was after eight, and the streets were dark and empty. Lights were on at nearly every house as families had dinner and settled in for the evening, but their glow didn't continue far past the closed curtains and planks of wood.

One very nervous fellow, Ben Linus, stepped out of his house to grab some toys his children left in the yard. Looking down the street, he saw two pirates, the large one carrying a third pirate, followed by two young men in soccer uniforms, one covered in blood.

He hurried inside, shutting and locking the door behind him. The other toys could stay out there.

"Arr, so, they was comin' after one o' ye, eh?" the Captain asked.

Uelese quickly turned his head to look behind the group; Paxton's head followed, but he saw and heard nothing. Turning his head forward again, Paxton nodded and admitted, "Yes, Captain, they were after me. If that means that you would rather not give us passage, I understand. I don't want to endanger anyone else."

"Ehh, you don't need to be worrying none about that. The beasts don't do much traveling by ship, heh heh."

At this Ueleses seemed to cough, but the upturned corner of his mouth gave away the laughter.

"So, you're all Freelancers, huh?" Terrance asked, trying to hide his disgust.

"Aye, for now we are. We live by the code of the Dead Men. Known more than a few, I have, and the only outsider to be told the full code as well."

"Yeah, I've heard some of it," Terrance began with a sarcastic tone. Then he continued with a child's sing-song voice, "'*We don't rape. We don't murder. We're the Ghosts of the Sea. We don't pillage or plunder or bring misery. Our commerce, respectful, our manner, polite. Dead Men of the Sea arrive every night.*'"

"Hahaha. Haven't heard that jingle in years. Your tone be a little off, and the code not be... "

The Captain stopped, his eye patch covering his left eye. There was nothing wrong with his left eye, but he had learned a trick from the Dead Men who wore eye patches over good eyes so that eye adjusted to the dark. When they went below deck, they would move the eye patch to their other eye, allowing them to see much more clearly in the dark. The Captain moved his eye patch over to his right eye now. The First Mate laid Jeff on the ground and both pirates turned, looking at the same dark corner behind them.

Hearing breathing coming from the corner, Paxton started, "Wha—"

"Shhh," Uelese politely, but firmly warned them.

Jeff sat up and looked around. He saw Uelese next to him with the Captain on the other side. Terrance and Paxton were a couple yards to his left. He blinked several times and rubbed his head.

"Around the corner there, Uelese. I'll come straight," the Captain said.

Paxton caught Terrance's eyes and whispered, "Who?"

Terrance shushed him and gestured that he didn't see or hear anything. Uelese turned and motioned for the two to stay where they were, and Jeff jumped to his feet.

Uelese looked at him sharply.

"I'm fine, Big Man," Jeff said and pointed to the corner, "Little girl over there?" Jeff made his way quickly and quietly around the house. Meanwhile Uelese joined the Captain and walked steadily and calmly up to the corner. Terrance thought he saw movement and heard the Captain saying, "—here? It's—follow us. Know better?"

Suddenly the Captain turned and walked back toward the group. Uelese appeared from the darkness carrying a little girl and Jeff followed.

"Please, take me with you." The girl pounded on Uelese's back, "And let me down. I have to get away. That girl… "

Terrance approached the girl, "What's your name?"

"That girl told me—"

"Be quiet," Jeff told the girl. Then, looking at Terrance, he added, "No closer. Not safe."

Uelese' look was stern and unwavering. The Captain put the patch back on his left eye and nodded sadly at Paxton, "You know this here Revenant?"

"I've never met her before," Paxton said. "How do you know she's one? If she was, couldn't she break free? Wouldn't she bring the others to us?"

"She attacked us outside your friend's house when we was lookin' for Jeff. I know she be Revenant. Can't answer yer other questions."

Uelese quickly snapped her neck and then popped it off. Jeff smiled a little, and Terrance nearly threw up, but Paxton just nodded sadly and turned to continue toward the docks.

Mara watched Uelese from the dark corner and smiled sadly as she watched her friend's head roll toward her, "Your death served us well, Penelope."

4. The Falcon

Terrance was uneasy and excused himself for a quick bathroom break. He ducked around the corner while the others surrounded the area to give him privacy and to keep an eye out for any more Revenant. He found a clear spot and fell down against the wall; with his face in his hands, he cried, "What is going on? What am I doing? Pirates?" His soul was in turmoil.

"I am here," a voice said.

Terrance shot to his feet and saw a man standing before him. He knew immediately this was the man from his dream and that this man was filled with power, "Are you going to kill me?"

"Fear not, Terrance. I told my father about you, and you've received his blessing. Now, go and stay by Paxton. The day comes when you won't be able to."

Terrance blinked and the man was gone.

Sara had a splinter in her thigh that she couldn't reach; it didn't hurt that bad, though, since her legs had been numb for the last hour. The crate she was in left her no room to stretch, and the men were rough even though it said "Fragile" on the side. *They probably can't even read.*

"Stop. Let me check that," Uelese called to the pirates.

Oh no. He knows I'm in here.

"That's a shipment to N'Orleans; an old man paid ten gold bars a few minutes before you arrived," the pirate said showing Uelese the paperwork.

Please don't check what's inside. Uelese shook the crate, but

Sara managed to hold on and keep quiet.

"Shoddy packaging. Tell him it ain't our problem if it breaks?"

"Yes, sir."

"Alright," Uelese slapped the pirate hard on his shoulder.

Thank Loki.

The other pirate handed the crate to Terrance, "Oomph. This is heavy for such a small crate."

Hey! Wait a second; that's Terrance; what if he knows I'm in here? Calm down, Sara; that's ridiculous. How could he know I'm in here?

"Man, we should have at least grabbed some clothes. I'm cold and we're gonna be ripe in a day or two."

"Sooner than that, mate." Jeff sniffed the air slowly and smacked Terrance on the shoulder hard enough to dislocate it, almost.

This jostled the crate and Terrance almost lost it. *Ahhh, what's going on?* Sara bit her lip to keep from yelping.

Jeff stared at Terrance like he was a thick steak, and Terrance glared back at him.

"Calm down," Paxton said and put his hand on Terrance's shoulder. "Just until we get to New Orleans."

"Yeah, calm down, man" Jeff said. "That's all water under the boat. So where you dudes headed after we drop you off?"

"That's our business, pirate," Terrance said.

"That's cool," Jeff raised his hands. "You stick with me. I'll teach ya' the ropes in no time, Terr."

Sara winced. That was *her* name for him.

"I'm glad to see you made it... uh... " Paxton tried to think of his name.

"Jeff, name's Jeff." He reached out to shake Paxton's hand, but Paxton didn't grab it. "Just find me in the morn' and I'll teach you all there is to know about this here ship. The *Falcon's* not the prettiest, but she's no piece of junk. And yeah, I feel great. Healthier than before."

"I don't remember asking." Terrance shifted the crate in his hands and headed downstairs.

A few hours later Sara heard only the ship creaking and the waves; there was no more shifting and tightening; no more singing and drinking. *They must be asleep. I just hope I can get out of here.*

She grabbed the crowbar her doctor friend packed with her and began trying to work it into the top plank. It was a bit longer than the box, and she couldn't quite get enough leverage. The plank popped loose and the crowbar dropped.

Sara held her breath.

Fortunately, the men weren't sleeping too close by and most were so far gone that they wouldn't have heard Chernobyl explode. Slowly she pushed the bar between the top piece of wood and the side. It wouldn't move more.

There must be something up there.

She placed the bar in the corner by the bottom of the box and pushed it. After a moment it moved some. She wedged it in further. Slowly, but deliberately, she moved the side out. It kept moving; finally she grabbed it and pushed it open enough to slide under the wood.

She was with the other cargo and realized she was fortunate to be at the edge of a stack. Throwing her legs out, she tried to stand up. Her numb legs cushioned her short fall.

She lay in a heap near some bunks, so she pulled herself toward them. She was still wearing her T-shirt and shorts and grabbed a pirate's shirt from the back of a chair, a pair of pants that was hanging off of a cot, and a hat that was stuck on a hook. *Oh, these smell foul. Don't they wash them?*

Putting the nasty disguise over her own clothes, the shirt wasn't too difficult, but sliding her legs into the pants was. When she finally had them on, they had to be rolled up, but they were small enough around her waist to fit well. Placing the hat on her head, she tucked her dark red hair under it and tried to stand again.

She was barely able to stay up. Her legs and feet tingled with pins, and her skin felt an inch thick. *Now for some boots.*

Looking around, none were small enough for her. She began to climb the stairs on all fours to look in the aft quarters. There, on the stairs, was a small pair of black shoes. *It's my lucky day. Oh, and they smell worse than the pants.*

She threw them on and tried to adopt a bit of a pirate swagger, and she stumbled like a drunk, unintentionally succeeding. She walked to the aft quarters and climbed into an empty hammock. Her legs were still tingling as she passed out fully clothed and hoping she could fit in.

"Can I do it? No. There's no way I could be the one. Or can I, the one who cursed them, save them? No. Not yet, but maybe I'm close... " Eugene was nervously trying to encourage himself and failing. His table was full of beakers, burners, matter separators, DNA Resequencers, two computers, and many odd looking ingredients.

On the table was also something that looked like the ear of a leopard, except it had snake skin and a single feather on the tip. That was lying next to a cage with five white mice curled up in the middle, sleeping. A knife was tied to the top of the cage, near the opening.

Next to the cage sat a vat of eyeballs; only one looked human; the others were reptilian, avian, ogrian, gnomerian, canine, feline, and a few others only Eugene could recognize.

An odd-looking, large jar made of thick diamond, was on a small table behind him. A refrigeration unit hung on the wall next to the table. There were many labeled tubes, but half of them were the same, *Revenant*.

He had to have a sample if he was going to create a cure.

It's almost ready... now I'll just put this here. Put that in there. Give it one more spin.

He put on thick, leather gloves. He wasn't concerned with hygiene as much as he feared getting a mouse bite or accidentally cutting himself. He reached into the refrigeration unit with a needle and took some of the Revenant blood. The leather gloves made it difficult, but this wasn't his first time; he barely noticed them now.

With his other hand, he picked a mouse out of the cage. As he lifted it out, he cut its back on the knife. He did this with one smooth motion and brought the mouse to the diamond jar as he did it. The animal wriggled and fought as the shallow cut burned its back. Eugene held it still but awkwardly as he held the back upright.

He placed one drop on the wound of the mouse, and it healed almost instantly. Eugene immediately dropped the mouse into the diamond jar. It tried to jump and climb out of the jar, but it couldn't. It leapt far higher than it ever could have before, but Eugene built the jar knowing of the mouse's increased abilities.

The separation unit stopped spinning. *Just in time.* Setting the needle in a sink to be sanitized later, he picked up a new needle and sucked up the substance from the separation unit. Then he squeezed it onto the jar floor near the mouse.

In the past Eugene would inject the mice with the serum, but after a few narrow escapes from Revenant mice teeth, he roughed up the bottom of the jar with a special acid, making it sharp and jagged. He squeezed the liquid directly onto that spot.

As the mouse lapped it up, the bottom of the jar made small lacerations that healed very quickly, but enough of the test batch made its way into the blood for the test to be accurate.

He put some of his own blood into the test batches to encourage the mice to drink it. This had the side effect of causing the mouse to bang its head on the wall trying to get more blood since their higher brain functions were not strong enough to resist the craving.

The mouse slowed and then stopped banging its head on the wall of the jar. The mouse looked up at him and seemed to calm down. It was docile and sniffing the air. *It worked. The cure worked. I can't belie—*

Then the mouse rolled over.

No, no, no, no, no! Not again. He pulled out his audio-scanner, held it close to the jar, and listened. There was no sound. No breathing. No blood pumping. Nothing. He opened the jar to confirm.

It was dead.

He didn't want to kill the Revenant; he wanted to heal them. He was guilty of their condition, so he was responsible for their cure.

"Damn it!" He was so close. "I need that damn egg. I'm certain it's the key."

Sara opened her eyes and saw two soccer players standing over her. They didn't look pleased to see her, especially the one on the left. The pirate over their shoulders, however, smiled fondly.

"What are you doing here?" asked Terrance.

"She came back for me," Jeff's eyes rolled down her body and up to Terrance's eyes. He caught Terrance's fist just before it connected with his jaw.

"How's your head?" Paxton asked. Jeff opened his mouth to answer, but Paxton interrupted him, "Look, I don't really care; just shut up; I'm not as nice as my friend here."

"Well, I hope you don't punch like 'im," Jeff laughed.

Terrance stared into Jeff's head and suddenly became confused. He could tell that Jeff was fighting something back. It felt like a thick, green, warm fog. His mind was there, beneath this fog, controlling the fog. Quickly, Terrance became lost in thoughts of finding something in the fog, a memory island, or a thought of lightning.

"Ya'll can't tell the Captain," Sara pleaded, and her voice broke Terrance's trance. "I can't go back home. Those things are there; they'll find me and kill me. They never let anyone go."

"They're not looking for you, Sara. They wouldn't even recognize you," Terrance said.

"Would too. They'd use me to find you," she said. "I know where the ship is going, so I know where you're going. You can't let the Captain take me back."

"If they wanted to, they could get to us here," Paxton said. "They may even be following behind the boat now."

"I think we should tell the Captain. Maybe we can send her back," Terrance said.

"Don't worry, Chicky; they won't follow us. We're safe now," Jeff reached to touch Sara's hand, but she pushed it away.

Terrance shot his hand out and grabbed Jeff's wrist in a vice grip. His eyes never left the side of Jeff's head.

"What do you mean?" Paxton also stared at Jeff.

"They never come over the water, Dude," Jeff's eyes explored Sara's body.

"Yes, of course. And I'm certain that this fact has been scientifically proven, which is why the government built a moat, instead of a wall," Terrance said and looked at Paxton with his eyebrows raised and pushed together.

"Didn't you know they were like witches, Terrance?" Paxton asked.

Jeff began to open his mouth, and Terrance's mind swirled, but before any sound came, Sara said, "I don't care. There was nothin' for me in that city except you, Terr, and I'm not goin' back. I'm sorry for what I did, but I will do whatever it takes to get you back."

Terrance had no reply. He just wanted to know what was happening in Jeff's head. He'd never felt anything like he did now. He wanted Jeff to go away, to stay, and to be alone with him, so he could ask him what it felt like.

Jeff yanked his wrist away from Terrance.

"Get your mangy selves up on deck," the First Mate called down. Uelese was a large, dark-skinned man that none would dare to disrespect. "Now."

"Yeah, yeah. We're coming," Jeff turned and marched up the stairs.

Paxton encouraged Sara to get up and stay behind them. The three walked up the steps to join the crew on deck.

"What the hell is that?" yelled one pirate.

Sara froze.

"Am I wearing the wrong uniform?" asked another.

"Can I be a captain of one team?" asked the one next to him.

"Alright, that's enough now. Someone be gettin' them real clothes," the Captain said. "Jeff. What do you think you be doing? You were going to 'show them the ropes' right? Get our soccer players some clothes. Now."

5. Caught

The days passed quickly; the winds were favorable; and it only took three days to get to Haiti. The ship had a gas-powered water-wheel, but with the price of gasoline, it was only used in extreme cases of bad weather.

Sara kept trying to talk with Terrance alone, and was almost discovered by Uelese. More than once Terrance avoided Sara and spent any free time studying Jeff and talking to Paxton, who was inconsolable.

That morning, with land in sight, Terrance was sitting on his bunk with Paxton.

"Yeah, and have you noticed he's never tired?" Terrance asked.

"I don't know about that; he just seems to be friendly and helpful. I think Uelese got to him about helping us out," Paxton replied.

"I don't know; he just seems odd."

"Odd?" Paxton thought about it. "Yeah, maybe. He keeps asking where we're going after New Orleans."

"Me too."

"You don't have to come with me, but I can't tell you. It's not safe. Anyway, when are you going to forgive Sara? You and her have been together a long time."

"Yeah, we have, but she slept with a *pirate*," the last word dripped off his tongue and left a sour taste.

"Don't dodge the question."

"A pirate, Paxton!"

"I know, but you were about to propose to her."

"P." Paxton sighed, but Terrance continued, "I." Paxton opened his mouth, and Terrance held up a finger to finish, "Rat."

"You two are good together."

"Not just any pirate, Jeff the pirate."

"I think you should listen to her and give her a chance, at least."

"Pirate, Paxton. Jeff the Odd Pirate."

"Terr, you're a pirate now."

The two sat in silence for a few moments. Terrance thought of Sara and how he was going to propose. He fondled the box in his pocket and was glad he'd had it in his soccer uniform.

He thought of how Cynthia was so nice to help with the proposal, even though she didn't like Sara. *I guess she was right.* Terrance wanted to ask about Paxton's mother and grandmother. He was building up the courage. He opened his mouth.

It was dry.

He needed to lick his lips. *Ok, now I can ask him.*

He opened his mouth again. He closed it. He opened it and finally made a sound.

He burped.

"Excuse me." Terrance covered his mouth, but at least it was loose now. *Better just ask now rather than wait and let my mouth dry up again.* "Hey, man... how are you doing with the whole... y'know... I mean... your mom and granny?"

The silence that followed the question was killing Terrance. He hoped that Paxton was glad to have the question asked, but knew he would never be ready to answer it.

"They were all I had," Paxton stared hard at his hands, wringing them together. "And I know they were close to you too."

"They treated me like family," he nodded.

Paxton looked at Terrance. Tears welled up in his eyes.

"I mean, they're still out there, like that. I can't imagine... "

"Me either," Terrance said. "I'm here for you, if you ever want to talk about it. I know it helped to talk about my parents when they died."

"They're not dead, Terrance, my mom and granny are— It's worse than that." Paxton seethed now, and the tears welled up as he thought of who to blame.

Terrance could feel the anger in the air, "Why be angry, though? It was a monster that did it."

"You're right. He is a monster."

"And I'll stay with you until we find him."

"Terrance, you know what I plan to do. Are you sure you want to stay with me for that?"

Terrance realized who Paxton meant, "That's not the monster I was referring to, Paxton."

"But he has their blood on his hands," Paxton said. "Telling him may be enough to kill him."

"All hands on deck," Uelese called from above deck.

"I guess we better go," Paxton hopped to his feet and hurried up on deck.

"Yeah, we'll continue this later. Don't think I'm going to forget," Terrance called after him, as he sat down and slipped his shoes on. He was alone now and pulled the ring out of his pocket to look at it. *Maybe I can trade you for a bit of money here.* He put the ring back and ran up on deck to join everyone.

"A few of you be coming on shore with me," the Captain addressed the entire crew. "We have a delivery to be making. Jeff, Uelese, you both be going; pick three men each, fifteen minutes."

Jeff looked immediately at Paxton, Terrance, and Sara, and then walked over to the three.

"You three will come with me," Jeff turned and walked straight to the Captain to report his pick.

"But we... " Sara stopped short as she realized Jeff was not slowing and considered this an order.

"Come on. We better get ready," Terrance said. "I want off this boat for a while, even if it has to be with him and her."

In the middle of the Atlantic Ocean, a rare site was witnessed by a mermaid out for her daily swim. She saw two ships tied together, one was flying the flag of the Dead Men, and the other was flying the flag of the Hell's Angels. She wondered briefly what they were doing and swam closer to listen.

"Captain Arnold, you will retrieve the package from the Dead Men's Captain," the Director of the Hell's Angels said.

"Y-Yes, sir. Director, sir."

A Director? This far out and meeting with the Dead Men?

The crew murmured about what it may be. She heard guesses from a mutant Russian baby to a clutch of ogre eggs. She swam around until she could get a better view of the package. As it was handed from ship to ship, she saw the crate.

She dove as fast as her fins could take her, deep under the water. She didn't want to be near the surface if the mother came looking for her egg.

Jeff approached the Captain who sat at a large desk covered with maps and star charts. His wireless was there, but that only worked in ports. The Captain continued to stare out the window.

"Son?" the Captain said this without turning around.

"Yes, Father, I have picked out the three."

The Captain continued staring out the window at Île de la Gonâve, waiting.

"Paxton, Terrance, and Sam. The three new guys from Miami."

"Don't you mean Sara?" His face didn't change.

"How did you—"

"You think I be stupid?" He turned to look at Jeff now.

Jeff's heart pounded. *Calm.* He settled. *Of course the Captain would know. A secret like that could only last so long.* He lowered his head, "No sir, I should have told you immediately."

"Yeah, you should've." He looked Jeff over for a second before continuing, "It's her what got you in this mood, eh?"

"Mood?"

"You ain't been yourself. Been working straight through the night."

"I thought you wanted me to be more serious with my work, Father."

"Yeah. Yeah, that be true. Just figured it'd take more time I guess," he said. He lowered his eyes and then looked deeply into a floorboard on his right.

Jeff left.

The ship docked in Port-au-Prince, and nine pirates walked off while the rest of the crew replenished supplies and made deliveries. The Captain, Uelese, Jeff, Paxton, Terrance, Sara, and three others walked through the market and port toward the center of town.

The Captain walked with a purpose and Jeff and Uelese followed one step behind him on either side. Everyone else was behind these two men, and it was clear from their conversation that none of them knew where they were going.

This was not just a common excursion.

As they walked out of the busy port area, they headed into town and down a quiet, dark street. The sun cast shadows over this street at all times of the day. Those who lived and worked on Dark Street liked it this way. The Captain entered a small, curtained door with no sign above it and the group followed him inside.

"Get him out of here; he's one of them," a voice screamed from the back room.

The store had only candles for light, and the front windows and door had curtains that blocked the little light that fell on Dark Street, not that any light would have made it past the assortment of shrunken heads, jars of plant and animal parts, charms, ingredients, and other strange concoctions piled in front of the windows. A doorway in the back had a curtain made from small bones.

The room smelled strong of incense.

A man came running out of the back room. Uelese caught him by the hair with one hand. Another man stumbled through the bones, a trickle of blood running down his face.

"Ah, Uelese, thank you," Azacca said. "Agwe will be grateful too. This man is one of those who press us down for protection money. I must put curse on him so others will not come back. If you would help me bring him upstairs, I would appreciate."

"Go ahead, Uelese. We'll continue in to see Agwe," the Captain nodded.

Uelese followed Azacca through the bones, dragging the man by his hair. The Captain also walked through the bones but turned left toward a small round table; the stairs were to the right. Jeff followed, hesitating at the bones, fluttering his eyes, breathing in their aroma, and then continuing. Terrance was next, followed by Paxton, Sara, and the other three pirates.

"Agwe, you scurvy dog, where ye be?"

An old, dark-skinned man shuffled down the stairs behind the group. His left eye was white with a pale scar that ran from the top left of his skull, across the middle of his eye, and ended in a slit that split his left nostril. At the bottom of the stairs, he stopped suddenly. He sniffed the air and reached into his robes with his right hand and withdrew an eight-inch knife. It was shiny and freshly sharpened. He raised it slowly and turned toward the group.

In a deep, dark voice, he said, "You will kneel, or I will kill you, zombie."

6. Death Metal

Eugene's turn in line finally came and he hurried forward. The rain beat down on him, and his hood only kept some of it off. The Port Delivery Stand was covered, but the walk-up-window wasn't.

"Eugene. It's your lucky day. Here's that package you've been waiting on," Susan said.

She handed him a box, nearly two feet tall and at least one foot wide and deep. He thanked her and grabbed the box by the ropes tied around it. Getting the box to his apartment wasn't easy, especially in the rain. *At least the rain keeps the streets clear.*

After struggling up the stairs, he carefully set the box on the ground outside his apartment. His neighbor, Roger, leaned out the door. "Yous going to join us for dinner, Buddy?"

"Not this week, sorry. Have to work through. I'll see you guys next week, though."

"We'll miss you. The kiddos love your magic tricks," Roger waved and went back in his apartment.

Eugene brought the crate into his apartment and easily removed the ropes. He went to the corner and grabbed his "letter opener," a small, black crowbar. Placing the prying end into a smaller plank on top of the box, he pulled back. The plank popped off easily.

Phew. I hope it's all this easy; wouldn't want to hurt it.

Straw that filled the inside spilled on the floor. He popped the other two top pieces just as easily and started on the sideboards. They were more difficult, but he placed the crowbar in a crack on one corner and pulled.

Finally it came off.

The other boards were easier, and Eugene was able to pull the box apart with his bare hands. He spread the straw and looked at the egg.

Nearly two feet tall and a foot in diameter, the outside was shiny blue with a pearlescent sheen. It was dimpled slightly and looked like the largest, most precious stone ever known. The egg kept itself upright.

It was impossible to tip it over unless it held a baby. Eugene was glad; he specifically requested one like this. He was excited to drill into the egg. *Now, I can complete the serum.*

He picked up a hand drill and placed the pointy bit on the top of the shell. He carefully placed pressure on it and slowly turned the crank.

Terrance's head swam. He knew what the Haitian man was saying and knew that the Haitians called the Revenant, *zombies*, but what surprised him was the voice. He recognized that voice.

It was his voice.

Sara was surprised by the voice too, but even more by Jeff falling to his knees. "He's a Revenant?" she whispered to Paxton.

Paxton pulled Sara away from Jeff and nodded.

"A Revenant Pirate," Terrance said. His face was stone.

The three other pirates were shocked and backed away from Jeff, drawing their swords. One of them began to swing at Jeff's neck and another prepared to jump at Agwe. The Captain caught the arm of the pirate before he connected with Jeff's neck, "Stop. He just confirmed what I be thinking."

Jeff's eyes were trying to focus, but he was still kneeling, and his hands hung limp by his sides. Agwe moved closer to Jeff, preparing to kill him. He was struggling and sweating.

"No, Agwe. We be needing to save him," the Captain said.

"An elixir for his condition not be on this island," Agwe responded. "However, since you have a speaker with you this time, I will make a releaser as before."

Terrance, Paxton, and Sara looked at each other, then at the other pirates. None of them gave an indication that they understood. The Captain, however, was grateful and had only one question. He pointed at Terrance, "This one here be the speaker?"

"Yes," Agwe answered.

"May he be staying with you, so as you can teach him how to use the voice?"

"It will cost you, Captain. More than the releaser will."

"Aye. We be unloadin' the goods now."

"Here is way to pick what you need," he handed the Captain a map. "Only he stay, though. Others must go with you."

Minutes later, Jeff was back under the Controller's influence. He was in a small cell in an upstairs room of Agwe's shop.

The cell was built for this purpose and was made of an odd, bluish substance Terrance didn't recognize, but thought it might be stainless steel. Stainless steel wouldn't hold a Revenant any more than paper would hold one, but upon closer inspection, Terrance saw the blue color radiating from it.

The metal was blurry and he couldn't focus on it. Terrance blinked his eyes several times, trying to focus. He moved his hand in close to it, and the blur reached out for him. He could see the metal more clearly now through the blur.

It filled his vision. He wiggled his fingers near the bar, but the blue blur did not move like a cloud would.

Terrance touched a bar of the cell.

He felt safe with Jeff sitting quietly in the center on a piece of cardboard, far from the bars. The skin beneath Terrance's fingers seemed to go into the metal, as if it were soft, wet clay. This unnerved him at first. He then began to feel fine about it and wrapped his whole hand around a bar.

The metal pulled him into another dimension. Terrance felt like a child again, carefree and playing with sand on Miami beach. His parents were there, and they waved for him to get up and come to them. He stood and ran toward them. He was so happy. Then he saw their eyes.

Dark.

The voice they used to call to him became dark too. Not like his voice, but like a Revenant's voice. A band of pirates formed out of the sand and ran toward his parents. He reached for them, but they were too far away. The pirates took his parents' stuff—they took everything—and shot them both in the head.

Terrance felt himself drowning in the water, but he could still clearly see what was happening.

The pirates were telling the police that his parents were Revenant, that it was a mercy killing. He was now in the deepest despair of his life. He couldn't breathe; nor did he want to. He was ready to die now and join them.

He gave himself over to the water.

Suddenly his hand was jerked away. Azacca had a cane around Terrance's wrist and had his eyes wide open, staring at Terrance with disbelief.

"You got a death wish, boy?" Azacca's tall, thin frame was not intimidating, but his presence was. He rapped his cane on Terrance's hand. "Death Metal is sure way to kill yourself. Never touch that stuff. Very rare. We only lock up zombies with it. Most of them have enough sense not to touch the stuff. Why you idiot?"

"Why is that?" Terrance rubbed his hand. "I mean, I know why I would never touch it again, but Revenant wouldn't necessarily know better, would they?"

"Terrance, my boy, you have lot to learn. They are intelligent when belly is full. They even have self-control. At least these American zombies do." He stared at Terrance to see if he understood. Then he continued. "If someone is controlling them, though, they not let the zombie touch the Death Metal. Vodoun zombie or American. It would affect them just as much. A mindless zombie or hungry Revenant likely not care, and that be the end of them."

"So, why don't we just make it touch the stuff. Then the Controller would be in a living hell, right?"

"Yes, but we do not want that," Agwe joined them. His robes were brown, red, and white, and most every color in between. He dragged them along the floor as he walked. Terrance was certain this was not by design but because of the old man's stoop.

"Why wouldn't we want that? I think we'd be better off without him and the Revenant."

"Why do you think that?" Agwe asked.

"They kill people. The farms alone are disgusting. They raise people like cattle. Not to mention they're trying to kill my best friend and his father."

"I understand, but you do not see the fault in your logic."

"And what is that?"

"You must find it yourself," Azacca interrupted. "This is silly. There is no way you hurt him, and if you use Death Metal, he break the hold. He has in the past. The Captain is paying Agwe to learn your voice, not speak of the Controller and nonsense crusades."

"Well, I've used it once. I told Jeff to do something when I was angry. I said, 'Come back here' or something like that."

"Yes, I felt your patterns growing strong, as I always feel the Controller's strong patterns," Agwe said. "You may develop those senses; for now, we work on your voice. An afternoon is not long."

"So, what do I do?"

"Reach down in yourself. You have the voice, but it not come from your mouth or lung. It come from your very being, your essence. Feel the depth of your passion. Let's start there. What do you feel passion about? What made you angry?"

"I saw that," he pointed at Jeff, "in bed with Sara."

"So, Sara. Is that the girl pirate with you?"

"Girl? You knew she... yes."

"You like her. Think about her. Imagine her scent. Her skin. Her lips. Her eyes. They all long for you. You want them. Close your eyes and picture it. Now, that feeling in your gut—tap into it and tell Jeff to jump."

"Jump," Terrance said in a voice he tried to make sound deeper.

Nothing happened.

"I don't think that will work. I'm still mad at her."

"Anger is not good to use, but for now it will work. Look at him. Think of him in bed with her and tell him to jump."

"Jump," Terrance said in a voice slightly deeper than his normal voice.

Jeff stood there, but his eyes darted at Terrance for one brief moment, then returned to staring at the chipped paint on a panel of wood outside the cage.

"Very good; you felt it. We can work with this."

Paxton and Sara were drenched. Their clothes were salty and wet with sweat, and clung to them like a second skin. The pair was used to thick heat, but this was an exceptionally muggy day.

"How could you climb in bed with that pirate? I don't know if he'll ever forgive you," Paxton said.

"That bastard forced me to do it, though," she pleaded.

"Forced you? Why are there no marks from a struggle? Why did he leave and not attack Terrance? Just tell him you were weak and admit the truth. He deserves that."

Paxton looked down at Sara. She was hunched over and wearing a jacket to hide her breasts. She was the only one not carrying her jacket, and she was miserable.

He saw her sigh and knew she was really sorry. He softened his tone a little, "He loved you so much."

"How would I know? Ya'll just played soccer."

"And he never shut up about you."

"He could have invited me to play, or somethin'."

"Would you have gone?"

"I guess not," she said.

"You could have talked to him about it."

The two walked along, staying about eight feet behind the others. They stared ahead at the ground. The Captain knew what they were looking for and where it would be growing. They were already a couple of miles into the thick forest growth.

"I guess I kind of wanted it—"

"Kind of?" Paxton's tone was gentle now. He could hear the pain in her voice.

"I was upset. He's just been ignorin' me so much recently," she was quiet for a moment. "I was a little jealous of you. Why didn't he want to spend time with me? Why— Why didn't I just talk to him about it?"

The question hung in the air. It tried to climb into Paxton's open mouth as his lips parted and came together, then parted again, soundlessly.

"I know it's stupid," Sara said. "I value your friendship too, and I couldn't be alone in Miami. After my parents died, you two were all I had. I still love him, you know?"

"But are you really sorry?"

"Yes. Especially now that Jeff's a damn Revenant."

"Now that he's a Revenant?" Paxton's voice was angry again.

"No. That's not what I meant," she looked down. "There are things you don't understand."

"Instead of talking to him about spending more time with you, you go to the port, find some strange pirate, and bring him home. Did that seem like a good idea to you?" Paxton allowed more anger to creep into his voice.

"No. I didn't know what to do. I just wanted to make Terrance jealous. We didn't even do nothin'."

"Because Terrance came home too soon, right? He was in your bed, half-naked."

"Yeah, I guess he was, but we hadn't done anything. I—I just—I messed up. I'll have to talk to Terrance when we get back to the ship."

They walked in silence for several seconds.

"So, why are we going to New Orleans?" Sara asked. "Is that where your dad's at?"

"No, it is just a place that will get us away from the Revenant. Or it would have. Now that Jeff is one and knows where we're headed, well, the Controller will have more there. Waiting."

"I guess that's my fault."

"No. If it hadn't been for the Captain, we'd all be Revenant by now. As horrible as it was, your screw up may have saved us."

"It's anger." Terrance told Agwe how he felt. "After sleeping with that, I can't help but be angry at her."

"Are you innocent? Is it all her fault?"

"She's the one who slept with that thing; I was just playing soccer."

"That's not what I meant. Relationships are like Luatu plant. When you pick Luatu leaf, it is poisonous. One prick from the spike on Luatu leaf can leave you asleep forever. Care is necessary. When you are careful and carry Luatu leaf with you, spend time with it, caress it, take care of it, a seed will grow inside.

"The elements for Luatu seed are already there, but it cannot grow until it is removed from its family. The other leaves. Care must be taken to plant Luatu seed as well. Luatu seed cannot be forced into ground; it must be coaxed. It uses its tendrils to escape if it is spooked.

"Now with Luatu seed; if you do not care for it, it will die. There is another thing about Luatu seeds. They can do great things, but there are always sacrifices. You will see, if you forgive her, and sacrifice pride, you can heal something dead."

Terrance sat, staring at Agwe for a moment. He watched Azacca help Agwe prepare a pot with herbs and liquids. He didn't recognize most of them.

Azacca cut Agwe's scar and Agwe allowed the blood to drip into the pot. Azacca then helped Agwe patch his eye with a bandage. Terrance knew that Agwe was sacrificing some of his own life for Jeff's.

"Well, she had mentioned that I didn't spend enough time with her, but I guess I didn't listen well enough. I—I'll work on forgiving her, but I need anger to use my voice."

"You do not need anger. You need only passion." Agwe was patient. "You must control passion inside. Reach into core of self and pull it out. Control emotions. Feel them and control them. Do not let any emotion control you."

"It's easier said than done," Terrance replied.

"Yes, now you begin to understand."

Terrance angled his head, looked at Agwe and creased his eyes in confusion; then he realized what Agwe meant, "I guess I have to forgive her and everyone else."

"Yes. Like those seen when you touched the metal. The pirates from the beach."

"I can't... "

Agwe stared hard at him.

Terrance slowed his breathing and stared intently at Jeff. It was difficult not relying on anger to make it work. He took a deep breath, filling his lungs. It was unnecessary, but it helped him to picture the force he could sense. It seemed to lie in the middle of his chest, just beside and below his heart.

"Jump," his voice was commanding and dark. Not as dark as it had been at home, but it did make Jeff look up again.

Jeff stiffened, and Terrance felt it, a presence inside of the pirate Revenant. It was brief, but it was a strong, sharp, piercing feeling. He recognized the sensation, but had no clue how he knew it. His eyes were wide with shock and his mouth hung open.

"You felt him."

"That was... " Terrance's voice was rough and uneven. He struggled to get those two words out, and was unable to bring more to his lips.

Agwe took pity. "Yes, that was the Controller. He surely sensed you too. I felt it when you walked in my store, just as he felt me when I commanded Jeff."

"How can you command him when he's under the Controller's power?" Terrance pointed toward Jeff.

"The Controller is very powerful, but the incense I burn weakens that connection so I take control long enough to get them in here." He raised his hand toward the cage, "or dispatch them quickly." He touched the blade on his hip with the same hand. "It also helps you control him now. The herbs your friends bring, the Luatu leaf, will help break the connection completely. Enough for you to control him."

"I can't, though, I'm not ready."

"You may not need to often. He will have control of himself when he isn't hungry or injured."

"How do you know this?"

Agwe smiled.

"They much like our Vodoun zombie, but they have more of their self left. The herbs and medicines that make a Vodoun zombie wipe out those memories. We *must* control them or they will be consumed by constant hunger.

"Several years ago, we had Vodoun zombie outbreak. Many of them attacked others and most of Haiti became infected. When the men came from America, they help us. But as payment they take the Bonifacy's to help them; they studied our methods, but when they added other things... well the results were very different."

"Did you say, 'Bonifacy'?"

"Yes."

"That's my name."

"Well, this was many decades ago. The family was brought to New Orleans well before you were born."

"Oh, I grew up in Miami," Terrance let the subject drop.

They continued to practice, and while Terrance couldn't reach what he did in Miami, he was able to make Jeff jump. Each time, though, he felt something more familiar from the powerful voice of the Controller inside Jeff's head.

The group of pirates followed the Captain and walked within yards of an old hut that none of them saw. That was what Alfred, the man inside, wanted. He had put together his hut from bushes, branches, and leaves, and each corner was a large, living tree. Even Paxton didn't notice the structure.

Alfred was dirty and wore few clothes. He had twigs in his long, knotted hair and wore a necklace made from seeds of the Luatu plant. The seeds writhed and moved and held on to each other. They were round with red tendrils and he regularly treated them so they wouldn't dry out, die, or worse.

He stalked out of his hut after hearing the group pass and moved through the trees looking for something left behind. After only a little searching, he found a single hair. It was dark and he could tell who it belonged to when he touched it.

This will work.

Alfred returned to his hut and began the ritual, grinning wildly.

The Captain stopped. The jungle was thick around them. They didn't feel very isolated, however. Haiti had long ago become a united island after the *Zombie Uprising*, but it was still small. It was difficult to walk very far in any direction without finding a small village, port, or hermit. The Captain had stopped for none of these things, however: His nose was up; he sensed something else.

"Does he hear something?" Paxton asked one of the pirates.

"No, I think he smells something. He always says he has an excellent sense of smell, can't stand rotting fish anywhere on the boat. And he can smell a rat on the boat too," the pirate said.

"Ahh. I wonder if it's that musty scent. It's almost wood like, but with some nut, mildew, and a little blood mixed in."

"What was that ye just said, boy?" The Captain's ears were well worn, but he heard Paxton's quiet description from over ten feet away.

"I was describing a smell sir. One that seems stronger than it should."

"And ye were describing it quite well, me boy. Can you find where it's coming from?" The Captain squinted at Paxton with his one uncovered eye.

"Sure, I believe it's that purple leaf over there," Paxton pointed at a small plant.

It was a Luatu plant.

Four purple leaves spread out from a dark center. They lifted up about two inches in the middle, then fell to the ground, as if they'd been draped there. The leaves were each about thirty centimeters long and thirteen centimeters across at the thickest point. The leaves also grew thick near the center, almost four centimeters. They had pointed edges, but the points looked soft. The middle was a pitch black circle.

He walked closer to the plant and noticed the middle wasn't there; a hole was there instead. He also noticed that the purple plant remained still, but not the large green plant that grew directly next to it. This green guardian plant covered the purple plant with protective green leaves that were the same size and shape as those of the purple plant. The green stem twisted its leaves toward Paxton.

He reached down to feel the hole.

"No," the Captain rushed forward. "Don't be using yer hands. It could bite ye. Let me use me blade. That green plant there be the Luata. It's the protector of the Luatu. Each must have the other or it not be long for this world."

The Captain pulled out a long curved sword which had a notch on the end. Paxton imagined what that would do on the way out if the Captain stabbed someone. It was there for that purpose, but it served another purpose on this occasion. He bent down and swung deftly to cut off one whole leaf; then many things happened very quickly.

The remaining three purple leaves snapped up and pulled into the hole. The green plant's fat bulb squeezed together, lengthening the stalk, and the leaves grew stiff. A sound, like rattling, came from the Luata.

The plant was screaming at them.

Simultaneously, the Captain turned the blade quickly to the notched side and hooked the leaf. He pried the leaf off the blade and shoved it into a large pocket in his pants, carefully avoiding the spikes.

When the leaves snapped up, Sara leaped back and tripped over a rock. She fell backwards and hit her shoulder on another rock. A small rip went from the top of her shoulder across her shoulder blade and rounded back to her armpit. The wound wasn't deep, but it was bleeding.

Behind her were four purple leaves and a tall green stalk that bent toward her. The purple leaves stretched toward the blood dripping from her wound. She reached back to push herself up, but as her hand moved toward the purple spikes, Paxton grabbed her arm and helped her up.

The green plant bent down to the blood on the ground and swept it toward the purple leaves.

"We got it; time to be gettin' back," the Captain smiled.

With Sara's injury the walk back was slower, but not much. Her back wasn't too bad, but she twisted her ankle, so another pirate helped Paxton with her.

"What's your name again?" she asked.

"Jean. Name's Jean," the pirate replied.

"How did he know what plant we were looking for?"

"Oh, he been here before. Hunted Luatu before, but not for Jeff." Jean lowered his voice as he said this, and his eyes made it clear that this wasn't a story she would hear from him.

"So, why did he do all of this for Jeff? Are they that close?"

"He and Jeff be close. They not really be father and son, but he found Jeff as a baby. He was left by our cargo and nobody around claimed him.

"Well, the Captain isn't no baby killer and didn't feel right giving it away to someone. I mean it wasn't the baby's fault he be left with us; so the Captain took the baby and raised him as his own.

"Jeff knows the truth, even goes off occasionally in N'Orleans; it's where we found him. He tries to find anyone who may recognize him."

"Wow. I didn't know."

"You don't know the half of it, really. He always be running off and getting into trouble. Jeff I mean, so this is just one more thing he's done. Though, I guess this will be his last mistake, huh?"

"But this will fix him, right? He'll be able to stay on the boat and make more trouble."

Jean stared at her like he didn't understand and then just looked forward.

The group continued the hike back in silence. When they arrived, Terrance was sitting at the table, eating.

"Hey guys."

"On your feet when the Captain enters, Terrance," Uelese commanded.

Terrance jumped up and swallowed the bite of bread that was in his mouth. He was nearly done and decided that if sitting was offensive, eating may be too. His eyes crept toward the bowl of soup and piece of bread.

Uelese' eyes squinted slightly.

Terrance noticed and looked to the group, "Did you get the plant?"

"Aye. Your friend Paxton here helped a lot. He has quite the nose on him," the Captain slapped Paxton's shoulder.

Terrance was relieved. He still hadn't been able to control Jeff fully, but with the progress he'd made so far, Agwe believed he would be able to once Jeff was separated.

Agwe and Azacca came downstairs.

"Let me have it. Everything else is ready," Azacca said to the Captain.

The Captain pulled out a shriveled red leaf that was already dry and crumbled around the edges. Paxton wondered what was going on; the leaf had been full and thick and purple not long before.

Jean noticed Paxton's expression, "It dries up quickly and turns red like that. Keep watching. You'll see why they need to harvest it quickly and close to when they use it."

"So that's a Luatu leaf?" Terrance said to himself. His eyes were on everything Agwe did, but his mind was on Sara. Her bandaged shoulder looked worse than it was, and Paxton was still helping her keep weight off her foot.

Agwe took the leaf, then walked to the stove. He grabbed a pot of steaming green liquid and moved it to the table.

Agwe grabbed the leaf with two hands, careful not to break off more pieces. Then he squeezed the edges. The middle bubbled up. He then broke the crusty outer shell, and a quiet shrieking sound could be heard as a round, red thing fell toward the pot. It looked like a large drop of blood with liquid tentacles stretching out from it.

Then, just before it reached the steaming green ooze, four tendrils shot out and grabbed the edge of the pot. The seed held itself above the ooze for a moment. The edges of the pot were very hot, though, and the seed couldn't hold on for long. The heat dried out the ends of the tendrils; they broke off, and the seed fell in the liquid.

The liquid in the pot then began to boil more. Red bubbles rose from the green liquid. The bubbles rose rapidly, but barely boiled above the rim. Agwe took the pot and a soup ladle and used the ladle to spoon the pot of soup into a bowl for Jeff.

Agwe headed up the stairs with Azacca, and Terrance followed instinctively. The Captain followed as well, but everyone else remained downstairs.

Agwe approached the cell. He grabbed his blade and used it to slice his finger open. One drop of blood was all he needed this time. He dropped it into the bowl. Jeff began to snarl and sniff in the direction of the bowl.

He fought himself over whether or not to eat it.

"The Controller is stopping him," Agwe said. "We may need to force feed him. Work with me, Terrance. Eat the food. Taste the blood. We command him together. Ready?"

Terrance nodded in agreement and both men spoke in dark voices; Agwe's was significantly darker and stronger. Jeff bent down, picked up the bowl, and lapped up some soup.

He eagerly tasted some more. Then, using both hands, he tilted the bowl back and dumped it into his mouth, licking the sides clean.

For Jeff the taste was like blood—not quite as wonderful as human blood, even with some of Agwe's in it, but far better than the ship rats he'd been eating. It was thick and made his mouth tingle. He felt the energy flowing into his body.

As the ooze reached his stomach, the seed inside took hold. Tentatively the seed stretched out its tendrils. The ends were still singed, and its skin was blistered, but the tendrils grew into the edges of the stomach. It would stay here for the rest of Jeff's life, expanding throughout his body.

Jeff curled up and sat on the floor.

"Jeff be seeded. The seed has anchored in his stomach," Agwe said. "He will be in pain for a short time, but now the Controller cannot call him across such vast distances. Terrance, you may command him at will, but remember, he is not an animal like our zombies; he will still have his own will and be the Jeff he was before. Only now he is different enough that the Controller cannot easily force his will on him. The Luatu seed will grow inside of him and protect him."

Agwe turned directly to the Captain and continued, "He will be himself when his belly is full, and his hunger should be less now, but it will be just like... " he caught the Captain's eyes. "Well, we must say goodbye old friend. I will have Azacca remove him and bring him down to the *Falcon*."

"Aye. Thank you, Agwe." The Captain nodded and turned to walk down the stairs. "Come, Terrance; they be delivering him soon."

Alfred sat in his hut and dropped the dark hair into the pot on his propane hot plate. As it hit the mixture inside, a Luatu tendril reached up and grabbed the hair, pulling it down into the stew. He grinned and knew it was now just a matter of time before it was ready.

There was more than one way to use the Luatu plant.

8. Jump

"Listen up, crew. Ye heard what's happened, no doubt. We have a *speaker* on board, and everything be fine. Jeff be seeded." The Captain dismissed everyone with a wave.

Even though nobody talked about it, Jeff's arrival that evening drew many stares. Terrance, Paxton, and Sara were on deck when Jeff boarded the *Falcon*. He looked at them as he shuffled by, focused on Paxton; then he looked away. He continued past them; then he stopped and turned back to Paxton, "I'm sorry. I never meant to let him know." He turned and went straight to his bunk.

"What's that about, Paxy?" Terrance asked.

Paxton flinched at the nickname, "The Controller knows we're going to New Orleans. He'll have someone there to follow us or kill us. They're probably already waiting."

"Did that bastard tell him?" Terrance asked.

"No, Terr. The Controller can read Jeff's mind, or at least he could read it until they gave him that awful stuff," Sara said.

"I wouldn't call it awful, Sara," Paxton said.

That evening, before setting sail, Paxton approached the Captain's door. Jean was speaking to Uelese outside of it, but he left as Paxton walked up and pulled the door handle. It wouldn't open.

Uelese hand was on the door, holding it closed. "Captain's busy."

"I need to speak with him, Uelese," Paxton said.

"Can't let you in there tonight."

"I'm not waiting for tomorrow. I'll keep it brief and you'll let me in now."

Uelese blinked slowly as he looked at Paxton. His pale, pallid skin, average height, average build, blue eyes, and brown hair stood in stark contrast to Uelese's dark brown skin, extreme height, large build, brown eyes, and black hair. The source of Paxton's confidence wasn't obvious. "Ok, I'll let you in there, but if he gets upset, it's on your head."

Paxton opened the door slowly and noticed the drapes around the walls of the room. Fine fabric covered every inch of the room, and the Captain sat at his desk gently weeping into a handful of them. "I said I don't want to be bothered tonight." He looked up, "Oh, Paxton. I told Uelese not to be letting anyone in here; I'll talk to you tomorrow. Please go—"

"Captain, please hear me out; I understand what you're going through. I know he was like a son to you, but I have to ask you something."

The Captain looked at Paxton. This wasn't the best time, but he waved for Paxton to continue.

"My mother and granny were infected too," he rushed the words. He choked back a sob and continued, "I want to save them like you saved Jeff. Can we go back to Agwe and get him to make enough of that stuff for the two of them? They're all I have in my life.

"My father ran out on us. It was his fault all this happened," Paxton took a moment to breathe. "I almost had to shoot them— my own family. My only family. I just want to save them. I want them to be like Jeff. I want them back."

"He is me son," the Captain said.

Paxton looked at him confused.

"Don't you go tellin' him. Ever. Do ye really want them to live like Jeff? He can't stay on me ship. He be needin' a speaker with him.

"I lost me son. When we get to New Orleans, he'll no longer be allowed to remain on me ship, and I don't know what will happen to him. I should be putting him down," the Captain struggled to continue. "I be too weak to do that. Don't be so weak as me, Paxton. Ye have your father. Hang on to him. Your ma and granny are gone now. They'll never be the same."

"I just want to know if I can get that stuff and bring it to save my family," Paxton said.

"No," the Captain answered him directly. "Ye can't bring it to them. Ye would have to bring them to Agwe, but I see you don't understand, so let me tell ye a little story. Sit down."

Paxton sat in the chair across from the Captain next to a thick, green curtain.

"Many years ago, I be a married man. Me wife and I be pirates, sailing the Caribbean and we be very successful. We had a little boy, Jeff, and we were very happy until one quiet night in the Houston Port.

"When it still be open at night before the Lutadors be protecting it, me wife went to pick up a shipment and didn't come back. Uelese helped me look; took all night, but he saw her after a Revenant attack. She be unconscious. He picked her up and brought her to me ship. To our ship."

He lost focus for a moment as he thought about their ship and stroked the drapes next to him. Paxton noticed then that the drapes he thought were hung along the walls were actually dresses. Dozens of beautiful dresses.

"We brought her to Agwe. Sailed straight to Haiti. Even used the gas engine to get there fast enough. Uelese knew what she'd become, and he guarded her day and night on me ship; only man alive who could. She did little other than eat rats and sit on her bunk.

"After Agwe seeded her, she be me wife again, mostly," he paused.

"A month later we be stuck at sea, no gas, no wind. We ran out of animals on board and she be hungry. She looked at young Jeff like he be breakfast.

"Finally, she eat Jean's father. But, you see, she be herself again after eating him and couldn't handle it; begged me to kill her. 'Put me out of me misery,' she'd say," he dabbed away tears with her dress.

Paxton cried, but wouldn't dare make a sound. Listening was hard enough, but he vowed to commit this story to memory, every syllable.

"I couldn't do it; me will failed me again and I let her live. To her this be unacceptable, so she threw herself in the ocean. She swam so fast and me ship had no power. That be the last time I saw her.

"Jeff be young, so I told him he be found in New Orleans so he wouldn't miss his mother. I be figurin' that if he thinks she just be his adoptive mother, he wouldn't take it too hard. He wouldn't go after her."

The two sat in silence picturing that last moment for a while. Finally the Captain finished up, "So, I guess I be just as weak now. I cursed me son to the same fate as me wife."

Eugene withdrew samples of the Dragon egg yolk using a large needle; he inserted it into the hole, and the yolk came out a deep blue color. He transferred it into small test tubes and sealed them.

He removed his latest test batch and added a sample of the Dragon egg yolk. His burner was warm enough, so he held the tube above it for just a few seconds. The yolk glowed white and burnt down into the deep red liquid below.

Eugene removed the tube quickly and looked at it. The liquid was all one color now, a deep, sickly yellow. This surprised Eugene, and he worried that the solution wouldn't work. He grabbed a sample of Revenant infected blood and a mouse.

As he put on the leather gloves, everything moved quick. He was on autopilot now. It took only a moment for him to infect the mouse and drop it into the diamond jar. It healed and Eugene took off his gloves.

He picked up a small, sterile scalpel and sliced his finger. The mouse smelled the blood and clawed at the diamond wall. As the blood dripped into the tube, it slowly spread and dissipated into the top portion of the yellow liquid. He poured it into the diamond jar and waited.

The mouse devoured the solution and everything slowed down. It finished the liquid and turned around. Standing still, it fixed its eyes on Eugene. Its breathing slowed. Minutes passed and the mouse just stood there. *This is it. None of them lasted more than a minute before.*

The mouse finally tilted its head up and looked again at Eugene. It twitched its nose and backed up until its tail bumped against the diamond wall. Then it ran forward and leapt higher than any of the mice had jumped.

Its claws pierced the diamond. It was stuck. It pulled at its left front paw, trying to free it, and climbed higher.

Eugene's mouth dropped.

Several pirates flooded toward the stairs to return below deck and grab a bite of fish and haven hash. On the way, Jeff grabbed Paxton's shoulder and pulled him aside, "I'll pay you back."

"What?"

"I'll pay you back for what you've done."

Paxton crouched and widened his stance, "Try it, Revenant." Paxton threw a right hook toward Jeff's nose.

Jeff caught it and gently held Paxton's fist in place, "No, I'll follow you off this boat and pay you back."

"Just do it here, in front of everyone. After what your kind did, and what you've done, I would rather die now fighting you."

"No, you don't understand," Jeff laughed. "I owe you, dude. It's my fault he knows, and I'll pay you back for that and for finding the Luatu."

Paxton relaxed his arm and let his anger fade into melancholy, "You don't owe me anything." He struggled against taking all his anger out on Jeff right now. He blamed Jeff, but what could this pirate do for him?

"I'm the reason they'll be there, waiting. I owe you," Jeff let go of Paxton's fist.

"There's nothing you can do."

"If they're waiting, I can help protect you. I must. You need me there."

"You can't—"

"Gail? What was she right about?" Sara yelled from across the ship.

Paxton and Jeff hurried to investigate the commotion.

Sara cornered Terrance moments before, "I know you can't forgive me yet, but I still care about you. I messed up, Terr, and I can't take it back, but it wasn't all my fault. I need to be the love of your life again."

"The love of my life," he turned from her to look over the water. "How could you ever be that again?" He turned back to her, "Not your fault? Did I put that *pirate* in your bed?"

"You may as well have, always running off with Paxton. Ya'll should have lived together, and I should have gone to the Great United States of Africa like my folks wanted me to."

"You're on a pirate ship now. I'm sure the Captain will stop there someday."

"But I—" she choked on her words, "I can't be alone."

"Alone? That's all I am to you, someone to keep you from being alone? There are plenty of pirates here to keep you company, or are they not enough like zombie Jeff?"

"I didn't want Jeff, Terrance. I wanted you to want me. I wanted you to be jealous and stop ignoring me."

"So you went to that pirate scum for more attention? You cheated on me for attention? Well it worked, but I don't think it's quite what you wanted. Maybe Gail was right," Terrance said.

"No. You don't under... Gail? What was she right about?"

"She said I should just leave you. That it was a mistake to—"

"What about Granny?" Paxton rushed up with Jeff behind him.

"Nothing, man. I shouldn't have brought it up," Terrance said.

"No. You're not dropping this, Terrance. What was a mistake?" Sara asked.

"Granny and Mom are Revenant and you two want to bring them into your quarrel? How dare you?"

"I'm sorry, Paxton," Sara said.

"I wouldn't expect this from you guys. What were you thinking?" He turned and left, "I'm going to eat, and I don't want to hear this again."

"Hey, if he's being rude to such a fine woman as yourself, maybe you'd like to join me for dinner? Or we could finish what we started in Miami," Jeff looked directly at Sara and held out one hand while placing the other behind his back.

"Off the boat," Terrance commanded Jeff.

Jeff leapt off the boat and into the water.

"Man overboard!" Terrance laughed as he walked to dinner.

Paxton stopped before going down to eat and watched several pirates throw a rope in the water to help Jeff out. When he got back on the boat, he ran at Terrance. Paxton picked up a bottle and threw it in front of Jeff who smirked and juked to dodge the bottle.

"I wasn't trying to make you hit it," Paxton said.

Terrance turned and saw Jeff speeding for him. "Jump."

Jeff jumped again, but since he was running so fast and dodged the bottle, he missed the mast and flew ahead of the boat several hundred yards.

"Thanks, Paxton," Terrance walked over to him. "I'm sorry about bringing up Granny. You know I love her, and I didn't mean any disrespect."

"I know, Terr," Paxton said. "Just don't let it happen again."

Sara followed them down to eat, but sat alone.

9. A Sea Monster and a Revenant

"You can't be serious. This again?" Paxton said.

"Yes. I'm going with you, Terrance, and Sara. You need protection," Jeff said.

"But, wait! Protection?"

"Yes. And if you object, I'll do it anyway. Besides, you'll have Terrance with you in case I need to be," he winced, "reigned in. I need a speaker, Dude. It's just not safe without one."

"You're right, but Terrance won't like it. Who knows what he'll make you do?" Paxton laughed at the possibilities.

"I know he hates me, but maybe Sara will appreciate it," Jeff winked.

Paxton glared at him, "I don't want a Revenant around either, even if it's cathartic for him to torture you. You're not coming with us."

"Stop. I'm going. I need Terrance around, as much as I hate to admit it. Now I need to go eat before I get too hungry." He turned to leave.

"If you do come, then do me one favor, since you owe me."

Jeff stopped and raised one eyebrow at Paxton.

"Stop with the Sara comments. She made a mistake with you and it needs to end."

"There was no mistake, Paxton," Jeff said. "She paid me to be there."

"Paid you?"

"She wanted to make him jealous. I told her I'd do the real thing for free," Jeff winked at Paxton. "Don't pretend like you wouldn't.

That dark red mane of hair, those green eyes, and that... " Jeff stopped when he noticed Paxton's glare.

"She insisted that I keep my sandals and undershorts on and that we weren't going to do nothing. We lay there for a good thirty minutes, and she wouldn't shut up about that boy."

Paxton was speechless.

Jeff started to walk away and turned back, "She loves him; there was no mistake, and I'm coming."

Alfred woke in his hut; it was time. Canton told him to act as soon as it was ready, so he walked over to the kettle. A small glob remained in the bottom, pulsing like a heart. He picked it up with a stick and placed it in a small, dirty rag. He tied the rag up into a bag, his poppet-bag. It was exactly what he would need.

He wasn't sure why he was told to do this, but the poppet-bag Alfred held didn't care about that. It didn't care about Canton, or his plans. It only cared that it could connect to its counterpart, Paxton.

Under his pillow was another bag, one with a blue glow pouring through it like liquid through mesh. This one was heavier, and it didn't move like the pulsing poppet-bag.

He held up each bag in front of him and slowly moved them together until they touched. They began to screech, writhe, and dance in his hand. Alfred knew Canton would be happy. *Enjoy the Death Metal, Paxton. You've earned it.*

Paxton shot up in his bunk, eyes wide open. The boat was pitch black. Slowly, he turned and stretched his feet toward the floor. His legs cracked as he stood up.

Thud!

"What the... " he stretched his hands in front of him as he walked forward, found his way to the hatch, and climbed up on deck. The full moon shone on the boat like a spotlight revealing an empty deck. *Men should be here watching the boat,* he thought.

"Hello, who's on watch?"

He was afraid of waking the Captain or the pirates below deck, but if those on watch were asleep, he had to wake them up. He looked around the deck for a moment before noticing the blue-gray color of everything and the calmness of the water. The still wind and eerie calm gave Paxton chill bumps.

Thud!

Paxton jumped. *It's coming from the bottom of the boat.* He walked cautiously to the port rail and leaned over. A large fish was swimming toward the surface so fast that he knew it would land on the deck of the boat.

He wondered what kind it was as it rushed toward the surface, but he couldn't see the whole fish. The body stretched down into the ocean further than he could see, and he could see very far. It broke the surface of the water and kept going; soon it rose over the side of the ship. It was blue-gray like everything else.

Paxton looked closely for the eyes, fins, mouth, or anything that would determine the kind of fish. It stretched out of the water as high as the mast and kept going. It slowly bent away from the ship.

Paxton thought that it was strange for a fish to stretch so high out of the water, but for it to bend over backwards was downright perplexing. The fish then flipped itself around and crashed on the ship.

"Tentacle. Sea monster." Paxton whispered the words to himself.

It grabbed at the ship and crushed the railings. Paxton panicked. He needed to find someone else. "Sea monster!"

The tentacle squeezed the ship and pulled at the mast. It flexed and a rail flew at Paxton, slicing his arm. The massive appendage was between him and the stairs leading to the bunks.

Why is nobody up here yet? Don't they hear the noise? Don't they hear me yelling? He picked up the rail and ran at the tentacle, plunging it into the sea monster. It loosened its grip on the mast, and he pulled the rail out to jab it again.

"Paxy, what are you doing?"

He turned and raised the rail, ready for another attack. He dropped the rail when he saw his mother behind him. She was standing on the boat with her arms open.

"Mama," he said.

Then J'Nou came behind her and bit her neck.

"No."

"You will tell me where your father is, or I will kill her," J'Nou said.

"Pax tona daru du ink," a voice said behind him.

Paxton couldn't understand the voice behind him and looked back. He saw nobody; then he faced the Revenant again, but his mother was gone.

"Tell me, Paxton," J'Nou said stalking him, refusing to let up.

Paxton knew he couldn't let the Revenant find his father. He picked up the rail and held it to his stomach. He heard a buzzing again and couldn't understand, "Stop or I'll kill myself. Then you'll never know."

"Paxton, wake up," Terrance said in his dark voice.

Paxton opened his eyes and realized he was holding a sword to his stomach, lying in his bunk, and Terrance was pulling the blade away from him.

"What happened?" He let Terrance take it.

"You yelled out 'sea monster' and now every pirate is up on deck looking for it. I came and found you holding that sword," Terrance said. "It looks like your pillow took the worst of it, but you scared me when you said you'd kill yourself."

"Then I guess I can forgive you for commanding me like that."

"I hope so, but everyone's going to be pissed when they find out there's no sea monster. You can't yell something like that, even in your sleep."

"Like I meant to, Terr," Paxton replied.

Terrance glared at him as they ran up on deck. When the pirates figured out that it was a false alarm, most were too tired to be angry, but a few threw eye darts at Paxton. He couldn't go back to sleep, but he needed some privacy, so he went back down to his bunk.

Terrance spotted Sara on deck; she was looking over the side, and he walked up to join her, "So, no sea monster."

"I guess not," Sara stared into the water.

"His nightmare seemed really bad. It had Revenant and his mother."

"Sounds bad."

"He even had a knife and was about to kill himself in his sleep," Terrance made a gesture like he was stabbing himself in the stomach.

Sara stared at the water for a while. Terrance grew uncomfortable and started to go below deck.

"Look, Terr, you and Paxton are all I have now," Sara said.

Terrance stopped where he was and listened.

"I can't lose you guys." She bit her lip, unsure what to say until she settled on the one, simple thing she knew was true. "I'm so sorry for all this."

Jeff checked rigging on the other side of the boat, but he could hear every word the pair said. Terrance walked back to the railing, "Look, Sara, I don't know if I can ever forgive you. Every time I think about you and that thing over there, I cringe."

"I can't be a pirate, though. Do you know how many of these men have hit on me? Maybe I can start over in New Orleans or something. I just need you to know I'm sorry."

"Sure you are, but you aren't staying in New Orleans."

"I just thought—"

"Thought what? That I wouldn't protect you? You hurt me," Terrance pulled one large splinter off and threw it overboard. "You hurt me a lot. I'll always take care of you, though."

He looked at her and stepped back to lessen the intimacy.

"I may have to kill your new boyfriend, though, if he tries anything again."

Jeff paused with rigging in his hand. *If only you knew how much she paid me to be in that bed.* He walked over to Sara and Terrance as they stared at the reflection of the moon on the water.

"Terrance," Jeff's voice was slightly dark as he said this. The darkness in his voice was not the same as Terrance's dark voice, but it was still intimidating.

"Jeff."

"I may need your help, man, so I don't eat someone."

"Are there no more rats?" Terrance sounded apathetic.

"Do you want him to eat someone before you act?" Sara said.

"No. I just don't know why we keep him around. He's dangerous."

"I don't know why the Captain keeps me around either, man. It would be better if he just killed me, but he raised me. He loved me like a son, and he won't see me again after New Orleans." Jeff sighed. "I won't disappoint him on our final voyage together. Please, dude, help me."

Jeff pleaded with his eyes. Terrance was taken aback by the emotion in them. Though he wouldn't admit it to anyone, he pitied Jeff.

"Fine," he looked at Jeff. "Count to a million out loud." His voice was dark and cold and Jeff immediately turned to look at the ocean off the port side rail of the ship; numbers flew from his mouth faster than anyone could comprehend.

"Well, that should still keep him busy for a little while," Sara said.

"Next time I'll have to go higher."

Terrance sent Jeff into the ocean to feed after Sara had turned in, leaving him alone by the rail. He looked around and pulled out the box with the ring. *Should I just toss it in?*

He held the ring out over the water and thought about it. This was Sara's ring, but he couldn't give it to her. Selling it might help them get wherever they were going. Where would he find someone who could afford it though? And how would he explain it to Sara?

Below deck Paxton rolled over in his bunk and murmured, "Mama."

10. Family Reunion

The *Falcon* docked in New Orleans, and the crew readied shipments for delivery. Most of the crew ran through their routine, except the Captain. Under normal circumstances, he would hustle a few more shipments or even offload a few not-really-extras for a higher price, then later claim they were lost or never picked up.

Tonight, however, things weren't normal.

He stood on the deck, lost in thought. Earlier he'd told Uelese he would oversee the preparations, but his first mate knew better. The Captain was waiting to say goodbye.

Uelese stopped with a box in his hand and watched Jeff approach the Captain. The other pirates did the same. Terrance, Paxton, and Sara were behind Jeff; bags were slung over their backs. Terrance pressed his lips together and crossed his arms, standing as far from Jeff and Sara as he could.

The Captain looked into Jeff's eyes, his lips quivering. The Captain flipped up the patch on his right eye, placed his hands on Jeff's shoulders, then pulled him close. The pair stood there, embracing each other for nearly a minute.

Paxton and Sara turned their eyes away and noticed that most of the pirates did the same. Terrance continued to stare. He was anxious to leave the boat, but the embrace reminded him of losing his parents.

He winced. No emotion for a zombie.

Uelese resisted wiping the tears from his cheeks. He would miss his nephew.

The Captain opened his mouth and then closed it again. He coughed and pulled back from Jeff. "Ye will always be me son, boy. And ye'll always be welcome here. Now, don't go getting into too much trouble. I love y—" The Captain choked the last word, wiped his eyes, and placed the patch back on his left eye.

"I love you, too," Jeff paused, "Dad."

"Now, get going! The lot of ya," the Captain waved them off the ship, but he looked hard at Paxton.

"I won't," he said to the Captain.

Well-kept buildings crowded the port here, but windows were few. Hurricanes on the Gulf of Mexico were often devastating, but the buildings were well designed to protect their occupants with port holes and sealed doors.

The evening rain blew in sheets against the hotels lining the port. It wouldn't get into any hotel, but it emptied the streets. They were eerily quiet and deserted. Most cities in America shut down for the night to avoid the Revenant hunting, but there was little threat of Revenant in New Orleans, so many enjoyed the night life.

Rumors spread about why the Revenant ignored the *City That Care Forgot*, but despite what they believed, people were still cautious in such a large city. People were forgotten in such a large city. People went missing in such a large city.

Often it was just a pirate passing through or a local who liked to party. Almost always, it was a shady character that didn't play well with others.

Jim didn't play well with others.

Jim crouched below one of the few windows to the Hurricane Hideaway, a popular, sturdy, beautiful hotel near the port. *Mmm, I hope it's a young one in there. Gloria's getting old, and I miss that tight skin.*

He pulled himself up to look in the window and heard his joints popping. *I'm not as quiet as I used to be.* He laughed to himself. *Haha, yes! That old hag would never forgive me if she knew I still liked this kind of adventurous stuff.*

He saw a door to a bathroom and caught it closing. A little girl was getting dressed next to the bed; Jim's heart began beating really fast, "I can't believe it. This could be the jackpot."

"What kind of jackpot, pervert?" a sing-song, high-pitched voice asked from over his shoulder.

"What was the name of the inn Uelese told us to check?" Paxton asked.

"The Hurricane something," Terrance said.

"It's the Hurricane Hideaway," Jeff pushed by him, "Should be this way."

Paxton spotted the inn and approached the door. He squeezed the lever on it, pulling hard. It resisted at first and then popped open making a suction sound.

"What's that about?" Sara asked.

Paxton noticed the rubber seal around the door jamb and the door itself as he stepped inside and smiled, "This place should do well."

Sara stumbled as the door pushed her inside. Jeff grabbed it from behind. Terrance's arm flew toward it a moment late, and he seethed.

"Thank you, Jeff. Is that a lounge?" Sara asked of nobody and rushed over to look inside. She saw a large room off to the left with a few pirates and a stage inside. Nobody seemed to be performing, but the sign on this side of the wall read, "Madame Ashleigh, next performance:" No time was written on the board.

Paxton walked up to the front desk. It was dark cherry with a white, marble countertop, and it stretched out from the wall and wrapped around the area behind the desk, leaving room for two people to help customers and a third to sit at a small, low desk. There was nobody to help them.

Paxton spotted the bell and slammed it down. Immediately a tall, skinny man shot up from behind the desk.

"Hello! May I—" He spun around after realizing he faced the wrong way. "Oh! Yes, what can I help you with?" He was clearly oblivious to the matted hair on his head. It stood outward and upward, like a sun rising from behind the small planet that was his head. He impatiently tapped fingers on his pen; then thinking he needed the pen, he picked it up and tapped the desk with it.

"We need a room with four beds," Paxton said.

"Three," Jeff's voice boomed from behind Terrance.

"Well, let's see," the clerk flipped through his book.

"Paxton, get us two rooms, ok?" Sara said.

"No, Sara. We need to stay together," Terrance said. She opened her mouth. "We'll discuss more in the room," his eyes darted at the clerk and then back to Sara.

"Ahh, here I found one." The clerk was bent behind the desk. He quickly popped up holding a key on a ring.

"Thanks," Paxton said as he reached to grab it.

The clerk pulled his hand back and smiled slyly as he looked at Paxton, "One night's stay up front; you can settle the rest of your bill each morning."

"Oh, of course. How much?" Paxton asked.

"Five Naughts."

Paxton reached into his bag, grabbed five Naughts and handed them to the clerk. He placed the keys in Paxton's hand.

"Enjoy. Madame Ashleigh is about to perform in a few minutes. I recommend you don't miss it." He turned around, slid down, and sat on the floor again, with his back against the desk.

"Why couldn't I have a separate room, Terrance?" Sara crossed her arms.

"It's too dangerous. I'm not leaving you in a room alone," he said.

"Why couldn't Paxton watch me and you two share a room?" Jeff winked at Sara, "Or I'll share with her, if you don't want to, dude."

"I don't trust you, *dude*," Terrance said. "And I don't think Sara would want to share one with me anyway."

"You mean you don't want to share a room with me?" she asked.

"No, that's not the reason. It's because we need to stay together. We need to protect each other. They know where we are, and they're probably here waiting for us."

"Fine. I don't want to talk about it anymore. I need something happy. We're going to watch Madame Ashy perform," Sara said.

"Ashleigh," Paxton said.

"What?"

"It's *Madame Ashleigh*, not Ashy."

"Whatever," she grabbed Paxton with her right hand and Terrance with her left and pulled them out of the room. Jeff followed behind the three as they passed into the lounge.

The group sat at a table directly in the middle, at the end of the empty stage, which was T-shaped, with the top of the T at the curtains and a runway protruding from the middle.

"What did you mean when you said you weren't trying to make me hit that bottle?" Jeff asked.

"Me?" Paxton pointed to himself.

Jeff nodded, "Yeah, you threw it at me, said you didn't want me to hit it; then I ended up jumping into the ocean, but I'm pretty sure I would have been able to grab the mast if I hadn't juked away from the bottle when I did."

Terrance and Sara nodded and leaned in to hear Paxton's response.

Paxton sighed, "You would have. That's why I threw it."

"But how did you know I wouldn't just slow down or knock it out of the way or something?"

"I've always been able to sort of see or know what would happen. Kind of a cause-effect chain-reaction sort of thing. I used to think it was luck, but it's gotten stronger over the past couple of years." Paxton took a drink just as they introduced Madame Ashleigh.

Madame Ashleigh, a tall, skinny, Haitian woman, walked to the end of the stage with confidence and grace. She looked at every person in the audience, one at a time, and then raised her hand slightly. Her off-white dress was a little tight on her frame and layered. It flowed to her ankles, folding in on itself without impeding her dancing.

The trumpet began to play. It was soft and quiet, slowly building. Then a guitar started the melody. The drums came in unnoticed at first; then they built beyond the song, only to settle back to a steady beat.

She swayed to the sound. It had a decidedly slow, swinging tempo. She swayed more, and then started singing, deep and smoky. The song was about her man and how he kept her down. She sang about leaving him. It climaxed when the Revenant attacked and killed her man; the song ended with her regret.

After the first song, she looked around and welcomed the small crowd. It was just Sara, Paxton, Terrance, Jeff, and three more tables of pirates and businessmen.

"I guess this isn't the busy show?" She waited for a few laughs and got one from Sara. "As you may have guessed, I am *the* Madame Ashleigh. My evenings are here on stage, and my days are in there," she gestured back to a curtain near the other end of the stage. The sign next to it read, 'Madame Ashleigh, Fortune Teller.' "But for now, let's heat this place up with our next song, *The Heat in Centralia.*"

The band hit its cue and she started into a more upbeat song about the burning city of Centralia.

"We should go tomorrow," Sara said.

"Centralia's pretty far away, and I heard there are fire goblins," Terrance struggled to keep a straight face. "I don't think it's a good idea."

Sara glared at him, "She can tell us if we'll get where we're going." Sara thought for a second, "Where are we going?" When she knew Paxton wasn't answering, she whispered, "Or if we'll run into Revenant."

"Hey Paxy, you hear how she whispered that? Next time you think there's a sea monster... " Terrance let a small smile through.

"I don't know," Paxton said. "There's something funny about her. I don't think we should go."

"Oh please, can't we stay just a little bit to ask her?" Sara smiled.

"It wouldn't hurt," Jeff said. "Besides, she may not be a fraud. If she is, we can call her on it. Maybe start some trouble. We all know we'll see Revenant, but she doesn't."

Terrance's head turned to face Jeff like a turret locking onto its target, "You really think there's a chance she isn't a fraud?" He couldn't hold it anymore; he smiled and snickered.

"Yeah, my experiences don't disprove it."

"And you've experienced so much," Terrance looked at him with tears in his eyes, unable to stop laughing.

"Listen, I'm speaking to her tomorrow. I don't care what you think about Jeff or how much you ignore me, but I want to know what she has to say," Sara swallowed. "If you leave without me, I'll find a way to catch up with you." She held her breath.

"I'll—" Terrance stopped for a second and calmed himself. He looked at Paxton and continued, "We'll go with you."

Sara eyed them both; she didn't expect it to be this easy, "Why? Are you poking fun at me? I won't let ya'll make fun of me, or Madame Ashleigh." She pointed toward the stage.

"No," Paxton grabbed Terrance's shoulder. "We're not making fun of you. We won't let you wander off by yourself, though, and Terr knows that." He smiled at Terrance who groaned and focused on Madame Ashleigh.

Jeff turned to watch an older lady approaching a group of pirates a couple of tables down. Sara looked at each of them in turn, "Then it's settled."

The lady saw Jeff watching her and approached the table.

"Excuse me, have you seen my husband? His name's Jim. He's about this tall and sixty years old." The woman held her hand a foot above her head to indicate his height.

"Nah, the old man's probably lost. I'm sure it's nothing," Jeff said.

She looked away from him and refused to make eye contact. *Is she ashamed?* He wondered. *Or just scared?*

"Are you sure? He was wearing a striped shirt and blue jeans," she said.

"Maybe he snuck out to find some lovin' from a younger woman," he said.

"Stop it, Jeff." Sara turned back to the woman. "What's your name?"

"Molly. Have you seen him, miss?"

"No, I haven't seen him. I could help you look, if you'd like?" Sara stood.

"No, thank you. I don't wanna interrupt your evening. He

wanders off at night sometimes. I'm sure he'll be back soon," the lady, Molly, moved quickly toward the next table. "Thank you, miss."

"Are you sure, Molly?"

"I'm sure," she called over her shoulder. "Thanks again."

Sara watched the old woman shuffle to the next table and ask them. Each "No" caused Molly to hunch her back more, and the disappointment slowed her down. Finally she ducked out of a side door and was gone.

"We should have helped her," Sara said.

"Yeah, but I'm sure Jeff's right for once," Terrance said. "He probably wandered off, or maybe he's sleeping outside, or inside, somewhere away from her. It'll be fine."

"You are so rude," Sara hurried upstairs and locked herself in their room. *They can sleep in the hall.*

Eugene stared at the mouse. It dug its left paw back into the diamond jar, a little higher than before; then it struggled to pull its right claw out. It was halfway up the very large jar and climbing.

Slow but steady it climbed. The Revenant mouse pulled its claws out one at a time and moved by millimeters up the diamond jar.

Its claws are stronger. Its claws should break on that wall, not cut through it. The only thing stronger than diamond is...

Eugene leaned closer and looked at the claws. They were blue and cut clean through the diamond. The mouse was almost to the top now. He realized the lid was off and slid it into place on top of the jar.

"This may suffocate you, Mr. Mouse, but I can't let you out. If you're contagious, it would be far worse than the Revenant problem we have now."

He left the mouse in the sealed jar overnight and set up a cot nearby. Sleeping light, Eugene woke up to check the jar many times, and each time the mouse was digging. When it was finally time to get up, he was surprised to see the limp mouse lying next to a small ditch in the jar.

It made it halfway through the jar before collapsing. I did the right thing. Eugene needed to convince himself. *At least it suffocated. It probably fell asleep and died peacefully.*

He slowly slid the lid off of the jar, and the mouse opened its eyes, looked up at him, and stumbled to its feet. He threw the lid into place and fell back.

Sara pushed the beads aside and leaned her head into Madame Ashleigh's waiting room. It was small with two couches and a hostess stand. On the stand was a piece of paper asking for a name and time. She wrote both and sat on the couch.

Long, dark fingers came around the side of the beaded curtain and pulled it back. Before he entered, Sara beamed, "Terrance, how was your breakfast?" She nodded toward the stand, "I signed us up."

"It was good, though the floor wasn't very comfortable," he said. "Paxton and Jeff are on the way. Jeff ate this morning, so he should be ok most of the day."

"That's good. Ya'll deserved the floor, though."

Silence dropped like an elephant. Terrance tried to push it out of his mind, but the thought of her in bed with that pirate forced its way in.

Finally, Paxton and Jeff showed up. Madame Ashleigh came around the corner and approached the stand at exactly the same time. She didn't look down at it, but instead locked her eyes on Terrance, "Now that you're all here, please follow me." She turned and walked back down the hall.

The group looked at each other and followed her. None of them knew what to expect, so the comfortable chairs, couches, and resemblance to a psychiatrist's office were only a mild surprise. Sara sat on a couch, facing a large, purple, puffy chair that Madame Ashleigh floated to. Terrance and Paxton sat on either side of Sara while Jeff sat in another chair across the room, perpendicular to everyone else.

"Leather," Sara said. "Very nice." She ran her hands over the couch and looked at it.

"Yes, I have a friend with a spider cattle farm; he's very generous," Madame Ashleigh said. She looked around the room at each person, then stared a long time at Terrance before continuing. "Though I doubt you came to discuss my furnishings." She said this as she looked again at Paxton.

"I understand your doubts, Paxton. However, have you considered all you've seen?" Madame Ashleigh looked deeper into Paxton's eyes. "Perhaps it's more difficult for you, knowing what you do about the origin of the Revenant. But then you're a seer yourself."

Paxton's eyes opened a little wider, but he composed himself quickly. Jeff glanced at him and Madame Ashleigh grinned.

"How much will this cost us? Before you start, Madame," Paxton's voice dripped with resentment now.

"Normally I charge forty, but, for family, there's no charge," she looked again at Terrance as she said this.

Paxton and Sara also looked at Terrance.

He looked at them and shrugged, "What? Just because we're both black, we're the ones who are related? Maybe she's *Orphan's* mother. He's awfully tan," he threw his arm up toward Jeff.

Ashleigh continued looking at him and Jeff laughed.

"I'm sorry, Madame. I don't know you. Are we related somehow?" Terrance asked.

"Yes, Terrance. Your father was my brother. He had the same name as you, Terrance Bonifacy. I always called him *Terr*."

Sara smiled and Paxton laughed.

"He was quite the boy, always playing soccer and doing well in school. And he loved your mother very much. I sort of introduced them." Ashleigh paused and her eyes filled with tears.

No tear fell, but her eyes were clearly wet as she continued. "When I learned of their death," she hesitated, "I didn't want to disrespect your father's wishes, and he never wanted me to visit you because of, well, my abilities and some other family things." She looked at the carpet, just beside her left foot, and touched her cheek.

After a moment, she looked at Terrance again, "You look like him. His eyes, nose, and height at least. You have your mother's mouth, though; your lips are much thicker than his." She breathed deeply. "He loved you so much," she brightened a little as she remembered something. "And he even sent me a picture once. Here. I keep it in this drawer."

She stood and walked to the wall behind Jeff, to the bookshelves that filled it. She pulled one of the books toward her and that shelf of books moved, revealing a large drawer. Rummaging through its contents, she finally pulled the picture out to show him.

She also grabbed a revolver.

"What do you think you're doing?" Paxton asked and jumped to his feet with pistol in hand and aimed squarely at the back of her head.

She slowly raised her arms to her sides. The picture was in her right hand, and she loosely held the revolver in her left.

"This was his grandfather's revolver, Paxton. His father learned to shoot with it, and I thought he could use it now, considering your plan." She turned slowly, walked toward the group, and handed Terrance the gun and the picture.

Paxton sat down and put his gun away. Jeff also returned to his seat, though no one had seen him leave it.

Terrance was on a soccer field with nobody else in the picture. His right foot was on the soccer ball, and his right hand was on his knee. His left hand was on his hip, and he was smiling, with two large saucers for eyes. He was about six years old in the picture, wearing the uniform of his first team. The picture itself was like new, only slightly worn on the edges.

"Wow, that was so long ago. I remember the team though. The Miami Sunsets. I can't believe you have this." Terrance's eyes brightened as he leapt to his feet examining the picture. The others crowded around him to also have a look.

"So you're my aunt, huh? Aunt Ashleigh," he said to Madame Ashleigh.

"Leisha, Aunt Leisha," she corrected. "But call me Madame Ashleigh. You have to keep who I am a secret." She looked around and seemed to consider something. "May I have a few moments with my nephew? I'll continue the session when we are done."

"Sure," Sara said. "We'll wait out in the reception area." She grabbed Paxton's arm and eyed Jeff.

"Will you flip the sign on the door to *Closed* please?"

"Yeah, I got it," Jeff said as he left the room.

Madame Ashleigh turned toward Terrance and grabbed his hands.

"Now, Terrance. You don't call me Leisha, but even more, don't call me Aunt. Tell your friends this as well. Oh, and your," she paused to drip out the last word, "zombie. I am Leisha Bonifacy, and no human or Revenant may know this."

She looked at him, and examined his face as she swung his arms. He was a foot taller than she was. His eyes filled with tears as he smiled slightly. He could see some of his father in her.

He knew it was quick and maybe he shouldn't trust a stranger, especially a fortune teller, but he'd seen the picture and knew it was him. His mind raced with scenarios of the deception and scheming she may be plotting, but in the end he knew he could trust her.

He could feel it coming off of her.

She let his hands go and took a deep breath.

Paxton didn't like to be wrong; nor did he like someone he didn't trust knowing so much about him. If he weren't in a bad mood already, this would have done him in, "So when are you going to tell Terrance the truth, Sara?"

"What do you mean?"

"Don't play games with me, Sara, and don't play games with Terrance."

Sara was nervous now. *Does he know? How could he?* "I'm not playing games."

"Jeff told me, Sara. I know what you did."

"What? What did that lying pirate tell you?"

"Now I'm a lying pirate?" Jeff said.

"He told me why he was in your bed. That you *paid* him to get in bed with you and do nothing, Sara," Paxton said. "And that you sat there for thirty minutes waiting for Terrance to come home, and even though Jeff wanted to do more, offered to *pay* to do more, you just talked about Terr."

"Oh," Sara looked around for an opportunity to get away from this discussion.

"He also told me you made him keep his sandals on."

"Sounds about right," Jeff said.

"So when are you going to tell Terrance?" Paxton asked.

"There are those who hunt us," Madame Ashleigh said.

"Who?" Terrance asked.

"Revenant."

"Why would they want us? Do you think you're seeing this wrong? I mean, they're chasing Paxton—"

"No. I don't need my visions to see this," she said.

Her voice was as smooth as it was on stage and it calmed Terrance.

"They hunt for our family. I can't go into detail now, but I wrote a letter to your father many years ago that will explain it. He didn't know the truth either, but when I found out, I had to try to tell him."

Madame Ashleigh placed a letter stamped 'Return to Sender' in Terrance's hand then grasped his hand between hers, "Open this alone."

He took his hand back and put the letter in his pocket.

"Just don't tell anyone your last name. Changing your full name would be best, but at least do not use your last name."

She thought for a second.

"Well, maybe one time, to one group. Yes, you should tell them. And you can tell them that your Aunt Leisha sent you. They're the Luminati. They'll convene tonight. Do you know your way around the city?"

"No, this is my first time here, but I think Jeff knows it pretty well. Who are they? The Luminati?"

"Oh, Jeff... well I'll draw you a map," she pulled a piece of paper and pen out of the corner desk, scrawled a map, and handed it to him. "Follow this, and arrive just after dark. Tell them immediately that I sent you. It's very important that you don't hesitate to tell them this. As soon as you enter, tell them I sent you and who you are."

"Why? Who are they?"

"They're friends of mine and they've protected me and the city from the Revenant since the war. They—" she cut herself off, turned her head, and bit her lip.

"They what?" he grabbed her arm and made her face him. "They what?" he spoke each word slowly and separately.

"They'll explain who they are. Just don't arrive before dark; leave your zombie outside, and tell them I sent you. Immediately."

Terrance turned and looked at the wall before he responded, "Ok, I will. I still don't unders—"

"You don't need to understand everything. You need to trust me. Get their help to leave the city safely. They have something for your trip."

"Fine, I will, but... Hey! How do you know we're leaving?"

She smirked at him, "I could see that without my gift, but you must convince Paxton that the Luminati can help you. Now, your friends are waiting. Tell them to open the store and come back in."

11. Votaries

J'Nou and Mara sat on a rock next to each other. The desert stretched in every direction as far as even they could see. She ran her right hand along her left arm, lightly tickling herself and looking at the goose bumps as they formed, "When are you going to tell me why we're waiting here? I'm hungry."

"The Controller's orders," he said.

Mara looked at him and rolled her eyes impatiently.

"Votaries are making a delivery."

"What are Votaries?" she asked.

"The Votaries are," he paused and considered, "friends. They hand over many of their children for our Farms."

Mara's eyes widened and her mouth fell open. Her hand paused halfway up her forearm. "I can't imagine anyone just giving us children, especially their own. I thought we just took them."

"No. Well," he thought for a second, "we do, but only sometimes. The Votaries believe we will change their children or even themselves, so they can *evolve* to be us. They very nearly worship us, calling us gifts from the gods, vengeance on the white man."

"The white man? Are they Natives?"

"Most of them are, but some are asian, white, black, hispanic, and more. They all believe we are the payback to what was once the ruling elite of America. They feel a kinship with us. When they arrive, one of them and a child will come with us; the rest we must allow to leave. When the four of us are alone... " he trailed off, smiling at Mara.

She smiled back. "Don't they know what will happen to them?

I couldn't imagine sending someone I cared about to a Farm. Especially my fam—" she lost her train of thought. "We do convert some of them, huh?"

J'Nou smiled. He knew the Controller wouldn't let her think about her family and would protect her, "We will keep the baby safe, no matter what. Farm 42 is only a few dozen miles south of here, so we will run it there."

"I understand. The baby will grow to be food or Revenant."

They both stood as the Votaries came into view. With the sun behind them, they were just long shadows on the horizon, stretching almost to J'Nou's feet. As they came into view, Mara noticed that they all wore the same long, tan ceremonial robe, and they had long, straight, black hair.

There were two women, each with a black veil that covered their face, though they walked taller and with more energy than the men. Each carried a small baby and there were three men with them, one with each woman and a taller man in front.

Stepping away from the group, the taller man held his hand up and said, "Hail Master Revenant. We have blessed news. We bring two children for you."

He dropped to one knee and bowed three meters away from J'Nou who motioned for Mara to get the babies. She took one in each arm. The baby in her left arm cried, but the other rolled over and nuzzled into her right arm.

The kneeling man spoke to the ground, "My man would join you as well, Lord Revenant, and, since we offer you two children, we humbly request that you take his bride, so the couple may come with their son, if it pleases you."

"That would be reasonable," J'Nou moved away with Mara and the children.

The parents of one child hurried to catch them as the others walked back toward the sun. The adult Votaries had difficulty keeping up with J'Nou and Mara.

The woman peeled her veil back and kept trying to steal glances at the child in Mara's right arm. "Can you believe it, Billy?" she asked her husband quietly.

"It's amazing. We'll be on the farm soon," he said.

"Actually it'll be a long walk," Mara didn't stop or turn around.

"Oh, that's ok. We're just happy to join you," he said.

"Our pleasure," Mara laughed a little.

The group went on in silence for another twenty minutes before J'Nou stopped and turned, "Would you like a rest?"

"I think we're ok, Master Revenant," Billy said; then he caught his wife's eye and amended his words, "but I guess unless we're close, we may as well rest here."

J'Nou pulled a blanket out of his pack and laid it on the ground. Mara laid the babies carefully on the blanket and watched the Votary couple. They approached the blanket and sat down, adoring their child and playing with it for a long while. The baby had Billy's finger in her right hand and Lilly's finger in her left hand. It began to coo and tried to open its eyes, blinking against the light wind.

Lilly smiled down at the child and caressed its face. She ran her hand over the thin, dark hair that barely covered the baby's head. Billy tickled under its arm and blew on its belly. The other child began to cry as a small gust of cold wind blew across the desert and hit them with sand.

"It is growing cold; we must hurry and get the children to the Farm," J'Nou said, lowering his voice so only Mara could hear him.

She walked over and picked up the cold, crying baby in her left arm, and then reached out for the other baby. Lilly bent, picked the baby up, and placed it in Mara's arm. The doting parents then stood and stepped off the blanket. They watched as Mara carefully wrapped the children in the blanket, ensuring they would stay warm, and then stood, leaving them on the sand.

Lilly felt a dull ache in her stomach, then a sharp pain; Mara was eating her intestines. Lilly looked down in horror.

J'Nou grabbed the back of Billy's hair and ripped his head off, shoving his hand into the skull to retrieve the brain. He savored every delicate bite.

Lilly, still alive, fell to her knees. She couldn't scream, but watched as Mara finished eating her handfuls. She was in complete shock, but Mara noticed J'Nou and how he slowly ate the brain. Then the smell hit her, and she craved it like nothing before. She looked at Lilly and grabbed her hair, pulling her head back.

Madame Ashleigh shook her head, "I will not see the future of a Revenant."

"So your visions are limited and he's the first one to volunteer, huh." Paxton made it obvious that this was a statement, not a question.

"I do not see Revenant. It's a choice." Ashleigh was used to sceptics.

"Then please," he faked begging, "if you won't do him, do me."

"Of course. It is surprising that a seer like you would doubt me so—"

"What do you mean, a seer?" Terrance interrupted her.

"Has he not told you that he can see what will happen?" She smiled at her nephew.

"I've told them, but that's different. I just see how things are going and can tell how some minor changes or series of events will unfold. I can't see the future." Paxton shook his head at her.

"What do you think I'm doing, Paxton? I'm just better at it than you. If I wanted to be able to tell exactly how a ball will bounce were I to throw it right now, that would be simple, but stretching events and choices out into the future is harder. You may get there, or you may just get much better and more accurate at seeing the immediate future. Either way, you're a seer, just like me." She lowered her head and closed her eyes.

Everyone sat silent for a moment. Paxton looked at Sara and Terrance; then he looked at Jeff and opened his mouth, preparing to speak.

Before any sound came out, Madame Ashleigh spoke: "Your future is clouded with indecision. You know my predictions are not as precise as some may desire, but I speak truth. You will fight a dragon and save your friend. You will find where your father is, protect his home, and sink into an abyss.

"You will be saved, and then you will search for your father. It's getting murkier, but I see you meeting the—" She stopped.

Her face brightened for a moment and she smiled. Then her mouth dropped and her eyes deadened. She opened her dead eyes wide. Blood poured from her eyes and she stopped breathing.

"What is it?" Terrance ran to hold her, but she jerked and put her hand up for him to stay back.

She stared at Paxton, forcing herself to breathe again. "You will do a great deed." Her voice was monotone.

Paxton's mouth was opened, but his eyes refused to believe her.

Madame Ashleigh breathed harder. "You will free the slaves of the one,... but there will be drastic consequences," she finally concluded as she tried to catch her breath. "I cannot look any more into your future. I must rest. I did see that you will leave the city safe, but sad. I must go to the back. Please, Terrance, help me." She lifted her arm toward him. "I'm sorry that I haven't read your future and Sara's, but I will on your return."

He helped her up and led her through a curtain he hadn't noticed. It was in a dark corner behind and to the right of the couch that he, Sara, and Paxton were sitting on.

In that room was a bed and a side table. He helped his aunt lay down on the bed and turned to leave.

"Wait. We won't see each other again before you leave. You must meet the Luminati tonight. Also, about Paxton, you must remain with him."

"You mean when he does this 'great deed'?"

"Yes."

"That's what the man said."

"Listen to him. The seer and the speaker must fulfill their destiny together."

"What's the deed, though? What destiny?"

"I won't tell you, but you will see me again before it happens. You must practice speaking. Control your zombie as often as possible; Sara or Paxton may also let you use them,"

Terrance started to say something, but she hushed him.

"That seeing wore me out. What I saw," she paused for a moment. "What I saw was too big. I need to tell you a little more before I fall asleep." She fought to keep her eyes open and took a deep breath. "Don't attempt to use your voice on the Luminati, and keep that zombie away from them." Her eyes fluttered. "I love you, Terrance. I'm glad I finally met you. You remind me so much of your grandfather. Come see me again. You're always welcome here; be careful," she slurred the last few words.

Terrance closed the store on his way out.

Madame Ashleigh opened her eyes one more time and looked toward the curtain, "I hope you can handle the truth about your grandfather; otherwise we are all doomed." Then she rolled over and went to sleep.

12. New Orleans' Finest

Paxton, Terrance, Sara, and Jeff stood in a dark alley, just off a busy street in the Ninth Ward. The map Madame Ashleigh gave them was difficult to decipher, but Jeff knew the city well, and they found the alley that morning. Later that evening, just before sunset, they returned.

"Luminati? Who are these people?" Sara asked Terrance.

"I don't know, Aunt-uh... Madame Ashleigh told me they would help us. She said they watch over New Orleans."

"Yeah, you've said that, but who are they?"

"I don't know. Some floating eyeballs." He'd been telling them all day that he didn't know who the Luminati were. Each time he guessed something more absurd: vigilantes, cops, ogres, freed Revenant, children, shape-shifting reptiles, etc.

"Well, why did we have to wait until tonight?" Sara asked for the fifth time in an hour.

Terrance stared at her. She tried to keep a smile from her face and failed. He shook his head and rolled his eyes; then he turned to hide his smile. She knew how to keep him from getting in a bad mood, and it even worked sometimes.

The alley was getting darker. Terrance held the railing and stood at the top of a set of stairs that led down to a black door, one floor below street level. A sign above the door read, 'Coroner Nightclub.'

It buzzed and flickered on.

"I guess that's our signal," Paxton pushed in front of Terrance.

"Wait! I told you already, Paxton. I have to go in first. Give me just one second," Terrance shoved his way past Paxton and pulled him away from the door.

"I don't like that. I'd rather go in there first. It doesn't smell right around here." Paxton darted around and in front of Terrance again.

"I agree," Jeff added. "It smells rotten and makes me nervous."

"Well, too bad." Terrance pushed past Paxton and through the door. Immediately and loudly he said, "My name is Terrance Bonifacy and my Aunt Leisha Bonifacy sent me."

As he began to speak the words, he felt a rush of air toward him. It stopped as soon as he said 'Bonifacy' and as he mentioned his aunt, the air rushed away from him.

He stood with his hands out and palms forward. The room was pitch black, except for a faint light from the exit sign above the door behind him.

"I thought you weren't supposed to tell anyone that," Paxton pushed in behind him.

"She said this was the one exception. You guys need to wait outside, though."

After a long moment, he heard, "Smells like a Bonifacy, but what is the other smell?" The voice was a woman's, and it sounded smooth and sweet, more beautiful than any Terrance had heard before.

Jeff started to push in behind Paxton, but Terrance tried to hold them back, "I have friends, and a Revenant." He turned and added over his shoulder and directly into Paxton's ear, "I've tried to tell them to stay outside."

Someone hissed.

Quickly, Terrance added, "He's seeded and under my control. I can make him remain outside, but may my friends join us?" He held his breath, staring into the darkness.

"Your friends may enter, but the Revenant will stay outside." This voice was different, deeper, and a little rough, but just as beautiful. It was like dark chocolate when compared with the honey of the voice before.

Terrance stepped forward and let Paxton fall inside. Jeff stumbled in too, but Sara stepped over Paxton and walked in gracefully.

"You two can come in." Terrance darkened his voice and addressed Jeff, "Stay on the stairs, or die." The pitch black of his voice made the room look brighter.

"Why do you warn him when you can command him?" the sing-song, high-pitched voice asked.

"I guess it's habit; I'm not used to commanding a Revenant. I really don't know, though; I guess I don't mind much if he does die. I mean, after what he did. Hadn't thought about it, I guess."

"No, I guess you've led a normal life, huh? No boogie men?" the sing-song, honey voice perfectly mimicked Terrance's voice when it said, "I guess" which drew a laugh from Sara.

Paxton heard a smaller laugh at the end.

Terrance didn't hear the laugh and just gave Sara the side-eye, "Haven't most of us? I guess—I mean, I'm sure you've dealt with more Revenant than most, guarding the city, but otherwise... "

Paxton could hear more sniggering.

"Why are you laughing?" Paxton asked.

The laughing stopped.

"Good ears," came another sweet voice, though definitely not the honey voice. She was slightly awed.

"This is enough. Are we going to get to see you? My Aunt told me you would help us," Terrance stepped forward.

"No." The many voices of the Luminati said this in unison. The sound was like a choir, in perfect harmony.

"B... " Terrance wasn't expecting that answer.

"We wasted our time, Terrance," Paxton said.

"We will help, but you will not see us," the dark chocolate voice said.

"We'd feel more comfortable if we could see you, other than just the shadows," Paxton said.

"What shadows? I can't see anything," Terrance asked Sara.

She shrugged, but he couldn't see that either.

This time, after a moment's pause, all three heard snickering.

"Why the hell do you keep laughing at us?" Sara took a couple steps forward before Paxton stretched his arm out to restrain her.

"You would not feel more comfortable." It was the chocolate voice again.

More laughing.

"That's it; this *is* a waste of our time, Terrance," Paxton said. "They're just a bunch of military grunts playing games with our heads. Why don't you command them to turn the lights on?"

"Good idea."

"No," an even deeper, richer voice spoke. It was one that had not yet spoken. "It will not do to have this. We will turn the lights up, but you must promise to remain where you are and not move. And do *not* try to use your voice on us, Bonifacy. Even your name can't save you then."

"We'll see."

Neon lights buzzed as they came to life in rows going away from where the three stood. Large, square support columns stood about ten meters from the wall and then ten meters from each other. A row of couches lined the wall to the left. A bar ran across the back wall while stairs in the center led up to private rooms. Neon signs flickered to life on the walls, signs for alcohol brands, local bands, and a couple of sports teams.

Terrance and Sara didn't notice most of this, and Paxton only briefly took it all in. The five Luminati in front of them grabbed all of their attention.

There were two women and three men. Each wore fashionable, yet understated clothing. The women wore pants perfectly fitted to their tiny frames and blouses that covered them well; yet Terrance and Paxton felt the need to look away. The men wore jeans, fitted to their legs perfectly, but not tight, and T-shirts that stretched tight on the chest.

They looked like brothers and sisters, each with deep black eyes, pale skin, and perfect bodies.

They stood alternating, male, female, in a line facing the three. None of them moved, not even to breathe or blink. Their skin sucked in the light. For a long time, the groups stood staring at each other.

"They're beautiful," Sara stepped forward.

"We told you not to move," the man in the center said. He was a little larger than the others, and they recognized the first chocolate voice that spoke earlier.

Terrance grabbed Sara and held her back, but kept his eyes on the Luminati. As soon as she felt his tug, the words registered and she stepped back, slapping Terrance's hand away.

The women laughed, and the sound was like beautiful wind chimes.

"My name is Lawrence. This is Maurice, Susan, Lydia, and Sam." The man with the first chocolate voice pointed to the others from his far right to his far left. "I do hope you're not scared."

"Scared? Why would we be scared? You're beautiful," Sara said breathlessly, her mouth open and eyes wide.

"Well, be assured that a Bonifacy and their friends are safe with us, despite our nature."

"Why is that?" Terrance asked.

Maurice tilted his head to the right, not understanding, "We respect what the Bonifacy family has done with the Revenant problem," Maurice said. His voice was full of bass, and it vibrated through them. His was the second, deeper voice, "The sacrifices your family made are very significant, and your Aunt is a dear friend to us."

"Sacrifices?" Paxton asked, looking at Terrance who shrugged.

"You don't know?" Susan asked.

"This is a story that must be told right," Lawrence gestured to the couches, "Have a seat, and I will tell it."

"That father of yours is an ass!" spewed the lady behind the counter. She was looking back toward the door behind her. When she noticed Eugene, she straightened her shirt and put on her sweet voice, "Sorry 'bout that, honey. What can I do you for?"

"Just this, thanks." Eugene gestured to the eggs, aspirin, seaweed, and other odds and ends.

"That'll be eight Naughts. You sure you don't want some smokes?"

"No, thanks," he smiled. "Actually do you have any cold Coke?"

"Yeah, here you go. That'll be eight and a quarter Naughts."

He handed her the money and bagged his stuff. Leaving with the bag in one hand and his Coke in the other, he thought about how long it had been since he'd held one of these glass bottles, the cold, wet feeling on his skin. On his way out, he used the bottle opener that was screwed on the wall, next to the door.

He stopped to take a sip.

The bubbles burned his tongue and opened his eyes. The real sugar brought him back to the last time he'd had a Coke. He and Paxton sat on their front porch in Los Angeles, watching the sun set behind the Pacific. He put his arm around his son, and they both took in the scene. It was the last time he'd seen his son happy. Not even an hour later, the Revenant came looking for him.

Eugene sighed, took another sip and continued home.

He put his stuff away and then sat with the rest of his soda in front of the diamond jar. The mouse was still alive. He knew this because every morning he would slide the lid off the jar, and the mouse would begin to breathe and stand up.

Eugene lifted the bottle to his lips, then paused. He jumped up and grabbed his latest batch, with dragon egg yolk, crushed dragon shell, ogre eye, Luatu seeds, and many other ingredients. He'd manipulated his own DNA and added that to the mixture. He opened the beaker and poured some Coke into it. Foam bubbled and some of it spilled over.

Sliding the lid halfway off the case, he poured the mixture into the jar. He didn't replace the lid as the mouse stirred. The mixture wet its paws. It opened its eyes and twitched its nose. Slowly it stood and squinted at Eugene; then it noticed the liquid on the ground. It sniffed the liquid and looked again at Eugene.

Does it know? Did that other mixture make it smarter? What am I doing? What if this increases the effect?

Continuing to look at Eugene, the mouse lowered its head closer to the liquid and sniffed again. Then it licked the liquid. The bottom of the diamond jar sliced small cuts in its tongue, and the liquid soaked through. As it entered the mouse's blood stream, the animal jumped back.

It looked at Eugene and opened its eyes wide. Then it looked up and stared at the opening for a moment, crouching like it was about to jump. *If it gets out, this could be a worse epidemic than the original.*

Eugene was about to shut the lid on the jar, but then the

mouse began to sway its head. It looked like a drunk pirate trying to walk on land, during a storm. Slowly its eyes glassed over and it sniffed around again. Following its nose it returned to the puddle and licked the cage clean.

Eugene smiled euphorically. *I'm sorry, little guy.* He slid the top of the cage back into place, locking the seal. The mouse looked up at the noise, then returned to the liquid.

I have to be sure.

13. Family History

Lawrence insisted that the three sit down and listen.

"Get comfortable. Lawrence loves to tell a good story, and this is one of his favorites," Lydia rolled her eyes.

"You're just jealous you can't tell it as well as I," Lawrence said. "Your family's story, Terrance, begins with a man who moved his family here in 1947 and immediately joined the army. Making a name for himself, he was fast-tracked to Officer. His talent and drive propelled him to be the first and only black General in the US Army.

"He developed a reputation for knowing what was going on before he received any communication from the field, and he often had orders ready before his troops contacted him. Some were afraid because they thought he was a speaker like you, Terrance. Others were in awe because they thought he was a seer like Madame Ashleigh or Paxton, here.

"A couple Generals just cared that his skin was too dark. Most of them were members of the Dixie Mafia, and this was before the Revenant War of the 1960s, when people became too focused on survival to worry about race, so they conspired against him."

"I told you he likes to talk," Lydia said.

"And you love to interrupt when the story is getting good," Lawrence glared at her.

"Oh, it's getting good? I hadn't noticed." She smiled and dodged as he moved to shove her.

"One of them, General Hammond, considered the rumors to have some basis in truth, so he recommended him for a project at Einstein's Area 51. The Stargate Project. He and the other Generals knew most volunteers didn't return from EA-51, so they were happy with the plan.

"The Project, as I'm sure you know, investigated the development of spies that could see through the eyes of people around the world, particularly in Germany or Russia. This was before Japan—"

"We all know about Japan and that all this was a long time ago," Sam interrupted. "Don't go off on one of your tangents."

"I find it difficult to tell a story when there are so many interruptions," Lawrence glared at Sam.

Paxton noticed Lawrence and Sam both had red eyes.

"The Project had their first real breakthrough with this talented black General, but it wasn't his destiny." Lawrence continued, "The Revenant Project, which we all know about, was begun to evolve ourselves beyond harm. *Prevent other countries from being able to hurt us, and we won't have need for an army,* as Einstein used to say. Others in the government wanted to use these evolved persons for more traditional reasons. I'm sure you're all familiar with this story, no?"

"Actually, I'm not. I only know that the government created them and about the Roswell aliens being a part of it, not much else," Sara said.

"The aliens aren't a real part of it, Sara," Terrance said.

"Well," Lawrence continued, "At EA 51, after the 1947 Roswell crash, they did have a live alien."

The three of them gasped. The government had been so open about the alien ship and the remains of the dead alien. They even sent it on tour around the country, and it was still in the Smithsonian Air and Space Museum, but only rumors persisted of a living alien.

"Yes, and it's still there, alive today," Lawrence said. "Or that's the rumor."

"Wait. So the Controller has a living alien there at EA51?" Paxton asked.

"If the rumors are true, yes. The group examined the DNA of this alien and our own DNA, throwing together pieces of each, and using radioactivity to change it. Then Chernobyl happened.

"The Russians told everyone it was only a Nuclear Reactor that went critical, but the Stargate Project knew better. They learned the truth about Russia's experiments, thanks to the General, so they stopped them."

"They caused the explosion," Sara said.

"Yes."

"So the General is the one to thank for the Universal Bears, the Watchdogs, and the Iron Curtain?" Paxton asked.

"The super-beings on those teams would never have been made had he not interfered, and Nazi Europe would have over-run the world by now," Lawrence said. "Of course, at the time, the Stargate Project was happy that he'd done so well, but the Revenant Project was having trouble.

"Einstein was dead now; it was 1961, and the project struggled to produce anyone who did not lose their mind immediately. Each victim of the serum lasted a little longer before they just attacked anything around them, but eventually they all became mindless zombies."

"I'm sorry, but what does this have to do with my family?" Terrance interrupted.

"You will see; be patient," Lydia said. "You must be patient; Lawrence is old and set in his long-winded, story-telling ways."

"Finally," Lawrence ignored her barb, "A breakthrough. They created a Revenant who maintained self-control *until* it grew hungry. What they didn't expect was for the Revenant to ignore the spider calf and attack the man who brought it in."

Lawrence paused and placed his hands together, "After eating, it scratched the word *cannibal* into its arm with the calf's fang. It had full memory of its actions and became depressed when it wasn't hungry. They needed a way to give it control over its urges.

"Then they learned about the General. He was given control over a ten-man team that was to be made into Revenant. It was time to produce real results, so the government brought in their best soldiers and injected them. These became the First Brothers.

"It took only moments for these First Brothers to feel the change. They were stronger, faster, and their senses were heightened. The General was given command, and told to help them work as a team and train for a mission behind Nazi lines.

"The General sat in a special chair deep in the EA-51 bunker and walked them through their training exercises. At first he allowed them to control themselves while he watched through their eyes, but as they grew hungry, he took control.

"It worked well, at first, but they soon grew stronger, and he needed to be closer to them so he could control them. Eventually, he could only control them directly with his voice. The scientists, knowing they would be unable to stop the ten Revenant if they failed, tried one last desperate act, hoping it would help the General control the Revenant.

"It worked, but it was the death of the General and the birth of the Controller. He went mad and killed nearly everyone at EA51. There are more details, but it ended with the Revenant War and the building of the Walls. "We believe that since then, he has regained some of his sanity, or things would not have calmed down since the war."

Paxton interrupted, "This history lesson is interesting, but where does Terrance's family come into this?"

The Luminati laughed lightly as if they were in on some larger secret.

"This whole story has to do with your family, Terrance. But for now, know that your Aunt helped us to broker a treaty with them," said Lawrence. "New Orleans is now safe from Revenant as long as we're around."

"And you couldn't just tell us that?" Paxton asked.

"Yeah, the history lesson wasn't necessary for just that. What gives?" Terrance asked.

"Impatient, imperceptive, or both? When your aunt was young, she saw visions of what we were and what we would become. She also saw the General's future, but there were alternatives that were far worse than what we have now. She helped us to shape most of the things I described," Lawrence said.

"Her visions of us, however, nearly ended her life," Sam added.

"She was nosy, and we knew she had figured us out," Lawrence said. "An eight-year-old walking into our coven in the middle of the night, after we fed, and when she knew we would be more patient with her—"

"Whoa there!" Sara said. "Coven?"

J'Nou and Mara arrived at Farm 42. This was a women's farm dedicated to breeding and care of young calves. Mara handed two babies to the human women.

"I thought we kept the males and females in different farms," Mara said.

"In general you will find that to be true," J'Nou gestured to two husky men drinking water out of a trough. He began to walk around them as if he were presenting a museum piece to children, "The two men you see here were brought for breeding and have done their job. We will bring them to the Roalds so they can fulfill their ultimate purpose."

Talking directly to the men, J'Nou said, "Come with us. We have need for you elsewhere."

The two women who were now breastfeeding the new arrivals, looked up and frowned. The two men shook the water from their hair and face, and lowered their heads as they walked up to stand in front of J'Nou and Mara.

Each man was shirtless with a spider-weave cloth wrapped around his waist. Their wet, greasy hair was unevenly trimmed about shoulder length and their faces were dirty and worn from the sun.

Each Revenant picked up a man and threw him over their shoulder. Running like this, they carried the men day and night, arriving outside New Orleans in only two days. They slowed before they were within sight of the city and a large willow tree. Two women sat beneath the tree.

"We brought you lunch, Cynthia." Mara said, looking at Paxton's mother. "Gail, I thought you'd enjoy this specimen. Finest cattle the Farm can produce," she pushed the one on her left toward Paxton's grandmother.

Cynthia and Gail stood and walked toward the men. Gail poked at her lunch, "A nice plump, juicy one, huh? My mouth's watering."

With her left hand on his right shoulder, Cynthia grabbed her lunch. He trembled and closed his eyes; he knew his purpose and was proud to serve. The Revenant farmers couldn't condition all fear out of him, but he was raised on a diet full of soy and carbohydrates, leaving him weak and suggestable. He was taught to know his role and accept it. He was fuel for the fire.

"It's ok," Cynthia said. "Be afraid, at least a little. It makes you taste so much better."

The women expertly consumed the two men, making sure to devour the brains first. When they finished, very little was left. They scooped up all the bones and ran to the Mississippi River to dump them and clean up.

When they returned, the group sat outside, looking from a distance for Paxton or his friends.

"Why don't we go in there and find them?" Cynthia asked. "I want to see my son."

"The Luminati guard this city. So we will wait until the group leaves their safety," J'Nou said.

"How many Luminati are there?" Mara asked.

"One would be too many."

"Yes, coven," Susan said.

"Your aunt figured out what we were and approached us," Lawrence said. "She told us about our past and our immediate future, which we confirmed. She even told us other things that she couldn't possibly know, including how we became a coven.

"Needless to say, we didn't kill her. She became a friend, and we value her advice. We offered to change her, but she refused and asked only one thing: that we attempt to consume only those with evil intent."

"We don't always stick to that," Sam added. "But that hasn't stopped her from trying to make us."

"Yes, that's a long story, however, and we have stuff to do," Lydia said trying to rush Lawrence along.

"We didn't know that she saw our distant future or that while we worked to shape the Revenant, she prepared us for what we would become. She groomed us, turning the Nightmares of New

Orleans into its guardians," Lawrence said.

"While the Revenant were not a direct threat initially, in large numbers they became one. And with how fast they reproduce, they are a threat to our food source." Lawrence focused on the blood pumping through the humans' veins.

"Speaking of which, we need to eat soon," Maurice looked at Sara's neck.

"Soon, Maurice," Lawrence said. "We became vigilant about killing any Revenant that attempted to enter New Orleans or the surrounding area. They stopped coming after we left their heads impaled on stakes outside the city. Then one day, a single Revenant child approached us with a white flag, walking backward. This was odd enough, but your aunt let us know, days earlier, that the Controller was sending a peace offering."

"Since that day," Lydia rushed to the end of the story, "We have had no issues with Revenant appearing within sight of New Orleans. We are the Guardians of New Orleans; we are the Luminati."

"We owe your aunt," Lawrence said. "Her help is the only reason you are safe and the reason we help you tonight."

14. Witch Doctor

Paxton stared into the deep red swirl that filled his vision. He saw the lighter color of fresh, thin blood mingling with the thicker, darker, congealed blood. His nostrils filled with iron, and he heard Terrance's heart pumping more and more blood. That wasn't the only sound, though.

The sucking sound was like rushing water.

He heard Terrance's blood pouring down Sara's throat and then a soft sigh as she stopped and turned to smile at Paxton with blood dripping down her chin. He knew she wanted to feed on him next, and he saw the Luminati behind her, encouraging her.

He tried to stand, but was stuck to his seat and couldn't close his eyes. Finally he opened his mouth and screamed.

"Paxton, what's wrong?" Terrance turned his head toward him. Blood spurted out of the two holes in Terrance's neck.

Paxton saw the drops as they separated on their way to the floor, and he heard them splash. He felt Sara's breath on his neck and saw Terrance's confusion. Her hand pushed his head to the side, exposing his neck more as her breath grew hotter. He felt the sharp points of her teeth pressing on his neck. The snap of his skin as she punctured it was like crisp sausage.

"Snap out of it!" Terrance commanded.

Paxton blinked his eyes and slapped his neck. He felt two wet spots and pulled his hand away to look. Two spots of blood were smeared on his fingers. "She attacked me," he pointed at Sara who now sat innocently on the couch to his left. He then noticed that Terrance was directly in front of him with a wound-free neck,

"I saw her drink your blood."

"You were right," Terrance said to Maurice.

"You were under the influence of Death Metal, Paxton," Maurice's voice was deep and velvety.

"But where is it?" Sara asked.

"It was probably a Vudoun curse. You came from Haiti, right?" Maurice asked.

"Not all Haitians practice Vodou, Maurice," Terrance said.

"That's not what I mean, Terrance," Maurice laughed. "A Vudoun Priest could have easily taken something from Paxton and performed the curse from anywhere. However, when you broke Paxton's connection through your voice, well, let's say they're not likely to try that again soon."

"You'll want to watch him, Terrance," Susan said. "If he begins to have a nightmare like that again, you may have to break him free from it before it kills him."

"Why would someone do this, though?" Terrance asked.

"My Dad," Paxton replied.

Eugene removed the top from the large diamond jar and held his breath. After a minute, when the mouse didn't move, he reached in with a needle and poked it. He yanked his arm back and prepared to throw the lid closed.

The mouse didn't move.

He picked it up with tongs and began to dissect it. It had the normal parts one would expect from a mammal, Revenant or not, and his nails were no longer blue, but an extra organ was also there between its heart and stomach.

What could this be for?

Eugene made a few notes and set the organ aside to come back to it later. He completed his dissection and found no other abnormalities. The mouse was healthy and completely normal. Its DNA showed no signs of Revenant virus.

His solution worked. Now he just had to repeat it, but he was certain it would be a success. *A little celebration is in order.*

It wasn't too late for a drink, so he pulled on his brown coat, went outside, and walked down the street to the Net Café. He didn't usually drink, but this was worth the exception. *I can go back to Miami and see my family again. Be the husband Cynthia deserves and the father Paxton needs.*

It's all been worth it.

His doubt and guilt melted away. His nightmare was finally over; 1980 would be a new beginning for the Roald family and a new era for America. Eugene was beaming with excitement as he sat at his usual table and ordered a Flaming Grog.

"Not your usual, sweetie?" the waitress asked.

"I'm celebrating, tonight," he winked.

Even the news coming over the Net—the Nazi's fending off the Universal Bears—wouldn't get him down right now. He was prepared to single-handedly bring America back to its former glory.

He noticed that the man sitting next to him wore a biker jacket with a Hell's Angels insignia and bore the mark of a Director on his neck. It wasn't unusual to see some pirates or their land-based gang in a Net Café; they mostly kept to themselves, but to see a Director *alone* made Eugene uncomfortable.

His mind went back to the man he bumped on the street. He looked around, planning a casual exit, but realized he was alone with the man. *This isn't good.*

"Eugene?" the Director looked down into his mug and motioned for Eugene to take a seat.

"What's this about? My name's not—"

The Director looked Eugene in the eyes and took a long drought of Flaming Grog. Then, daring Eugene to deny it again, he set the mug down and motioned for more.

"Who are you? And how do you know who I am?"

"I'm Bruce; as for how I know about you... Now, that's something I'm not at liberty to tell. What I can say is that you're a difficult man to find. In fact, if I hadn't bumped into you the other day, I never would have known you frequented Hell's Kitchen."

"That *was* you."

"Yeah, you're lucky I was drunk. I didn't realize who you were until almost an hour later. Then I saw the package. I don't know what you're up to, but an egg like that costs a lot."

"Look, I don't have much money. I spent everything I had on

that egg. Mostly I trade in services. I'm a doctor and if you're injured—"

"I'm not looking for money and I'm not injured."

"So, what do you want from me?"

"I don't want nothin'. I just need to deliver you where you're going."

"And where is that?"

"Chicago."

Terrance, Paxton, Sara, and Jeff followed Lydia and Lawrence into the garage.

"Whoa, I want that one," Jeff ran away from the group.

The two Luminati looked down at him. It took all of Sara's persuasive power to convince them to allow a Revenant to enter their garage, and he was determined to push it.

"No way. It's mine, zombie" Paxton took off behind him.

"Can we turn on the lights? Some of us can't see in the dark," Sara said.

"Sorry," Lydia flipped a large switch, and the lights flickered on in long, fluorescent rows, flooding the garage with bright light for a moment. The lights faded to a more moderate look, something the Luminati were more comfortable with.

A large collection of vehicles, mostly motorcycles, filled the garage. Jeff and Paxton stood on opposite sides of an orange bike with black flames down its sides. Its motor was unlike anything the two had seen, but they both sensed it was the fastest and best in the bunch. The engine was a clear sphere with a blue glow.

"Wheeled vehicles? What is this, 1940?" Terrance teased.

"They all have modified lifts," Lawrence said. "They'll run fine on wheels, but when you need to leave the road, they have repulsor lift technology. I modified it from the norm, though, so they'll handle as well as any wheeled vehicles. You'll lose no handling in the corners."

"None? Even this one?" Paxton asked.

"Even that one, and there's a Hydrolized Nucleic Reactivator engine on that one, Paxton. The HNR 2 will rocket you up to super-sonic speeds in under twelve seconds. I recommend neither of you drive it, unless you have a death wish."

"Why is it HNR 2, Lawrence?" Sara emphasized the 2.

Maurice laughed as he entered the garage. "Well, Lawrence, answer her question."

"The first one ripped right out of my hands," Lawrence eyed Maurice. "It flew out onto the ocean and continued on top of the water, unmanned. At least until I lost sight of it."

"Yeah, he never did find it. It may still be out there, flying across Aztec America," Lydia elbowed Lawrence.

"I'll take it," Paxton said.

"I'm not sure you can handle it," Lydia said.

"I can handle it, as long as it doesn't blow up."

"Sure about that?" Lawrence slid around behind Paxton and began to take the keys out of the bike. He moved faster than Terrance, Sara, or even Jeff could see.

Paxton followed the movement with his eyes and grabbed the keys first.

Lawrence was a little surprised that Paxton moved that fast, almost as if he'd started moving before Paxton saw him move. Lawrence was far stronger, pulling the keys from him, "Those are some fine reflexes. I guess you're a seer, like Madame Ashleigh, no?"

"I'm no—," Paxton worked some words in his mouth, trying not to insult his best-friend's only family, "fortune-teller."

"I mean no offense. You have a natural talent for short-term seeing and that can be far more accurate than fortune-telling. I knew a seer once; he was a friend. He could see the immediate future very clearly and used it to save my life—" Lawrence said and noticed Lydia tapping her wrist. He stopped his story and continued, "Embrace your seeing ability, Paxton. Being a seer will serve you well." Lawrence tossed the keys in his hand a couple times. "You can take it," Lawrence tossed the keys back to Paxton and strolled around the bikes and behind a large cabinet.

"Fine, I'll take the green one over there." Jeff gestured to a Nuclear Rocket, the NR 299. It wasn't custom built like the HNR 2, but it would be fast enough, and he was sure its top speed was faster than anything Terrance and Sara would drive.

"Is that pink one good?" Terrance asked.

"Yeah, you like it?" Lydia laughed.

"I thought it looked safe enough for Sara."

"Thanks," Sara smiled at Terrance. "I do like it, but does it handle well, Lydia?"

"Yes. I've driven it, and its lines are perfect. You should be fine on it," she handed Sara the keys to the pink PRF 231. "I think Lawrence is getting something special for you, Terrance."

Lawrence came around the corner with a modified, black Harley Davidson Rocket Runner 913. It was sleek and sporty, not your traditional chopper. The Harley line was known for quality, speed, handling, and weaponry. Also, like all Harleys, it had a Harley Heuristics Unit. The HHU mostly helped with maintenance and local information through a constant net connection, but it also helped the handling of the bike to make it smooth and fast over any terrain.

"Is that a Harley RR 913?" Terrance asked.

"Yeah, I made a few small adjustments to it, though," Lawrence said. "Madame Ashleigh let us know you'd need them. Mostly I added a few extra balancing servos for high speed turns, some adjustments to the seat, including allowing it to slide back and adjust for the fastest speeds and turns. There isn't much out there that will move faster or better than this."

"Sweet. I can't wait."

"You'll like this last thing, too. I built it especially for you. I accessed some of that alien technology from EA 51 with Sam's help, so these plates can read your thoughts. I upgraded the HHU to work with them, too; the bike will react before you even know you want to turn. I've tested it and it works well, but I think with your powers it'll work far better."

"Wow! We can't thank you enough for all this help," Terrance said. He was slightly distracted as he ran his fingers along the contours of his new ride.

"Don't thank us yet," Sam said as he walked down the stairs, "There are some Revenant at the boundary line, about eight kilometers and one meter outside the city. I didn't get a good look. I don't want them to know we've seen them. As long as they remain outside the line, they know we won't touch them, and I don't think they'll cross it. You better arm up and be prepared. Even with these bikes, you're not likely to outrun them both before they could jump you."

Terrance checked his pistol and his grandfather's revolver. Sara and Jeff were unarmed, but Jeff wasn't concerned with that. Paxton still had his handgun from Miami, but he knew they were outmatched unless the Luminati helped. He turned to Lawrence and asked, "What kind of help can you offer us?"

Death Metal. Alfred reeled from the pain of being suddenly torn free from Paxton's mind. *It's too powerful, but Canton is impatient.* He wiped the blood from his nose and lip.

This is going to hurt.

Alfred carefully tied his right arm to a large tree and yanked away from it. Birds escaped the forest in large flocks when he yelled. Setting a bone may be painful, but he couldn't afford the side effects of painkillers.

His skin was covered in several spots with Death Metal burns, blue patches of scabbed skin. Each patch was slathered in a mixture of Luatu oils and Finu juices, giving the patches a purple, wet look.

A professional witch doctor didn't run into these setbacks. Never had his connections been broken, let alone twice. And with the same person? Something weird was going on.

One time was surprising, but now I know: Canton is hiding something about the boy. Paxton Roald was becoming a nuisance and Alfred didn't like nuisances.

Alfred's employers wouldn't be happy about this, but he couldn't hide it from them long. Besides, how was he supposed to deal with this boy if they didn't tell him everything? It was time to heal, so he rolled into bed. He'd need to try again before Canton returned for an update. *That Revenant won't leave until it's handled.*

15. The Big Easy

ew Orleans' gate, *The Big Easy*, loomed over the group and blocked the light of the moon. It was forty meters tall, and each door was nearly ten meters wide and at least two meters thick. The doors weren't ornate, but at the bottom were many carvings, messages for loved ones, signatures, offensive messages for the Revenant, and every form of graffiti known to man.

Two large guard towers stood fifty meters high on either side of the door. They were approximately five meters in diameter and armored with Kevlar, metal, and cement. Small shards of death metal were shoved randomly throughout and along their top edge. The towers were well prepared for a massive Revenant attack.

Standing in the shadow of the Big Easy, however, the group was far from being in the dark. New Orleans was one of the only American cities with nightlife. The citizens knew that the Revenant never came, though only a handful knew of the Luminati. For most people in New Orleans, they were only a children's bedtime story, something to scare them into behaving.

The gates wouldn't be opened at night, even for the Luminati. Though the city was safe, no one was brave enough to open the Big Easy during the night and invite the Revenant or, arguably worse, a horde of shambling zombies inside. Maurice stood at the guard tower, waiting for the group. He gestured for them to come over.

They wheeled their bikes toward the tower. The noise of the engines didn't concern them; the bikes were quiet. Fission, fusion, and nucleic power didn't create the noise that old gasoline powered engines did, but driving the bikes through the small doors in the gate tower wasn't something they planned to do.

Maurice helped Paxton first, picking up the bike for the few steps needed to climb. When he emerged, he wasn't alone. Sam and Susan had just landed after jumping over the Big Easy.

"If you can jump over that, can the Revenant too?" he asked them.

"Probably," Susan replied, "we've never let them get close enough to try." She smiled at him.

Looking her over, he felt his heart beat faster, "I bet you don't."

"It's impressive enough to let the city feel safe, though, without them knowing we're vam—err, blood-suckers," Susan winked.

"I'm sure jumping over the wall helps keep your secret, too." He blushed as she smiled back at him and nodded agreement.

Maurice ignored Jeff, letting him carry his own bike, and instead helping Sara, then Terrance. Soon the four were outside the gate with a Luminati on either side of each. Each was excited for the hunt and the prospect of killing a First Brother of the Revenant, but Sam was less so than the rest. He had lost by picking the shortest straw, and he stood next to Jeff.

"I don't need your help, Sam," Jeff said, "if you want to—"

"Be quiet," Terrance commanded him.

Sam laughed.

"Ok, we have no chance of sneaking up on them; in fact I'm certain they've seen the bikes already," Lawrence said.

"Was it a good idea to put glowing engines in all of them?" Susan asked.

"Really, Susan? Really?" Lawrence continued, "We need to be straight forward. If we can tempt them into crossing the boundary, we can take them out. If not we'll have to follow through with what we discussed."

"Ok, I see them; let's get it over with," Paxton said.

"Where are they?" Jeff asked.

Paxton pointed at a tree eight kilometers away. None of the other humans saw where he was pointing; nor could Jeff.

"I don't see them," Jeff said.

For the first time, all the Luminati paid attention to Jeff. "That means they shouldn't be able to see us either." Lawrence smiled and looked at his coven.

Immediately they disappeared toward the sides of the road. Terrance motioned for the group to move along and ignore the Luminati. He understood what they were doing. The group hopped on their bikes and lined up, wheeling them slowly north.

As far as anyone could see, the grass stretched out from *The Big Easy* with no trees to interrupt it for several kilometers. Except one. A single willow oak grew beside the road to mark the boundary. Under the large tree, two Revenant stood alert and looked in the direction of the wall.

Cynthia and Gail watched for Paxton.

They stood like trees in the wind, arms at their sides, feet planted, and eyes facing forward, but each of their bodies were continually in motion. Gail noticed something to her left and turned her head. She tilted it slightly and shifted her weight to run. Though she appeared to have the body of a seventy-year-old woman, she took a stance that showed how lithe she truly was now.

The Controller stopped her just short of moving. He wouldn't let the instincts of one of his Revenant ruin the truce with the Luminati; nor would he let her die for no reason.

Lydia realized she'd been spotted and walked purposefully up to the pair of Revenant. Cynthia's eyes only briefly fell on the tiny frame of Lydia, taking in the way she stood like an immovable object. While Cynthia and Gail were fluid, Lydia was stone.

The Controller knew and shared with the women what Lydia was capable of despite her unimpressive figure. Cynthia's eyes immediately returned to watching for Paxton. She wanted him to join her, to be more than human, to feel healthier and more powerful than ever before. Power burned through her, tempting her to move, daring her to stand still. She wanted that for her son.

"What are you doing at our border, Revenant?" Lydia asked.

"Nothing that concerns you, Lydia." Cynthia pointed back toward the Big Easy, "Now, go have a drink on us. We have no intention of crossing the boundary tonight."

"But you could join us over here," Gail said. "I'm curious what vampire meat tastes like."

"For such an old woman, you have no class," Lydia turned and walked along the border, pretending to be walking the line, protecting it. All the while, she was signaling to the other Luminati and Paxton about what she'd seen.

Two Revenant.

Alone.

"Don't pretend that you don't want my blood, life sucker," Gail replied.

Lydia stopped and turned back. "We are not allowed. Nor would I want to taste the putrid, expired blood that fills your old veins, zombie," Lydia said.

"She upsets me," Gail growled. "I want our Paxton with us."

"Calm down, Mother," Cynthia said. "We'll handle them in time. We just need to collect Paxton and find my husband. Then we'll be ready."

"Ready for what, Cynthia?" Lydia asked. "What does the Controller have planned for Mr. Roald?"

Cynthia smiled and ignored Lydia's question.

The group slowly wheeled their bikes toward the tree. They bought enough time for the Luminati to take up positions and scout ahead. When they were in position, the group rode their bikes the rest of the way, to within twenty meters of the women.

The bikes were fast, but they didn't want to see how fast yet. There was time to stretch the engines later. The groups were at the line of the neutral area, a border around New Orleans that stretched from the Willow Oak tree to the tree line. The Luminati kept the area clear of trees, except the one.

Paxton watched the women as he rode, but when he got closer, it hit him that this was his mother and grandmother.

His mother was the one who raised him while his father was working on his *project*. She was the one protecting him and shepherding him to the ship while his father saved his project. LA opened Paxton's eyes to this, the months at sea that the family spent, mourning his sister, apart in such close quarters, and again, when his father left them in Miami.

For his project.

Paxton had only one *real* parent. When they arrived in Miami, his father stayed on the boat. Paxton didn't cry, but turned and took his mother's hand. He would protect her like she protected him. When his grandmother joined them, he began to feel like he had a real family.

He had to talk to them. He had to see if they were strong enough to repel the Controller's hold. They were the most important people in his life.

And they stood ten meters away now.

16. Guns, Guilt, and Gail

Terrance took the shotgun from his shoulder and left his grandfather's revolver at his side. Sara took the 9mm pistols out of her holsters and had one ready in each hand. Jeff crouched, nearly on all fours, prowling up toward the two women, unarmed.

Paxton walked with his hands out to his sides, open and weaponless within six meters of the women. He motioned for the others to stay back.

They didn't listen.

Paxton stopped 3m away and Terrance stood at his right shoulder with Sara beside him and Jeff on Paxton's left. He stared at his mother and grandmother with tears rolling down his cheek. He wasn't sobbing; he'd done that already, but he couldn't deny the emotions he felt.

"Paxton, baby. Give me a big hug," Cynthia stood and reached her arms out looking like the woman who had been there for him his entire life. "I missed you so much."

His grandmother hunched over a bit, "Come here, boy. We haven't seen you for a while." She looked as frail as when she was in Miami, and her voice trembled with her age, but he knew she was putting on a show. Paxton saw how she approached Lydia, even if they didn't see him at the time.

"Controller, release my family. If you don't, I'll find you and kill you myself," Paxton said.

"You can't do that, Pax," Cynthia said. "It's better to have him around. Come on. It feels great to be so full of life. Look at your grandma; she can walk upright and even run. You were helping her off the couch only weeks ago."

Gail stood taller and healthier. She looked like a woman half her age.

"Controller, I will find my father and kill him before you get to him. Then I'm coming for you."

"He healed me, Paxy. He's the good guy in all this; don't you see it?" Gail said.

"I want a reply from the Controller, Mom."

Terrance winced and looked at Paxton. He had recommended that Paxton not call them *Mom* or *Granny* when he talked to them.

"The Controller isn't doing this, son. He's only keeping us from running to you. My urge to run and hug you is unbearable, but those blood suckers are around, and if I take one step closer to you, they'll tear me apart. You can't let them hurt me, Paxton. Please, just come with us.

"If you don't want to become one of us, we can just travel together. Then we can find your father and see what he wants to do."

The Luminati growled so lightly that only Paxton heard it, and only they heard his heart beat faster, or so he thought.

Cynthia smiled a little more. She heard his heart and knew she was close, "We can live together forever. Your father can join us, and we can be a family again. We won't have to be afraid of anything or need to run anymore. We can be a family forever together. Don't you understand what the Controller is offering?"

"Yes, he'll even allow your friends to join, if they wish," Gail said, "and if not, he will leave them alone forever. You can verify with the blood suckers that we're good on our word."

"I don't want to join you. I won't become the very thing that tore our family apart. Mom. Granny."

Terrance winced again.

"You're strong enough. You can fight this. You can return to me. Please, don't leave me like Dad did," Paxton fell to his knees.

His mother took a step toward him.

Terrance raised his weapon, and Sara followed suit. Jeff prepared to pounce, and the five Luminati took a step closer. Twenty seconds passed and nobody breathed or moved, except Paxton.

He stood slowly and said, "You are not my mother—"

"Of course I am, son," she tried to interrupt him.

"—and you are not my granny."

Gail crouched, mirroring Jeff.

"You both are monsters now, and the only thing to do with monsters is destroy them. I'm sorry. My family is *all* dead now." He raised the Magnum in his hand and aimed it at his granny. He heard a small thudding sound and a whistle in the air.

He turned his head, along with the Luminati and Jeff. Cynthia and Gail heard it and didn't look but turned to run.

Suddenly the four motorcycles exploded in huge fireballs, singeing the backs of their necks and knocking the three humans to the ground. Jeff quickly placed himself between the three and the explosion which burned off most of his skin as shrapnel cut his right leg in half, stopping just before it would have ripped into Terrance.

Jeff could feel his Revenant nature as it rose to the surface and he lost control. He felt Sara beneath his head and arms and grabbed her side as he reared back his head, mouth open.

"Jeff. Off," Terrance shouted darkly.

Just before his mouth dug into Sara, he leapt off, fighting the words. He stalked back toward Sara.

"Jeff, feed on those monsters!" Terrance pointed toward Cynthia and Gail who were almost to the tree line.

Jeff jumped toward the Revenant.

"No," Paxton yelled, "We'll find them again later."

"Jeff, stop. Sit," Terrance commanded him again.

Jeff immediately sat in midair and fell to the ground, skidding on his butt.

Eugene was buckled into an NJ-950; the jeep was well suited for off-road travel, but it was not armored. The tan paint was scratched and the body was banged up. It made its way slowly through Pennsylvania, heading west on an unpaved roadway.

"Why are you doing this?" Eugene asked. "Are you a Votary? You're not Revenant, and I see the Hell's Angels Director tattoo on your neck."

"Call me Bruce," the Director replied.

"Ok, Bruce. Why are you doing this? Do you even know who I am?"

"You're Eugene Roald."

"Well, yeah. But... "

"You know, there's a city on fire about a mile, sorry, about a kilometer and a half south of here," Bruce pointed out the window toward a smoky horizon. "They say it's been that way for a hundred years. Ever been there?"

"Centralia? No, can't say I have," Eugene had little desire to talk about the place.

"Good. Don't."

The pair drove on in heavy silence for another hour.

"Do you work for the Controller?" Eugene asked.

"No."

"Then why are you doing this?"

He slowed down and looked at Eugene out of the corner of his eye. He weighed the pros and cons of telling Eugene why he was doing this, "I have to."

"Oh come on! That's what I get? I'm trying to create a ser—" Eugene stopped himself and sat quiet for a moment.

"I'll tell you what. You tell me what you needed the egg for, and I'll tell you why I'm taking you or where I'm taking you. Your move."

Eugene thought for a moment, "You go first."

Bruce raised his eyebrow and stared harder at the road. He didn't bargain.

"Ok, ok. I had the egg to complete a serum. Now it's your turn. Why are you taking me?"

"Because of someone I care about."

"That's it?" Eugene stared in disbelief.

"The more you give me, the more you get. Don't play games with me, pal."

"Fine."

"It must have been a silenced 45mm explosive round, fired from that direction. We searched and couldn't find anyone," Lawrence said. "There was evidence they were there, and it smelled like Revenant, or maybe that was just Jeff feeding nearby, but they must have shot from beyond the line, then they immediately ran. We'll figure it out, and if it was a Revenant, then the truce is over."

"They were probably gone before the shot even hit the bikes," Lydia explained.

"We can't go back in and get more bikes; we can't risk it. We'll have to continue on foot," Terrance said.

"That's too dangerous; besides, your aunt is a seer, and told us this would happen. I thought we could prevent it, but we've learned to trust her and were prepared. We have a jeep ready. I'll run and get it." Lawrence disappeared after the vehicle.

"A jeep? We'll be exposed and slow. We may as well just walk the whole way?" Sara said.

"You haven't seen the jeep yet, honey." Lydia smiled.

Sara pursed her lips and narrowed her eyes. She leaned into Terrance, "How do we know that we can trust these bloodsuckers?"

"I trust my—Madame Ashleigh, Sara. That's enough. Wait a second. You're just now thinking about this? We could have been their dinner hours ago."

"Well, what if the bikes weren't shot? What if they were sabotaged?"

"It would have been a more effective sabotage if they had blown the cores," Jeff said. "The bullet only blew the converters, causing a massive explosion, but nothing as bad as it could have been."

They heard a motor approaching, and the jeep came into view with its lights off. It was black and well armored, fully covered and protected, riding a meter off the ground. It was heavily modified by the Luminati and looked like it would take them quickly and safely over even the toughest terrain.

"A modified NJ-1300. Sweet," Jeff said.

"So, what did you do to this, Lawrence?" Terrance asked. "Repulsor lifts I assume? Or are we stuck in a wheeled vehicle?"

"Not me, This one was all Maurice. It's nuclear powered, so you should be good to go for a few decades; just don't let the engine shielding get damaged," Lawrence said. "I think he threw in a few tricks. No repulsors, though. Just hit the screen inside for some directions on the specialties." He tossed the keys to Terrance and went to examine the bike remains. "It looks like a few large pieces are left, and fortunately the cores are all intact. We'll work on rebuilding these for your return."

"Return?" Sara asked. Paxton's head turned as well.

"I guess she didn't tell you. No matter. We'll have them ready, but it's time for you to go."

They all knew he was right and packed up. After some quick goodbyes, they packed into the NJ-1300. Terrance helped Sara up into the jeep and then climbed in after her. Both of them sat in the front while Paxton and Jeff sat in the back.

"Where are we headed, Paxy?" Terrance asked.

Paxton wasn't in the mood and stared at the tree line, where Gail and Cynthia disappeared, "East."

They sat there for a moment, waiting for Paxton to say more. Terrance turned the headlights on and drove east, into Dixie Mafia territory.

"Poor timing, no?" a large man said as he entered Alfred's small hut wearing a long coat with the hood over his head.

"I'm sorry," Alfred replied, visibly shaken. "Where's Canton? I thought he would be here to—"

"Canton is occupied elsewhere. I'm Captain Oliver. I'll be your envoy for as long as I let you live."

"But you're a First Brother."

"Yes. You look like you're not doing well," Captain Oliver didn't move.

Alfred grabbed his arm, rubbing it over the bandages, "Yeah, I don't know how, but they broke the connection. Twice."

"It doesn't matter. You failed and now he's moving on." Captain Oliver walked further inside the hut and stopped next to Alfred's bed.

"You'll have another chance. I'll remain here to let you know when it's time."

Alfred knew there was no point in protesting, and he merely rolled over on his cot and went back to his trance. Revenant weren't known for their patience.

17. Civil Rights

In a small village one day's drive east of New Orleans, somewhere in Alabama, the Beaumonts sat down for their evening meal. Sean, his wife Casey, their son Simon, their daughters Elisabeth and Julie, his parents, and his mother-in-law talked about the day.

"Daddy," Elisabeth said, "I helped Mommy make dinner tonight."

"And you did a wonderful job, Sweetie. The bread is soft and warm. It soaks my soup right up, just the way I like it," Sean said.

"I helped Daddy shoot the deer that's in the stew," Simon said. "With a real arrow," he mimed shooting an arrow at his sister. Then he adjusted his shirt and sat taller.

"It tastes great, Simon," Casey said, patting her son's hand.

"What did Julie do, Mommy?" Simon asked.

"She slept all day. I think she'll still be doing that for a while. She's not even two weeks old," Casey's mother said.

"So, did you get to shoot the arrow a lot, Simon?" Elisabeth asked.

"Just a few times, but I hit the deer once," he replied.

"Wow! Daddy, can I go hunting with you sometime?" she asked.

"We'll see. Maybe tomorrow, Sweetie. Now eat your dinner."

Two hours later, the moon was high and full, but deep in the woods where J'Nou, Mara, Cynthia, and Gail crouched; no light reached the ground. They were in the thick trees and very alone.

The ground was moist with dew, making the dirt soft.

J'Nou could have drawn in the air or shared his thoughts with Mara, but he drew in the dirt. He always appreciated the way it felt to crouch and draw lines on the ground. It reminded him of his days in the Rangers, before he went to EA 51.

The lines were faint, and the wind cleared them almost as fast as he drew them, but as his fingers traced the lines, they burned into the other Revenants' retinas.

They had to let the group of humans out of their sight after following them for a day, but they would easily find them with Jeff's scent. The plan was to get a visual on the group today, but first they needed to make a stop.

A run-in with a Revenant alligator cost J'Nou his arm, and Mara still had cuts and bruises. They needed to feed and recuperate, but they were fortunate that Cynthia and Gail showed up to help out before too much damage was done. The other women were following a kilometer away, on the opposite side of J'Nou and Mara.

J'Nou abruptly stood and nodded to Mara. She ran quickly through the trees, and he followed behind and veered slightly to her left. Cynthia followed behind that, veering to Mara's right, and Gail followed directly behind Mara. They came to a small village with seven buildings grouped in a circular shape.

The crude wall around the buildings would keep out a Sasquatch, but it was no match for a Revenant. They silently jumped over the wall. Sniffing the air, Mara gestured toward a building to their right.

They crept to the door and slid inside. J'Nou noticed a sign that read *The Beaumonts* carved in the door.

A family of eight was asleep inside. One older couple slept together, while another even older woman slept alone. Another younger couple slept in the same bed with their youngest daughter, not even a month old. A brother and sister, around six and four years old, slept together in the remaining bed. The resemblance of the individuals was undeniable.

"This will be a feast," J'Nou whispered.

"I can't wait," Terrance said, sarcastically.

"Oh come on," Paxton said. "Nobody really acts like that any-more, do they? Besides, there's too much to worry about with Revenant to harass you."

"I hate to say it, Paxton, but I think Jeff's right," Sara said. "I used to live around here, well, a bit north of here, but I heard stories. And I knew more than a few people like that, especially the Dixie Mafia."

"The Captain used to deal with them," Jeff said. "And we'd only be allowed to bring our palest pirates to the delivery. They never said that, but the Captain is one smart man. As soon as he figured it out, we cut off all dealings with them.

"It wasn't easy, either. They paid well, and it hurt us for a while until we picked up some more regular customers. I'm glad he did it, though. Those dudes saw Uelese once and got really angry."

"Wonderful, so we have a bunch of bigots to look out for. Anything else to add to the list?" Paxton asked.

"Sure. There are always the Caterwalls and the Chuntrices," Sara said.

The four rode in relative silence for a few miles. The only sound was the engine, tires, and other parts of the NJ-1300 shaking, rubbing, and sounding like they would barely stay together.

The road was very bumpy, still paved in a few areas, but more often the roads were patches of dirt and worn grass that kept large trees from growing there. The old roads were built during the War of the Others. President Roosevelt built an interconnect-ing highway to increase travel between states and act as emer-gency travel in case the Nazis attacked us. After the Revenant War, most highways and roads were left to crumble.

"So, Paxton, where are we headed? And why?" Jeff brought the subject up first.

Paxton stiffened and focused on driving. Sara watched birds heading north, but Terrance looked at Paxton expectantly.

After a few minutes, Paxton answered. "We're going to New York. That's where my Dad is." He took a deep breath. "I have to give him to the Revenant."

Sara gasped and Terrance's eyes narrowed, but Jeff just stared blankly.

"I understand," Jeff answered.

"No, I'm not sure you do!" Paxton snapped. "He helped create the Revenant virus. He's responsible for all of the death and destruction over the past decades. The worst horrors ever. And if I give him to them, they'll only make themselves stronger."

Paxton sped up and the ride became bumpier.

"But he is the only bargaining chip I have."

He began to focus on the road and the ride became less bumpy, but he didn't slow down.

"He is the reason they were there and infected my mother and grandmother."

He sped up.

"He is the reason they're chasing us."

"Paxton, I don't think—" Sara started.

"He is the reason that I have to trade his life for theirs," Paxton began to slow the NJ-1300 to a normal speed. "After they're safe and seeded, like Jeff, I'll hunt down and kill every last Revenant."

Little was left of the family. The Revenant finished them so quickly that the humans didn't even stir in bed. The rest of the village would wake with a grim discovery. Many carnivorous birds were already flocking to the village, though. J'Nou left the door and windows open so the birds could pick at the rest of the gore.

Perhaps the villagers would blame this on the birds.

Probably not.

J'Nou and the other Revenant followed Jeff's scent as they ran through the woods.

They found the jeep traveling along an old road and scouted ahead of it.

"We do not want any sign that we are following them, but we must help them get wherever they are going," J'Nou said. "If Cynthia and Gail cannot convince Paxton to join us, and it is obvious they are prepared to fight us, then we will allow them to find Eugene. Then we will pounce before they know what is happening."

"I'd rather not harm my grandson, if we can prevent it," Gail said. "But I'll gladly tear that hussy apart if I get the chance."

The Revenant split up again. One pair ran along the road on each side, scaring off the animals and finding nothing that would slow the group.

Then they came to a patch of road that was stuck twenty meters in the air, an old bridge that no longer reached down to the ground. There would be no way for the NJ-1300 to cross this or easily go around it. Going around, without a path, would put them out at least three days.

"We will help them, Mara," J'Nou said. "Run and find the others."

She returned with Cynthia and Gail and they jumped to work on the overpass and began to bring it down. Mara knocked out one of the pylons, while Cynthia and Gail worked together to slowly bend it down. J'Nou piled rubble into a smooth ramp.

"They will just think they are very fortunate," J'Nou said.

"Or that there are strangers nearby with a talent for fixin' up roads," Cynthia said.

They continued down the road, ran into a few obstacles to remove, and soon found a small town. They figured the group would stay there for a night and they staked it out.

Sara sighed. What were they doing? A bunch of kids who thought they could make the decision to turn a mad scientist over to some super-human zombies? This was the type of stuff she read about on the net.

She wanted Terrance. He was the only reason she was here, and he wouldn't look at her for more than a moment. Sure, she could turn to the zombie next to her, but why would she do that?

Ick. He was looking at her. She should pretend to notice, maybe make Terrance jealous. That would make him look at her. *No! I can't do that again.*

She reached forward to touch Terrance's hair; then she pulled her hand back. He was talking to Paxton about something. She couldn't be bothered to pay attention to what it was; she was too busy being sidetracked by the thought of Paxton.

He would tell Terrance when he had the chance. She couldn't let him be the one who did it. She knew it was wrong, but now she would lose either way. The setup didn't make him pay more attention to her, and admitting it was a setup could make him hate her more.

Sara sighed again and looked out the window. A deer ran by and mouthed the word 'scared' at her.

She jumped and hit her head on the roof of the jeep.

"What was that?" Terrance turned back and asked.

"Nothing. I just... I don't know. I hit my head on the roof," she said.

"How did you do that?"

"I thought... I must be hungry or tired."

"No, what did you see?" Jeff asked this time.

Terrance glared at him briefly, and then looked back at Sara. Was he jealous of Jeff being nice? Could he still have feelings?

"I saw a deer."

"Oh, that's no big deal. I saw it too." Terrance said.

"Did it say anything to you?"

"No." Terrance grew concerned and looked at Paxton and Jeff. Paxton slowed down so he could hear this, but Jeff didn't seem too surprised.

"I've seen this before, Sara. It's nothing to worry about." Jeff said. He lay back in his seat and acted as if that settled the discussion.

"You've seen everything, haven't you, Jeff?" Paxton looked to Terrance who smiled.

"Traveling with the Captain, I saw a lot."

"Damn pirates," Terrance mumbled. "You all think you're so worldly and smart."

"I met this dude, once. He could speak to animals," Jeff said. "Dr. Uhh, I can't remember his name. Dude! What was his name? Anyway, they talked to him and he talked to them," Jeff said. "I know! I thought he was crazy, but he told me stuff only the Captain, his parrot, and I knew. And he only had a few moments with the parrot."

"Parrots talk, moron," Terrance said.

"Yeah, but I was there and couldn't hear anything. It was like he heard it in his mind." Jeff pointed to his head and looked around at all of them.

"That's what it was like for me, Jeff," Sara said. Terrance glared at Jeff. *I wonder what bothers him most about Jeff, that he's a zombie, a pirate, or was in our bed?*

"Well, listen to the animals," Jeff said. "The Dr. always said, 'They never lie.'"

"What did the deer say, Sara?" Paxton asked.

"He said one word, 'scared'."

"'Scared?' That's weird. Why would it say that?" Terrance said to himself.

"How am I supposed to know, Terr?" Sara nearly cried. "I just saw a deer mouth the word to me. I was a little too shocked to follow up."

"Are you sure?" Terrance asked.

"Yes, I'm sure!" *Slow down, Sara. Don't let yourself get angry at him; you're just scared.* "Don't you think I would tell you?"

"Whoa, Sara. Calm down, I—"

"'Whoa?' I'm not a horse, Terrance." She quieted her words, but they dripped with venom. "You should just be quiet."

"Hey you two. There's a town up ahead. We're all tired; let's see if we can get a room and stay the night. Maybe some sleep will help?" Paxton resumed driving at a steady speed.

Terrance faced forward.

"Yeah, maybe," he pushed the words out through his clenched jaw. "But first, we need to feed our pet. Jeff, go feed on some animals, no humans, and return. Quickly."

Jeff immediately opened his door and hopped out of the NJ-1300. He tumbled, then stood and ran into the woods.

Sara clamped her mouth shut and stared out the window. *How did this go so wrong?*

Jeff was a mile outside of the town and deep in the woods when he smelled a large buck close by. It was time to eat, and the strong smell brought drool to his lips. He wiped his face and crept toward the scent. Another scent hit him and it was stronger. He felt like a starving dog. This smell was better than the deer. It was tastier. His mouth watered like a grandma with her garden. He recognized it immediately, human blood.

Through the trees Jeff saw a group of men around a campfire. One of them was injured. He could see the blood soaking through the bandages and cloth on the man's leg. Jeff took a step toward him and stopped. The command from Terrance was to feed on animals and no humans; Jeff couldn't do it; he took another step, fighting the command.

To his left Jeff saw the buck grazing, and before it finished its last breath, dinner was served. He was satisfied for now and relieved that he had Terrance to command him. The thought of devouring those humans brought prickles to his back and brought his knees to the ground.

What am I now?

Jeff's desire was so great that he knew he needed Terrance. *This won't happen again; I couldn't resist the temptation alone.*

He stood and turned back toward the village when it hit him hard. The smell almost knocked him on his back. He couldn't place it, but he recognized it.

It wasn't the human's, or the buck's remains. He was sure it wasn't another animal. The smell was death and life, human and animal. He recognized it and took off back toward the town.

"We want to stay the night," Paxton said.

The bearded guard reminded Terrance of the fried chicken tycoon from the Civil War. "We don't allow visitors, sir," the guard said "We will oblige you with safe passage around our fair town, but I cannot allow you to enter. I do hope ya'll understand."

"But sir, we only need a night," Terrance said. The guard looked him up and down with a scowl on his face. *Is he shocked that a young man would talk to him like this, or a black man?*

The guard's stare grew uncomfortable and Terrance looked around for Sara. She was looking at a squirrel, trying to read its mind, but getting nothing from the furry creature.

Jeff ran up to them, startling the guard, who in turn pointed his rifle directly at the newly arrived Revenant.

"No, not me! Revenant!" Jeff pretended to pant, even putting his hands on his knees and leaning over. He pointed back toward the forest, "They're behind me, killed my wife. Please, let me in!"

"B-but, we can't, Revenant?" The guard paused. "Are you sure, boy?"

"Yes, do you know anything else that can leap over a full grown tree?"

"No, I guess not."

I do, thought Terrance. The guard stepped away and called into the radio. After a quick back and forth on the radio, he returned and addressed Paxton, "Ok, you all can stay for the night." Again he looked at Terrance carefully, "but at dawn, or after any attack befalls us, you'll continue on your way. Also, you boys will be expected to help with defending our town."

"We agree," Paxton said.

Terrance nodded.

"Now, please, let us in before they come!" Sara panicked.

The man sighed and waved them inside.

"Good bluff, Jeff," Paxton said.

They were alone in their room, the only one available for the group to share. They packed in and gave Sara the bed. Paxton and Terrance made do with pallets on the floor while Jeff prepared to stand watch through the night.

"Yeah, even I can admit that wasn't bad, but lying comes naturally to your type, doesn't it?" Terrance said.

"Who said I was lying?" Jeff asked.

"What do you mean?" Terrance stopped making his pallet.

"I smelled them. Not sure how many," Jeff said. "I didn't get a look at them."

"And you're just now telling us?" Sara asked.

Jeff's head lowered slightly, "Sorry, Sara."

"Is it the same smell from New Orleans? The smell of J'Nou and my family?" Paxton asked.

"Yeah. And that creepy girl. I think so."

"How can you know that it's them?" Terrance asked. "Or even that there's more than one?"

"I just do," Jeff said. "My senses seem to be getting stronger."

"Great, so they can probably smell you," Sara said.

"Dude, you're right. I hadn't thought about that," Jeff said. "It's probably how they found us."

"Maybe, but at least we know. And they don't know that we know. We need to split up," Paxton said.

"But we can't do that. Jeff could go crazy, and they'll know if we don't leave here together," Sara said.

"Yes, but we'll have to risk it," Paxton said. "Terrance can command him. We'll leave together tomorrow morning, then split up later on. They must not be staying within sight, or I would have seen them."

"Sara, you can talk to the animals, too. Find out where they are," Jeff said.

"No, I tried to talk to that squirrel outside the door, but I can't do it. I think the deer was just a fluke," she said.

"No, I don't think so," Terrance said. "You've always loved animals. I agree with the zombie-dude. I think you just need concentration and practice. Tap into the feelings you had when the deer spoke to you and try again when you can."

"Ok," she smiled at him before looking away.

Terrance blushed and his ears felt warm. Maybe they could move past all of this if they survived to New York.

"Ok, after Jeff leads them away, I'll break off from Terrance and Sara," Paxton said.

"Why?" Terrance and Sara asked.

"So I can kill J'Nou and that little girl. Also, I need to make a deal with the Controller."

"What kind of deal?" Terrance asked.

"Don't worry, I'll make sure he leaves you guys alone too. Jeff and I will flank them, and you can continue on your way. We'll catch up with you afterwards."

"No way!" Terrance said. "That's too dangerous. We've been ahead of them. We can stay ahead of them."

"I'm not putting you in more danger. I'm the reason they're following us."

"We don't know that for sure," Terrance said. "It could be me."

The others froze and looked at Terrance.

"What do you mean?" Paxton asked.

"It's just something Madame Ashleigh said. They may be after me, or both of us. The Revenant have been after my family for years. Now that I say it out loud, it makes me wonder about my parents... I just think we should stay together if we're going to do this."

Sara put her hand on his shoulder.

"Never mind," Paxton said. "If they're after me, I may be able to convince my mom and granny not to harm me, but... "

"I doubt it," Terrance said. "We need to put them out of their misery, Paxton. It's the only way."

Paxton stared at Terrance. How could his best friend suggest something like that? "No." He wouldn't consider that. Now that he knew of the Luatu and saw Jeff here, he knew it would be just as bad as murdering them. "I'm not ready for that. I can get them back."

"At what cost?" Sara asked.

"Dude, trust me; this isn't the easy life," Jeff added.

Paxton turned and stood there. Silence settled over the room. Finally he said, "We'll just keep moving forward then."

"Great, man, now that we have a plan, I have a question. Did anyone wonder why there was only one room left when they don't take visitors?" Jeff asked.

"I hadn't thought of it," Paxton said.

"I had. The way the guard stared down Terrance, I wanted to rip his head off. He didn't want us to come into the city," Sara said.

"I didn't think you would notice since you were lost in that squirrel's eyes. I was getting a bit jealous," Terrance smiled. "I got that feeling off of him too, though—almost radiating from him."

"I guess I hadn't thought of it, but he did stare at you a lot," Paxton said.

"I'll be extra vigilant tonight, man, just in case. Birmingham may be small, but the Dixie Mafia have a lot of pull here," Jeff said.

In the morning, Paxton and Jeff packed up while Terrance

and Sara walked to the market. No one was in a hurry to cram back into the jeep for their long trip.

The market was full of flowers, clothes, and food. The shop-keepers tried to sell their wares to anyone but Terrance. He didn't feel comfortable approaching many of the stalls, even as he smelled flowers and reached for a Blue Bonnet. The shopkeeper yelled at him that it would be two Naughts for that particular Blue Bonnet.

"I just wanted to—" he started.

"I don't care what you wanted to do," the shopkeeper inter-rupted. "You will not touch my flowers until you pay me, boy."

Terrance reached into his pocket and withdrew the Naughts. He put them in the shopkeeper's hand.

"In the jar! In the jar! How dare you try to touch me."

Terrance noticed a jar with a label. He couldn't quite read it because it had faded, but he got the gist. This was a cleansing jar for money from people like him.

He dropped the money in and took the flower. Turning to Sara, he put on a brave face and handed the flowers to her.

"These are sweet, Terrance. Thank you," she said.

The two sat on a bench next to each other in the middle of the market.

He didn't notice that she was hunched over and quiet; he was too busy watching the shopkeeper look around for something.

Sara stared into the flowers, but didn't focus on them; her mind was very much somewhere else.

"There's something I need to tell you," she said.

"What is it?" he asked.

"It's about Jeff." She had to tell him now, or it would kill her.

Terrance stiffened. He didn't want to hear about that zombie-pirate, especially when it was so difficult to forgive Sara.

"It's ok. I think it's time to leave that behind us," Terrance stroked her hair and smiled at her.

She was still lost in her flower, counting the pollen as it fell on the leaves.

"No," she said. "I have to tell you."

He took his hand off her head and gave her all of his attention.

What if she was going to tell him exactly what they did in that bed? What if she thought she had to confess every detail? He didn't want to know.

"Well," she was taking too long to say anything. "When you found us, in bed, well, we hadn't done anything."

Terrance watched the shopkeeper walking over to a town guard. This wasn't the first time she'd told him this. He still wasn't sure he believed it, but at least she didn't tell him something that made it worse.

"I know, Sara. You've told me that already."

"That's not it." She had to force the words out like bad medicine. "I paid him to be there." She couldn't look him in the eyes.

He jumped off the bench and smacked the flowers out of her hands, "You what? It wasn't enough to cheat on me, but you paid him to do it?"

People began to stare, and the shopkeeper pointed at Terrance while talking to the guard. Sara noticed that every person in the market was looking at them.

"No. Calm down. Sit. I didn't finish yet." She tried to touch his arm, but he yanked it away.

"You paid some gigolo to cheat on me, Sara!" He was yelling now. "A zombie-pirate-gigolo."

"You don't understand, Terr, I—"

"Don't call me that." He turned and saw the guard and shopkeeper looking at them and talking.

"I paid him to wear his sandals and lay in bed with me." She stood now and tried again to calm him by touching his arm. This time he let her. "We didn't do anything."

Terrance saw the guard and shopkeeper start to walk toward them. Terrance turned back to her, "Am I supposed to believe that, Sara?" He spoke quietly now, but with more poison in his words, "You were both hot and sweaty and half naked. Why would you pay him to just lay in bed with you?"

He deliberately pulled his arm out of her grasp.

"I wanted to make you jealous; I guess it worked too well."

Terrance fumed; he didn't know what to believe.

"Hello, ma'am," the guard stood tall and straight in front of

Terrance, but talked to Sara. "Is this boy causing you trouble?"

She didn't expect this. Trouble? She was the one causing the trouble. She should have just waited to tell him after they left.

"No," Terrance said. "We're fine here."

He looked hard into Terrance's eyes. "Ma'am?"

"No," she said. "He isn't causing any trouble."

Sara watched another guard rush up to the first and whisper in his ear. What could he be saying? The guard obviously understood; he nodded, but he seemed more irritated than before. "You two follow me. You're leaving."

"We were shopping. I'd like to finish," Terrance said. He had no plans or need to buy anything else, especially after this scene, but he couldn't let them get away with this.

The first guard shoved Terrance down, "Please give me a reason to do more," the guard smiled.

"Don't do that! We'll go," Sara said and tried to help Terrance up, but he pulled away and stood on his own. She put herself between him and the guards, "We're going."

The two followed the guards to their jeep. Two more guards were there making sure Paxton and Jeff remained in the vehicle and were prepared to leave.

Terrance climbed in the back seat with Jeff, letting Sara go up front, and the group was escorted out of town.

"Dude, are you ok?" Jeff asked Terrance.

"Yeah," he said.

"What happened?" Paxton asked.

"That southern fried racist pushed me down. The big one," he said, pointing out the window.

"Why would he do that?"

Terrance held up his arm and pulled his sleeve down, pointing at his skin, "Because of this." He boiled beneath the surface. Any provocation would set him off.

"I just thought they were anti-social," Paxton said.

"Anti-social, Paxton? They were racists! Probably have slaves here somewhere," he said. "When we're done finding your father, I'm going to come down here and teach these Brummies a lesson."

"Brummies?" Paxton asked.

"Brummies. People from Birmingham, Paxton. Do they not have names for people from a certain city or racists back in Los Angeles?" Terrance said this with all the venom he could muster.

Paxton bit his tongue as they left Birmingham and continued east.

"Oh, Paxton, get this: Sara paid Jeff to sleep with her," Terrance said.

"I know," he said.

"You know?"

"I told him on the boat," Jeff said.

The tension in the jeep was suffocating Sara. She wanted to jump out the window right that moment.

Terrance's stomach dropped out of his body and ran away. He was empty and confused. Paxton was his best friend, but he knew. How could that be?

"I thought you were my best friend. How could you keep that from me?"

"I am, and I didn't keep it from you—"

"You didn't tell me, Paxton!"

"No, I didn't; I gave Sara a choice. She had to tell you or I would. If I didn't think it was better for you to hear it from her, I would have told you myself."

Terrance turned on Sara, "So you only told me because he made you?"

"No, Terrance. You have to believe me. I wanted to tell you. I realize it was stupid and immature. I just wanted you to pay attention to me; I never thought that you would give us up."

"Well you were wrong about that, huh?"

A heavy silence filled the jeep for most of the day.

The group stopped for a break and Paxton pulled Jeff aside, "Jeff, I have something I need you to do for me."

"Dude, let me have it. I'm sure it won't be a problem," Jeff said.

"I want you to track down those Revenant and make them an offer," he lowered his voice more, "Tell them I'm willing to give them my father, but my mom and granny have to be seeded like you and they have to leave the four of us alone."

"Are you sure? That doesn't sound too safe to me."

"Yes. When we stop tonight, I want you to go find them. Will you do it?"

"I guess so, man."

18. The Rain

The group found a cave and settled in, but Terrance needed some space and found a private corner. A cool rock would have served well as a seat if the Bible in his back pocket weren't irritating him. He pulled it out and remembered his aunt's letter.

He opened the Bible to Psalms, pulled out the letter, and carefully unfolded it. He began reading from the top. It was addressed to his father with a mention that his Aunt had received the other returned letters, but needed to send this last one.

After that, the tone changed. The next paragraph began, "When Dad became the Controller, everything changed for both of us."

Wait, what?

He read it again, "Dad became the Controller... "

His grandfather couldn't be the General.

One more time, "Dad became the Controller... "

I can't be the Controller's grandson. This can't be true.

But he knew it was; that was what he felt when he spoke to Jeff in Haiti and the reason Agwe recognized him so easily. It was all coming together now.

Terrance continued reading, "I stayed and changed my name; you ran and took your family to Miami. We're not that different, Terr. We both tried to escape his reach, but we can't; he'll find us both and it's time to tell your son about him."

That was why they didn't want him to see his aunt. She wanted to tell him; wanted him to know why the Revenant would be after him and who he really was.

"I've felt your son's power from here, and I know he'll grow to be a speaker more powerful than Dad, but, Brother, I've also seen that he will grow up without you."

She knew.

"You have to tell him now, or he may not be prepared for everything he'll face: betrayal, pain, lost love, and being a speaker. Most of all, he may not be ready to replace—"

Replace what? What could she mean?

The letter ended. Terrance flipped the letter over. Nothing. He looked in the envelope for a second page, shoving his hand inside. Nothing. He flipped through the Bible. Nothing. He scrambled around for a dropped paper. Nothing.

Sara walked up, leaving Terrance no more time to search for a paper that wasn't there. He shoved the note back into the pocket Bible and stood up quickly, hitting his head on the cave wall.

"Effin Ai."

Sara bit her bottom lip to hold back a laugh.

"What are you doing here?" he said.

"We're almost done setting up for the night. Jeff will be back soon," Sara said.

"Where did he go?"

"I guess Paxton wanted us to talk."

"Great! More time with not one Judas, but two."

"Judas?"

Terrance lifted the Bible, "Yeah, he's in here. Why don't you read about him?"

"Maybe if I had one, I would," Sara started to storm out toward the main cave area.

Before she made it out, Paxton came in and placed his hands on her shoulders, turning her around and walking her back toward Terrance.

"Well, we won't last long like this. Your petty bickering could kill us."

"Look, she paid for some zombie-pirate-gigolo to come 'play house' and you knew about it. It's not 'petty bickering' and there's nothing more to talk about." Terrance put the Bible in his back pocket and pushed past Paxton on his way out.

"They didn't do anything, though," Paxton said.

Terrance stopped and turned back on him. He knew Paxton was goading him so he would stay and talk, but right now he was angry enough to give in to it, "And just how do you know that?"

"Jeff told me," he said.

"Oh, so now we trust this 'dude' to tell the truth? What next? Do we trust the Revenant to be our Benevolent Overlords?" Terrance put his hands together and bowed.

"It's not like that, Terr," Sara said.

Paxton interrupted her with a hand on her shoulder, "Sara, I think you need to let me t—"

"Paxton Eugene Roald! Don't you dare," she turned on Terrance. "I made a stupid mistake and never should have used Jeff to make you jealous. I've apologized a million times. I've suffered through your jabs and prods; heck, I thought I deserved them."

"You did," Terrance said.

"Be quiet and listen, you big idiot. I can't get a word in without you inserting some little comment like that. What's your problem?"

"I'm too honest."

"That was rhetorical. You were ready to forgive me in Birmingham. I didn't have to tell you that I paid Jeff; blast it. I could have denied it if Paxton said it. I mean, would you believe me or Jeff? Don't answer that.

"Look, I didn't do anything with him and I just—" she stared at Terrance.

Nothing was getting through. He crossed his arms, stared over her head, and remained expressionless. He was a barrier of anger.

She ran out of the cave.

"Good job. I'm going after her," Paxton said.

"No, don't. She needs time to cool down," Terrance said.

Paxton hesitated, then trusted that even if he was mad, he wasn't lying, "Jeff told me that he wanted Sara, you know? He offered to pay her for the privilege, but she wouldn't let him touch her. She paid him to keep his hands *off* her."

"They were all hot and sweaty when I got there, Paxton,"

Terrance finally relaxed some. "I know they weren't just lying in bed."

"It was Miami. The heat... and they were in that bed, under the covers, for more than half an hour." Paxton dismissed the concerns with a wave. "It was stupid of her, but she didn't cheat on you, Terrance. You can't go on hating her."

"I can't help it."

"You were prepared to forgive her earlier today. Then she confesses this to you and now you can't? What's wrong with you?"

"Every time I look at her, I see that... thing. He's not even human, if he was before." Terrance sat on a rock and rubbed his neck. "And now I see her paying him for... but I guess that's not really it. I just... " he pulled out the letter.

"The letter from your aunt? What was in it?"

He put it back in the Bible, "Just some bad news."

"We'll talk about that later. She's trying to be honest with you; think about that. Stay here and calm down, man. I'm going to go find her. I know she needs her space, but those Revenant could be out there."

Jeff was looking for the other Revenant. He needed to find them and give them Paxton's message before he grew so hungry that he would do something that he'd regret.

He thought back to the forest and that buck. Maybe he should eat something now, before smelling a human.

He smelled something; was it them? Could he have found them already? The smell grew stronger with each passing hour. Were they that close? What if they took advantage of him being alone?

No, that wasn't it; this smell was the best smell he ever smelled and his worst fear. He began salivating and could taste it on his tongue.

Jeff punched a hole in a tree trunk, "Damn! I ate a deer before I left them. I knew I shouldn't stay away this long."

A camp between him and the cave came to mind. *No! I can't think about that.*

It was a small camp with just a handful of people, and he

could easily pick up a quick, tasty snack. They were all outside and soon someone would step away far enough. *Stop it. I can't do that.*

Nobody would have to know, and he could finally have a satisfying meal, but he would regret it. It was his nature anyway; why should he deny it? *I need something now!*

Deer and rodents tasted like cardboard; they couldn't satisfy the same way human meat would. His stomach felt emptier than ever. *But if I eat an animal, the people in that camp will live. I need Terrance here.*

He'd never eaten a human before, but somehow he couldn't get the taste out of his mouth. Instinctively he knew how much he would enjoy this meal.

Jeff walked into the camp.

Sara ran out of the cave, crying. The rain came down in sheets and she slipped, tearing a hole in her jeans. She scrambled to her feet without a thought of the mud caking her jeans and shoes.

Her mind was filled with the thought that she was still too close to the cave, too close to Terrance. The forest was her only refuge. Thorn bushes yanked at her skin and clothes while branches whipped her face and caught in her hair, but her mind was still in the cave.

What was behind that stone face? He hid so much from everyone. Everyone except her, but now he pushed her out too. Why would he do that when she was being honest with him? Something else was going on; she knew him too well to miss that, but what was he hiding?

Her foot caught beneath a leaf-covered rock, turning her foot too far toward the outside of her body. The pain ripped through her mind, taking Terrance out of it completely. She screamed before she hit the ground, hard.

Consciousness trickled into Jeff's mind. He lay on his back, under some trees. Was it a bad dream? He remembered feasting on humans, with two other Revenant. J'Nou and his ever-present-nightmare-child, Mara, joining him in a macabre supper for three.

He must have fallen asleep from hunger; he would never do such a thing, especially with those monsters, but he never slept and he felt comfortably full.

"I see that you have finally accepted your true nature, Jeff. That is a good thing," J'Nou said.

Jeff shot up and looked around. The campsite was a bloody disaster. Tents were ripped open like bags of granola; sleeping bags were peeled back like banana skins.

There was no nightmare, only reality.

"We cannot undo your seeding, Jeff, but if you wish to join us, that may be arranged."

"I don't want to join you monsters," Jeff said.

"We're the monsters?" Mara held up a bloody sleeping bag and threw it on him. "Then I think you'd fit right in," she laughed like she was teasing a nerd at school.

He fought to pull the bag off his head and muttered, "I couldn't... I didn't... " He still wasn't able to process the situation. How did this happen?

"You looked for us and now we are here," J'Nou spread his arms as he smiled. "We even shared a meal, so now we are friends. What did you want, Jeff, if not to join us?"

"Paxton... " He had to focus on why he was here, but he couldn't shake away the images from last night.

J'Nou stopped smiling and walked straight for Jeff, "What about Mr. Roald?"

"He wanted to make an offer." Why though? If he could do this, how much worse could they be? They had no remorse, no conscience.

"He wanted a deal with the Controller? Interesting. Please continue."

Jeff tried to continue, but couldn't make himself. If Paxton made this deal, he would condemn all of mankind to become prey, or worse, cattle on a farm.

"Ahh!" Sara screamed as she fell a couple miles away. The Revenant heard her and turned to look.

"Don't worry, Jeff, Cynthia and Gail are close; they'll help her,"

Mara said. "What was the deal?"

Jeff shook himself out of his daze, "What do you mean *help her*?" He took off toward the sound.

J'Nou and Mara were fast after him and quickly caught him. J'Nou picked him up and stuck him on a branch like a waiter sticks tickets on a spindle.

"You may hang around here if you wish. We will go in person to see what this deal was."

A small doe nibbled grass near a bear cub. His mama was scratching her back on a pine tree, knocking needles onto the cub and doe. The rain barely reached the ground here, but even if it did, the animals would hardly care.

Mama bear pricked up her ear and stopped scratching. The doe and cub looked at her. They heard what she knew was coming a moment later, a human scream. Normally this would send the three running the other direction, but there was something else, a subtle undertone.

She was hurting.

Whoever screamed this needed help, and the animals could help. Mama bear took off through the forest with her cub and the doe close behind. She pushed through brush and jumped over gorges. The cub and doe struggled to keep up, but they pushed their young bodies onward.

The three animals found her, a red-faced, red-haired girl, sobbing gently. The girl looked up and said thank you, hugging mama bear; she didn't hug back, afraid she would hurt the human girl.

"How did you know to come here?" she asked them.

"We heard your yell and knew you needed help," mama bear answered.

Sara, the girl, pulled herself up, "I did. I'm so scared and feel so—"

A large rock flew toward Sara. It seemed like slow motion, but she couldn't stop as she finished the word 'alone.' She managed to step back, but she watched as the rock cracked mama bear's head open. As the beast fell, much of her weight landed on Sara's hurt ankle.

She screamed in pain again.

Before the rock hit the ground, Cynthia leapt onto the doe and ripped it apart. The animal never saw the Revenant. Right behind her, Gail flew out of the trees and grabbed the cub. It wasn't as easy as the doe, but she took care of him and threw his carcass into the trees.

"You're welcome, hussy," Gail said.

"Welcome?" Sara cried out in pain, both emotional and physical.

"Yeah, that bear would have torn you apart."

"She was comforting me; she wouldn't hurt me."

"How'd you know that?" Gail said.

"I think she may be like Captain Oliver," Cynthia said.

"We could always use a sister like you, but you could be even more useful if you brought Paxton and Terrance to us. We'll even leave you alone," Gail said, "Though you don't deserve it."

Sara was in pain. She understood what Paxton's mother and grandmother were saying, but didn't have the strength to fight back, or even give in. She saw something moving behind them and managed to push some words through her tears, but it wasn't understood by either Revenant.

Cynthia leaned in, "What was that, honey?"

Sara said it again, "Men. Ten. Lie. On."

Gail shook her head, "Must not be too important."

A mountain lion pounced on Gail, pinning her to the ground and sliding her, face first, through several feet of mud, leaves, and grass. He roared ferociously and clawed at the back of her head. She had suffered several gashes before she managed to push up hard, throwing the large cat off her back and against a tree.

The cat caught the tree trunk and turned around; it pushed off and back toward Gail, but this time she was ready. She caught the cat's head and slammed it into the soft ground.

It didn't get up.

"Enough of that, you little tramp," Gail said to Sara.

"If you won't help us, it's time to join us," Cynthia said. She held Sara up like a living rag doll. "Terrance may be upset, but he deserves so much better than you. However, you'd be no help dead, so—"

Paxton showed up. "Wait, Mom, don't." He was breathing only slightly heavier than normal but was soaked from head to toe. "I want to make a deal with the Controller."

Cynthia pulled Sara close with her right arm and grabbed her throat with her left hand, "Don't move, son."

"Tell us where your father is and we won't kill her. How's that for a deal, Paxy?" Gail stepped between Paxton and Sara.

Paxton was confused. He wanted to make the deal, but now he wasn't so sure. Would they keep it? They were about to kill Sara to find his dad; what would they do if he handed him over?

But he knew this was the Controller's influence; it had to be. His mom and granny wouldn't act like this if that Master of the Revenant didn't make them. There was only one thing left to do. He pulled his gun out slowly. Both Revenant tensed and Cynthia tightened her grip on Sara.

He lifted the gun with two fingers, keeping it pointed down. Then he flipped it and pressed it under his chin, "Let her go, or I kill myself now and you never know where he is."

Terrance was soaking wet. He should have followed Paxton, but he had to cool down before he could think clearly. He was upset about his grandfather and what he could become. What he *would* become.

He was scared.

Why did he take so long to leave the cave? If he found her, he would forgive her in a moment. He knew how much she needed him and should have been more attentive. She needed that. After losing everyone, she had only him.

Sure, she was a little crazy, but he needed her. He had to believe her and he would, but first he had to find her. He slipped on some mud and jumped up, starting to run even faster.

Then he stopped.

He couldn't move anymore because it was back: the hand on his shoulder. He looked down and saw it there. Was this a dream? Was he really out there, or was he asleep in the cave? He had to wake up.

He turned and saw a Middle-Eastern man in his thirties with a beard, "Who are you? Why did you stop me?"

"You need to know something; then you can find Sara," the man said.

"What? She could be in danger. Please tell me."

"You will become what you fear, but I will be there."

Terrance stopped breathing and stared at the man.

"Do not fear," the man said. He put his hand back on Terrance's shoulder and spun him around. "I am with you."

Terrance was running as if he'd never stopped, and he could hear Sara. He would dwell on what happened later, but for now he had to get to her.

He heard Paxton now, offering a deal; he couldn't let him do that. Their lives weren't worth what the Controller would do with Dr. Roald's help.

The mud caked on his shoes, but he trudged through it. His legs were heavy and tired when he heard Paxton, much closer this time, telling them he would kill himself.

That was all the motivation he needed. Terrance was on the scene in seconds. He quickly took it in and saw Gail ready to pounce on Paxton. Cynthia was holding Sara.

"Let her go, and both of you sit down. Now," Terrance's voice was dark and powerful, but in that moment, he felt his grandfather.

The Controller pulled him into that dark, powerful force, and he lost control. He saw the Farms, children, women, and men all separated. He saw them going about their lives in a palpable melancholy. Then came flashes of other places, Nazis, Pirates, and more. They weren't just images; he heard the crying baby in the Farm; he even felt the thoughts of a Revenant undercover in Nazi Europe.

He was losing himself, drowning in the sea of images, audio, and thoughts. He had to break free. His head hurt and his eyes blurred; then, just as suddenly it ended, and he saw Gail and Cynthia lift their legs and sit in midair.

Sara ran to him and he grabbed her, but he was scared to use his voice again.

Paxton took the gun from under his chin and pointed it at Gail, "Now, as I was saying, I have a proposal."

"Yes, Mr. Roald, I am curious what this offer is," J'Nou walked out of the forest, followed closely by Mara.

"It seems you are no longer in a position to dictate terms to us, so I will let you know what you must do now. You will first put the gun down; then you will tell us where your father is. The Controller has graciously decided that you will still be allowed to leave. This is a generous offer, Mr. Roald; I do recommend you take it."

Paxton was about to talk, but Terrance'd had enough. He would put up with his grandfather one more time for this. J'Nou was dangerous, but Terrance knew that Paxton's offer was more dangerous.

Terrance's voice rustled the trees and vibrated the ground, "J'Nou, go—"

J'Nou pulled something out of his pocket and threw it at Terrance, "As I was saying."

Terrance fell to the ground, clutching his face as blood poured between his fingers. Sara helped Terrance, cradling his head and asking him how bad it was, but he didn't respond.

"What did you do to him, zombie?" Paxton could feel his senses heightening, and he heard something coming toward them in the forest.

"He will live. I have only protected myself from his influence." J'Nou stood at ease.

It must be Jeff, Paxton thought; *the damn zombies can't hear him over the rain.*

"Ok, J'Nou, I could tell you where he is, but wouldn't you prefer something better?" Paxton asked.

J'Nou stood there, clearly waiting for Paxton to get to the point.

Just need to keep him distracted a little longer. "I know you'd rather have him than just know where he is, right?"

J'Nou was not playing along.

"Right, so if you would rather have him, I am willing to make you a deal. You seed my—"

Jeff jumped out of the woods toward J'Nou, but Jeff still had a hole in his midsection, and J'Nou was too well trained to be taken completely off guard.

J'Nou shifted his weight to one leg; then, as Jeff nearly hit him, he used the momentum and grabbed Jeff, one hand on his shoulder, the other in the hole in his middle, to throw him through a tree twenty meters away. "I grow impatient, Paxton."

Cynthia and Gail finally stood to join in; only moments passed since Terrance controlled them. The four Revenant lined up, ready for battle.

Across from them, Jeff picked himself up slowly; Sara held Terrance's head, and Paxton stood with a gun pointed at J'Nou.

"Do not hurt—" Cynthia began to say something, but the Controller stopped her.

"Mr. Paxton Roald, I wished to make this easy on you, but you insist on muddying the waters. You will now submit to us one way or another. Will you tell us, or must I make you one of us? You are clearly outmatched here," J'Nou gestured toward his fellow Revenant.

Paxton didn't know what to do. He would trade his father for his friends and family, but to turn him in with no guarantees right now, he couldn't do that. It was a gamble, and he wasn't a gambler.

Jeff ran toward J'Nou again, but this time, Paxton saw something nobody else did.

The tree next to J'Nou was tall and large, but dead and petrified. It was an oddity in this living forest. His mind felt all the possibilities; he saw the strengths and weaknesses; and he knew that he could use the tree to his advantage. It wouldn't win this battle, but with one step, the seer would engineer their escape.

Paxton stepped once to the left before Jeff passed by, forcing Jeff to sidestep and come at J'Nou from an altered angle.

The new angle meant that when J'Nou threw Jeff, he hit the tree hard. It was enough to crack it and it crashed on top of the Revenant, not killing them, but they were pinned. It would take only moments to get out from under it, but that could be enough to escape.

"Jeff, carry Terrance," Paxton said, "Sara, come on. You can help him in the jeep. We have to go."

I have to get my father first. That's the only way to have leverage.

The group made it to the jeep quickly, despite Sara's ankle and the mud. It wasn't easy for Jeff, either; he was hungry and Terrance smelled good.

He wouldn't do this again, so he laid Terrance in the jeep and ran ahead to find an animal. "Go on, dude. I'll catch up."

"Good luck, Jeff," Paxton climbed in. Terrance was in the back of the jeep with his head in Sara's lap. "How is he?"

"I'm bandaging him up now," Sara put herbs the Luminati gave them on Terrance's face. "It's really bad, Paxton. Whatever he threw at him cut through his cheek completely and all the way back."

She kissed him on the forehead and he looked at her. She never saw fear on his face like she did now, "You'll be ok; don't worry. We're going to get you to Atlanta; it's close."

Paxton ran over a large fallen branch and the jeep bounced.

"If Paxton doesn't kill us first."

"So, this serum would actually cure all of the Revenant?" Bruce asked.

"Yes. It *will*. I just need to test it more, but you're taking me away from my laboratory," Eugene said. "That kind of makes it hard."

"I'm sorry about that. I truly am." Bruce ran his hand through his hair, "I have to do this, though. They have my daughter."

"Who has her?"

"The Mafia."

"The Mafia? What would they want with me?"

"From what I could tell? Nothing. I believe they were hired by someone else. I'm sorry. I wish I could help you, but it's my little girl."

"But couldn't the Hell's Angels just go in there and take them out?"

"We could. And we'd win, but I don't know if my daughter would be alive afterwards or not. And it could start a war that may last decades; the Mafia has more than a few connections and they're very powerful." Bruce sighed. "Besides, I couldn't do that."

"I understand," Eugene said. "I would do anything for my son."

"So you understand?"

"Yes, Bruce, I understand and I can even forgive you, but I would also give up anything to protect him, and the greatest threat to him and all of humanity is the Revenant. You're keeping me from getting rid of all of them."

The two sat quietly for a long time.

"So. You want to tell me *where* you're taking me?"

19. Georgia Nightmare

Jeff caught up to the NJ-1300 and climbed into the shotgun seat. Paxton had only slowed a moment when they saw Jeff running toward them.

"They're following close, Paxton; we can't lose them. What now?" Jeff asked.

Sara ran her hands along Terrance's hair and tried to calm him. His head was still on her lap and his eyes were closed. He shivered constantly.

"We head to DC," Paxton said.

"DC? What's there?" Jeff asked.

Paxton glared at Jeff before driving onto the road.

"Idiot, it's heavily militarized. There's no way they'd be stupid enough to come anywhere near that fortress," Sara said. "I thought someone raised on a pirate ship would know more about the most secure port in America."

Paxton smiled. He knew Terrance would have loved to hear her say that to Jeff.

"Exactly, Sara. We can hide out there for a few days. Maybe even get some more help," Paxton said. "I may be able to use a few of my dad's connections."

"To give your dad to the Revenant," Jeff said. "Who's going to do that?"

"I'll worry about that; you just try not to eat anyone, ok?" Paxton said.

Jeff shut his mouth and turned to look out the window. They didn't know, but what Paxton said brought painful and fresh memories to mind.

"First we need to stop in Atlanta," Sara looked down at Terrance. "He can rest there, and we can redress his wound. This cut is all the way through, Paxton; I can see his skull. We'll head to DC when Terrance can make it, but first we need to find a doctor to stitch him up."

Captain Oliver woke Alfred in the middle of the night, "It's time, Alfred."

"Huh? This early?"

"Yes. Now," Captain Oliver smiled.

Alfred groaned. His arm still hurt, but he would push through the pain. The bowl, doll, and Death Metal were all prepared, so Alfred shuffled to them. He lifted the doll and began chanting. Carefully he touched the doll's head to the Death Metal and with his other hand, he poured a strange liquid on the doll.

Alfred saw a dirt road ahead of him and felt a steering wheel in his hands. He saw a small house on the right side of the road and turned the wheel toward it.

Paxton saw the wall looming 1000 meters high. It stood in the desert, surrounded by Farms as far as he could see. The gate was open, though, and many Revenant stood in the way prepared to stop the jeep from entering.

Paxton sped up, pressed a button on the console, and spikes came out of the hood. They were each one meter long and very sharp.

The spikes bore into the Revenant, stacking them on top of each other. Paxton could see the entrance to EA 51 ahead of him and pushed the NJ-1300 as fast as it would go.

"Paxton, what are you doing?" Jeff asked.

"Stop, Paxton! Jeff, grab the wheel and hit the brakes!" Sara yelled.

The jeep flew through the air as it left the dirt road in a remote part of Georgia, knocking down more trees. The NJ-1300 went through the porch of a small cabin and took out some chairs, poles, and most of the front side of the abandoned house before Jeff could stop it.

"Paxton, what's happening?"

He pulled out his pistols and aimed them at Sara and Jeff, "How did you get in here, J'Nou?"

"Paxton, what are you doing? Wake up!" Sara yelled.

Paxton saw J'Nou reaching for him.

Jeff lunged for the pistols as Paxton squeezed the triggers.

Suddenly, everyone froze. Paxton blinked and Jeff held as still as a statue. Sara looked beside her.

Terrance was sitting up looking at Paxton with his mouth wrapped shut. None of them heard anything, but they all felt Terrance's will upon them. He'd done it without speaking and they couldn't fight it.

Terrance laid down, and passed out.

"It happened again," Paxton said.

"Yes, but he saved you again," Jeff said.

"Now, let's get him some help," Sara said.

The four Revenant looked on as the group backed the Jeep out and left the house.

"We should have finished them in the forest," Mara said.

"No. It is good that the Controller keeps a tight hold on you. You have much to learn," J'Nou said. "Captain Oliver had a problem and this did not go as planned. We must separate them ourselves."

"Why didn't we attack Paxton, though?"

"He's my son. I don't want to hurt him," Cynthia said.

"It doesn't matter; Terrance still has control. He could turn us away or stop us long enough to let the zombie or Paxton kill us," J'Nou narrowed his eyes. "We have to separate them, without killing Terrance."

"Why can't we eat him?" Mara said.

"The Controller has other plans for him, my dear," J'Nou said. "We only need them to think we want to hurt them, and they will rush to Dr. Roald. Then we will walk up and take what we want.

"Cynthia, Gail, you two are required in Charlotte. You will rejoin us with Captain Oliver later."

Atlanta was still two days away on this road. In the mean-time, Sara made Paxton stop every couple of hours. At each stop, Sara had squirrels, raccoons, and other furry creatures bring her herbs or large leaves to redress Terrance's wound after they ran out of bandages. Jeff asked her to bring some animals for him to feed on, but she refused, so he went out to hunt his own.

She still couldn't control her ability, but the animals seemed to know what she needed and where she was. She kept Terrance's face clean and dressed, but signs of an infection began to appear. The leaves were not as sanitary as the bandages, and the herbs were more effective as pain relievers than antibiotics.

Sara was very concerned.

"Terrance, this is going to burn." She poured the last of a bottle of alcohol on his cut and winced along with him. She hated to hurt him, but she knew it would help.

"I'm sorry, Terr. We'll get you some help soon."

They arrived at the gates of Atlanta three nights after they left the cave. This large town would be their best chance at finding a doctor soon. The wall, the first one built during the Revenant War, rose nearly five hundred meters.

It once protected a bustling city until some Rangers captured several living Revenant and brought them to the researchers in the CDC for study. The researchers were not prepared, though, and became the first victims of a Revenant-induced zombie outbreak. How the Revenant created zombies instead of other Revenant was still not known to most.

Not being a city on the coast, the outbreak caused an immediate exodus, and the bustling city became a small town overnight. Most left for Charlotte or Jacksonville, but the *Pride of Dixie* stayed, and now the wall served to protect the headquarters of the Dixie Mafia.

Another prominent feature of Atlanta was the field of crosses by the gate. They weren't for decoration; the Dixie Mafia liked to make examples of the African missionaries who visited America. White or black, they were hung up there and left for days to suffer. A lucky few were chosen for sacrifices and quick deaths.

"Business?" a guard asked as they drove up to the gate. He eyed the NJ-1300 suspiciously. It was grimy enough to not look new, but any vehicle in America that wasn't military or breaking down brought plenty of attention.

Paxton noticed the shield on the man's jacket. It was white with a red border, and on the shield was a red X.

"My friend. He has a nasty cut. We just need medical services and we'll be on our way. We can pay."

"Good." He reached out his hand.

Paxton handed him a box of .35 ammo. The guard hefted the box and looked at Paxton who put another box in his hand. The guard smiled; then he looked in the back again.

"That your friend?"

"Yeah."

The guard stopped smiling and gestured for more. Paxton gave him two more.

"That'll do," the guard leaned in close. "Check out the Underground for a room, and I would ask for Dr. Carlson. He's the only one who might help that," the guard looked back at Terrance.

"What's that supposed t—" Sara said.

"Never mind, Sara," Paxton said. "Thanks."

The guard picked up his radio and squinted at the jeep as it passed through the gate.

They arrived at the Underground. It was a hotel and shopping center built under old railways, but now that no trains passed through, the top was a fresh marketplace. They were able to help Terrance to their room without much attention. It helped that Jeff could carry Terrance with one hand, and they covered him with blankets to hide his wounds and skin.

"This is what I meant before," Jeff said.

"Are these the ones you delivered for?" Paxton asked.

"Yeah. I recognized the patch on that guard. They're the Dixie Mafia."

"What did you say, boy?" a large man asked. He had a scruffy red beard, and he wore a tight, white shirt and jeans.

"I said, *Dixie Mafia.*"

The man dropped his cigarette and stepped on it. He walked right up to Jeff and staring him in the eyes, he whispered directly in his face, "I wouldn't say that name too loud. You get overheard talking about them and you'll draw unwanted attention. They're a little sensitive about how people perceive them, if you know what I mean."

"Nope, bro', I don't," Jeff said.

"Their supply problem," the man opened his eyes wide and nodded his head as if this should be obvious.

Paxton stepped in and directed Jeff to back up, "I'm sorry. We're not from around here."

The man grunted and nodded, "They used to get supplies from a port southeast of here, but the pirates that delivered just stopped one day. It hit 'em hard, and they weren't able to take care of their territory. More than a few towns kicked them out, but they're still welcomed here. By all of us. Just be careful, and hide him." His eyes darted to Terrance, "Or he may be their latest example."

Then he walked away.

"Hm. I like to think I had something to do with that," Jeff said.

"Great, but now we're in *their* territory," Sara said dryly.

"Yeah," Jeff said.

"Did you see those men outside the gate?" Sara asked. "They were hanging on crosses, still alive."

"They dislike other religions around here, almost as much as they hate dark skin. We better keep Terrance and his Bible hidden, man. Paxton, we're going to have to bring that Dr. Carlson to us."

"I agree. I'll go first thing in the morning," Paxton said. "The sooner we leave Atlanta, the better."

"We're here," Bruce said.

"Chicago?" Eugene asked.

"Yep. And now I can get my daughter back," Bruce stopped the car just outside the town. "Is there anyone I can tell that you're here? Someone who would maybe be able to help you or something?"

"I don't think so. But if you run across my wife or son, let them know I'm ok. Don't tell them to come after me, or where I am, though. I don't want to put them in more danger."

"Ok," Bruce thought for a moment. "Look, I'm really sorry about this. If there's any way—"

"It's your daughter, Bruce. I understand," Eugene was upset

and didn't think he would see his lab again. He couldn't let that research go to waste, though. Maybe his son could complete it, but he'd have to know one more thing. "Do something else for me, Bruce. If you find Paxton, let him know that our last drink together was important to me."

Bruce nodded and continued into town; his Director status let him pass the guard's gate without hassle. The Mafia may run this town, but the Hell's Angels controlled a good piece of it too.

He pulled up to the back of a restaurant, Luigi's Pizza, and climbed out of the jeep. He walked around, took Eugene out of the passenger side, and led him in the back door. Quietly he pulled out a revolver and aimed it at Eugene's head.

"What are you doing?" Eugene yelled. He began to struggle and tried to pull away.

"Good. I want to get my daughter back; they have to believe I'm willing to kill you if I don't get what I want. They need you alive," Bruce said.

"Hey! Don't harm the moichandise!" a surly voice yelled. A short gentleman in a suit, came through the back door. "We wants him unharmed, or your daughter gets it."

A large, olive-skinned man, also dressed in a suit, followed him out the door with a little girl held at gunpoint. She was six years old with blond, curly hair down to her shoulders. Her jeans and Mickey Mouse T-shirt were both from the '60s. She was very frightened, but not of the large man, Pasquale, who held a gun to her head.

She stared at the short man and clung to Pasquale's leg in fear, until she saw her Daddy. When she saw him, she squealed with delight and tried to run to him. Pasquale held her back and whispered in her ear. After that, she calmed down and smiled at Bruce.

Bruce raised the gun slightly away from Eugene. Pasquale did the same, lifting his gun slightly away from Bruce's daughter.

"Let her walk over here; when she gets halfway, I'll let Eugene go," Bruce said.

"That's reasonable enough, and I'm nothing if not a reasonable man. Pasquale, let her go," the shorter man said.

Pasquale let the little girl go, and she began walking toward Bruce. She'd obviously been well taken care of. Her clothes and hair were clean and well groomed.

Bruce let Eugene go. He stared straight ahead as he passed Bruce's daughter.

"Come here, baby!" Bruce called out.

She ran to him, and jumped into his arms, hugging him.

Eugene blinked away a tear and kept walking.

Their room had two beds. Paxton volunteered to sleep on the chair and gave Terrance one bed and Sara the other.

When morning came, Sara went to the market to grab soft, fresh fruit for Terrance. Jeff waited to feed again until she came back.

Paxton was out asking questions about Dr. Carlson, and it wasn't long before a man came up to them. He was wearing a jacket like the guard at the gate. Paxton noticed the Dixie Mafia shield patch, but this one had a dragon clinging to the X. The man was pale with light brown hair and green eyes. He carried his large build and tight clothes slowly, but with confidence. The tattoo on the left side of his neck had a red circle with a red K in it.

"Name's Buford Whitmore. What's yours?" the man stepped directly in front of Paxton.

"Paxton."

"Well, Paxton, what brings you to these parts?"

Paxton noticed the slight bulge on the right side of Buford's jacket and the way he walked. It was an obvious sign that the man carried a weapon, and by Paxton's estimation it was a 9mm.

"Just passing through."

"Where are you headed?"

Paxton noticed a few more men, most with similar tattoos and patches, but none with a dragon. They surrounded him and Buford, trying to stay casual.

"Just heading east."

"Hmm, cause I heard you've been asking around for a doctor. My buddy here is a doctor. I'm sure he could help whatever ails you." He pointed to one of the other men in a white jacket.

The man in the white jacket walked up to Paxton and reached out his hand, "Dr. Buchannan." His shield was like Buford's but instead of a dragon, it had a red cross on top of a black K. "I used to work at the CDC, so I'm pretty good."

"That's ok. Thank you, but I'm looking for a Dr. Carlson," Paxton shook his hand. Paxton wasn't sure if this would offend the man, so he decided to offer a slight bow with his reply.

"Dr. Carlson is a decent man, but I wouldn't let him treat a one but my servant," Dr. Buchannan spit on the ground to emphasize his point.

"It's more of a personal reason. If you know where he is, I'd appreciate it. If not, thank you, anyway."

Dr. Buchannan and Buford stopped smiling and looked at each other.

"His office is about three streets that way on the left. There's a sign out front." Buford pointed down the north street and watched as he walked away.

Paxton noticed that the people who were shopping in that area were all but gone. He began walking up the north street, but before Paxton could reach the corner, Buford jogged up to him.

"One other thing. If you're heading east, do you think you could deliver something for us to Charlotte? We would pay you well for it. Of course, half now, and half upon delivery," Buford slung an arm around Paxton and smiled. "Come on, do it for your brother, eh?"

"Sorry, we're not heading to Charlotte," Paxton shrugged out of Buford's arm. "I'll pass. Thanks for the information, though."

Buford stopped and stared, his eyes on Paxton who continued down the street. Buford was not used to being denied. Especially twice. He motioned for another man in a Dixie Mafia jacket to come over and then whispered to him.

His eyes remained on Paxton as he spoke.

Terrance felt himself rising out of bed and through the ceiling. He touched his cheek and it was split open, but not bleeding or hurting. He tried to speak, but couldn't make a sound as he floated through a cloud.

He blinked and suddenly was on the beach in Miami. Kneeling in the sand, this time from behind his parents, he watched as pirates attacked them in front of him again. He saw himself running out of the water to his parents and heard his other self crying, but he wasn't able to understand or change what was happening.

He didn't want to.

A hand grabbed his shoulder and he looked back; the glowing figure was there. He still couldn't speak, but he felt the touch of the figure and its warmth.

"I was there too, Terrance," a deep voice came from the figure. "I felt your pain and your sorrow."

Terrance wanted to ask who he was, but he already knew and still couldn't speak.

"Yes, I could have stopped it, but it had to happen. I weep for what must happen now, but it will shape the man you must become before your destiny begins. I am with you, Terrance. Rest now. You have a long night coming."

Terrance blinked and saw Jeff standing at the foot of his bed, guarding him again.

Paxton approached the 'Dr. Carlson, MD' sign and went inside. It was a simple office with a small waiting room and two chairs. A pale woman in her thirties, with long, strawberry-blonde hair sat at a desk and waived him into the room.

"What can I help you with, darling?" she said.

"I need to talk to Dr. Carlson."

"Oh, you can sign in, and I'll call you when he's ready for you. What kind of symptoms do you have?"

"Oh no. It's not for me. I have a friend at the Underground who needs help from a doctor. His cheek was ripped open."

Paxton made a motion pointing from the left corner of his mouth up to his left ear.

"Oh! I see," she stood, revealing her dirty, ripped jeans and bare feet. The contrast between her dirty jeans and her starched white button-up shirt was striking. "My name's Rosa. I'll be right back; you have a seat."

After waiting several minutes, Rosa and a tall skinny man,

wearing a long, white coat, walked in. Paxton stood and reached out his hand.

"Dr. Carlson?" he said.

"Yes. Bring me to your patient, please. I have another appointment in an hour."

Dr. Carlson was a freckled man with red hair and a slightly crooked nose. He also had many scars on his face and neck.

"I expect payment in full, up front."

"Will this do?" Paxton pulled out a bottle of pure grain alcohol.

"Yes," the Doctor grabbed the bottle and held it up to the light. "Where did you find this? Wait, let me check it first." He opened the bottle and sniffed. "Can't say for sure this hasn't been diluted, but it's good enough. More than enough; this could help a hundred patients."

"Just heal my friend. Please."

J'Nou and Mara waited outside of Atlanta. The petrified tree had crushed them, leaving them like wild animals. The Controller had to step in, even for J'Nou, until on the way to Atlanta, they came across a family heading the other way, to Birmingham. It was a small family of six, but they were enough for the Revenant to fully recuperate from all the damage and come to their senses.

They stood outside and watched as the Dixie Mafia performed silent and not-so-well-hidden auctions of dark-skinned men, women, and children. It was the second time in as many days that the Controller had to hold J'Nou back. Without it, he would ran in there and tried to kill all of the Dixie Mafia.

To storm the city.

They killed his mother before he became a Revenant, and he would never forgive that.

"They said her eyes were slanted, so *she* must be one that their god messed up," J'Nou told Mara. "They slit her throat right in front of me. I was only eight."

"I'm sorry. I would help you, but there are so many of them."

"Too many. I am thankful for the restraint of the Controller in times like this."

"You're right. I'm beginning to see why you're thankful for

him. Maybe we should wait to the east of the city, out of sight, until we smell Jeff pass by."

"They may have come here for reasons other than his cheek and may not continue east. I do not want to get too far ahead. We cannot be too sure that Eugene is not here. We will stay close. The Controller will strengthen me to not rampage through the town. And he will reward me later when we return."

Dr. Carlson and Nurse Rosa tended to Terrance's face.

"This alcohol will help keep an infection out, but it's gonna hurt every time, and don't use it too often or you'll dry out his cheek. I want you to dab some on his face every two hours or so, Sara, and be sure to give him those sedatives for the next few days," Dr. Carlson said.

"Watch what he eats, too. Give him soft food for now, so he doesn't strain the stitches," Rosa said.

"You can cut them off in about two weeks, no sooner," Dr. Carson said.

"Thank you, Doctor," Sara said.

"Don't thank me yet; the Dixie Mafia's out there. They're more dangerous than this cut. They may sell him or sacrifice him, so keep him out of sight and get him out of this town," Dr. Carlson said.

"We will, Doctor," Jeff said.

"Wait, is that what those people were outside? Sacrifices?" Sara said.

"No. Those are criminals," Dr. Carlson said, "Missionaries. They string up every missionary they find."

Sara looked at Paxton and he nodded. They would have to get rid of Terrance's Bible before someone saw it, or he'd end up out there.

"Thank you, again, Doctor, and here, have this." Paxton offered him a small pistol.

"No thank you, Paxton," Dr. Carlson replied. "I use a shotgun. My aim's terrible."

Paxton held up a finger and ran to look through a sack.

"Here you go," Paxton tossed a box of shotgun shells to the

Doctor. "I hope you never have to use it."

"Thank you," Rosa said.

The Doctor and Rosa left the room quietly. Jeff left to feed again since he was only able to get small animals around the town. Sara refused to let him eat pets, so he was eating very often.

Paxton remained awake as a lookout over Sara and Terrance while they slept and Jeff fed. The night went by slowly, and it grew cloudy as the moon rose and the room darkened. Paxton was comfortable and pulled out the documentation for the NJ-1300 that the Luminati gave them. It seemed to him that this thing could do quite a bit. His eyes were a little heavy as he read.

Four men broke down the door and overpowered Paxton, tying him to the chair he sat in. One of the men tied Sara to her bed before she woke up. Terrance didn't wake up at all; the drugs were in full effect as he was thrown over one man's shoulder and carried out of the room; blood dripped from his cheek onto the man's back.

21. Dragon Sacrifice

Terrance was groggy and asking for Sara when he woke up. Disoriented and drugged, it was difficult to focus on the blurry shapes in front of him. He felt the sting on his stitches, and it blurred his eyes with red. When he finally pushed away the pain, his eyes began to clear, and he saw where he was: in a basement.

But they don't build basements in the Deep South. Then his eyes focused more and he saw that it wasn't a basement, but a barn and he was lying on hay.

"So, it's awake?" a gruff southern voice said. "Ask it what it's called."

"What are you called, boy?" a pale, fat man with white hair asked him, bending into Terrance's face and dripping sweat on him.

The man's sweat burned his cheek where the stitches held it together. He tried to open his mouth to answer, but it was very stiff and difficult. He pushed through, stretching the stitches and pulling at his dry lips.

"T—" he said. "Trence."

"Trence? Odd name," the first man said. "You can call me *Master* Buford."

Jeff was surprised to find Sara and Paxton tied up. He ripped their ropes off and asked them what happened. They filled him in, "We need to find him."

"Yes, but maybe you should stay here," Sara said. "He may be bleeding and—"

181

"I just fed. I'll be fine, Sara. I'm going to find him. Look, I know he hates me, but he's my self-control. He's my Controller, the only one that can keep me from hurting others," Jeff said.

"But, Jeff, if you're injured... "

"Sara, I'm going," Jeff was uncharacteristically serious. "I messed up."

"What do you mean, 'messed up'?" Paxton stepped between Jeff and Sara.

Sara pushed him out of the way, "I can handle this. What do you mean, 'messed up'?"

"When I was looking for J'Nou and Mara, I... " he didn't know how much to tell them. Would they think he was a monster? Would they hate him for it, like he hated himself? The camp-site smelled so good, but could he tell them that? "Look, I need Terrance. If they're trying to take him away, I'm going after them."

Sara nodded at Paxton, "We may need him when we find Terrance."

"Fine, but we all follow my lead. Got it?" Paxton asked.

They agreed and Paxton and Sara grabbed some weapons.

"First we need to find him. Jeff, you and I will look for tracks or some sign and find where they would have taken him. Sara you stick with me," Paxton said.

"Ok," Sara said.

"We'll regroup when we find him," Paxton continued. "Let's hurry."

The three of them headed out into the night, but before they split up, Paxton found the tracks of the man carrying Terrance. The tracks were obvious, deeply imprinted in the mud from the weight of the two men. They followed the tracks to a gate near the southern wall, hidden away from the main roads.

"Halt. Ya'll can't go through at night; come back tomorrow," the large guard said.

"No," Paxton replied.

"If you'd like, I can persuade you to leave," the guard raised his shotgun and smiled.

Jeff grabbed the shotgun and twisted it into a loop before the guard knew what was happening.

"He has a tattoo like the others; let's tie him up and leave him for them," Paxton said.

Jeff took the shotgun and tightened it around the guard's hands. Then he tied his legs together and gagged him using the guard's pants.

On the other side of the gate, Paxton found the trail again. They followed it all the way to a large, circular clearing with a well-kept barn in the middle.

"What is this?" Paxton asked.

"One of their temples," Jeff said. "They worship and sacrifice in those. They have no clue who they're messing with."

He started toward the barn and Paxton stopped him with a hand on his chest.

"Calm down, Jeff. We need to be smart about this. If we're not careful, they could kill Terrance before we can save him, so, we're going to have to get in there without them knowing." Then he proceeded to lay out a plan to ambush the barn.

"Your *friend* shouldn't have turned down my offer. You're going to pay the price," Buford said.

"Yeah, we'll hang 'em good, Buford," a short, wiry guy said. He could hardly stand still.

"Quiet, Lenny. We're sacrificing him to the Great White Dragon," Buford said. He turned back to Terrance, "Your kind doesn't deserve to be healed. You're infected."

He pulled out a butterfly knife and opened it with a flourish. Deftly, he cut one of Terrance's stitches.

"You're one of the Dark Dragon's mistakes."

He snipped another stitch.

"Your kind should be serving my kind."

And another one.

"Your kind should be our pets."

Snip.

"You should never be coddled by our women."

Snip, snip.

"You should be killed for touching that girl."

Snip, snip, snip.

"Tonight."

He cut the rest of Terrance's stitches.

"We're not going to kill you, Dr. Roald," Santori said. He was a tall, tan, dark-haired man with a sharp Roman nose and thick lips. His suit was black with gray stripes and a white shirt and black tie. He stood above Eugene in a walk-in cooler at Luigi's.

Eugene was loosely tied to a wooden chair in the middle of the cooler. He was not being entirely cooperative, but his captors had fed him, so he was talking.

Some.

"If you're not going to kill me, why did you kidnap me?" Eugene asked.

"Haha," Santori spoke the laugh. "Dr. Roald, we are not at liberty to give you this information. We were hired for a job, and they were explicit that you must be safe and alive. However, you will be with us for a while. And bruises heal, Dr. Roald."

Santori let that sink in.

"What do they want with me, though? Can you tell me anything?" Eugene asked.

"Pasquale, if he gets hungry, stuff his face. I think he'll enjoy Mama's meatballs," Santori said as he left the cooler.

Pasquale's suit was a little too small for him, but it held together as he walked over to Eugene.

"Hungry?" he said.

"No, I just ate half a pie. I think I'm ok," Eugene said. "Can you tell me anything about who hired you or why?"

"You don't give up, do you?" He laughed. "I like that."

Pasquale lumbered over to a stack of boxes and leaned up against them. He looked over at Eugene and nodded. When Santori left the cooler, Pasquale took on a more intelligent look. No longer just the muscle, he was in control of himself in every way. His eyes brightened and he smiled to himself.

"I'll tell you what, Doc," Pasquale said, "I'm not supposed to know much about who wanted you or why, but I do know it's a group from Texas, and they're really anxious to have you."

Paxton hid behind a tree. From where he crouched, he saw Sara waiting at the back of the barn, but Jeff stood on the side of the barn opposite of him. Paxton heard the shifting of the lookout on his side of the barn.

The impatience and boredom in his movement was obvious. Paxton listened closely and heard the slowness of the man's heartbeat. He wasn't expecting anything to happen tonight.

Paxton quietly said, "Go."

Only he and Jeff heard it, along with two other Revenant who were within earshot.

"Why don't we get him now?" Mara asked.

"We must keep the Controller's grandson safe. After that, we will try to separate them again, despite the protests of Cynthia and Gail," J'Nou responded. "Perhaps we will have the good fortune to kill some of these cretins in the meantime."

"So why don't we go save him? We could take them all out."

"Paxton and his friends showed up first. We will stay out here and watch. It is better to observe them before we must confront them again. If they need our help, or if an *opportunity* arises, we will take advantage of the situation."

Jeff waited impatiently for the signal. Paxton would take out the guard on his side with a large hunting knife, and Jeff would use his bare hands. They would be inside a moment later, and Sara would follow as soon as she noticed the doors opening.

But he smelled *them* nearby.

The smell was not getting stronger, though, so he put it out of his mind. Just then he heard it. Barely a whisper, but the word was clear in his ears.

"Go."

The guard stood twenty meters away from Paxton. The distance between them offered no cover.

Paxton made it half that distance before the man noticed him coming. He saw the man's head turning in his direction. He heard the guard's heartbeat increase and saw his pupils dilate. He also saw the fear crossing the man's face as the guard noticed a shining blade flying through the air toward him.

The blade was the last thing the guard saw.

Back on Jeff's side, the guard heard something and began to look toward Jeff; then he felt pressure on his neck, and then he felt nothing. He saw his feet and the ground coming closer. Then he saw nothing.

Jeff silently slid inside the door, opening it only enough to fit through. It took him a moment to examine the barn.

To his right, at the back of the barn, one end of a piece of rope was tied to a beam and hung down. The other end was tied around Terrance's neck, forcing him to stand upright on top of two hay bales. Around the hay, wood was stacked and ready to burn within a pentagram. Large and small, hand-carved, wooden statues were stacked along the back wall.

One man, with a pointed white hood on his head, stood in front of Terrance, facing him. The man's back was to Jeff. Two men stood on each side of the hay bales, facing forward. Each wore a white hood that looked as if it would come to a point but instead ended abruptly as if it the tops were cut at the same angle, but different heights. Jeff wondered if this indicated a different role for each of them.

All five men wore white robes with the shield symbol on the front and back. The men beside Terrance had the plain symbol while the man in front had a dragon on his robe.

Jeff heard the man in front speaking, but it stopped abruptly as Paxton threw open the door on the other side of the barn. He dove in and rolled toward Jeff with his pistols firing.

Jeff quickly ran toward the guards on Terrance's left side and dove at them. His arms ripped through the first man and grabbed the shoulders of the man behind him. He pulled the second man through the middle of the first man as his teeth dug into the second man's neck. He then grabbed both heads and twisted them off at the neck, one at a time. Reaching into the skull, he scooped out and ate the brains.

He did this for more than hunger, though it tasted good. If any stray bullet, or knife cut into him, his blood could get into the men's wounds and turn them. They did not want to face Revenant racists.

The thought that he was a vicious, brain-eating monster lingered, but he was too focused on saving Terrance to allow that thought to surface.

Paxton rolled along the ground and mid-roll, while upside-down, he took in the scene, including the two men to his right and Jeff running toward them. Paxton aimed and shot the two men on his left in the chest, but did not fire at the man with the pointed hat.

The man in front was too close, and Paxton didn't want to shoot Terrance. He recognized the man, Buford, as he saw him drop and kick the hay bales out from under Terrance.

Paxton's roll stopped and he righted himself, aiming at the rope Terrance hung by. He missed with his first shot.

Jeff turned after eating the brains and attacked Buford, but he moved quickly and tripped Jeff. This stunned Paxton and Jeff; neither expected him to be so fast.

While Sara waited, she called as many animals as she could. Unfortunately it was only three squirrels.

Jeff probably scared them all away.

She saw the door open and ran to it. Not moving as quickly as Jeff or even Paxton, she arrived after most of the fight was over. Looking inside she saw Paxton kneeling and shooting at the back of the barn. She also saw Buford rushing toward Jeff with a knife. It took a moment, but her eyes finally focused on Terrance who was hanging from a rope with two hay bales beside each other a foot below him.

Without thinking, the three squirrels rushed toward Terrance.

Jeff rolled backward and hopped up on his feet as Buford rushed him with his knife and sliced Jeff's right arm off at the shoulder. Grabbing Jeff's hair with his left hand, he yanked Jeff's head back and cut it off with one clean move.

Alfred's body lay lifeless on his floor. His neck was broken.

"You're no use to us anymore. I'll do what you and J'Nou couldn't," Captain Oliver said to Alfred's corpse.

He left the body there to be found by wild animals. A man as crazy and useless as Alfred didn't deserve to be consumed. Beasts and insects would feast on the worthless flesh.

Captain Oliver put on his sunglasses and ran a hand through his hair. Leaving the small shack, he ran to the nearest port. He saw Agwe and Azacca walking out of their shop, sneered at them, and ran the long way around town to grab a snack before leaving Haiti.

Behind a shop, he saw an old man and his daughter. She patted the man's head with a wet rag. Smiling to himself, he casually walked up to the two.

"Is your father ok, ma'am?" he asked.

"Yes, he's just warm out here, but some sun is good for him. Are you ok? You look ashen," she replied.

"Oh, I'm fine, just been in the sun a bit long. May I help?"

He reached down and slowly took the towel from her hands, keeping eye contact with her the whole time. He dabbed it on the sleeping man's head. He could smell the blood pumping beneath his skin.

He was hungry.

"My name is Oliver; what's yours?"

"I'm Pacey. I was about to bring him in, though, so that's not necessary. Thank you, sir," her uneasiness showed through her smile.

"Let me help you bring him in, Pacey."

"Oh no. I'm sure you have places to be."

"Not at all. I have a while before my ride leaves."

"Well, thank you," she looked over his chiseled body and warm face.

He lifted Pacey's father, making it appear more of an effort than it was. The warm skin and pumping blood in the pair was nearly more than Oliver could handle.

He wondered, sometimes, why he tortured himself like this. Most Revenant would attack and eat, but he liked to play with his food first, putting them at ease. Their flesh tasted better when a flood of hormones and fear didn't taint it.

When they entered the house, though, he couldn't wait any longer. He pinched the old man's spine, killing him quickly, painlessly, and silently. Then gently, he laid him on the couch Pacey pointed to.

"Would you like a cold drink before you go? I have some tea and lemonade in the refrigerator," she said.

"No thank you. A warm meal sounds better."

He slid behind her and ran his hands from her shoulders up to her neck. She wasn't scared, but goose bumps formed all over her skin.

Well, some hormones taste better than others.

He enjoyed his dinner.

Paxton aimed at Buford and shot his calf. This slowed him down, but not much. Buford threw Jeff's head into a corner; the head split open as it hit the wall. Jeff's body dropped to the ground.

"So, you came to save your friend, did you?" Buford said. He didn't stay still, but remained next to Terrance. "You interrupted a sacrifice to the Great White Dragon, boy. Do you know what happens when you murder our priests and interfere with our sacrifices?"

A little more to the right, Paxton thought.

"Do you, boy? When you interfere, you get crucified outside town. Just like you—"

Buford moved away from Terrance just enough and Paxton opened fire and hit Buford between the eyes and in the nose; then another bullet ripped through his mouth, rattling around inside his head. Two more bullets ripped through his head and went out the other side, splattering blood and brains all over Jeff's body and head and the entire corner.

Buford's heart didn't stop for a while. Paxton heard it continue pumping as his body fell toward Jeff's and blood pooled out of Buford's body.

Terrance's body dropped to the ground with one squirrel on his head. Two more clung to the rope that had held him up. Only one minute had passed since they'd entered the barn.

Paxton ran to Terrance, loosened the rope and bent down, listening for breathing.

He didn't hear anything. He placed his ear on Terrance's chest and heard a heartbeat, but it was faint.

Quickly he tried to breathe air into Terrance's mouth, but it was difficult with his cheek open again. Sara was right beside him, holding Terrance's cheek shut.

The pair traded off several times, breathing air in and pushing it out. Finally Terrance coughed up blood and cried out in pain.

He began breathing.

J'Nou and Mara heard most of what was happening in the barn, but they didn't know all the details. They did smell blood, though. After a moment, they also heard a clamor near the city wall where the group had been.

"Carl's down; they may find the barn. We have to get those slave lovers before they find Buford." The voice came from the wall. "I think I heard gunshots; let's go."

Mara looked at J'Nou and raised her eyebrows, "We can't let them die here. We must follow them to Paxton's father, right?"

J'Nou smiled at the excuse. The Controller would allow him this small group of racists.

Mara and J'Nou stalked toward the sound of the Dixie Mafia. There were eight men in total. This would be easy for the two Revenant.

They rushed the group, comprised of one man with a pointed hat and seven with hats that looked cut off on top. The man with the pointed hat wore a dragon as his symbol, while the other seven had only the circle with a K. Mara crept around the right side of the group while J'Nou positioned himself on the left.

Mara and J'Nou leapt from cover and attacked the group. They had the drop on them, but planned to kill first and eat afterward.

The man in the pointed hat had another plan, however. He pulled out a long, sharp knife and sliced off J'Nou's left arm as J'Nou killed the second man in his circuit.

After killing her third victim, Mara stopped for just a moment.

"Revenant are not welcome here, especially slant-eyed mistakes like you," the Dixie Mafia Dragon said.

J'Nou leapt back, leaving three men in the group, including the man with the pointed hat.

Mara did the same on the other side of the group.

They would have to rethink how to take out this group of men before rushing in.

"Can you even see me clearly through those eyes, or does it look like I'm leaning?" the Dragon continued. The other two men laughed.

J'Nou reached out to the Controller to see if he knew what was happening here, but nothing like this man had been encountered. He was obviously not a Revenant, or Vampire, but he wasn't human either. He moved fast enough to counter J'Nou.

But J'Nou had experience. He trained with an elite corp in each branch of the military twenty years earlier, along with extended visits to the samurai and ninja clans in the Japanese Empire. He wasn't rusty.

Mara lunged in low to take out the legs of all three individuals. At the same time J'Nou jumped to attack from above. He left himself purposefully open to attack by the Dragon. Mara's attack took down two of her targets.

The Dragon jumped to avoid Mara, while lunging up with his knife toward the one armed assailant from above. J'Nou expected this and used his training and experience to roll to his left side in the air, pointing his stump toward the man and forcing him to miss J'Nou entirely.

Twisting back while still in the air, J'Nou's arm reached around the man's arm and broke it off clean at the shoulder. Then, before the hand dropped the knife, he whipped the arm around and cut the man's jugular vein.

J'Nou panted and looked into the city. A fire raged inside of him, and he stalked toward the wall. He stopped, mid-stride, and stood straight.

Mara stared at him, unsure what was happening.

He felt the Controller in his mind, trying to stop him.

He put his left foot forward, slowly.

Do not do this, J'Nou.

His right foot went forward now.

J'Nou. You will be slaughtered, and I don't want to lose you. Please stop.

It was more difficult, but he slid his left foot through the dirt, moving it forward slightly.

I promise you, J'Nou. I will let you handle this. Just not now. You must follow them. Captain Oliver, Cynthia, and Gail will join you again shortly. We will wipe out the Dixie Mafia, but first we need Dr. Roald. Please do not make me use Mara to stop you.

J'Nou stopped struggling and looked at Mara.

After looking at her a moment, J'Nou said, "Let's get this cleaned up."

22. Cowcatcher

Terrance was on the beach again with the glowing figure before him. The figure was gently weeping.

He was unable to move, breathe, or speak.

"Remain calm, Terrance. I'm still here," the figure said. "You are meant for more than this."

The figure gestured behind him. Terrance looked back and saw the waves hitting the beach. His parents were there, but this time they were looking at him and there were no pirates.

Behind them, he began to notice more figures. As they came into focus, he saw that they were all his parents. There were hundreds of sets of parents on the sand.

"Your family will always be waiting when you're ready to take your place. And I will be there with you."

Paxton placed his arms under Terrance's neck and legs and lifted him. He strained, but Sara helped him. Once Paxton was standing, he was secure in carrying Terrance. Sara walked to the corner where Jeff's head was and knelt. Paxton looked at Sara and then at the head and began walking toward the door.

She missed him, even though he was a monster. He'd given his life for Terrance, and she would remember him for that. She leaned over and whispered something nobody heard.

"Sara," Paxton said, "we need to be going. We've got to get Terrance out of here and there's nothing we can do for Jeff anymore. There could be more of them; we won't be ready for that."

She nodded and pushed herself up.

On the way back into town, they saw a grizzly sight. A group of men, Paxton estimated eight, lay in a heap on the ground, ripped to shreds with their brains removed. One head, however, was gone.

"Revenant," Paxton said.

"Why would they do this? They didn't consume them," Sara said.

"Maybe they were like Buford. He moved as fast as any Revenant I've seen and he was just as strong."

"How could he do that?"

"I don't know. He wasn't Revenant though, or he wouldn't have died so easily."

"Easily? You put a bullet in his leg and several in his head. I think that would have killed any Revenant."

"No. If you don't separate the brain from the spinal cord, it will regenerate. There's something about the cerebellum or thalamus and where it connects to the spinal cord. They can heal from anything unless you destroy the brain or separate it cleanly from the spine. My Father taught me that when we lived in LA, and it helped when they invaded."

"Oh. I didn't know."

"Yeah."

"So, do you think Jeff will heal?"

"His head was removed pretty clean, and broken open. I doubt there's any chance he'll heal."

The two continued through the gate and walked back to the Underground. The sun was rising over the horizon, but they were in no mood to watch it. Paxton laid Terrance down in the back of the NJ-1300 and ran off to find Dr. Carlson. Meanwhile, Sara packed up their belongings.

They had to hurry before it was too light outside.

Paxton found Dr. Carlson and Nurse Rosa opening their office. He told them what happened as briefly as he could.

"We'll go with you. We can't stay here if Buford's dead," Dr. Carlson said. "As bad as he was, he tolerated my presence, but with him gone, Joseph will be in charge, and he's far less tolerant. Pull your jeep around to the office; we'll need to grab some stuff."

"Wait. Can we fit in there? There will be six of us, plus our stuff, and Terrance needs to lie down as much as he can," Rosa said.

"Buford ripped Jeff's head off," Paxton said. "We'll have enough room, and there's storage in the back. Pack up and we'll be back in a few minutes."

Rosa's jaw dropped.

Dr. Carlson lowered his head and whispered, "Hurry."

The doctor and nurse went inside and grabbed everything they needed.

The sun was coming up on Miami Beach, casting an orange glow that rivaled any beauty in existence. Nobody saw the waves as they crashed against a moving tower. The waves split in two and broke on its back.

The tower was Captain Oliver. He was over eight feet tall and about three feet wide at the shoulders. His skin was dark and smooth. Water dripped off of his bare chest between the waves.

He loved swimming even before he had become a Revenant, but now he could swim underwater for miles without surfacing. He watched the marine life as he propelled himself faster than any boat and slowed to swim around some sharks. He circled them and commanded them to swim in unison around him.

But this was the part he hated.

Surfacing.

He walked through the dry sand and it stuck to his bare feet. The grit of the sand rubbed against his feet and legs. He wore his shorts only to appear modest if anyone was watching when he surfaced.

Now he needed to find some dry clothes before running North.

J'Nou panted.

He wanted to go back and kill every last Dixie Mafia member. If it weren't for the Controller and Mara, he would have attempted just such a thing.

That Dragon who pulled his arm off made him angrier than

ever before. *How could such scum get power like that?*

He consoled himself with the fact that he did take out a group of them and had its head as a trophy. Or was the Controller consoling him with that fact?

He would worry about that later.

He would return.

For now, he needed to find a way to track Paxton. He thought that he knew where they were heading, but he wondered if the group avoided the subject on purpose or if Paxton didn't tell them. He attempted to eavesdrop on their conversations, but everything was about taking care of Terrance now.

In the meantime he found himself sniffing the air and wrestling with following the group. Mara had discovered Jeff's body in the barn, so the two knew it would be more difficult to follow them, especially inside a vehicle.

Blood continued to poor from the hole in the back of the body's head. It was no longer pumped out; the heart had stopped hours earlier; but the blood flowed slowly, thickening over the dirt and hay.

It picked up dirt as it moved and carried it along, down the shallow slope of the ground. The blood took multiple routes, around this piece of hay, through that divot in the ground, or over a dirt clod.

As it pooled in the dirt, it was soaked up.

A very quiet sucking sound was heard by nobody.

Paxton was sitting behind the steering wheel while Rosa sat on the other side, next to the window, and Sara sat between them. In the back seat, Dr. Carlson sat behind Rosa, making it easy for her to hand him the many items she had in the containers and bags on and around her and Sara. Terrance's head lay on Dr. Carlson's lap.

Paxton tried to blend in with the horses and carts and the few trucks that left on the four-lane highway going out of town. While the NJ-1300 already stood out in the crowd, he would not hurry and unnecessarily draw more suspicion.

They had to get out of Atlanta before someone discovered the bodies.

Dr. Carlson kept asking him to slow down, though. He examined Terrance's neck and found that nothing had been crushed or collapsed.

"Terrance should heal fine from the hanging. I see no permanent damage to his throat or neck," Dr. Carlson said. "However, his cheek ripped more, and I'll have to stitch it again while he's drugged."

"So those pills you gave him—he won't feel it?" Sara asked.

"No, he'll sleep through it, honey." Rosa patted Sara's hand.

"You'll need to pull over while I sew it up, though, Paxton," Dr. Carlson said.

"It'll have to wait then. I'm sure another hour won't hurt it much; am I right?" Paxton asked.

"You're right. If they catch us, it won't matter, and another hour will only worsen the scar at the most. I can still re-stitch and help him then."

"Ok, we'll pull over as soon as we get out of Atlanta."

They were almost through the gates when a bell began ringing. Paxton and Sara tensed.

"It's just the Church of the Great White Dragon," Dr. Carlson said. "It's time for the market to open; that's all. We're still safe as long as—"

Another sound chimed. This one was much louder and sharper.

"Paxton, go. Now," Rosa yelled.

The gates were closing and most people were trying to turn around if they hadn't passed through. Paxton laid on the horn and pushed the gas, bumping through carts. He was only feet away from the gate when Rosa yelled. The gate wasn't far and he thought they could make it to the other side just in time.

Some guards pointed guns at them and yelled for them to stop.

"Paxton, we have to escape. They'll kill him this time," Sara said.

"I know. That's what I'm doing."

He pushed through the gate only moments before it shut completely, but they weren't in the clear yet. Several guards climbed in jeeps and trucks to chase them. A lot of carts and horses had made it through the gate, preventing Paxton from speeding up and escaping. The guards would surely catch them if he didn't do something.

Then Paxton saw the crucifixes. Turning right and pushing a few buttons on the console, the jeep pushed out a cowcatcher.

"How did you know it did that?" Sara asked.

"Where'd you get this thing?" Rosa asked.

"Our friends who built it gave us some documentation. I read up last night," Paxton said.

He began plowing through the crosses and knocking them down, left and right. The jeep and trucks behind him tried to follow, but couldn't keep up with the NJ-1300. Eventually they were clear of any Dixie Mafia.

Terrance was waking up, but he was still groggy from the drugs. His first thought was that his cheek and throat hurt like hell, and he wasn't sure which one hurt worse.

He raised a hand to touch his cheek, but slapped it instead.

"Ouch," he whispered.

"Oh, so our patient is finally awake," Rosa said.

"Yes, it's been funny seeing him try to sit up and open his eyes. The drugs must still be in his system," Dr. Carlson said.

"You're terrible, Doctor, letting him do that to himself. What kind of bedside manner is that?" Sara scolded him.

The Doctor laughed.

"Do you remember what happened, Terrance?" Dr. Carlson said.

"I—Uh," it still hurt to talk. "A basement and some trolls," he winced.

"Close enough," Sara said.

"Not trolls. It was those Dixie Mafia bastards. They tied you up and tried to sacrifice you," Paxton said. "We killed every one in there, but when we finally got you down, you weren't breathing."

Terrance struggled to sit up, but Dr. Carlson held him down,

"Now, now, you need to rest, son."

Terrance looked around to see where they were, "Wait. Where Jeff?"

"He's dead, Terrance," Paxton said.

"He died saving you, Terr," Sara said.

"He attacked the guys who took you, but one of them was as quick and tough as a Revenant, maybe more so," Paxton said. "He ripped off Jeff's head and... Well, I got him before he could hurt the three of us."

Terrance didn't have words for this. He was shocked. He'd never liked Pirates or Revenant, let alone this zombie-pirate-gigolo that was in bed with Sara when they met. *It's like fate wanted me to hate him.* He would never have saved the man's life or even passed along a nice word to him.

"He saved me?"

They drove along in silence for a couple of hours.

"It's time for some more, Dr.," Rosa offered Dr. Carlson some cotton soaked in alcohol.

"Thank you," Dr. Carlson took the cotton. "Terrance, this will hurt a bit. I need to disinfect the stitches." He dabbed Terrance's cheek carefully.

"I have family in DC if you're heading that far," Rosa said.

"We are," Paxton said.

"Would they have room for us?" Sara asked.

"Sure, they'll have a room or two."

"I appreciate it, but I may have a military connection. It's a good idea to stop there, though," Paxton said.

Captain Oliver no longer enjoyed eating the oranges that were plentiful throughout middle Florida. He did enjoy their smell, however. They were much better than the ones in California.

He continued on, through grove after grove. He had to meet Cynthia and Gail in Charlotte; they had a message to deliver. After that they would rush to meet J'Nou and Mara. With Jeff out of the picture, the five Revenant should easily be able to get what they wanted from three humans.

After the groves ended, he ran into the marshes. The mud

and water came up to his knees, but he was making good time until something rushed at him from under the water—the largest alligator Oliver had ever seen. It was at least twenty meters long and six meters wide.

It was Revenant.

Oliver leapt out of the way just before the jaws snapped shut. This was real swampland now, and he was buried up to his waist in mud. It wouldn't be easy to get out in one piece. He smiled.

Perhaps I could use a break.

Captain Oliver bent over and dove into the mud. He swam under and behind the creature, kicking up mud, plants, and debris until finally he had the alligator's tail in his hands. He planned to throw it far enough away that it would no longer be an issue. The Revenant alligator had other plans though. It tore off one of Oliver's arms, swallowing it whole.

With the one hand he had left, Captain Oliver threw the alligator twenty feet away, spinning to disorient it. Then he jumped on its back.

Pulling the top of the alligator's mouth up, he tried to rip its head open. It was nearly impossible with one hand, and the alligator used its tail to swat Oliver away.

Oliver skidded across the swamp on his back like a well-skipped stone.

As soon as he stopped, the alligator was upon him.

You're a tough one, huh?

He reached up and held the alligator's mouth shut, bending it to his will.

"I think I'll call you, Alexander," he continued North to Charlotte with his new pet. "Now let's go leave a message for our old friends."

23. Washington Post

Washington's lights glowed over the ten-story wall. The wall wasn't as awe-inspiring as Charlotte's one kilometer technological marvel, but the light at the top of the New Washington Monument provided hope the banks never could.

President Kennedy had extended it near the end of his first term in 1956 to be 1776 meters high in celebration of the 180th birthday of the United States of America. During the Revenant War, the military added a very strong light that shone at night like a second sun.

However, outside the modest wall, the light quickly faded, and another wall came into view. The first defense of the Capital City was a wall of Rangers and their A41 tanks. Each A41 had its headlights facing away from the city, and was just close enough to the next one that it was nearly impossible to tell which two lights belonged to one tank and which two were the space between.

The tanks were each manned by six soldiers. One, the commander, acted as navigator and field coordinator. Another, the pilot, was privileged; the tank's speed and maneuverability was legendary, even when compared to the technology from the Armies of the Great United States of Africa and the Japanese Empire. The last four soldiers were gunners, and each man sat below a rotating pod on one of the four corners. Each pod had a 38mm gun which rotated in nearly a complete sphere, except where it pointed back toward the tank itself.

The guns fired at a rate of 4 per second. Each round was

explosive and would tear a Revenant in half, but now five tanks had their twenty weapons trained on an NJ-1300.

Paxton slowed the vehicle and flashed his lights. One tank flashed its lights back in the same pattern and pulled forward quickly. Even over the flat terrain, the smooth movement and the speed with which it closed the distance stunned the group.

"For a wheeled vehicle, it moves amazing," Terrance said with difficulty. His cheek hadn't healed the way it should over the past week and was becoming infected. He wasn't doing too well and spent most of his time sleeping.

"Yeah, but it's not wheeled; it just appears that way. They use a combination of the tracks and repulsor lifts to give it that speed and smoothness, without losing maneuverability," Paxton said. "Something Maurice told me about. It's where he got the idea for the bikes."

"Slowly step out of the vehicle and approach the tank with your hands up," a voice said over the tank's speaker.

The group stepped out of the vehicle. Paxton, Sara, and Nurse Rosa lifted their hands. Dr. Carlson gave Terrance a hand getting out of the vehicle and helped him remain standing. Dr. Carlson held Terrance's left arm, while he held his own left hand in the air and Terrance held his right hand up.

"State your business."

Paxton slowly approached the tank. Ranger Mercer climbed out of it and walked toward the group.

"My name is Paxton Roald. My friend's hurt, and we're being followed by two Revenant. You're going to do your scan, and then we need to get some help in the Capital."

Ranger Mercer spoke quietly into his com. Then he looked back at the group as they continued to approach him.

"Stand still and do not move. The men in the tank are instructed to shoot through me to kill you if they need to."

The ranger approached the group one at a time with a small device. It looked like an open book, but the top piece had a hole in it, and he held it in front of Paxton with the hinged side facing him.

"Place your hand on this," the Ranger said.

Paxton placed his right hand through the hole and onto the other piece. Ranger Mercer pressed the top down to the bottom, and the device pricked Paxton's finger. On the scanner yellow lights around the top piece blinked slowly and the scanner chimed.

Ranger Mercer lifted the top piece again, and the device stopped blinking and chiming. The yellow lights changed to green and it dinged. Ranger Mercer pressed a button and walked toward Sara. He repeated this with each person. When he finished testing Terrance, he gestured to the A41.

"Return to your vehicle and follow us to the post ahead," Ranger Mercer said.

The group climbed back into the NJ-1300 and drove along as the tank sped toward the empty spot in the wall of tanks.

"Proceed through." Ranger Mercer's voice came over the tank's loud speaker. His tank waited to take its place until they drove through the hole in the wall.

On the other side, their eyes adjusted. For the first time, they noticed that the flat, treeless ground between the two walls was not empty. It was filled with many Rangers, bunkers, temporary shelters, larger mounted turrets, towers, and various, less threatening vehicles.

"Welcome to Washington's tent city," Paxton said.

They slowed and drove along the path to the right. A soldier gestured for them to follow him and walked the vehicle to a command tent twenty meters away. The soldier turned and signaled the jeep to stop, and the group began to climb out.

"One of you comes with me. The rest will stay in the vehicle for now while we search it," the soldier stated.

Paxton began to open his mouth, but the soldier had already turned and entered the tent. The two standing outside the opening did not look ready to listen to anything Paxton would say, so he closed his mouth, determined to talk to whoever was in command about getting help for Terrance.

Inside the tent, three soldiers, two Generals, and a Colonel looked over a table that had a hologram of the Capital City in the center with the surrounding terrain also shown. The A41 tanks were also there, in a solid line around the city, except in the bay where boats of a design Paxton did not recognize lined up to guard the holes in the ten-story wall.

General Wallace and Colonel Gordon looked up as he entered.

"Come forward, Paxton. It's good to see you alive," General Wallace said.

General Morrison pursed his lips and kept his eyes on the hologram.

"You know me, General?" he asked.

"Of course. I'm General Wallace," he nodded and reached out to shake Paxton's hand. "I knew your father when we were at EA-51, and we've been keeping an eye on your family until LA. We thought you were all killed, but our intelligence was apparently wrong." He threw a look at General Morrison.

"General Morrison." The other General nodded and shook Paxton's hand. "We were relieved when you turned up. I do hope this means your father is safe as well?"

Paxton gave no indication. Something felt wrong, and he feared the reaction if they knew his plan for his father.

"Hmm," General Wallace said, "I understand that you don't know us from Adam, son, but you can trust us. Would you tell us if the Revenant had him?"

"They do not have him. Now, I have an injured friend who could use some help," Paxton looked back at the door.

"Private Richardson," General Wallace addressed one of the soldiers standing guard at the door.

"Sir," Private Richardson saluted.

"Fetch Colonel Gunthrey for me."

"Yes sir."

He turned and left immediately.

"Now, Colonel Gunthrey will be here in a moment and can bring you to Medical. In the meantime, Paxton, where have you been and what brings you this way?"

Paxton didn't feel like telling him everything, but he had to play nice so Terrance could get help.

"We've been down south, and now we're on our way to visit some friends here in town," Paxton said.

"Friends? Here?"

"Yes."

Just then Private Richardson returned with Colonel Gunthrey. General Morrison squinted and his upper lip twitched, but General Wallace smiled. Paxton wondered what Morrison's problem was, and if he could trust General Wallace.

"Colonel Gunthrey," General Wallace said. "Please take Paxton's friends to Medical. Do not allow them into the city for the moment, but take them directly to Dr. White and instruct him to give Terrance the best care possible. Do not tell them his real name."

Colonel Gunthrey snapped to a salute and then immediately exited the tent.

"Why can't he tell them who Terrance is?" Paxton asked. Then, thinking again he added, "And how do you know who he is?"

He wondered if the Revenant scanners did more than detect infected individuals. Perhaps the government's DNA database was more thorough than they let on.

"I would have thought he'd tell you. It's not my place, though; you can ask him later. For now we have more to discuss," General Wallace said.

General Morrison focused on the table again and General Wallace asked him about the Revenant. Colonel Gordon paid more attention as Paxton told them about J'Nou and Mara, conveniently leaving out his mother and granny. He also shared the events with the Dixie Mafia and the group of members they found killed, but not consumed.

"It seemed very atypical of Revenant. I've never seen them attack, and not feed," Paxton said.

"We've run into that before, but rarely," General Morrison said and stared at Paxton. "It seems that the Controller isn't controlling them at all times, giving them some autonomy, especially the more mature ones, and First Brothers. We believe that sometimes a younger Revenant, given too much freedom, will attack, and the Controller will pull the Revenant back and not allow it to feed," General Morrison said. "The young Revenant you described would fit this explanation."

"Or it may be a training exercise to exert self-control," Colonel Gordon said.

"That may explain it. The young one probably lost control," Paxton said, though he wasn't sure he believed it. "Now, if you don't mind, I thank you for helping Terrance, and we'll be moving on as soon as he's ok. So, if you're finished, I'd like to see how he's doing."

General Morrison looked at him sharply. *What about your friends outside, Roald? Or do you expect us to deal with your problems?*

"You all may remain here for as long as is necessary, but we'll want to talk again before you leave," General Wallace said.

Paxton turned to leave.

"And don't forget to tell your friends in the city hello from us," General Morrison said.

Damn! Paxton didn't like being caught in a lie. He had no friends in the city and no intention of staying here longer than necessary. General Morrison knew this and was letting Paxton know that he knew.

24. Drugs and Love

A rat scurried across the open field. It smelled something rotting in the building ahead of it and its mouth watered. It twitched its whiskers and found a hole in the building, covered only by some hay. He easily scurried through the hay and then the hole.

There it was, ahead of him, a head, with only a little of the spinal cord sticking out the bottom and skin growing over the neck hole.

The rat moved closer and sniffed the air. It licked at some blood that congealed near it. He moved in closer to the bits of flesh ahead and picked up a piece of skin with his tiny paws. He nibbled a bit and stopped.

He heard something.

The rat tore back into the skin, twirling it around as he ate.

He barely saw the blur just a moment before it ended his little rat life.

As Dr. Carlson helped Terrance into the Medical Tent, Colonel Gunthrey stopped them and said, "Dr. do not divulge Terrance's real name. Please tell them his name is Terry Connor."

Terrance nearly fell; he wasn't expecting Dr. Carlson to stop abruptly and stare at the Colonel. The drugs he was given were severely messing with his mind and body. He needed to get inside and the Colonel was right, but how would Dr. Carlson know that it was dangerous to use his real name? They hadn't discussed his family's status with the Revenant.

On that note, however, how did the Colonel know? Were there Revenant nearby? Or worse, Votaries? He used to think they were just as bad as the monsters they worshipped, but after his time with Jeff, he knew they had one thing the Revenant didn't: a choice.

Would these crazies be after him or know he was here? He heard they gave their children to the Revenant. What would they do with him? What if—

"That's no problem, Colonel," Sara said.

Terrance looked at her, surprised; then he remembered that she knew his family was wanted. She may not know everything, but that was probably enough. He liked it that way; nobody need-ed to know why the Controller would want him.

Inside, the beds were straightened and empty. Terrance de-cided it must be the most sterile place in America and it was devoid of patients.

"Who do we have here, Colonel Gunthrey?" asked a short, stocky man. He was wearing a long white coat as he approached Terrance and began examining his cheek.

Terrance turned to nuzzle the doctor's hand.

"This is Terry Connor and Dr. Carlson. I'm sure he can answer any questions, Dr. White. General Wallace said to treat him with the best care," the Colonel said.

"The best?" Dr. White's eyes snapped to the Colonel's.

"The best."

"The best." Terrance's drowsiness showed in his speech.

The Colonel turned and brusquely exited Medical.

"Alright, the best it is. Dr. Carlson is it?" Dr. White asked. "They told me you've been treating him."

Terrance continued trying to nuzzle Dr. White's hand while he performed an examination of his cheek.

Dr. Carlson nodded and Sara laughed.

"This looks a few days old and not healing well," Dr. White continued. "Was the slice completely through the cheek?"

"Yes, Doctor," Dr. Carlson said. "He came to me about a week ago with a slice, all the way through and almost up to his ear. Sara was there when it happened."

"What happened, Sara," Dr. White asked as he removed his hand from Terrance's reach.

"Well, a Revenant threw a rock at him and it sliced through his cheek all the way to his ear," she said.

Dr. White didn't seem too sure of the story Sara told him, "A rock? Don't Revenant usually do more than throw rocks?"

Terrance snapped awake for a moment. He sensed the implications aimed at Sara and didn't appreciate it. It only lasted a moment, but Terrance commanded Dr. White's attention, "Usually."

Sara smiled.

"Ok. And you took care of him, Sara, until you found Dr. Carlson here, right?"

It took a moment for his question to register. Sara was still thinking about Terrance protecting her. Even when she didn't need it, it still meant a lot to her, "Yeah, it was a few days old before we could reach Atlanta. If it weren't for Dr. Carlson and Rosa, Terrance might be dead now."

"You did well, Sara." Dr. Carlson turned to Dr. White. "I stitched it up and provided alcohol as an antiseptic. Unfortunately, the Dixie Mafia got hold of him and strung him up in a barn outside Atlanta.

"That's also where the bruises and abrasions came from. They weren't there when I first examined him. I've tried to keep him as healthy as possible, but it's all been downhill since a couple days ago. I gave him some Nectometophin to numb the pain, but it also caused severe drowsiness and loopiness, which is why he seems fascinated with your hand."

"Nectometophin?" Dr. White asked.

"Yes, it's a drug I developed in Atlanta while I was a researcher at the CDC, before the outbreak. It has mild antibiotic properties and strong pain relief. It also makes the patient really tired and loopy. The best part, though, is that it can be made simply from several plants in a few minutes using common items."

"Tell me more about this."

While Dr. Carlson explained, he laid Terrance on a bed.

"Well, this isn't too bad. It's too late to keep it from scarring, but we can have him up and ready to go by the morning; in fact, he should be mostly healed within the hour," Dr. White said.

Sara and Dr. Carlson looked dumbfounded at Dr. White.

"Dr. Carlson, I think you've been holding back on me," Terrance said, smiling with his good cheek.

They all chuckled and Dr. Carlson asked, "Tomorrow morning? How is that possible?"

"We've made major advances in medicine here. In fact, I'd love to have your help advancing it more," Dr. White said. "With what you've told me about Nectometophin, I think we could use your talents."

"What is this method that will heal in an hour, Doctor, if I may ask?" Nurse Rosa had been quiet but she was cautious of 'miracle cures'.

"Bio-heal."

Dr. White held up a jar with green gel inside.

"No. Not that," Nurse Rosa said.

"I've heard of it and its side effects. Wasn't that banned even before the Revenant War?" Dr. Carlson asked.

"That's nothing to be concerned with anymore. We've nearly perfected it, and there are no side effects. With a wound this severe, that's been there this long, he will still have a scar," Dr. White said. "It's no miracle, but it works."

"When you say 'nearly' what do you mean?"

"Well, we have a two-step process that couldn't be used in the field yet, and the gels are difficult to create and they break down easily."

Dr. White carefully put on two pairs of gloves and scooped his hand into the Bio-heal gel and brought out a small dollop. He smeared this on Terrance's cheek. With one finger he wiped some on the inside of Terrance's mouth, walked over to a sink and washed his hands, removed his gloves, washed his hands again, and then sprayed a blue liquid over his hands and arms.

"Nurse Rosa, would you mind wrapping his head? Be sure to cover it all and spray some of that blue bottle onto the bandages when you're finished. Soak it until the bandages are completely blue all the way around his head," Dr. White said, "and soak another rag and put it on the inside of his cheek."

"What's the blue spray?" Dr. Carlson asked.

"That is the inhibitor. It prevents any of the unfortunate side effects of the Bio-heal," Dr. White explained. "It will kill the gel slowly, but quickly enough that the patient, after healing, will not suffer 'outgrowth'."

"Outgrowth?" Sara asked.

"The Bio-heal works by instigating uncontrolled growth, almost like causing cancer. When we first tested the idea, most people were covered in tumors from head to toe by the end of a week. It sounds like this inhibitor should prevent that," Dr. Carlson said.

"Sha da ba bana?" Terrance mumbled through the rags. His face was creased with mild pain.

"What did he say? Don't move, Terrance. You'll heal faster if you stay still. It may burn a little, but it's just the cultures and organisms doing what they need to do. If it becomes too much, let us know," Dr. White said.

"O A," Terrance nodded and gave a thumbs up.

He looked over at Sara and tried to smile. His other hand felt in his pocket. The small box was still there, contents intact. How it stayed through everything that happened, he didn't know, but he was glad he didn't toss it in the ocean when he had the chance.

"So, you and sleepy here had something?" Nurse Rosa asked Sara.

Sara had been standing outside the medical tent for a while when Rosa showed up. She was shivering and thinking about Terrance.

"Yeah, we did. Until I screwed it up," Sara said.

"What happened?"

"Well, it's a long story, but let's just say I let my jealousy and loneliness get to me, and Jeff showed up at the right time."

Rosa frowned and Sara realized what that sounded like.

"We didn't do anything. I mean, I paid him to lay in bed with me. Oh, that sounds bad. I just wanted to make Terrance jealous, so he'd know how it felt. I didn't want to cheat on him."

"Did he cheat on you?"

"Not really, but it felt like it. He spent all his time with Paxton. If it weren't for Paxton, Terrance would have killed Jeff. Then some Revenant showed up, and we all would have died if the Captain hadn't arrived."

"The Captain?"

"Yeah, the Captain of Jeff's ship broke the door down and shot one of the Revenant in the gut, and that kind of started the whole thing. Anyway, we were close for a long time before that."

"Yeah."

"Yeah, when I arrived in Florida, I had nobody. My family all died on the way there, and I finished the trip alone. I planned to hop a ship to the Great United States of Africa, land of freedom and prosperity, but I found Terrance first. He'd lost his parents, so he knew how I felt and we connected. I never wanted to leave again."

"Sounds like you still feel something for him," Rosa said.

"I've never stopped."

"Well, at least he'll be ok. You can tell him how you feel in the morning and hopefully he'll realize what a wonderful thing you two have. We can't put love off." Rosa looked off to the office where Dr. Carlson and Dr. White talked.

"You and Dr. Carlson?"

Rosa's eyes went wide.

"How did you guess that?"

"I've seen how you look at him, but I wasn't sure until now," Sara smiled.

"Yeah, neither was I until all of this," Rosa looked again at the office. "It was dangerous in Atlanta, but Buford kept us safe. He hated that we helped people like Terrance, but he had to protect us, or our mother would have climbed out of her grave and killed him."

"Mother? You mean?"

"Enough about me; what do you love most about Terrance?"

"Good try, but no. You're Buford's sister? And Paxton killed him?"

"He had it coming. The only good thing he ever did was protect us from the Dixie Mafia. I wanted to run away with Dr. Carlson, but he wouldn't leave. He said that he had a mission there. Paxton killing him was the best thing that ever happened to me. Now, what's your favorite thing about Terrance?"

"Ok, his eyes. They're so kind and gentle, but they've always had this power. When he's protective of me, like even on the ship," she smiled to herself. "On the way to New Orleans, everyone knew I was the only girl on ship and one pirate got a little too fresh. Well, he was there and heard it, so he jumped up and sent the guy off the ship, into the water. Even when Terrance was mad at me he still protected me.

"And he's always been protective of me; I guess I just forgot that. I miss it so much, but I think I miss his friendship the most. Maybe we should just be friends."

The two women sat there quietly discussing Terrance and Dr. Carlson until Paxton showed up.

"Where's he at?" a large man with a blue jacket and a black cowboy hat bellowed as he threw open the door to Luigi's. His voice sounded metallic.

"Pasquale, get in here," Santori said. "And bring Dr. Roald. We have visitors."

The large man with the blue jacket was followed by two more men. Each wore a blue jacket, but their hats were yellow. They also had holsters with what looked like old six-shooters in them.

As Pasquale entered the dining room, with Eugene following, he noticed the six-shooters and how they were modified. A large attachment was on the top of each weapon. This attachment read the intent of the user and adjusted the line of fire. Using gyroscopes, it turned the weapon slightly to aim where the user was looking.

Auto-Aimers. AA6s were nasty weapons.

Pasquale had heard of some of the technological advancements that groups in the Greater Texas Area had developed, especially the Lutadors with their steam powered toys. He studied some smuggled documents of an AA6, but decided that anyone who relied on that would lose something in a fight.

One wrong look and I'd clip Santori instead of shooting Black Hat.

Pasquale did not trust cowboys, but he wasn't the boss. One hand remained within quick reach of the unaltered Glock in his vest while the other gently pulled Eugene along. His eyes never left the cowboy on his left after he noticed the man's shifting eyes and nervousness.

"Wayne. It's been a while. How's the wife?" Santori asked.

The man in the black hat, Wayne, looked at Eugene, sizing him up. Then he looked at Pasquale and asked, "What's your name?"

"Pasquale."

"Pasquale, how've you been treating Eugene?"

"Well as we were able. He's mostly refused to eat since he arrived."

"Mostly? But he eats when he's hungry enough, right?"

The metallic tone in Wayne's voice increased as he grew worried, and Eugene began paying more attention. That's when he noticed the glint of metal under one man's hat, where his ear should have been. The others had ears, but this gentleman had only one.

That's Japanese technology. What are Lutadors doing with it?

"No, he'll eat when Pasquale joins him," Santori said.

"Well, then we may need to borrow your man, Santori," Wayne said.

Pasquale tensed, but he was too well disciplined to speak his mind.

"That wasn't a part of the deal, Wayne," Santori threatened him.

The other Lutadors put their hands on their AA6s.

"Deal's changed, Samuel."

Santori glared at Wayne.

"The Lutadors will pay for this, Wayne."

"We can afford it. Come on, Pasquale; it's a long way to Texas," Wayne said.

Colonel Gordon's fresh uniform made it obvious that he was recently promoted. He led Paxton to Medical through the organized chaos that was the tent city of the First Defense. Paxton finished explaining his plan for their departure.

"—then we get out of the A41 tank, switch into our NJ-1300 and we're home-free," Paxton said.

"I like the idea," Colonel Gordon said.

"So, the Revenant alligator… "

"Did you see it on the news? It's in that tent over there," Colonel Gordon said, "We've found that even animals, especially Revenant animals learn quickly what Death Metal is."

"Wow. I couldn't imagine that thing. Is it large?"

"Fourteen meters long, snout to tail tip. It's also over two meters wide, not including its feet. We figure it's been eating well, and they never really stop growing. At least this one hasn't. It's already two meters longer than it was when we captured it."

"Just a couple of weeks ago?"

"Yes."

"No wonder they promoted you so quickly," Paxton said.

The Colonel smiled, "Your friend will be right in this tent. I'll discuss your plan with the Generals. I think it's a good one. If you see your dad, tell him I said *hi*."

Colonel Gordon stretched his hand out. Paxton felt slightly ashamed at the mention of his father and hesitated a moment. He then returned the clasp with a firm grip.

"Thank you, Colonel."

When Paxton entered the tent, Terrance walked up and embraced him. With the bandages gone, he was left with a noticeable scar from the left corner of his mouth up to his left ear. It still looked raw and red, but Dr. White had assured him it would be less sensitive in the morning, though it may never regain its color. Terrance told Paxton about it; his speech had been restored and with no sign of an impediment.

"So, you're staying here?" Paxton asked Dr. Carlson. "Thank you for what you've done to help Terrance, Dr. Carlson. He might not be alive if it weren't for you."

"It was my duty and pleasure. I'll miss helping the slaves the Dixie Mafia has now, but my work here with Dr. White could help all of us. With some of the drugs I've been working on and his gel, we may be able to clear our country of the Revenant menace.

Then we can restore it to its former glory. The US will rise again."

"I hope you're right, Doctor." Paxton was again pained, knowing that if he had his way, the Revenant would become a much stronger threat to humanity across the globe.

"Don't worry, Dr. After we're finished, we'll go take care of the Dixie Mafia," Terrance said.

"That's a little ambitious, Terr," Sara said.

He smiled at her.

"Yeah, maybe you're right, but I plan to try."

They all embraced. Nurse Rosa would remain with Dr. Carlson, and they both were so full of hope and happiness. Even Paxton felt lighter inside. Sara began to tear up a little. She was very happy for Rosa and Dr. Carlson.

It was late, though, and Paxton wanted to leave while it was still dark, but Dr. White insisted that it wasn't a good idea.

"He'll be fine to leave tomorrow, but we'll want to keep him here over night. Like I said before, we haven't had any side effect issues, but I still should keep an eye on him, and he needs another round of the inhibitor to be safe. You're both welcome to stay here with him, though," Dr. White said.

Terrance rolled his eyes, "Dr. White, I feel fine. I don't think I need—"

"Terr, you're listening to the doctor. Wrap him up, Nurse," Sara said.

He smiled and reached back into his pocket. The ring was still there and after everything, maybe he would get to use it.

25. From Charlotte With Love

Eidan Nogmi stood on the corner of a bustling city street in the banking capital of the United States. After the Revenant War, money still needed to flow and be controlled. Every major bank still had a main branch in Charlotte even though most moved their headquarters to New London, banking capital of the Great United States of Africa.

All this money afforded a luxury most people in the US had lost. Security.

Security in the form of the Great Wall of Charlotte, a white, concrete, 1km high engineering marvel; complete with Death Metal runners, gun turrets, and a gate 200m high and 160m wide at the bottom.

"This is Eidan Nogmi reporting from the scene of that grizzly attack in Charlotte, NC. The Queen City is one of the largest fortified cities in America, and it is the single largest inland city left. Security is high in this town, and the cameras on every street capture all crimes.

"It's these cameras, like the one I have here," Eidan held up a small, black camera with a green and red light. The camera was off and neither light was shining, "that have earned Charlotte her most recent nickname, Big Sister. But regardless of the controversy they instigate, they also help the folks of this town feel safe every day. I have with me local Michael Koster. Michael, how often do you think about the Revenant threat?"

Michael was a short man with a red tan. He seemed very confident and had his black hair slicked back like a helmet.

"Well, Idan—

"It's Eidan."

"—we really don't think about it too much around here," Michael continued without stopping. "I mean we see them on the Net and stuff, but the past few years, we been pretty safe. Hell, we ain't even had a murder in years."

"But yesterday's events have changed that?" Eidan said.

"Well hell, yeah! We want to BBQ and live our lives, not be afraid some group of Revenant gonna come in and attack us."

"And that's what makes this so strange, Emily. The security footage has been viewed and it seems that one Revenant has done all this destruction and murder with the help of a Revenant alligator.

"Often Revenant attack to feed, but this one in particular only consumed one of the victims, killing many of the others and doing things we will not share on the Net Broadcast. For details deemed far too raw for NB, visit my newsfeeder. My article, additional videos, and interviews will all be available there."

Back in the studio Emily stared into the camera a second too long before composing herself.

"Eidan, I hear you do have some of the footage of the destruction downtown that you *can* show us," Emily said.

"Yes Emily. And this footage speaks for itself," Eidan said.

The footage rolled and showed an intersection at night lit by traffic lights, street lamps, and the security camera's light. A shadow grew large as something moved in front of the security camera's light and then jumped down. A black shape fell into view.

Then it became clear what was happening. The shape became a man; he was larger than most people and moved like an animal. He no longer moved like a human.

This was the Revenant.

This was Captain Oliver.

Next to him a huge alligator, Alexander, walked into frame.

He looked straight at the camera and ran away quickly with Alexander following, as if he were no more than a blur or smudge. The time in the bottom right sped quickly ahead ten minutes until he returned with a small girl.

She was limp.

He laid her on the road, in sight of the camera, and walked over to a light pole. Ripping it from the ground, he barely reacted to the sparks as it winked off. He bent the pole around and then, with one hand, he reached down and gently laid the little girl in it. He proceeded to bend it more, wrapping her in it as if he were swaddling her.

You could make out her breathing on the camera now as he held her closer to it for a good look. The top of the pole stuck up along her back; using this he hung her off of a building where the security camera couldn't quite see her.

Then, as if he knew it was just out of view, he ran to the camera and, laughing into it, he moved it to the side to show her clearly.

He was toying with someone.

"That little girl was unharmed and fortunate, but she is now an orphan," Eidan said. "Her family was the first group of victims found this morning. They were found dead, propped up under the security camera as a twisted danse macabre. An audience macabre."

"I guess she's not so fortunate after all, Eidan. Does anyone there have any idea why this one Revenant would do this?" Emily asked.

"Well, the Chief of Police is here and I've heard that Colonel Gordon is on his way. You may remember Colonel Gordon. I spoke to him recently when he was still a Ranger dealing with a Revenant alligator in Florida.

"He is now a Colonel and considered the Ranger's foremost expert on animal Revenant. We've been assured this alligator is not the one from Florida, and we'll have an interview with him tomorrow.

"Chief Walters, are there any leads as to why this lone Revenant would do something like this?"

The Chief shifted his eyes around quickly; then he took in a deep breath and puffed out his chest.

"Well, Mr. Nogmi, if he weren't a Revenant, we'd say he were psychotic or sending a message to someone. For the moment, we are assuming that the Controller wants to send a message, but to whom we do not know."

"And this is the first time a Revenant has entered the Big Sister—"

"We prefer the Queen City."

"Of course. It's the first time a Revenant has entered the Queen City, but with your security wall, cameras, and more, it was thought impossible that a Revenant could ever get in here, let alone, one with a twenty meter alligator. Many have referred to your city as Revenant-proof. What would you say to them?"

"We are investigating the situation still, and will have a response to that after we talk with our representatives from Lu Tech."

"Lu Tech built the wall, right?"

"That's correct."

"How do you believe he got inside?"

"Well, as I said before, we're following a few lines of inquiry on that, and we don't wish to discuss them at the moment. The most concerning one to us is that dang alligator he brought in with him."

"Is there any truth to the rumor that he was helped in by Votaries or other Revenant already here?"

"We're not speculating on such things at the moment. There is no proof that any other Revenant were here, or have been. Those ideas are… they're pure speculation."

"One last question, Chief. How much security footage is there of the attack?"

"Almost all of it is on one or another security camera. The piece you showed was the first clip, based on the security time stamp. From there it seemed he wanted us to see every step. That is one point against him having help."

The Chief puffed up a bit more, "At one point he grabbed a battery-powered camera and carried it around setting it here or there to record his acts. He was very blatant with this footage and left it on the front step of the Police Station."

"Wow. That doesn't say a lot for the security in this city. Well—"

"Wait! I mean—" The Chief tried to grab the microphone.

"I'm sorry, Chief; we're out of time for now. If you like, we can have a full interview later tonight," Eidan said while keeping the microphone out of reach and sound of the Chief.

The news cut to Emily in the studio, "This will not bode well for the Chief's reelection this fall, Eidan. In other news tonight: Are the Corsairs Modern day Robin Hoods or just Robbers? After this message from our sponsor, Lu Tech."

"So, how is the superstar doing?" J'Nou asked.

"Great! And how's the sneakiest man I know?" Captain Oliver replied.

He grasped J'Nou's hand and pulled him close for an embrace.

"It's been a long time. So, who's the runt?" Captain Oliver said.

"My name is Mara," she said.

"Well, Mara, I'm Captain Oliver. The Commander of the First Brothers."

"I thought the Controller was the commander."

"He's more of a General."

"Well, why didn't J'Nou salute you?"

Captain Oliver laughed, "She has a point, J'Nou."

Captain Oliver jumped up to a branch and looked around the trees to see the line of A41s. It was night and the headlights were on, so the Revenant couldn't see past the lights.

"Cynthia. Gail. I trust you were helpful for Captain Oliver."

"I hope so too," Gail said. "Captain Ham wouldn't share the camera time."

J'Nou laughed, "Yes, he likes the limelight. So, what was the message in Charlotte?"

Captain Oliver turned around and smiled at J'Nou. He hopped down and landed directly in front of J'Nou.

"Don't worry; he'll know what it was," Captain Oliver said. He pointed back to Washington, "What are we going to do about this? Do you think his father is here?"

"I do not know. I do not feel like this is the place, but if we wait here too long, we could lose our chance," J'Nou said.

"So let's just go in there," Mara said.

She turned toward the Capital City and began to walk. Captain Oliver picked her up by the shoulders and turned her around to face him.

"We must be more patient, Little One," J'Nou said to her.

"Why didn't the Controller stop me?" Mara asked.

"He doesn't always control us. He could, but he teaches us to control ourselves," J'Nou said.

He glanced at Captain Oliver and added, "Plus you had two First Brothers with you, so you were pretty safe. Even we can't take them head-on, though."

"But they'll recognize us if we walk in. Or at least you." Mara looked at Captain Oliver, waiting for his reply.

"They would not only recognize both of us First Brothers, but their scanners would figure out that you were Revenant. I have that covered, though. Come on out, ladies and gentleman," Captain Oliver.

Four women and one man came running to the group quickly. Their clothes were torn and clung to them with sweat.

"Who are they?" Mara asked. "Is it snack time?"

J'Nou walked over to the group, looking each one up and down. He touched their shoulders, arms, and cheeks, making a mental note of each one. The group stared forward and tried not to move.

"We do not eat Votary Scouts."

26. Conspiring

I t was the darkest part of the night, and both the sun and moon were absent; the only light came from the A41s and the Washington Monument. Lieutenant Daniel Thorne stood in Watchtower Bravo, behind the line of A41 tanks, expecting that all the night's excitement was behind him.

He wouldn't let his guard down, though.

All towers and tanks received a warning about the two Revenant that followed the group earlier, and the Revenant attack in Charlotte, but none of them knew of the other Revenant and Votary Scouts waiting nearby.

"There!" Lieutenant Daniel's lookout, Cedric, yelled.

Daniel dashed to the railing of the watchtower and grabbed a pair of night vision binoculars. As he pulled them to his eyes, he pressed a call button and ordered a group of A41s to investigate. The other tanks nearby trained their guns ahead of the ten advancing tanks for added protection.

The tanks quickly covered the 300 yards of cleared terrain between the line and the trees. Stopping abruptly, the drivers and front gunners saw the group Cedric spotted from the tower.

A single man stood in front of the group, his hair sopping wet with sweat. His button-up shirt was torn and partially unbuttoned, and his pants were ripped at the knees. Four women stood behind the man; each was as sweaty as the man and wore shirts that were also torn. Their pants were ripped up their legs, and blood stained the shirts and pants where the rips were, and gashes showed through the holes.

Ranger Mercer hopped down from one of the tanks and looked at the group.

"They look injured, sir," he said into the walkie-talkie on his shoulder. Keeping an eye on the group, he said, "Just stop where you are. Don't move. The men in the tank have orders to shoot through me if necessary."

He pulled out his scanner and used it with each man and woman in order. Each of them passed, and Ranger Mercer made a gesture to the tank.

"Alright, listen closely. We'll walk to the line of tanks. Follow the first tank; walk in front of me, and tell me what happened."

"Revenant, that way," he pointed back into the trees, still catching his breath. "They attacked our village. There were two of them. A girl and a man. We barely escaped."

"How did you escape, uh... "

"Name's Randolph."

"How did you escape, Randolph?" the Ranger grabbed his rifle and followed behind the group and the other tank.

The hairs on the back of Ranger Mercer's neck stood up. There was something odd about this man.

"They attacked the camp and we ran away. Most of our injuries are from the trees, bushes and falling, but they did follow us. We know they're out there in the trees now."

"How do you know that?"

"We could hear them taunting us, chasing us," Randolph said.

"So how did you get away? Why didn't they kill you?"

"I don't know."

Ranger Mercer held his rifle tighter. Something felt wrong here.

He brought them through the wall of tanks and directly to Medical. Paxton, Terrance, and Sara were there, in and out of sleep, as they waited for Terrance to be released. They watched as the five people came in and stood around one of the beds.

The new people stayed to themselves, but often looked over at Terrance and Paxton. Doctor White approached them, looked each one over, and then he turned to his assistant.

"Clean their wounds; bandage them all up and give them

some dressing gowns. Tomorrow they can get fresh clothes. Their wounds are superficial and should heal in a few days, except this one and this one."

Doctor White pointed to a wound on the thigh of one of the women, Susan, and another on Randolph's chest.

"They'll each need stitches; I'll scrub up and do those," the Doctor said.

"Why don't they use the gel, Paxton?" Sara whispered.

"Probably don't have enough of it for just anyone," Paxton whispered. "Now, go to sleep, Sara. We need to leave early."

Sara grumbled, rolled over on her cot, and grabbed Terrance's hand.

Doctor White began stitching up the wounds while his assistant bandaged the others. When they were all taken care of and given dressing gowns, the Doctor went to his office. Four soldiers stood guard in the room while the patients took turns getting dressed. The assistant waited outside the closed curtains of a bed.

Susan went first.

She sat on a chair and carefully took off her right shoe. Reaching inside she pulled out a small vial of red liquid and held it up to the light. Her hand trembled and vibrated the liquid inside.

She knew this day would come, and she had looked forward to it for years, but to have it within her grasp made her tremble with excitement. She savored the moment and would remember every part of it.

Carefully, she set the vial on a side table and undressed. Before she put on the dressing gown, she pulled down the bandage on her thigh and exposed the torn flesh. She pulled her skin, tearing the stiches open, and poured the vial on her wound.

She could feel the skin on her thigh growing together. It was warm and raw. Her other wounds began to tingle and warm up. She felt them healing, but paid no attention to that anymore. There was a small pressure in her abdomen, and she felt thicker. Then it was as if suddenly her entire nervous system caught fire.

She didn't scream, but for a moment, she thought she would. Then the fire was over almost as soon as it began.

She noticed how fast a fly on the end of her bed beat its wings and she could almost count each movement as it flew up into the air. She heard the heartbeats in the other room and smelled the blood in their bodies. Her mouth watered and she knew she needed to feed.

Now.

Suddenly she wasn't alone in her own mind. She sensed the First Brothers and even Mara, but another presence was far more powerful.

A horrific, all-encompassing presence.

The Controller would not let her feed.

"Each tank must leave at the same time," General Wallace said.

He and General Morrison were discussing Paxton's plan. Colonel Gordon was almost in Charlotte, responding to the attack.

Morrison and Wallace leaned over the war table.

"Leaving us undefended? I disagree, Wallace," General Morrison said. "If we send them out staggered, the Revenant are likely to follow one of the first. But, if we send them out at the same time, we'll be guessing which one the Revenant will follow or where their attack on the city will come from."

As he described his plan, he moved the tanks to match his description.

"Yes, but if they leave at the same time, it's less likely for the Revenant to guess which group Roald and Bonifacy are in. The point is—"

"The point, General, is that we want to flush out the Revenant. The best way to do that is to use the group as bait," General Morrison said.

Morrison showed the NJ-1300 moving toward the tree line, alone.

He stopped to look at General Wallace as this sunk in. These were kids and General Wallace couldn't believe what he heard.

"We won't let them get hurt. Don't worry about your old friends' children if you still consider them your friends. We just need to draw out the Revenant." The General began moving tanks again. "They'll leave with one A41 escort. At the tree line, we pull back the A41. We'll put three soldiers in there with them, and when the Revenant begin to follow them, we'll send more tanks in as backup."

"General Morrison, you've already killed the Bonifacies and led the Revenant to Paxton. We're lucky they don't know where Dr. Roald is already or we'd be overrun."

"All the more reason to get rid of Paxton anyway."

"And what happens if they capture him and he becomes one of them?"

"You're right. We shouldn't let that happen."

"It has to be a Revenant," Jimmy told his brother.

"But it can't be, Jim. It has to be a Vampire," Sonny replied.

"But Vampires don't exist. It's a Revenant coming in and taking people at night."

"It can't be! They're disappearing from right in front of people. They'll be out in that barn and then they're just gone," Sonny said.

"A Revenant could do that."

"No way. It's not possible. Don't you watch the Net Casts? They move fast, but you can still see them. This Vampire is a blur."

"It's not a Vampire, Sonny."

"How do you know?"

"I—I guess I don't."

The pair walked into the barn, knees shaking. Jimmy had a slingshot in his back pocket and Sonny had a baseball bat. They were supposed to be finishing their homework, but the mystery of the barn called them.

As they opened the door, a stench hit them. It was the smell of dirt, hay, blood, and rot. Both nearly fainted.

They looked toward the back of the barn and immediately knew what the stench was. There was a pool of congealed blood and bones from humans and animals, but the flesh was gone.

"I told you it wasn't a Vampire, Sonny," Jim whispered.

"Why do you say that?"

"Vampires would drink the blood, not eat the flesh."

They were pulled further into the barn by the steel grip of curiosity.

"Maybe, but—"

"Shhhh! We don't want to bring out the Revenant," Jimmy said.

They heard a movement in the corner and looked over. Jimmy thought he saw a blur.

"Vampire," Sonny whispered back.

They couldn't stop. They walked further in and noticed the hoods and jackets of some Dixie Mafia members. Jimmy saw the symbol of a Dragon on one and realized where they were.

"Let's go and do our homework, Sonny."

"Yeah."

Both children, their faces as pale as snow, left the barn and ran home.

27. Capital Exodus

Paxton heard some noise and woke up. He'd been a light sleeper since Los Angeles and things had only worsened since then.

He sat up. Terrance was asleep in the next bed with his head still covered in blue wrappings. Sara lay on a bed pulled up next to Terrance and holding his hand. They were both to Paxton's left, but the sound came from his right.

Looking around, his eyes adjusted to the darkness. They were alone in Medical. There was no doctor or nurse, and only two of the new people were there now.

He heard another sound to his right.

What were these new people doing? They all seemed fine and very awake considering the ordeal they'd been through.

Paxton closed his eyes and took in a deep breath. It was there, a faint smell that floated on the air like death in a kitchen.

His eyes shot open.

Eidan sat in a chair across from Colonel Gordon in the Charlotte studio. The live, net-wide interview was being broadcast at the top of the 7 a.m. episode, "This is Eidan Nogmi, here with Colonel Gordon."

"Last time we talked, you were *Ranger* Gordon, and your team caught a Revenant alligator. May we ask what happened to that alligator?"

Colonel Gordon was fresh from Washington and in charge of the government's response to the attack, "It's classified, Eidan.

I'm here to discuss the response to the recent attacks here in Charlotte."

"So, does that mean that the alligator on the footage may be the one you captured?"

"I can say it's not the same one; that alligator's whereabouts are known, but I'm here to discuss what we know so far about Charlotte."

"Yes, the recent attacks. What about those? Do you still think it's the work of one Revenant who was sending a message as the Police Chief said?"

"We believe the Chief was correct about there being a message. The question is who the message is from and who it is for."

"But he may not be correct about the Revenant working alone?"

"We are looking into those claims, but nothing has been confirmed."

"Is there a reason to believe the message is not from the Revenant who left it?"

"As we all know, the Controller is more than the leader of the Revenant; he can exert his will on them beyond anything you or I have experienced. We've learned that he can make the individuals do anything he wants, even if it is against their own deepest held beliefs.

"His ability to control Revenant in such a way means he can control them absolutely; therefore the message may be from Oliver or from the Controller," he said.

"Oliver?"

"We have identified the Revenant on the tape as former Captain Oliver Johnson. He is one of the first Revenant."

"A First Brother? Colonel, are the rumors about First Brothers true? Do they have greater power and intellect? Are they *Super Revenant*?"

"There is no evidence to support that. Obviously they had military training and have been around longer, so they are likely more talented in certain areas and have the benefit of experience."

"Do you think this is a message to President Olmos from the Controller?" Eidan asked.

"We're unsure if it's for the President, but we have moved him to a safe location. As far as we know, the message could be for you. We are quite confident, however, given the way Oliver was purposefully appearing on camera, it was a message from the Controller," Colonel Gordon said. "We think if Oliver were sending the message himself, it would have been more subtle, or the Controller would have subdued his behavior."

"Will the military be increasing its presence in Charlotte?"

"We have considered doing this. Charlotte currently has one A41 tank, but they also have the Great Wall. In light of the recent events, however, we are preparing to send two more A41 tanks within the week, not only here, but also to New York, Chicago, Miami, and Philadelphia. Those will be delivered within the week."

"Isn't it true, Colonel, that Washington has a line of A41 tanks that encircle it, a line that consists of over one hundred tanks?"

"Yes. That's common knowledge."

"And what would you say to the people who comment that there are too many tanks protecting the Capital City and not enough for the other cities and towns?"

"It's our official position that protecting the government and the most populated city is paramount to our nation's stability."

"But would a few more tanks be that detrimental to the safety of the Capital City? And what about the West Coast? There are rumblings about seceding from America over there."

"I was here to discuss the response to the recent attacks. Now, if you'll excuse me, I must take care of Charlotte."

Colonel Gordon stood and removed his microphone.

"Well, thank you, Colonel."

Eidan turned and faced the camera.

"Up next, Chief Walters defends the actions of Charlotte's police force."

Paxton knew what the smell was, but not where it came from. It was close, and now he wasn't going back to sleep. He needed coffee.

A breeze brought a fresh wave of the scent; was it that close or was a window open?

When he got to the coffee, Susan was there. He hadn't seen her before that, but he was preoccupied with the smell and dismissed it.

"Oh, early riser too, huh? My name's Paxton." He held his hand out and smiled.

She shook his hand and the corners of her mouth turned up slightly, hiding her smile. The smell was stronger, much stronger.

"Susan," her grip was strong. She continued, "I'm a bit wound up after what happened. I feel like I won't sleep for days."

"What happened?"

Paxton already knew what she told Dr. White, but he let her go into great detail about the attack and the chase. She showed him the many bandages as she told him about each one and if Paxton weren't so aware of every facial movement, he would have believed her.

Why was she lying and why was that smell so strong?

"Well, at least you're safe here now. There's no way any Revenant could get through the line of tanks outside."

Susan tried to hide her amusement, but Paxton saw through her false fear.

"That does make me feel better. So, what about you? Why are you here?" she asked as she moved in closer to him.

Paxton realized what she was, but he hadn't decided what to do about it. Maybe he could buy them some time and force the Revenant to face an armada of A41 tanks, "We're just visiting my Dad." *As long as they didn't send Mom and Granny.*

"Really? Is he with the military?"

"Yeah." Paxton didn't want the tanks to hurt his family, but they were Revenant and it was too late. "He's a doctor here. We're going to see him in the morning, when my friend heals up."

Paxton took a look at Terrance, sleeping soundly and still holding Sara's hand. He had to let them know, but how?

"Yep, we should be good to go in the morning." He looked back at her as he said this.

"That's excellent news," she said.

"Excellent news?"

She stuttered for a moment, stiffened and then her eyes grew slightly distant; most people wouldn't notice the difference, but Paxton had experience and saw more than the average person. He'd seen that with Jeff on the way to Haiti and with his granny and mom. He knew this meant the Controller had her.

"Excellent news that Terrance will recover so soon."

"Oh, of course."

Paxton's smile faltered. He couldn't see a lie in her face anymore, only the Controller.

"Well, I better go check on him; it was a pleasure meeting you, Susan," he walked away wondering how the Controller knew Terrance's name.

Eugene and Pasquale sat next to each other in the back seat of a Horn Rimmer, a long car that rode high off the ground and had the eight horns of a single Spider Bull lined up on the front hood. It was considered bad luck to mix the horns from several cattle or not to leave them all together.

Wayne leaned back on the second-row seat with his AA6 resting on his knee. There was plenty of room inside. Three rows of seats, the second one backwards, provided plenty of room for meetings or kidnappings.

This was not a meeting.

"So, where are we going?" Eugene asked.

Wayne looked out the window and laughed, "South."

"They're Lutadors, Eugene," Pasquale said.

"Lutadors?" Eugene pretended this was news. It was better if they didn't know how well he remembered them. "I thought you were supposed to be vigilantes who worked against the Revenant."

"We are," Wayne said.

"Then why are you kidnapping me? What do you want with me?"

Eugene felt his energy returning. Maybe he could explain it to the head of the Lutadors, if his old friend would listen.

"I'm not the one in charge. All I know is that your presence was desired in Houston, so we called in a favor from Santori. How he got you, we didn't care, as long as you were safe," Wayne said. "We do want you to stay safe, Eugene. We have big plans for you."

"But you said you didn't know what they were," Pasquale said.

"No. I said I'm not the one in charge," Wayne said as he pointed his AA6 at Pasquale. "And you're not the one we need to stay safe, so shut up."

Eugene felt his energy draining quickly.

Paxton was standing in the command tent again, sharing his plans, "General Morrison, I believe I can get the Revenant to come to us. First, we make ourselves look weak, and second, we put up with allowing five Revenant to roam within the line. Then—"

"Five? There is no way we're going to allow five Revenant in here," General Wallace said.

"They're already in Medical."

"That's impossible!" General Wallace said.

Paxton stared at him, "It's not only possible, General. It happened."

General Morrison was moving his models around on the command table and didn't look up, "So, you're suggesting we feed them false information and then make ourselves vulnerable?"

"Basically," Paxton watched General Morrison move five tanks off the line. "We'll really need to send most of our tanks out in multiple directions. They should see this as an attempt to fool them into following one set. Then, as soon as they show themselves, we pounce from both sides," Paxton said.

"What about the five already inside the line?" General Morrison said and finally looked at Paxton with no expression on his face.

"Don't you think they'll go with their brothers and fight the tanks?" General Wallace asked.

"No. They're more likely to present a unified front to attack Paxton," General Morrison said as his hand lowered toward his weapon. "We can't let them find out where your father really is, son. I hope you understand that."

General Morrison pulled his weapon. Paxton saw this and snatched it out of the General's hand. General Wallace looked at Paxton and nodded. Wallace grabbed Morrison and held him back. Paxton knew Wallace had only given them a few minutes to get their group out of the city.

As he hurried back to Terrance and Sara, Paxton heard General Morrison yell for guards behind him.

Paxton ran to the medical tent and woke Terrance and Sara. He knew Susan and the other Revenant could hear what he told them, but there was nothing he could do about it. Sara began taking Terrance's wraps off.

"Don't those need to stay on until morning?" Paxton asked.

Sara saw no doctor or nurse in the immediate area, "I hope not."

As soon as the bandages were off, Terrance massaged his jaw and said, "Me too."

They needed a way out, so they hurried toward the NJ-1300, ducking behind crates and corners. When they got there, a guard stood at each wheel of the vehicle.

"I can make them leave," Terrance said and started out from behind the crates, but Paxton held onto him.

A soldier's radio crackled, "All soldiers, be on the lookout for the visitors from last night. All of them are considered enemy combatants. Attempt to take them alive, but if that is not possible, lethal force is authorized. Some are Revenant. I repeat, some are Revenant."

The broadcast went on to assign particular groups to attack Medical and rearrange troops to make escape more difficult. Included was assigning more soldiers to the NJ-1300. Several soldiers came from nowhere to join the four at the NJ-1300.

They would have to find another vehicle.

"Some are now Revenant?" Sara asked. "They'll be gunning for us, instead of letting us turn ourselves in."

"I don't get how this could help them. They get us killed and still have five Revenant inside their line?" Terrance asked.

"I don't know; it doesn't make sense," Sara said.

"It does," Paxton said. "They figure they can take these five out with no problem, but if the Controller finds out where my Father is, they'd lose the war in a week. They probably think that if we're dead, the First Brother outside will pull back and leave the rest to fend for themselves."

"They're scared," Terrance realized.

"Yeah; that's what I said, and we are acceptable casualties. Maybe even targets."

"We can't take the jeep; they'll tear that thing apart in two minutes. We'll have to take a tank." Terrance stood as he said this.

Sara pulled him down quickly.

"You'll be seen!" she whispered.

"They're looking for him, not me."

"They're looking for all of us, Terr."

"Ok, I'll be careful."

He ducked and dodged about fifty meters to an occupied latrine and forced it open. It smelled terrible. A soldier sat inside doing his business.

"You will remove your clothes and leave them here. Afterwards, you will return to your barracks and sleep for two hours."

Terrance's voice was darker than it had ever been.

The soldier stood and removed the rest of his clothing. He streaked toward his barracks and Paxton snuck into the latrine.

"What if the soldier had been a woman?" Sara said.

"Then you'd have your uniform first," Terrance smiled.

After putting their uniforms on, the group marched toward the nearest A41. Terrance got rid of the soldiers nearby and sent three of the gunners to hide in a latrine for an hour.

"Does that mean they'll all be in the same one?" Paxton asked. "I think you need to work on your wording, Terr."

The other gunner and the driver remained under Terrance's control.

"So, where to, Paxy?" Terrance smiled.

"New York. No more stops, so I hope you all went to the bathroom," Paxton said.

"Three times."

They laughed nervously and Terrance directed the driver. The tank lurched and then raced away from the line. Immediately a voice came over the com.

"Red Five, what are you doing?"

Terrance, Paxton, and Sara tensed.

"Don't answer that yet," Terrance commanded.

Soon the com crackled again.

"Red Five, I repeat; what the hell are you doing?"

They would let this go for a little longer, but the tank was near the tree line. If the soldier on the other side of the com decided to do something about it, it could be too late.

"Captain Gniev! Turn your tank around now! That is an order."

The tank entered the trees too quickly to be stopped, but four tanks already followed in a staggered formation.

"They're going to shoot us out of here," Sara said.

"Tell me what they'll do to us, Captain Gniev," Terrance commanded.

"They will try to flank us and return us to the line. If that does not work, they will destroy us," Gniev said. He had been a tank driver for several years and was experienced with protocol as well as how to move the tank.

"Answer them, but do not tell them about us. Tell them you saw a Revenant."

Sara looked at him horrified. She worried that the driver may not be a decent liar, and now that would be the only thing that could keep them alive. Paxton, however, moved so he could read Gniev's face.

"Sorry, Antilles. I saw a Revenant in the trees checking it out now. Please have the other tanks hold their position. Gniev out."

Paxton saw nothing that gave away the captain's deception.

"Negative, Gniev. We need you to return to the line. There may be a stowaway with you. We need you to return to the line immediately. Copy?"

"Do not tell him about us. Tell him you see the Revenant now," Terrance said.

The tank was into the trees now, weaving between them.

"Negative, Antilles. We have no stowaways. We are within sight of the Revenant," Gniev said.

There was a moment of silence as Antilles tried to confirm that they were following a Revenant. When the other tanks could not confirm or deny, Antilles hopped back on the com, "Red Five, I will allow you to follow the Revenant for another five minutes. At that point, I expect verification from Red 1, 2, 3, or 4. They are assigned to assist you."

Terrance looked hard at the driver.

"Copy."

Five minutes passed quickly and Gniev was unable to shake the tanks following them. Every time he squeezed through a tight spot, the tanks made it through or found a quick way around.

The group had begun to fall behind a little, but as long as one stayed close, the others would catch up. Five minutes would not be long enough.

Captain Oliver's scouts raced to turn as many soldiers as they could, but as fast as they turned them, they were killed. The five Revenant only lasted long enough to turn eighty-three soldiers before they were overcome. No Revenant remained in the city limits, but the Controller was pleased. As each soldier was turned, he ripped all the useful knowledge he could from their minds and allowed them to mindlessly attack any other soldiers.

Knowledge of the tanks and tactics flooded Captain Oliver's mind as he raced to keep up with them and yet remain out of sight. J'Nou and Mara did the same on the other side of the group while Gail and Cynthia ran ahead to create a diversion.

The five of them would not be enough to stop even two tanks, so they had to help the group escape another way. They had not fallen for Paxton's ruse, but they would let him think they had and follow him straight to his father.

"We have twenty seconds; any ideas?" Paxton asked.

Nobody spoke up.

"Pilot Gniev, we have trees falling behind us. I think it's the Revenant. Do you want me to open fire?" the gunner, Porkins, asked.

"No, Porkins. We'll allow them to block the road behind us for now," Terrance commanded. Switching back to his normal voice, he added, "This is perfect. They'll get rid of our tails so we can get to New York."

"And they'll follow us there too. Wonderful," Paxton rolled his eyes. "What if they won't trade for him? What if they get there and take him and I lose everyone?"

"Don't worry, we'll have an A41 tank, and there are two more at the gate. It's the perfect leverage to let us get to your father first. Don't worry; everything will be fine."

"Did your aunt tell you that? Or are you guessing?"

"No, your mom did," Terrance said smiling.

Silence fell heavy inside the tank.

"I'm sorry, Paxton. I forgot. I shouldn't have said that. I think this medication... "

Terrance's pale scar flushed pink with embarrassment.

"Let's go." Paxton finally broke the silence. "I'll get to my Father before they do. And if they won't make the trade, we won't have to protect him for long."

The com remained silent.

28. Looking For Hell

A few hours later, Sara was the first to see the Statue of Liberty. While the crown and tablet were broken and damaged, the torch still reflected the morning light. It was an impressive sight, but New York's wall drew more of the group's attention.

The wall was only four stories tall, nothing like the Great Wall of Charlotte. It was also older and didn't stand nearly as high as the buildings behind it; yet it was world famous for its guards.

Volunteers manned every meter of its entire perimeter on each story with a large mounted turret. In red spray paint a famous phrase, large enough to be read from kilometers away, was written. That phrase was, "United we stand! Together *THEY* fall! Yankees stand together all!" A date, 3 May, 1971, was under it in smaller letters.

It was May Day now, nine years later. The day the entire world found out the Revenant could be dealt with.

They could be held off.

They weren't invincible.

They could fall.

It was the last day of the Revenant War, before the Controller called his Revenant home from their march across America.

People outside the city were celebrating with roasts, drinks, dancing, and singing. It was an unusual atmosphere for New York, and yet common on May Day.

With the crowd and atmosphere, Terrance realized that approaching the city in an A41 would draw a lot of attention. Even in their army clothes, they couldn't climb out of it without drawing even more attention.

Terrance commanded Gniev to let them out two kilometers from town and then to approach the wall and join the other two A41s at the gate. Terrance also instructed him to warn whoever was in charge that some Revenant followed them, "but don't tell them about us."

Terrance, Paxton, and Sara joined the flow of people entering the main gate. It was easy to enter the city.

Too easy.

This made Paxton nervous.

"All of this celebration is going to get my dad abducted. A Revenant could sneak right in here and grab him," Paxton said.

He spotted the Gate Keeper and was about to approach him when the siren sounded. People rushed inside, leaving food, drink, tables, and more outside the wall. The group watched as the main gate closed.

Gniev had completed his job.

Fillian's long, black coat dragged on the ground as he shuffled around the corner. It was barely open, and he buried his hands deep in his pockets. His eyes shifted back and forth, looking up and down the street for a mark. Then he spotted three of them walking toward him—two young men and their lady friend. He leaned back against a building and pretended not to notice them.

"Lost there, friends?" Fillian said and stepped forward to look them over as they passed.

"We're looking for Hell's Kitchen," Paxton said.

"Hell's Kitchen? Oh yeah, I know the place. I can help you with that." He opened the left side of his coat and gestured with his right hand, "I can help with other things too. I got stuff to calm you down, stuff to speed you up, stuff to help you remember, stuff to help you forget. I got stuff for when—"

"Do you know where Hell's Kitchen is or not?" Paxton asked again.

"Sure I do, I told you that. If you're going there, friend, you'll want some of this." Fillian pulled out a vial of blue liquid with what looked to them like an empty baggie taped to it. "I got some fresh Dragon Power. This stuff is the best you'll find anywhere. It'll have you more focused than ever. You know how to use it? You take this baggie—"

"He doesn't know where Hell's Kitchen is," Terrance said. He stepped up to Fillian and leaned down as he said this. He was only slightly taller than Fillian, but the effect worked.

Fillian looked at the scar on Terrance's face and wondered what could do that and who could survive it. He placed the Dragon Powder back in his jacket and shuffled his feet. "Hell's Kitchen you say?" Fillian looked around, "Nothing's free in New York, my friends." He looked back at Terrance with a little more confidence.

"How much?" Paxton asked.

Terrance stepped behind Paxton, crossed his arms, and stared at Fillian. He thought better than to use his power on the street. There were too many people out here and someone was bound to overhear it.

"Twenty Naughts."

Terrance squinted and Sara shifted to reveal her weapon. Paxton raised his eyebrows.

"Look, twenty Naughts and I walk you there myself." Fillian looked across the street and put his arm around Paxton, "Come on. I'll take you to the gate."

"The gate?" Paxton asked.

"Hey! You! Fillian, you thieving bastard! Give me my money!" The man who said this came at them from across the street. His hair was hard and spiked up. He wore a white wife-beater, jeans, and dark sunglasses. The five men behind him wore similarly tight, black T-shirts, wife-beaters, or sleeveless shirts.

Terrance uncrossed his arms and Sara reached for her weapons. Paxton eyed the group and reached for his weapon too.

"Who are your new friends? They haven't met the Impact yet, have they?" The Impact lifted his shirt and motioned to his abs. "Fillian owes the Impact some money, don't ya? So, who are they?"

"Listen, I just need some info out of this guy; then we'll get out of your way," Paxton said.

"Information? What sort of information do you have, Fillian?

Your daughter been speaking in her sleep again?" He took another step toward the group. "Come on, you're making the Impact angry."

Paxton noticed a crowd watching them. More and more people gathered and stopped, waiting to see what happened.

"What does he owe you... sorry. I missed your name," Terrance said.

The man looked at Terrance and stared at the scar. The men behind him tensed and readied themselves to grab their weapons.

"I'm the Impact. And he owes the Impact one hundred Naughts," he turned to Fillian. "You have one day left before the Impact brings his posse after your daughter."

"You can't take my daughter, Impact, please. I beg you. Just give me a couple more days," Fillian dropped to his knees.

Terrance was about to use his voice but he felt something. Like someone listening in on him. He looked around and spotted someone wearing goggles and staring at him.

"We'll cover him," Paxton said.

That got Terrance's attention again. Paxton reached into his pocket and the Impact's posse tensed even more. They relaxed as he pulled out several Naughts and Draughts. He handed the Impact one hundred Naughts worth.

"Now you leave," Terrance said as he took a step forward.

"You have some good friends here, Fillian," the Impact didn't look away from Terrance. "The Impact would keep them around."

They walked away and the crowd dispersed. Fillian looked at them with tears in his eyes, "I owe you so much. My daughter... she's all I have now." Fillian grabbed Paxton's legs. "I promise I'll pay you back. Anything."

"Don't deal with *the Impact* anymore. Men like that are only trouble. You have a daughter to think about; take care of her and stop selling those drugs," Sara said.

"I promise."

"And bring us to Hell's Kitchen," Paxton said.

"Ok," Fillian kicked the ground, "The truth is I can bring you to Hell's Gates, but Hell's broken up; I can't go in with you to Hell's Kitchen. It's too dangerous and I need to get back to my daughter."

Fillian led the group to Hell's Gates before leaving to take care of his daughter. He thanked them several times and promised he'd find a way to repay them.

The group walked between the open two-story metal doors. Each one was attached to a building and marked the entrance to Hell, a Manhattan borough.

"All I know is that he has an apartment here. I don't know exactly where it is," Paxton said. "We should be able to find Hell's Kitchen from here, though. How big can Hell be?"

Paxton smiled at Terrance as he said that.

"Looking for something, you say?" an old woman nobody had noticed scratched her head spreading dust with the rags on her arms and shedding dandruff like snow. "It's so hard to remember something on an empty stomach." Her stomach growled, as if on command.

They knew they were being played, but took one look at each other and nodded. Sara nudged Terrance and he pulled out five Naughts, but Paxton stopped him.

"First, where is it?" Paxton asked.

Her excitement and desperation turned to hesitation.

"What's wrong, old woman? Don't you know where it is?" Sara asked.

"I do," she said.

"Then what's the problem? Tell us and we'll give you the money," Sara said. "You want to eat, don't you?"

"Well, you see. It's, uh, kind of, uh, here."

"Here? We're in Hell's Kitchen? This run-down part of Hell?" Paxton asked.

She nodded to each question and then pointed to the gates, "Those are Hell's Gates and everything inside them is Hell's Kitchen... Can I still have my money, sir? That could feed me for a week."

"Sure, if you answer one more question."

"Please, sir, I'll try, but this time, uh, the money first?"

Terrance handed her the money.

"If she doesn't answer... " Paxton looked at the old woman closely.

Terrance nodded.

"I'll answer. I promise. I just need to eat." Fear filled her eyes now.

Paxton saw his granny in her and shook his head to clear it, "Ok, ma'am, have you heard of Eugene?"

"Eugene?" her eyes brightened. "Yeah, uh, he's that nice, quiet, old man. Always keeps to himself and his work, but he, uh, sometimes gives me a Naught." She scratched her cheek and skin flaked off. She looked at her fingers and flicked off the skin. "I think he lives in these apartments over here."

She shambled down the street, avoiding the trash and people. There was barely more grime on the streets than on her, and as she walked, the smell of urine and dirty hair filled everyone's noses. Paxton was certain the smell increased the more she moved.

She stopped at the second building on her right. They didn't even cross a street to get to it. She opened the door and said, "In here. He lived in this building. I don't know what room or floor, but I do know you need to be careful." She lowered her head and voice. "The Five Points have moved in there."

"Five Points?" Sara asked.

"Let's just go. They can't be as bad as the Revenant," Terrance said.

Terrance started into the building, but Paxton put out his arm to stop him, "You've never heard of the Five Points, have you Terrance?"

He shook his head.

"Well, they'll slit Sara's throat just to see you flinch, and then do worse to her lifeless body. That's after they cut off your eyelids so you see all of it. So, let's not underestimate them, ok?"

Terrance nodded.

The old woman turned to walk away, but Terrance stopped her, "Here. Thank you," he smiled and handed her another five Naughts.

They entered the building slowly. Paxton was in front with Sara behind him and Terrance was in back. Graffiti decorated the walls and everything smelled almost as bad as the old woman. Paxton didn't know what to do, but he was determined to find his father.

"Should we knock on some doors and ask about him?" Sara cocked a shotgun.

"I don't know what else we can do. I'll be ready in case we run into any trouble," Terrance said.

"So will I," Paxton toasted with his gun and walked down a hall to the first door. He stood in front of it and brought his fist up to knock, but Terrance stopped him.

He furrowed his eyebrows and pushed Paxton to the side of the door. Sara and he stood on the other side while Paxton knocked on the door.

No one answered.

He leaned in and listened closely. He couldn't hear any movement, so they moved on to the next door. They continued like this down the hall.

The first floor was empty.

So was the second.

They climbed the stairs to the third floor and opened the doors. As they looked down the hall, Paxton heard a door shut. He also caught a strong smell of sulfur. They continued down the hall, knocking on doors. The sulfur smell increased until they were drowning in the stench. Finally, someone answered.

"We already paid you. We can't afford more. Please go," a voice said.

"We're not looking for money," Paxton said.

Terrance and Sara watched down opposite sides of the hall, holding their noses, as Paxton spoke.

"Who are you? Five Points protect us. We safe." The voice was slightly muffled from behind the door.

"We're looking for a man; maybe you could help me," Paxton said. "His name is Eugene."

There was a stir and feet approached the door.

"Who you, that look for him?" a deeper voice said.

"I'm his son."

The door cracked open and an older man, Richard, looked out. "Ahhh. Yes. I see it. You have his eyes," he said. "You welcome here. Come in."

The three went inside the room, and Richard leaned out to

look up and down the hall. In addition to Richard, an older woman and two kids, each wearing a gas mask, were in the room.

"Name Richard. And you?" he took Paxton's hand.

"Paxton. This is Terrance and Sara."

He nodded. He motioned for them to sit on an old sofa and he sat in a large chair next to them. He did not introduce his family. His wife and kids removed their gas masks and hurried into the bedroom.

The three remained standing.

"We really just want to find my father. If you could tell us what room he's in, I'd appreciate it."

"His apartment next door."

Paxton began to turn to the door and thank Richard.

"But that won't help you, Paxton" Richard said.

Paxton turned back and waited for more. Richard motioned toward the couch again, and this time the group sat down.

"He gone," Richard said. "He been missing for more than a week now. It not odd for him to lock himself in room for days, but he always came over on Sunday nights for dinner.

"He hasn't been here the last two Sunday; nor have we seen him come and go," Richard said.

"The smell made my wife think he dead," Richard continued. "I don't smell, so I don't know, but I see you smell it. Anyway, I go next door and find only dead animals and a large egg. I try to clean it up, but apparently, it still smell. He nowhere in there."

Richard paused for a moment and looked at each of them.

"You drink something."

"No, thank you," Sara said.

The other two shook their heads.

"Not much else, except give you this key to his room. He left me with spare. Oh! Also, I tell you one more thing. He spent some night at Caf down street."

"Thank you," Paxton said.

The group accepted an invitation to dinner. It was Spider Beef Roast, corn, and potatoes. Terrance and Sara helped Richard's wife and children set the table while Paxton and Richard carved the roast.

"Excellent dinner, ma'am," Terrance said with his mouth full.

"Thank you," she said. "Your father not much of a talker, but we gathered that he doing something about Revenant. Sometimes he talk about how he had to take care of the problem, almost like he felt guilty about it. He always just a little crazy." She took another bite and blushed. "Always kind, though, so we listened politely."

"Yeah, he's quiet like that. We ran into a few Revenant on the way here. Terrance's scar there is from one," Paxton said, directing the discussion away from his father. "He threw a rock at Terrance and sliced his cheek all the way through. He had a mouth flap all the way up to here." Using his finger, Paxton drew a line from the corner of his mouth up to his ear.

The children dropped their forks and turned pale.

"I don't think that's the right kind of talk at a dinner table, Paxton," Sara said. "What were you thinking?"

"Sorry, ma'am. I just... I guess I'm not used to being around young children."

Richard calmed the children and got them to pick up their forks and begin eating again. For the rest of the meal, the conversation remained awkward.

29. Raising Hell

After dinner, the group went to Eugene's apartment to stay the night. They found many empty cages with rat droppings, a bloody jar, and a large, blue, gooey mess.

"It smells way worse in here; maybe we should get a room somewhere?" Terrance asked.

Paxton rolled his eyes, "If I can put up with it, I think you can, Terr."

Terrance glared at him and Paxton laughed.

"That must have been the egg," Sara said.

"Dragon's egg by the look of it," Paxton said.

"Dragon's egg? What would your dad do with that and where would he get it?"

Paxton snuffed and walked to the bedroom.

"Look, Paxton," Terrance placed himself in Paxton's path. "You may blame your father for what happened to your mom, but it's not his fault."

Paxton narrowed his eyes. Terrance continued anyway, "Don't squint at me, you pompous ass! It's the Revenant's fault this happened. It's my grandfather's fault."

Paxton's mouth dropped and he stared at Terrance.

"I was going to tell you before, but I never had the chance. He's the one who sent them after your family, and he should be the one you want to kill. You can't give your dad to him."

"Lot of good that would do me, Terr," Paxton said. "There's no way we can get to him. My dad, on the other hand... " Paxton stopped. Tears welled in his eyes. He wiped them away and stiffened.

"My dad is already dead to me. I'll trade his life for Mom and Granny. If they don't accept the deal, I'll make sure they can't have him; then I will find every other scientist who had clearance to EA51."

He moved around Terrance.

"Stop and face me," Terrance said darkly.

Paxton turned immediately to face him. Hatred was in Paxton's eyes.

"I could command you not to do it. And don't think I won't do it, if I have to."

"Then I'll have to take you out of the equation. You won't deny me the only chance to get them back. I don't care if you're the Controller's grandson."

Paxton went to the bedroom, slamming the door.

Several tanks were gone and fires burned in the Capital City. Cedric stood watch from his tower, carefully watching the horizon for any movement. As he watched the trees, his eyes began to feel heavy, so he wiped the binoculars and set them down. Then, reaching for his coffee, he felt wind, and a blur stopped in front of him.

It was a man.

A naked, tanned man.

He had brown hair and stood Cedric's height. He was fit and hungry. He looked like he wanted to eat Cedric.

Cedric realized too late what it was. It wasn't a man, it was a Revenant. It sniffed the air and jumped off the tower, running through the camp, in and out of tents, until finally it leapt over the line of tanks and took off North.

The next morning, Sara woke up a little stiff. She had commanded all rats and insects out of the apartment. It took a few hours to make sure she had sent everything out, but it was worth it. Sleeping on the couch was safe thanks to her, but that hadn't made it comfortable.

Paxton stormed out of his room as Terrance stood up. Nearly

walking into him, Terrance moved just out of the way. Without turning, he said, "I'm going to the Net Cafe."

"We're coming too," Terrance said.

Paxton whirled on him and stared up into his face.

"You ever do that to me again, and I'll kill you," Paxton said.

"I'm not going to apologize, Paxton," he said. "You were acting like an ass, and if you continue to do so, I'll continue to practice on you."

"Boys, please. Apologize to each other. Paxton was an ass and you *controlled* him. You both were wrong; now grow up," Sara stared at the two.

Paxton picked up his bag and walked around Terrance who dropped his shoulders, picked up his own bag, and followed Paxton out the door. Sara shook her head and followed behind Terrance.

The Net Cafe wasn't far from the apartment, and they found a table near the stage right away. They ordered breakfast while a tall Russian in metallic goggles leaned against the wall watching them.

Paxton waved the waitress over and they ordered drinks. When she brought them back, Paxton asked her a question. "Ma'am, may I ask you: Do you know a Eugene?"

"Eugene?" she said. "Eugene, no; don't think I've heard that name before."

"Thanks," Sara said. "How are we supposed to find him?"

Paxton scowled and stared at the Russian. Terrance told him about the person he'd seen with goggles when they met Fillian; now Paxton wondered if this was a coincidence and kept his eyes on the goggled Russian.

Nearby a large man in a leather jacket stood and walked toward them. He had a Hell's Angels Director's insignia tattooed on his neck.

"Did I hear you asking for a Eugene?"

Paxton was on his feet in a second and Terrance was close behind. Paxton was almost a foot shorter than the Director, but Terrance matched his size easily.

"Sit down, now," the man said calmly.

His eyes darted toward a group of Hell's Angels in the corner. They were paying very close attention.

Paxton and Terrance sat down, leaning away from the Director. They gestured to the empty chair between them and across from Sara. As he sat, the Director made a small movement behind his back with his left hand; Paxton noticed that his friends relaxed.

"Yeah, we were asking about Eugene. What do you know about him?" Paxton asked.

"Not too loud," the Director said. "First of all, who are you?"

"I should be asking that about you, Director."

The Director stared at him. Paxton saw that Terrance was about to open his mouth. He looked at the Russian and then back at the Hell's Angels in the corner. On top of that, the Net Cafe was getting busy.

Nobody needed to know what Terrance could do, yet.

"I'm his son, Paxton. Now, who are you?"

Terrance closed his mouth and looked at Paxton.

"I thought so. I'm Bruce... the guy who kidnapped him."

Captain Oliver was in a foul mood; he didn't like it when the Controller kept him from what he wanted.

J'Nou was standing beside him overlooking New York. They heard the siren and saw the gates shut. There was no scout inside the city that they could use; they knew this was where Eugene was and they needed to get inside.

The Controller, Captain Oliver, J'Nou, and the other First Brothers had discussed what to do. The Controller led and moderated this discussion, passing along pros and cons to the plan, but after allowing Captain Oliver's plan to be executed in the Capital City, he wouldn't budge concerning a full-scale assault on New York until Eugene's location had been confirmed.

J'Nou proposed a compromise and everyone agreed; the two First Brothers would get ten more Revenant, all former soldiers, and be allowed to make a minor assault to try and draw out Eugene. Captain Oliver also converted some animals as backup.

When the Revenant arrived the next morning, the army

consisted of the two First Brothers, Mara, Gail, Cynthia, the ten Revenant soldiers, and several Revenant animals including alligators, black bears, two sasquatches, and many smaller animals. Captain Oliver's pet, Alexander, was among them.

"You're sure you can keep this many animals under control?" Mara asked.

"He can. And when we get near the humans, he won't need to. They smell much more appetizing than we do," J'Nou laughed.

Cynthia and Gail snickered, but Captain Oliver was not in a laughing mood. He leapt onto a high branch in a tree next to him. He was thirty meters off the ground and watching the sun coming up over the Statue of Liberty.

"We attack at nightfall," Captain Oliver said.

Paxton's eyes flared and nothing stopped Terrance from forcing Bruce to tell them what he meant, using no words.

"I brought him to the Italians in Chicago, a guy named Santori. Met him behind a restaurant. I can give you directions," Bruce didn't want to give up so much, but couldn't keep from telling them more.

It continued to pour out of him, "They had my daughter. Nobody knows about her, but they found out and took her. I had to bring him there to get her back. Now that she's safe, though, I've given you all the information I could."

"Thanks; that was helpful," Terrance squinted at the man.

Paxton and Sara realized what Terrance had done, and neither of them had heard him speak. Paxton knew he hadn't said a word.

"How did you do that?" Bruce asked.

He looked at each of them and seethed. Paxton, Terrance, and Sara looked at each other innocently. Bruce calmed down, but only a little, "Ok, so now you know. I kinda liked the guy. We talked and had a lot in common. He was trying to stop the Revenant to save his son and wife; I guess that's you and your mom," he said and looked at Paxton.

"You look a lot like him and must have got your smarts from him too," he continued. "Look, I'm not going to tell you what to do, but if you want my advice, don't go after him. The Mafia isn't in this for themselves. There's some other group that wants him and if you go, it may be more trouble than you can handle.

"I promised him that if I ran into you or your Mom, I'd let you know what happened. That's it, though. I have nothing else."

"Thanks for the information," Paxton said.

The three stood and left the table. Paxton was more determined than ever as he walked out the door.

Sara whispered in Terrance's ear, "Do you believe him?"

"Paxton did," Terrance said and looked at Sara. "Thank you, Sara. For coming with us and helping me."

Sara blushed and looked down. The group left the Net Café.

"We're leaving for Chicago tonight," Paxton said.

They were not leaving for Chicago tonight.

30. Delayed Travel

"**A**re these the ones?" a scrawny man with thick, taped glasses asked.

"Yeah, it's that one there. The pale one," Gniev identified Paxton. Gniev was the driver of the A41 the group had hijacked.

"I thought you told him not to tell anyone," Paxton said.

"I did," Terrance said. "I guess it's not permanent."

The little guy held out a box. The lid had a hinge which he held toward himself as he opened the lid toward the group. The sound it emitted knocked them out, and the meeting was over before any of them knew what was happening.

Paxton woke sharply and remembered everything. He was bound to a chair in a dark room with the scrawny man, the driver, and a larger man who remained beside him, "What's this? A—"

He was promptly hit and quieted by the larger silent man.

"I'll ask you a question when I want you to speak, pale boy," the scrawny man turned to Gniev and asked, "How many were following him?"

"At least three; there may have been more, but I think our boys in the Capital City took care of those."

"So, you led them to us, huh?" the scrawny man said. He walked up to Paxton and leaned into his face.

"We didn't mean to," Paxton spit blood. "If you let us go, we'll lead the Revenant to Chicago. You won't have to worry about them at all."

"You think we want you to bring them there?" the scrawny man puffed up and looked out a window at the Statue of Liberty, "We're not cowards. We're the Yankees and we'll handle them here, but since you brought them here, you get to help." He turned back toward Paxton and smiled.

"But you don't understand. They're not even looking for me. They're looking for my father, but we can't let them find him."

"Why?"

Paxton paused. He didn't want to tell anyone, but he couldn't let his father be captured. He knew too much. *Which is worse?*

"Well? I'm not a patient man, and neither is my large friend here. Why?"

Paxton knew it was more dangerous to hide the reason than to share it. "He was one of the scientists who created the Revenant. They would use him to make themselves stronger or more powerful," Paxton said. "If he's captured by them, we'll all have much more to worry about than a handful of *these* Revenant."

The scrawny man paused. He walked over to a tall Russian with metal goggles that Paxton had not noticed before now. He knew he'd had a bad feeling about that Russian. Neither of them said anything; yet the little man nodded and approached Paxton again.

"Yet you want to turn him over to them? Why?" the scrawny man asked.

Paxton was deflated. How could they know that? Did Terrance or Sara tell them?

"No, they sleep. They are far too dangerous awake, particularly your comrade, Terrance," the Russian spoke in her broken English.

A woman? This surprised Paxton, though he'd never seen her move and she was covered from head to toe in leather and gadgets. "Great. You can read my mind, I suppose. You're one of those super freaks from Chernobyl, huh?"

The large man hit him again.

"He told you not to speak unless you answer us. Now, he ask you question," the goggled Russian had taken over the interrogation, and the scrawny man sat back watching.

"Shouldn't you already know?" It was pointless to even consider lying with her in the room, so he spilled it, "My mother and granny were infected. They're out there now and I wanted to trade him for them. I know a way they can be free from the Controller."

"And you wish to trade dead man for this?"

Paxton was stunned.

"Oh, you did not know that your father was killed?"

"You're lying." Paxton couldn't believe this. He wanted the honor of killing his father *after* he got the rest of his family back.

"The Lutadors, from what I *heard*. They did not want the Controller to get his hands on such impressive mind." The Russian woman turned back to the scrawny man, "We have all we will get from him; we can hang them now."

Eugene sat in a soft chair. It would have been comfortable if the suede didn't stick to his skin. Pasquale was more comfortable standing behind Eugene.

They were alone in a room overlooking the city from the twentieth floor of Lutador Tower. The view would have been nice, if not for the black smoke that rose from the many vehicles and buildings. The technology of the Lutadors, created to fight the Revenant, also invaded everyday life here and left the city looking like a large black tar pit with shining lights in it.

"What do you think they want from me?" Eugene asked.

"I don't know," Pasquale said. "Maybe they want you to help their fight with the Revenant."

"You're so optimistic. They could have talked to me if that's all they wanted. Maybe sent me a letter or messenger."

A large, tan man in a chair rolled in. The chair was black with smoke rolling out the back. It had pipes that ran around it in a dizzying maze delivering power to the thick, metal wheels. He wore a large, yellow hat, and his legs were gone from the knees down, but Eugene recognized him from EA-51. James Monroe.

"We didn't think you would listen," James said.

"You should have tried me, James" Eugene didn't get up or turn his head toward James. He watched him only through the reflection on the window.

"We need your help and expertise, Eugene. We have a couple of projects that have, well, stalled."

"And you think I'll help you kill our victims?" Eugene said. He stood and faced James. "After what we've done to them? I know what you and the Lutadors *do* here, James."

"Our victims? You still view them like that?" James laughed softly and powered his chair closer to Eugene. "After all of the attacks and deaths and the collapse of everything that was the great United States of America, you think they're our victims? After the Farms, Eugene! You couldn't be more wrong."

James moved his chair in front of Eugene and pressed a button. His chair unfolded upwards, placing James at Eugene's eye level. The wheels split apart further to balance the chair, and pipes shifted to continue powering them and the gears that were now balancing it. James stared him in the eyes, unblinking, "They're our greatest enemy."

"I'm wrong? You were there. We caused this and we should be fixing it, not exterminating them like some pests." Eugene was angry now and clenched his jaw. "Are we not to blame for their existence?"

"Technically? Yes. But they're so powerful and well organized, and murderous. Oh," James spun his chair to face away from Eugene and drove it toward the window, "and *mindless*. Can't forget that one. They must take responsibility for what they've become. We *are* to blame for their existence, and we should fix it," he spun his chair back to look at Eugene. "Especially Bonifacy."

"The Controller is probably our greatest ally."

"Ally?"

"If it weren't for him, we'd be neck deep in dead bodies and Revenant. He keeps *them* under control."

"Yeah, under *his* control. He sent one to Charlotte just to make a point. And I got it," James was pacing with his wheelchair. "He attacked innocent people in my home town, just to tell me that he's got the upper hand. And then, what he did to my brother and his family... and my niece was there, watching... As soon as he's ready, he'll come for us. There's no other option. We have to go after him first and that's what I was talking about. We've run into some trouble, old friend."

"I'm no mechanical engineer like you, James. I doubt I can help you."

"No, you're not. But you are the best damn chemist and DNA manipulator in the world."

He lowered his chair to ground level.

"We've been working on a suit to create an ultimate soldier to battle the Revenant."

James paused to gauge Eugene's reaction. Eugene sighed and looked down, shaking his head.

"James, we tried this before."

"This is different. The suit connects to the very DNA of its wearer, but it also has an override code and can be shut down remotely without affecting the wearer. The problem is that they're not working right and that's where you come in. You can help us improve the connection and communication between the user and the suit. We need them to anticipate the user's movements and enhance them. We've also been trying to develop a serum to prevent rejection, but so far that's not working."

"This is a bad idea, James. I think you should walk away from it. Powered up people with suits that tap into their very being. I don't think it's a good idea. Have you thought about what powers this would give a speaker or seer or even a mutant? How long before we're talking about the threat from the cyborgs?" Eugene prepared himself to leave. "I'm going back to New York to heal these people. They deserve that, not genocide."

James' bodyguards raised their pistols at Eugene.

"I'm afraid I can't walk away from it, Eugene. And I can't let you, either."

Eugene was tired of the whole situation. He walked toward the window. Looking over the city, he made a decision.

By tomorrow, he would be on his way home.

The wall around New York was only four stories high, but Paxton decided that it seemed much higher when one was being dangled by their feet high above it. They were each tied to one of the eight protrusions arching out from the top of the wall, just above the main gate.

Paxton, Terrance, and Sara were all hanging upside down from their own rope. The Yankees drugged them and hung them there. The drugs wore off quickly, but Sara had fallen back into unconsciousness from being up there, and Terrance was almost unconscious again. Paxton could feel the blood pooling in his head and knew he was slipping back into oblivion.

The sun was almost down over the horizon, and Paxton could see the Revenant Army congregating in the distance. He was surprised to see animals there with them.

Many animals.

Or were those spots from the blood pooling in his head?

No, he was sure they were animals.

These animals were lined up as if they were trained, but he didn't know of any alligators or sasquatches that could be trained like that, nor bears, or panthers.

Terrance finally closed his eyes. Paxton could hear his heart still beating, along with Sara's. Both were slowing, though.

Suddenly he saw a blur out of the corner of his eye, faster than anything he'd seen before. The blur moved toward the city wall. Weapons along the wall aimed toward the blur. Paxton knew that if he couldn't make it out, it was likely they didn't know what to do about it.

The blur ran up the wall and pushed off of it toward Sara.

She fell toward the ground, stopping when the blur caught her. Suddenly he wasn't a blur, though, and Paxton gave into the blackness as he recognized Jeff.

Jeff wore a DC soldier's uniform that had the name *Cedric* on the front pocket.

Jeff sat Sara down and ran back toward the wall leaping and grabbing Terrance next. Finally, he got Paxton down.

Once they were all down, Jeff picked up Terrance and Sara and jogged back toward the city gates. Paxton followed, unable to keep up. They weren't getting in this way, though.

"What happened? I thought you were dead," Paxton said.

"Yeah, well, whatever that guy did to change himself bled over into me and helped me heal. Don't really know any specifics, but we can talk about it later. They're coming," Jeff nodded toward the trees.

Paxton looked where Jeff indicated and could see the line of animals approaching. The people could barely be seen behind them as the sun set. Terrance's eyes opened and he began to regain consciousness. With Sara still unconscious and with no way inside, though, they were in immediate danger.

As Paxton tried to wake Sara, Terrance stared at Jeff who just smiled back.

"Is there anything you can do for her?" Jeff asked Terrance.

Terrance looked at Sara and struggled to be fully awake. Then he licked his lips and moved them.

"Wake up," he whispered darkly.

Sara opened her eyes and saw the approaching animals.

31. May Day

T ed rushed down the street toward the gate. He'd spent the last hour preparing his wife and kids and boarding up their apartment. The Yankees' call to defend the city came suddenly, and he didn't know if he'd be back for them. Most people knew about the criminals currently hung as offerings to the Revenant, but nobody suspected that an army of Revenant animals would approach the city.

He ran toward the wall without looking down. His focus was on the gate, less than a mile away. This time he would defend his town, like his father did nine years ago. His father died as a hero during Yankee victory on May Day—Barry Nugent, Hero of the Great Battle of New York, but Ted would return to his family alive.

He would see his children get married.

He would meet his grandchildren.

He would come home a hero.

He was a minute away from the gate, and it was the only thing on his mind, so he didn't watch where he stepped. He stumbled and nearly fell.

He looked down and saw a large rat under his feet.

Why is it running toward danger? Wouldn't it smell the Revenant and go the other way?

He began to run again and tripped.

He looked and saw more rats, some the size of small dogs. Then he looked behind him and across the street. He saw what he estimated to be every rat in the city, as well as every cat and dog, a few snakes, at least one gerbil, a turtle, and a small group of white mice. All were running toward the gate.

What the hell?

The line of Revenant animals approached, but Sara faced the city, hands up and head down, concentrating. Terrance looked beyond the Revenant animals to find the human ones while Paxton looked for his family. Jeff waited for a signal from Terrance.

Terrance glanced at the Sasquatches and nodded to Jeff. He ran off toward them and jumped at the first one, landing on its shoulders. He yanked at its head and could hear the tendons in its neck stretching.

The Sasquatch reached up and grabbed him. They struggled for a moment until they heard the first of the guns warming up on the wall. Jeff jumped down, and they both ran as the gunfire began.

Sasquatches weren't nearly as intelligent as humans, but it wasn't difficult for one to recognize the sounds of war.

The wall guns opened fire on the entire crowd of Revenant and animals. The two A41 tanks drove out to the line, on opposite sides and each took out a swath of alligators. Their low position, large size, and relatively slow movement made them an easy target for the machines, which were built to take out small, quick, human Revenant.

Good, thought Jeff as he easily stayed ahead of the guns. *I hate alligators.*

Jeff turned to look at the gate. He heard creaking and scratching. Gnashing and chewing sounds joined in. Then holes began to appear along the bottom of the gate. Rats, cats, and dogs all poured through the holes onto the battlefield.

Sara turned to face the Revenant and stuck her arms out to her sides, looking up. The animals congregated around her and the wall guns stopped. She then moved her arms forward and glared at the Revenant Army. Her animals ran forward, outnumbering the Revenant by more than a hundred to one.

The Yankee volunteers were mesmerized by this animal war. The alligators and bears swallowed many rats whole. The

Sasquatch that Jeff did not have chasing him picked up a dog and broke it in half. Then Sara felt it. The first one had turned Revenant.

It was a rat. In seconds, Sara could feel the difference and tried to use this feeling to affect the other Revenant animals. She tried first with the small black bear she could see running at her, and it paused, as if trying to decide what to do. Then it looked behind itself, then forward again. The bear clawed the ground and shook its head; then it snapped its eyes directly to Sara and ran straight for her.

Captain Oliver smiled as he saw the animals leave the city. *More for me to play with.* He directed most of the animals to quickly kill the pests, but then a rat was turned by accident, and he knew that was the turning point.

He would take control of all of the animals and turn them against this girl.

Who does she think she is? She can't compete with—

Then he felt it. She took control of a Revenant bear and was turning it back toward him.

She's good...

He focused his will on this bear and turned it toward her. He warped its mind to notice only her and desire her flesh.

I may have to be careful with Paxton and Terrance, but not you, little girl.

Terrance could do nothing with the animals, but there were human Revenant in the Army somewhere; he just had to find them. While Paxton looked for his mother and granny, he pointed out the other human Revenant as he saw them.

Terrance focused. He needed to be prepared to turn them all at once and with the Controller's presence still there, it wouldn't be easy.

Finally, Paxton said, "That's all the regular Revenant I see, but there's still no sign of anyone I recognize."

Terrance focused on all of them and spoke in a dark voice

that was heard by everyone in the city, "Revenant, return to the Controller immediately."

The human Revenant stopped. They looked directly at Terrance, then back toward EA 51. Terrance didn't want them to be destroyed; when he controlled them, he could feel more than just the Revenant people saw. Despite his wishes, stationary Revenant were tempting targets. A few fell to gunners on the wall; then one by one, the rest turned to retreat, but that's when Terrance felt the Controller, his grandfather.

And he felt Terrance.

The human Revenant slowed and turned back. They ignored Paxton and Terrance and went straight toward an A41.

Terrance collapsed. He barely held his eyes open and felt a pressure in his mind, telling him to sleep. The weight was like the whole universe sitting on his eyelids and all he heard in his head was, *You're safe, my boy. Go to sleep. I will protect you.*

Jeff was back on the Sasquatch's shoulders, trying to wrestle it to the ground. Jeff could only match its strength but was much faster.

He swung down and around the mammoth ape's back. It stood twice his height, with shaggy hair that he used to climb around its body. Dropping down to its left side, he swung behind it and wrapped his left leg around the Sasquatch's left leg, locking it. Then, with his other leg, he kicked behind its right knee.

The Sasquatch fell on its face.

He climbed up its back, grabbing its head and pulled back as the Sasquatch reached for Jeff's arms. That's when he heard Sara scream.

"There's no way I'm doing this, Pasquale," Eugene said. "I'm working on a drug we can use to restore their humanity. I'm not going to help kill innocent victims. I've made up my mind; I'm returning to New York."

"And how are you going to do that, Eugene?" Pasquale asked.

Eugene looked out the window.

"Well, we can't go out here." He turned to smile at Pasquale.

"A little high for that. I may have an idea, though. You come. Stand behind the door here. When I have the guards distracted, you go."

"Won't they notice I'm not in here?"

Pasquale walked over to the bathroom door and shut it, "You're not to be disturbed."

"This couldn't possibly work. They'll catch me."

"Trust me, Eugene."

Eugene moved behind the door, eyeing Pasquale who opened it and asked the guards to come in. They came into the room, only slightly suspicious.

"I need one of you guys to help me move some of this. Eugene's a bit particular about where his furniture is and which way it faces. Since his trip to the Japanese Empire, he's always talking about Feng Shui this and Feng Shui that. If we leave the couch facing the wrong way, he could jump out the window."

The two guards looked at each other.

"Where *is* Eugene?" the first guard asked.

Pasquale pointed to the bathroom door. "I wanted to get this room fixed before he comes out."

The second guard shrugged at the first.

"Alright, what do we need to move?"

Pasquale led them to help him with the couch while the second guard watched the bathroom with his back to the door and Eugene snuck out.

"Wait here," Jeff slammed the Sasquatch's head into the ground and jumped off its back. He then ran toward Sara and spotted the Revenant bear running toward her.

She strained to get control of it again, but couldn't. She was too scared to focus, and Captain Oliver was too strong for her.

The bear was feet from her and in a full run. It leapt into the air, flying toward her. Suddenly it went sideways.

Jeff slammed into the side of the beast pinning it to the ground. He wrestled with it, trying to get a solid grip on one arm. He almost had it; then Jeff yanked and heard the bear's shoulder pop.

The bear was angry now. Its other paw swung around and swiped at Jeff; its claw tore into his shoulder and sliced tendon and muscle. Jeff's right arm hung limp at his side.

Pushing with his legs and pulling with his left arm, he popped the bear's injured arm off completely. The ripping sound brought bile to Sara's throat.

The beast thrashed wildly and rolled over, almost throwing Jeff off. He whipped around and grabbed the other arm. The bear clawed and bit at Jeff. It dug its teeth into his shoulder and tore at his good arm. Struggling, Jeff ripped the bear's other arm off.

Sara focused and realized that Jeff needed her; he had one arm left, but it was in the bear's mouth. Her mind blazed as she came to. She commanded the bear to let go and it opened its mouth.

Jeff took advantage. He yanked his arm out of the bear's mouth. Then he grabbed inside its mouth with his good hand and wedged his right foot on the bear's shoulder. He kicked as hard as he could, ripping the bear's head off just below the brain stem.

"Twice in one day, Sara. You need to be more careful." He winked and decided to have a quick snack; he needed to heal.

Five of the Revenant soldiers ran toward one of the A41 tanks. The human soldiers inside it were ready and opened fire at them, but the Revenant split up and moved faster, two heading to the right, two to the left and one straight on, leaping.

The guns swung up and split their fire. The bullets trailed just behind the Revenant, but the tank pulled backwards and spun quickly. It moved faster than the Revenant anticipated, causing the leaping Revenant to land just short of the tank.

With one knee and one hand on the ground, the middle Revenant snarled at the tank.

The tank continued its spin toward the left group of Revenant. The two Revenant soldiers leapt in the air, aiming to land on the tank. One of them was split in half and torn apart as the incendiary rounds exploded through its body.

The other one landed on the tank where it could not be shot.

The designers never planned for Revenant to make it past the four guns, leaving the top of the tank open for attack. The guns could not swivel to shoot the Revenant off the tank.

It was the only blind spot.

Fortunately for the current occupants, the first soldiers to test the tank designed something to remedy the situation. A metal mesh was woven onto the top of the tank along with debris and other camouflage. This mesh was wired to a neutronian power source in the base of the tank.

The Revenant that landed on the tank was shocked with thousands of volts of electricity and jumped back off the tank as fast as it landed.

In midair it fell unconscious and landed flat near the two Revenant on the other side of the tank. The voltage couldn't kill a Revenant, and it began to wake up quickly, but just as it woke up, one of the turrets turned and fired. The other two scattered before the bullets left the barrel, but the sleepy one took an explosive round between the eyes.

The remaining three Revenant grouped together as they moved, and one of them took a leap at the tank. It didn't try to land on the tank, instead aiming for the front right turret. It grabbed the turret and pulled up to bend it.

The Death Metal it was made of had a very special coating. Regular paint would not stick to the precious metal, but this spray-on alloy made it look like any other painted metal. The barrel easily bent under the pressure from the Revenant, but the moment it held the barrel tortured every Revenant in America. The Controller immediately withdrew his presence from his family of Revenant and Terrance.

The tank made quick work of the two Revenant writhing on the ground. The incendiary round trying to exit the bent barrel exploded, damaging the tank and the Revenant that bent it.

The tank would make it to be repaired; the Revenant would not.

Terrance sat up as the Controller lost his grip. He knew what had happened. He knew about the Death Metal.

In those moments, the Controller made a mistake and lost

control. Terrance learned that his grandfather didn't want him or Paxton to die.

Renewed by this thought, Terrance was filled with energy and confidence he'd never felt before. He wasn't foolish enough to think he was invincible, but as he ran straight into the battle, Paxton yelled, "What are you doing?"

"I'm going to pay our Revenant friends a little visit." Terrance slowed only slightly and waved Paxton to follow. "Grandpa wants you and me alive and human, so we don't have to worry about the Revenant."

The fight lasted only ten minutes when Yankees poured out of the gate. As the men and women ran past Terrance, one of them handed him a long knife. Ted handed Paxton a handgun.

Paxton smiled, "I guess we're no longer criminals."

He darted through the mob, toward the Revenant with Terrance on his heels.

"Who is controlling these animals?" Terrance asked. "Last I heard, Revenant animals attacked Revenant or human and none of them were this well-organized."

"Him," Paxton pointed. "I noticed it when he sent a bear after Sara. He's definitely the one controlling them."

Terrance stopped and looked back, "A bear? Is she ok?"

"She's fine. Jeff took care of it immediately. It was while you were passed out on the ground." Paxton turned and pointed to a group of men, "You come with us. We're going to break up these animals."

Paxton and Terrance ran toward Captain Oliver with several Yankees in tow. They stopped when they saw Alexander. The alligator was huge and Captain Oliver was sending him their way.

J'Nou and Mara stood still at his side, ready to defend him. Gail and Cynthia were on either side of them.

Paxton raised his weapon and fired.

J'Nou grabbed the bullet just before it hit Captain Oliver, and Alexander stopped.

"You can't defeat us, Paxton. Have you come to sacrifice yourself?" J'Nou said.

"I want to make a deal, J'Nou. Call off this attack and I'll give you my father."

"That's it? We just get your father if we walk away?"

"No," Paxton said and looked at Terrance and the Yankees in the group. "I want my mother and granny seeded, too."

Captain Oliver stepped forward, "You want what?"

"You heard me. I want them seeded, like Jeff. Then I give you what you want."

"Where is he, Paxy?" Gail stepped forward.

What could he do? He never could lie to his granny, but he couldn't tell them that Eugene was dead.

"Paxy, you do know where he is, right?" She stepped forward again.

"He's in the city."

"Paxton Eugene Roald!" Granny took two more steps forward, "You know that I can tell when you lie. You can detect lies with the best of them, but you can't tell one to save your life. Now where is he, and the Controller will consider your offer."

Paxton lowered his weapon and blinked away a tear. "He's dead, Granny."

Paxton had no time before now to let this sink in, but saying it out loud hit him harder than he thought it would. "I let you down. Now they'll never free you."

"You're lying," Captain Oliver said and pulled Gail behind him.

"No, he's not. I know his face. This is real," Gail said.

"Then there's no need for either of you," Captain Oliver said and grabbed Gail and Cynthia and threw them to Alexander. "Feed, Alexander."

"Terrance, stop him," Paxton lunged forward.

Terrance closed his eyes and concentrated, "Sleep."

Eugene snuck around the corner with no idea how he would get through the lobby on the bottom floor. He made it to some stairs and entered the door. Twenty floors was a long way, especially at his age, but he was grateful he was going down and not up.

It took a while, but he made it to the bottom floor.

He peeked through the four-inch-wide glass window in the door. Seeing nobody near the door, he walked out. It was too late for many people to be entering and exiting the building, but the street outside was still busy.

He walked through the lobby with confidence, knowing it was less likely to draw suspicion. His heart pounded as he opened the front door. He felt his pulse in everything he touched. On the street he weaved into the crowd. He was far from free, and still needed to find a way to leave the city.

At this time of night, that would be impossible; nobody wanted to leave a city this late anywhere in America, but especially not inside the second fence.

He had to find a place to stay for the night.

Sara noticed Jeff's arm and watched him quickly feed on the bear. He devoured the entire thing and she watched as the tendons and muscles knitted themselves back together before the skin on his arm healed over.

Then she saw Paxton and Terrance running toward the human Revenant and the giant Revenant alligator near them.

"We have to go with them. This crowd and that wall can handle the animals," Sara said.

He agreed and slung her over his shoulder. Several animals turned toward them to attack, but Jeff ran so fast they could do no more than turn toward them before the pair was gone. Running toward their friends, she felt the air whipping in her ears and found it hard to breath.

They were there almost instantly and saw Captain Oliver slump to the ground. The other Revenant stumbled; then Terrance stumbled.

Jeff stopped abruptly and put Sara down.

Alexander didn't hesitate as he went for Gail and Cynthia.

Sara realized what was happening and stared hard at Alexander as Jeff leapt onto its head. His arms would not reach around its mouth. Try as he might, Jeff could not hold the alligator's mouth shut.

It fell to the ground. Jeff tried to pull its mouth back and take its head off, but he couldn't get it to budge. The alligator was nearly asleep, and had little fight left in it.

Paxton looked at his mom and granny. He knew he could never save them now, but he couldn't let them remain as slaves to the Controller. Ted and the rest of the Yankees were fighting off the animals from behind while Terrance struggled to stay awake. Sara and Jeff were wrestling with Alexander, but they were struggling.

His only time was now. Paxton raised his weapon to aim at his mother. His hand was shaky, but his aim was true. His mother, then his grandmother went to join his father in eternal slumber.

"Be at peace, Mom. Be at peace, Granny."

Terrance was woozy, but not asleep. He was done controlling the Revenant, and they stirred back to life. Sara focused on her loose hold over Alexander, but Jeff jumped down and looked at Paxton.

"I get J'Nou," Paxton said.

Jeff nodded and leapt at Captain Oliver.

Captain Oliver stood again and was ready for the attack. He caught Jeff and swung around, continuing Jeff's momentum into the tree behind him. Captain Oliver was far slower, but well trained. He smiled to himself as he realized this traitor Revenant was not off limits. He could fight to the death.

Jeff slammed into the tree, cracking it and himself in half. He then fell to the ground limp.

Mara pounced on Jeff and tore into his neck with her teeth. He shook her off and threw her several feet away.

Ted and the other Yankees turned to help Jeff. They fired at Captain Oliver. A few shots found their mark in his chest and legs as he ran at the group. He reached into the first one's chest with his right hand and ripped out his heart. With his left hand, he grabbed the next man's head and slammed it into his knee, breaking it open. Continuing down the line, he killed each man.

Ted's children would grow up fatherless.

Paxton fired and knicked J'Nou's neck. Then he walked up to him. He knew J'Nou was only wounded, and would heal from the wounds, but a gun wouldn't give him the satisfaction he wanted. He set his weapon on the ground and used his bare hands to finish the job, breaking J'Nou's neck.

Paxton felt more empty than ever. Now that J'Nou was dead,

he could only think of his father. He looked around for something to destroy the Revenant's head.

I have to be sure.

Sara had Alexander under control finally. Captain Oliver was occupied, so she turned to face the army of animals. The other Revenant soldiers were torn apart by the tanks, so the Revenant animals were all that was left. She held them back and confused them, making it easier for the Yankees to finish them.

There were still a lot of animals left, so she was only able to prevent attacks on humans. The animals wandered around, mindless. A group of panthers took on a few alligators while elsewhere the Sasquatch faced off against a group of alligators, bears, and wolves.

The Revenant Sasquatch was winning.

Sara noticed that the animals would attack any other species, but not their own, and the Yankees were attacking all of them in the confusion.

Terrance watched Captain Oliver, but the Revenant paid no attention to him. Instead, Oliver stalked up to Paxton as he bent over to grab a large branch. Terrance felt woozy from his last contact with the Controller, but he couldn't let Paxton be harmed.

He saw Jeff preparing to leap at Captain Oliver from the side, but it may not be enough this time.

"Behind you," Terrance said.

Captain Oliver began to turn around as Jeff slammed into his chest. The Captain was knocked on his back with Jeff on top.

Paxton turned and saw it; then Mara came at him from behind. She swiped her nails across his back, tearing his clothes and digging deep into his flesh.

Paxton swung around and Mara pinned him.

"Be careful, Paxy. I may not be allowed to kill you yet, but I can play with you," Mara said.

Ted, who wasn't quite dead yet, despite missing the left side of his head, aimed his weapon and pulled the trigger. He knocked Mara off of Paxton; then he dropped his weapon and stopped breathing.

He died a hero, like his father.

Jeff nearly destroyed another tree as Captain Oliver threw him into it and hopped to his feet, making a tactical retreat. Alexander followed his master and Mara. Oliver stopped only to grab J'Nou's limp body; then he jumped on the large alligator's back.

Jeff sat up and looked around. Terrance struggled to help Sara, putting his arm under her to help her. Jeff could tell how exhausted Terrance was, though and picked himself up. He inserted himself between Sara and Terrance, helping them toward the gate.

Jeff needed Terrance now more than ever, so he was glad not to be turned away. Where would they go now? If Paxton's father really was dead, then the Revenant should leave them alone, but what if he wasn't? And where was Paxton?

Jeff heard a soft thud and turned back to see Paxton digging a hole with a large branch. He turned around.

"What are you doing? The... " Terrance realized why Jeff was bringing them back. "Go, help him, Jeff."

Jeff hurried over to Paxton and offered to dig the holes. He had two perfect graves ready in a moment. Gently picking up each woman, he laid them to rest and began to cover them.

"Wait," Paxton said. "I need to say something first. When they were turned, I was too afraid to put them down; I couldn't let myself believe that they were Revenant.

"Then, when I found out about the Luatu, I was ready to turn my father over and put the world in danger. It was stupid of me, but I'd still do it if I could bring them back." He looked at Terrance now. "I would do it, Terrance.

"They didn't die today. J'Nou killed them in Miami, but now they can rest."

32. A Way Out

Eugene could barely sleep on the cold floor, but he was happy to be off the street. He knew Pasquale couldn't hold the Lutadors off for long, but he hoped his friend would play dumb long enough.

Eugene only needed to be safe until morning.

He was not going to be safe until morning.

The commotion outside his door was enough to rouse him. He knew the family who let him in could be harmed if he was found there, so he hurried to the basement window and tried to climb out.

Opening the window was easy, but he'd gained a few pounds over the years and the window was small. He pushed his head and arms through the window and began to pull his middle through.

This was more difficult than he imagined.

Unfortunately, he didn't have the several minutes it would take for his escape. The Lutador guards came in the door behind him and were greeted with the old man's bottom half hanging out of the window.

Terrance, Paxton, Sara, and Jeff sat at a table in the Net Café the day after the battle. Terrance and Sara had to make Paxton leave their apartment. He didn't feel like moving from his bed and had barely eaten. In the background the reports and interviews from Washington were repeated on the news.

"Sounds like the Revenant did some real damage in Washington after we left." Paxton tried to sound like it mattered.

"Yeah. I have a feeling they won't be so friendly next time," Terrance rubbed his scar.

"I just hope Dr. Carlson and Nurse Rosa are ok," Sara said.

Terrance grabbed her hand and squeezed it.

Jeff shushed the nearby tables before turning back to his own, "Hey, I think they're talking about us."

". . . and most of the reports about these heroes," Eidan Nogmi reported from Washington, "say that they're just kids, but they held off an entire Revenant army until the Yankees could come out and clean up the rest. The reports sound a bit too good to be true.

"It's just too bad they couldn't have been here to help the Capital City. As I said before, I'm heading up to New York and should have a report from there tomorrow. We'll see if I can find these heroes of May Day Two and get an exclusive interview with them."

"Ok," Paxton forced a smile. "That does it. I'm healed enough; that little girl barely scratched me, and I'm done thinking about my parents. Besides, we traveled with Terrance's cheek wide open. I think I can manage."

He hoped none of them would notice how much he was lying.

"I think he's right," Jeff said. "We should go. Especially if you think Washington may want a piece of us. An interview is the last thing we would want."

"Ok. We'll prepare today and leave first thing tomorrow," Terrance said. He didn't buy it, but he knew he had to get Paxton away from New York. "I'm sure that as the 'Heroes of May Day Two' we can find a ride and everything else we need."

After the fight, they were treated to an apartment—free drinks and food, and just about anything else they needed or wanted, so they all agreed to leave tomorrow. They would finish their meal and rest up before packing.

"So, Jeff, does it feel different? Do you think you could see farther than Paxton?" Sara asked.

"I feel more in control, but that's about it. And no, I'm much faster and slightly stronger, but I can't see any farther or smell better or anything like that." Jeff sipped his juice, "This apple juice tastes the same as it ever did." He winced.

The group had convinced everyone that Jeff was visiting Russia during Chernobyl and was a mutant. It was far more palatable than the truth and with his speed, he seemed more like one of them than a Revenant. Many didn't like or trust mutants, but their fear was less than those who wouldn't trust a zombie, especially after the attacks. And if people thought a Revenant could move as fast as he did, it would only scare them more.

It was simple for him to consume normal food, even if he didn't like it. He had to be careful, though; when it was time to really eat, he left the city to hunt.

"Jeff, Paxton and Sara told me what you did in the barn," Terrance said. "They told me how you sacrificed yourself."

"It was nothing, Dude," Jeff said. "I'm here and better than before."

"It was a lot and I'm sorry. I hated you from the beginning, and in the beginning, I had a reason, but I never gave you a second chance. You've earned it."

Jeff smiled and looked into his cup.

"I know I can't change the past, Dude, but I'm sorry. I wish we'd met under different circumstances."

"But if it were different, we'd be dead. Paxton would be a Revenant and America would be facing a much worse situation than we are now," Terrance said. "I hate what you did, but I forgive you. You're a different person now."

"That might not be so bad," Paxton mumbled. Only Jeff could hear him.

The four continued eating as a lady walked up on stage, "The Net Café is proud to welcome the Chipmunk Cherry Velcros."

The band took the stage and the Café went wild. They played some southern swing and encouraged the dancing that ensued. Terrance and Sara took a spin on the floor during the last couple of songs, and the Russian lady who helped interrogate Paxton entered the Café and walked over to an empty table near Paxton and Jeff.

She sat down and stared at Paxton. She was more somber than he'd seen her, and it made him uneasy.

Eugene still refused to work. He was happy to find out Pasquale was alive and safe despite his escape attempt. A few days later, however, he was surprised that James had not visited him.

Until now.

"Eugene, I respect you," he wheeled his chair over to look out the window. "I respect that you don't want to do this. But you have to know that if you don't do it, someone else will."

Eugene nodded.

"It would be far better for you to help us."

"How is that, James?"

James turned his wheel chair toward Eugene again.

"If you continue to refuse, we will be forced to the alternative, Eugene. We have intelligence that the Controller has been hunting down our team, every scientist from EA 51 that still lives. We've helped many escape and they're here helping us, but recently he's been focused on finding you."

James watched for Eugene's reaction.

"You would hand me over?" Eugene asked.

"No!" James said, appalled at the thought. "I hate that they captured any of us. If there was a way, we'd try to free them. But it's too late for that, I'm sure. There is no way we could let them get a hold of you, though. Especially with what you know."

"Why? Do they want a cure? I'll offer that to them freely."

"You and I both know what they want and it's not some cure," James said. "They want you to increase their power, and you are the only one who can do that."

"You couldn't know that."

Eugene remembered what happened to the mouse in the trial. Just before it worked, he'd created a super Revenant strain. The mouse cut through diamond with no trouble and its intelligence increased too. With that kind of power...

"We have plants in their farms and even EA51. The surveillance bugs work very well."

Eugene knew about the surveillance bugs. One of those gifts from the Japanese Empire was on his shirt when he escaped, making it easy to locate and extract him.

"So then, you'll protect me, and I can get on with my work here."

"I'm afraid that's not an option, Eugene. We have to get these suits working. We know that the others, the ones they captured, are hard at work on helping them improve themselves, so we're dedicating all our resources to this project and you'll have to help us. If you refuse," he paused and raised his chair up to Eugene's height. "Well, we have to keep you out of the hands of the Revenant." James looked hard at Eugene who finally realized what James was saying.

"You're going to kill me."

"Tonight."

As the music ended, Terrance and Sara sat down.

"You see her over there?" Paxton pointed.

He knew it would be useless to try to hide from the Russian what he thought and said, so he didn't whisper or lower his voice.

"Yeah, I saw her as we danced. I wonder what she wants," Terrance said.

"And why hasn't she busted us for Jeff," Sara said.

"Who's the Russian chick?" Jeff asked.

"She's that mind-reading mutant. She'll know anything we think, and she's the reason we were hung out."

The Russian rose from her table and walked toward the group. She brought a chair and set it down backwards, sitting with them as if she were an old friend.

"Vita Andreeva." She introduced herself and shook Jeff's hand, "The *Russian Chick*. I am sorry for other day."

Paxton stared at her, clearing his mind. She still wore the metal goggles, but now they were on her head, holding back her long, curly, black hair. He only now noticed her icy blue eyes.

She wore a brown leather jacket that would not button over her white button-up shirt and brown, utilitarian pants, with many pockets, chains, and tools.

"I understand your reluctance to talk with me, after I, how you say, hung you out to dry?" Vita continued, "I am here to share information with you, as apology, and to offer my service."

"What information could you have that would interest us?" Sara asked with more jealousy in her voice than she would have liked.

"It is about your father, Mr. Roald."

Paxton couldn't help himself now. He was undeniably inter-ested and impatient. His first instinct was to deny it, but he knew that would be useless. Instead, he stared at her and waited.

"I am afraid this will not be news to your liking, but I felt. . ." Vita stopped herself. "I felt that after what happened, I owe you this difficult news. Before he died, he help the Lutador build ma-chine. This machine make man move like your friend here."

Paxton's jaw dropped. He hadn't expected this, and even her face hadn't conveyed the severity of it.

"He made something worse than the Revenant?" he asked.

"I do not know any details. I only know that this exist now," she said.

"What does this have to do with me?" he stood and pushed his chair back, turning it over.

Several people turned to look at the group. They already drew a lot of attention; the last thing they wanted was more attention, but Paxton was in no mood for games.

"I tell you, comrade, I only think you want to clear family name. After what I have done to you, I offer my service to help." Vita was clearly ignoring what Sara was thinking.

"And how do *you* know this?" Terrance asked, leaning in.

"I know a lot of things." Vita turned to look at Terrance, and Sara's eyes narrowed. "I hear thoughts, and I overheard the thoughts of some men who work for Lutadors. Santanas, pirates from West Coast. They are gone now, though. They were by docks, leaving to return to Texas. It was special delivery of some metal or another."

"This doesn't make us even, Vita," he said.

"I understand."

"I don't think you do," Paxton left the table. The others fol-lowed him.

Paxton's mind wasn't empty any longer, and he was flooded with memories of his mother and granny. Memories from when he first arrived in Miami, all the way to covering them with dirt. Vita couldn't help but remain at the table alone, crying.

Paxton sat on a bed in their apartment. It was the apartment that his interrogators, Vita and Jonas, the Head of City Security, had provided for them. He had been in the bed since they left the Net Café.

"I was going to do it, Terrance," Paxton said.

"I know you were, Paxton," Terrance said.

"I was really going to trade my father," Paxton said. "Then, of all things, he made it worse... " He continued staring at the piece of egg shell he had taken from his father's apartment.

In the two days that passed since Vita told him what his father had done, he hadn't moved from the bed. The group cancelled their plans to leave and instead remained in New York, taking care of Paxton.

He drank and ate very little other than what his friends forced on him. He just sat where he was and didn't say more than a couple of words to any of them.

"Do you wish you had done it?" Jeff asked.

Sara looked horrified at Jeff when he asked this, and Terrance made his opinion obvious too, but Paxton looked up at them and thought for a moment. Then he shook his head. "No. Not anymore."

"You have us, Paxton," Sara said.

"She's right, dude," Jeff said.

"Yeah, Paxy. We'll always be here for you," Terrance said.

He smiled, hoping Paxton might too.

Paxton didn't smile, "I just need some time alone for now." He stood and walked out the door.

After leaving the apartment, Paxton walked down to the docks. He shoved his hands into his pockets and shuffled his feet along the pebbles near the water. Watching the oily water softly hit the dock wall, he considered the futility of the waves.

Why do they keep beating at the wall?

For a long time, nothing more passed through Paxton's mind. He sat on the dock and listened to the ships pulling in and out of the harbor, and the gangs unloading for their pirate counterparts, but he paid little attention to them.

He began to think back to his mother taking care of him, the smell of Granny's cooking, and the smell of mothballs in her room. Sitting on the edge of the dock, he thought back to when his family arrived in Miami.

As they pulled into the Miami harbor, Paxton picked up his mother's suitcase, and they began to disembark. He realized his father wasn't behind them and turned to look.

His mother touched his shoulder, "Your father's not coming, Paxton."

"But he has to, Momma. The Revenant will hunt us all down. He has to be with us to protect us."

"No. Your father is the one they're after. He'll be safe somewhere else, and we'll be safer without him. Come on. Let's go." His mother looked back at the boat.

The pair turned to leave, but Paxton heard a commotion behind him. It was Eugene pushing through the pirates to get to them. Eugene ran to them, picked Paxton up, and hugged him close, "Cynthia, I'm sorry. You know this is the only way for you to be safe." He moved to hug her now, but she smacked him on the cheek.

He took it and hung his head in shame, glancing around to confirm that all the pirates saw it. They were no longer trying to hide their interest. Not after so many weeks. This was better than the top-rated soap on the Net.

"How the hell can you say that leaving us could be what's best?" Cynthia looked like she could smack him again at any time.

"Look, baby, it—"

"Don't you dare, Eugene. It isn't. I know you blame yourself for Laura, but we could be a family together, run across the world to the US of A or the Japanese Empire. Even Nazi Europe would be better," she lowered her voice "if we were together."

Eugene put his hand over his mouth and looked down. The pain in his eyes was intense. He looked at Paxton and then down at the empty space next to him where his daughter should have been.

"Dad, I know you blame yourself for Laura, but you can make

up for it. Let's just be together," Paxton said.

"I can't, Paxy. I need to fix this. You're right and it's my fault Laura is dead and they're after me. I couldn't handle it if one of you... If I go away, you'll be safe."

"No we won't," Paxton yelled. "We need you with us. You're never with us. All you do is work on your stupid potions," Paxton turned away.

"You're not only hurting me; look at what you're doing to him? Shouldn't he have a father?" Cynthia said.

"He will. I just need to finish this. I could save us all if I can just get it right." He stopped and looked at Paxton, placing his hands on his son's shoulders, "I'll return as soon as I fix it."

Cynthia stared at him for a moment, "Don't bother," she turned and walked away. "Not if you get back on that ship."

Her mother, Gail, waited at a Café nearby to bring them to a new home. Paxton began to follow her, but his father held his shoulder and turned him around.

"Paxton, I know you don't understand what I'm doing now, but one day you'll know how painful this was for me. I would give anything to stay with you if I could, but I have to fix my mistake."

"No you don't. You need to be my dad," Paxton whispered poisonously as he stared at his own feet.

"Yes. Yes I do, but listen to me." Eugene was emotionless now. He waited until Paxton looked in his eyes. "Part of being your dad is protecting you and being responsible for my mistakes. I caused this trouble, and I have to do what's right and fix it.

"If you see any Revenant," Eugene said, "you find me. If they're looking for you or are around Miami, anything, come to me. You, your mother... even bring your granny. I'll be in New York, in a place called 'Hell's Kitchen.'

"It should be easy for me to hide there, but don't tell anyone where I am. Not even your mother," Eugene widened his eyes and spoke more slowly. "The Revenant cannot know where I am and they cannot catch me. If they found me... it could be a terrible thing for the whole world."

Paxton turned and pulled his arm away from his father. As he walked away, he heard Eugene whisper, "I love you."

But that was years ago.

It was the last thing his father said to him, and now he was here, alone with the flotsam and oil water of the docks.

He killed his mother and granny, the only people he truly loved, all because they were infected with a disease his father created. He placed the bullets and then he buried them. The anger toward his father, anger he felt for so long, drained from him, leaving him empty, hollow, and sullen.

Even in death you make things worse. I thought your death would end my torture, but it didn't. I have no purpose now. Not anymore.

Without anger or love, what's left for me?

He leaned over, closer to the water and watched a piece of rope create ripples in the rainbow of oil.

I bet that junk could hide a body under it.

He looked around and didn't see anyone paying attention.

I could slide in right there, in peace, and then when someone finds me, they'll know that it was because I was just like my father. They'll know that he always provided the same thing for his family.

Paxton pushed himself off of the dock and into the water.

A way out.

Epilogue: Nightly News

" ... and now to Eidan Nogmi, who is reporting live from New York," Emily read from the teleprompter. "Eidan, how is everyone there?"

"Thanks, Emily. Everyone here is talking about May Day Two." Eidan's report came from the harbor with the Statue of Liberty in the background. "I have with me Fillian and his daughter.

"Fillian, you met the heroes before the battle; is that right?"

"Yeah. They helped me when I was... uh, in trouble," Fillian said and looked at his daughter. "If it weren't for them, I may have lost the most precious part of my life. These guys are great. I couldn't believe it when I heard they were criminals and being strung up outside the city."

"Criminals?" Eidan looked into the camera dramatically, "What do you mean?"

"Well, I don't know what they did exactly, but I think it had something to do with the Revenant, so Jonas—he's our Chief of Security—he hung them out from the wall. So, when I heard that, I was surprised. Then they... hey, that's them over there!" Fillian pointed down the dock to Terrance, Sara, and Jeff. They were out looking for Paxton. Eidan and his cameraman ran down the docks.

"Terrance, Terrance, can I have a word? You're being broadcast live, worldwide, by our NB."

Eidan put the microphone in Terrance's face.

"No. I'm looking for our friend, and I don't have time right now," Terrance didn't slow down; nor did he look at Eidan or the camera.

"Is it Paxton?"

"How do you know our names?" Terrance turned and stepped closer to Eidan.

He stared straight at him.

"I... uh, your names were all given by the Yankees. Only first names, though. I hope that matters."

Terrance turned again and continued down the docks, looking for Paxton. Eidan followed him and tried again.

"Terrance, we wanted to know how you all did it, how did—"

"Look, dude, we're busy right now. Go away," Jeff said.

Eidan turned to look at the camera.

"Well, Emily, it looks like they're too busy at the moment, but I'll try to get an interview with them later today."

"Thanks, Eidan. Wait, Eidan, what's that commotion behind you?"

Eidan turned and saw Terrance in the water with Jeff; they were lifting something onto the dock, and Sara and Fillian were helping pull it onto the dock.

"Follow me, Steve," he said to his cameraman as he ran toward the group.

It was clear they were pulling Paxton out of the water.

"Go away; this isn't some NB special!" Sara yelled at him.

"Yeah, dude," Jeff appeared next to Eidan.

Eidan jumped back and so did Steve. They moved away to give the group space, but Eidan signaled for Steve to zoom in.

A kilometer away, Bruce Campbell made a routine check on one of the Hell's Angels' ships. He heard about Eugene. He tried to focus on the ship, making sure everything was loaded properly and running on time, but the guilt he felt made it nearly impossible.

"—Roald. He's in the tower with James, and we'll be ready for the Revenant soon," said a man wearing a blue cowboy hat.

"Good. You will let me know when to send the reinforcements?" said another man, a Santana.

It was odd to see a Santana pirate ship on this coast, but it happened from time to time. There were some items one could only get from the Santanas. But it was very odd to see one talking to a cowboy.

Bruce walked over. As a Director of the Hell's Angels he was afforded some privilege, and he wasn't known for throwing that around.

He stood no more than three meters away from the pair, staring at them.

"May we help you?" the cowboy said.

"Yes," Bruce said as six of his Angels joined him.

The Santana, who had his back to Bruce, turned around. His face was angry and full of disgust. But as soon as he saw that he faced a Director of the Hell's Angels and six other Angels, his face became apologetic.

"Sorry, Director," the Santana said. "My friend here was unaware of who you are. What may we help you with?"

The cowboy barely kept his composure. But most importantly he kept his mouth shut.

"I heard a name," Bruce said. "Who were you discussing?"

"Name? Did we mention anyone by name?" the Santana looked at the cowboy.

"Tell me what you know about Eugene Roald," Bruce demanded.

"We, uh... I don't think you heard us right," the Santana said.

"Yeah, we was saying Kathleen Mold. She's a Lutador," the cowboy squinted, "like me." He tipped his hat to Bruce. "It's an innocent mistake."

"No. It isn't," Bruce took a step forward. His fellow Angels did the same. "Now. Tell me what you know about him."

9 781959 677048